OXFORD WORLD'S CLASSICS

NOTES FROM THE UNDERGROUND
AND
THE GAMBLER

FYODOR MIKHAILOVICH DOSTOEVSKY was born in Moscow in 1821, the second in a family of seven children. His mother died of consumption in 1837 and his father, a generally disliked army physician, was murdered on his estate two years later. In 1844 he left the College of Military Engineering in Petersburg and devoted himself to writing. *Poor Folk* (1846) met with great success from the literary critics of the day. In 1849 he was imprisoned and sentenced to death on account of his involvement with a group of utopian socialists, the Petrashevsky circle. The sentence was commuted at the penultimate moment to penal servitude and exile, but the experience radically altered his political and personal ideology and led directly to *Memoirs from the House of the Dead* (1861–2). In 1857, whilst still in exile, he married his first wife, Maria Dmitrievna Isaeva, returning to Petersburg in 1859. In the early 1860s he founded two new literary journals, *Vremia* and *Epokha*, and proved himself to be a brilliant journalist. He travelled in Europe, which served to strengthen his anti-European sentiment. During this period abroad he had an affair with Polina Suslova, the model for many of his literary heroines, including Polina in *The Gambler*. Central to their relationship was their mutual passion for gambling—an obsession which brought financial chaos to his affairs. Both his wife and his much-loved brother, Mikhail, died in 1864, the same year in which *Notes from the Underground* was published; *Crime and Punishment* and *The Gambler* followed in 1866 and in 1867 he married his stenographer, Anna Snitkina, who managed to bring an element of stability into his frenetic life. His other major novels, *The Idiot* (1868), *Devils* (1871), and *The Brothers Karamazov* (1880) met with varying degrees of success. In 1880 he was hailed as a saint, prophet, and genius by the audience to whom he delivered an address at the unveiling of the Pushkin memorial. He died six months later in 1881; at the funeral thirty thousand people accompanied his coffin and his death was mourned throughout Russia.

JANE KENTISH works as a lecturer in Byzantine art and as a translator. She has translated *Netochka Nezvanova* by Dostoevsky and Tolstoy's *A Confession and Other Religious Writings*.

MALCOLM JONES is Emeritus Professor of Slavonic Studies at the University of Nottingham, and is the author of *Dostoyevsky: The Novel of Discord* (London and New York, 1976) and *Dostoyevsky after Bakhtin* (Cambridge, 1990). He is also co-editor, with G. M. Terry, of *New Essays on Dostoyevsky* (Cambridge, 1983) and with Robin Feuer Miller, of *The Cambridge Companion to the Classic Russian Novel* (Cambridge, 1998). From 1995 to 1998 he was President of the International Dostoyevsky Society.

D0993202

OXFORD WORLD'S CLASSICS

For over 100 years Oxford World's Classics have brought readers closer to the world's great literature. Now with over 700 titles—from the 4,000-year-old myths of Mesopotamia to the twentieth century's greatest novels—the series makes available lesser-known as well as celebrated writing.

The pocket-sized hardbacks of the early years contained introductions by Virginia Woolf, T. S. Eliot, Graham Greene, and other literary figures which enriched the experience of reading. Today the series is recognized for its fine scholarship and reliability in texts that span world literature, drama and poetry, religion, philosophy and politics. Each edition includes perceptive commentary and essential background information to meet the changing needs of readers.

OXFORD WORLD'S CLASSICS

FYODOR DOSTOEVSKY

Notes from the Underground
and
The Gambler

Translated by
JANE KENTISH

With an Introduction and Notes by
MALCOLM JONES

OXFORD
UNIVERSITY PRESS

OXFORD
UNIVERSITY PRESS

Great Clarendon Street, Oxford OX2 6DP

Oxford University Press is a department of the University of Oxford.
It furthers the University's objective of excellence in research, scholarship,
and education by publishing worldwide in

Oxford New York

Athens Auckland Bangkok Bogotá Buenos Aires Calcutta
Cape Town Chennai Dar es Salaam Delhi Florence Hong Kong Istanbul
Karachi Kuala Lumpur Madrid Melbourne Mexico City Mumbai
Nairobi Paris São Paulo Shanghai Singapore Taipei Tokyo Toronto Warsaw

with associated companies in Berlin Ibadan

Oxford is a registered trade mark of Oxford University Press
in the UK and in certain other countries

Published in the United States
by Oxford University Press Inc., New York

Introduction and Select Bibliography © Malcolm Jones 1991
Translations and Explanatory Notes © Jane Kentish 1991
Chronology © Ronald Hingley 1983

The moral rights of the author have been asserted

Database right Oxford University Press (maker)

First published as a World's Classics paperback 1991
Reissued as an Oxford World's Classics paperback 1999

British Library Cataloguing in Publication Data

Data available

Library of Congress Cataloging in Publication Data

Dostoyevsky, Fyodor, 1821–1881. [Zapiski iz podpolíâ. English]
Notes from the underground : and, The gambler / Fyodor Dostoevsky :
translated by Jane Kentish : with an introduction by Malcolm Jones.
p. cm.—(Oxford world's classics). Includes bibliographical references.
Translation of: Zapiski iz podpolíâ and Igrok.
1. Dostoyevsky, Fyodor, 1821–1881—Translations. English.
I. Kentish, Jane. II. Dostoyevsky, Fyodor, 1921–1881. Igrok.
English. 1991. III. Title. IV. Title: Notes from the underground.
V. Title: Gambler. VI. Series.
PG3326.A2 1991 891.73'.3—dc20 90–9378

ISBN–13: 978-0-19-283626-7

9

Printed in Great Britain by
Clays Ltd, St Ives plc

CONTENTS

INTRODUCTION

I

Notes from the Underground and *The Gambler* were both written in the mid-1860s. Each may in its own way be regarded as an overture to the novels on which Dostoevsky's reputation as one of the great European novelists rests.

Notes from the Underground was published in 1864, *Crime and Punishment* and *The Gambler* in 1866, and *The Idiot* in 1868. Dostoevsky's remaining major novels, notably *The Devils* and *The Brothers Karamazov*, belong to the following decade.

As with most of Dostoevsky's important works, these two were written during periods of acute personal crisis. In 1849 Dostoevsky had been arrested with other members of the Petrashevsky group by a Russian government made highly nervous by the revolutionary events in Europe. Dostoevsky's involvement in the political discussions and activities of the group had been marginal but he was nevertheless condemned to death and, when the last-minute reprieve was announced at the place of execution, the sentence was commuted to four years in the fortress of Omsk in Siberia, followed by four years as a private soldier. This last period was spent at Semipalatinsk where Dostoevsky fell in love with Maria Dmitrievna Isaeva, who became his first wife. The marriage was not a successful one and by 1864 Maria Dmitrievna was seriously ill with tuberculosis. She died in the same year during the writing and serial publication of *Notes from the Underground*, the second part of which was delayed owing to her death. A. P. Grigorev and Dostoevsky's brother Mikhail, who had worked with him on the journal *Time* (*Vremia*) since 1861, also died in 1864. This relatively successful journal had been of enormous importance in Dostoevsky's attempt to re-establish himself on the Russian literary scene following his return from imprisonment and exile. Both his literary and financial fortunes were tied up with it and it was also the vehicle for the evolving philosophy of *pochvennichestvo*—the philosophy of the Russian soil—in which he and his colleagues attempted to reconcile the warring Westernizing and Slavophile tendencies in the debates of the 1860s. The loss of these colleagues and relatives was a bitter blow to him, though the journal itself had had to close in 1863 following the publication of an ill-judged article on the Polish question. It was followed in 1864 by a short-lived successor, *The Epoch* (*Epokha*), in which *Notes from the Underground* was itself published.

The idea of *Notes from the Underground* as it came to be written seems to date from the end of 1862 when Dostoevsky was writing *Winter Notes on Summer Impressions*, in which he recounted and discussed his recent trip to Europe. But he had previously (1859) contemplated a long novel called *A Confession*, which is clearly related to *Notes from the Underground*. Moreover, Dostoevsky was reworking his early, second novel *The Double* (1846) at this time. There are clear echoes of this earlier text in *Notes from the Underground*, from the predicament of a lowly civil servant unable to raise himself from his position of social inferiority even down to details like the name of the hero's superior in the Civil Service (Anton Antonovich Setochkin).

The idea of the 'underground', as exemplified in this work, has furnished modern European fiction with one of its principal archetypes, recognizable not only in Dostoevsky's own later works and those of his Russian successors but no less in the work of such leading Central and West European writers of our time as Kafka, Hesse, Camus, and Sartre. The underground in Dostoevsky's sense is the consciousness of a hero (or anti-hero) morbidly obsessed with his own impotence in dealing with social realities. This obsession is usually accompanied by feelings of bitterness and resentment towards that society which forbids him entry.

The years since Dostoevsky's return to St Petersburg had been marked by other events. He had published a number of literary works, including *Notes from the House of the Dead*, a fictionalized version of his experiences in Omsk; a long novel, *The Insulted and the Injured*; and *Winter Notes on Summer Impressions*. During these years he had been abroad a great deal and until 1865 much of this time was spent in the obsessive pursuit of a neurotic, intelligent, and attractive young woman called Apollinaria (Polina) Suslova. This relationship, in which Dostoevsky experienced more torment than fulfilment, finds an unmistakable echo in that of the narrator of *The Gambler* with his Polina, and later in the personality and conduct of Aglaia and Nastasia Filippovna in *The Idiot* and other of Dostoevsky's 'predatory women'.

By the summer of 1865 Dostoevsky was deeply in debt and pursued by creditors. To be fair, this situation was chiefly caused by his responsibility for his brother's family and his own extravagant and irresponsible stepson. To attempt to extricate himself from it he sold the rights to an edition of his collected works to the unscrupulous publisher F. T. Stellovsky, who is now chiefly remembered for this episode. The contract contained a clause stipulating that he would also produce a novel for him by 1 November 1866 and, failing this, that Stellovsky would have the right to publish anything he wrote during the next nine years without payment. Dostoevsky was preoccupied at the time with *Crime and Punishment*, which began publication in the January and February numbers of the periodical *The Russian Messenger*. At first he planned to write the two novels simultaneously, one in the mornings and the other in the latter part of the day.

But the beginning of October arrived and nothing had been written of Stellovsky's novel. Dostoevsky was desperate. He even considered the possibility of allowing his friends to help him write it. However, he found a better solution. He engaged the services of a young shorthand typist, Anna Grigorevna Snitkina, and dictated the novel to her in twenty-six days (4–29 October), delivering the manuscript to Stellovsky on 1 November in the nick of time. Stellovsky was out when Dostoevsky called, so he took it to the police station and obtained a dated receipt.

The novel was entitled *Roulettenburg*. There is evidence that the idea for it had existed in Dostoevsky's mind at least since the spring of 1863 and that he had entertained the idea of writing the two novels at once at least since the summer of 1866. But it was Anna Grigorevna who saved him. In spite of the difference in their ages (she was 20, he 45), he proposed, she accepted, and they married. There is thus something to Marc Slonim's idea that the conception and execution

of the novel mark the conjunction of the three great loves of
Dostoevsky's life, Maria, Polina, and Anna. It is even truer of
the two works taken together.

2

In outward form neither of the works included in this volume
is typical of Dostoevsky's mature fiction. Nor at first glance do
they look very similar, though actually they have important
things in common. For instance, both are narrated in the first
person by the principal character. This principal character in
each case is socially disadvantaged and at times resorts to
expressing his resentment in excruciatingly petty and scandalous forms. Each text, moreover, may be described as a personal
confession by its narrator. The particular form of *Notes from
the Underground* is, however, unique in Dostoevsky's work. It
is divided into two parts, the first consisting of the philosophical polemics of a prematurely retired civil servant in the mid-
1860s and the second of his memories of episodes in his life in
the 1840s. The first is supposedly contemporaneous, the
second retrospective.

The Russia in which Dostoevsky wrote *Notes from the
Underground* was seething with debate and ideological polemic:
1861 had seen the Emancipation of the Serfs and the following
years saw the enactment of further major reforms, as well as
riots and disorders which led to the repression of dissidents
like N. G. Chernyshevsky. Abroad, the American Civil War
was in train, Schleswig-Holstein was invaded by Austria and
Prussia. Darwin's *On the Origin of Species* had appeared in
1859 and was glossed by Huxley's *Man's Place in Nature*,
published in English in 1863 and in Russian translation in
1864. The first volume of H. T. Buckle's *History of Civilisation
in England*, arguing that with the development of civilization
wars will cease, was published in Russian translation in 1863.
All these events are reflected in the text of *Notes from the
Underground*, and a full appreciation of the work is impossible
unless its contribution to topical polemic is taken into account.

But most important of all is the thought of N. G. Chernyshevsky, the politician of the Populist movement, who had been
arrested in 1862 and was at the time in the Peter and Paul

Fortress awaiting exile to Siberia. He was a significant and very influential, if not original, philosopher, who, in the spirit of the New Enlightenment, presented human beings as ultimately rational creatures, who have only to be shown their true interests to act in accordance with them, and who live in a world in which rational laws operate in the moral as well as the natural sphere. To be fair to Chernyshevsky, he lived at a time when determinist ideas prevailed in the natural sciences and he did wrestle, if unsuccessfully, with the philosophical problems of freedom and constraint. But the overwhelming impression left by his philosophy was that individual freedom is severely limited, perhaps even altogether illusory. He was, however, a historical optimist. While in prison he wrote, smuggled out, and had published a novel called *What is to be Done?*, whose heroine has a dream of a shiny new Utopian world, in which machines are people's slaves, associated with the image of the Crystal Palace at the Great Exhibition in London. This too is echoed in *Notes from the Underground*.

It is this philosophy and its analogues in eighteenth-century France which form the ideological focus of *Notes from the Underground*. However, readers and critics have varied on how to interpret their role. Some have seen the work as a Swiftian satire against Chernyshevsky in which the underground man is himself the prisoner of the ideas he seeks to refute. Others have seen it as a great statement of the claims of individuality and the will against abstract theories and thus as a prelude to modern existentialism and a companion to the works of Kierkegaard. Others have seen it as an expression of Nietzschean 'amoralism'. Not surprisingly, some have seen it above all as the self-exposure of a pathological personality and valued it chiefly for its psychological insights. Dostoevsky's own emphasis on the 'underground type' tends to give weight to this view, especially since he did not link this idea exclusively to *Notes from the Underground*. These views should not be seen as mutually incompatible, but rather as evidence of the work's continuing appeal to adherents of widely varying world-views and literary and philosophical preferences.

What the story undoubtedly reveals is the unhappy conjunction of a personality problem and a philosophical problem. The narrator is a person who experiences an oppressive sense of impotence and frustration in his dealings with others and encounters a philosophy which implies that everything is predetermined and any attempt to alter things by imposing one's will is foredoomed. This philosophy has the irresistible and oppressive authority of being fashionable and of being widely accepted as axiomatic by those who are supposed to know. In other words, a philosophy of individual impotence seems to confirm the feeling of impotence of this latest manifestation of the type of the superfluous man, so well known in Russian literature. It is a philosophy which he shares with those (of whom he supposes his reader to be one) who are more self-confident, but intellectually more limited, than himself, who accept the fashionable doctrines but fail, happily for them, to perceive their implications. The underground man perceives them, alone in his underground, weaving a web of self-analytical thought from which he cannot escape.

He reacts in part by petty acts of resentment in the outer world and partly by compulsive analysis of his own actions in the light of Chernyshevskian philosophy. As the reader will discover (or have discovered), the philosophical result is a reversal of the values of the New Enlightenment in favour of those of existentialism. The underground man rejects reason as the dominant faculty, on both historical and psychological grounds, and posits the individual will as the most important of human interests, even when it is exercised in the service of destructive impulses. Hence the famous passage in which the narrator claims that the prospect of the completion of the Crystal Palace, of the socialist anthill, is so intolerable that humanity might prefer chaos and destruction. Most certainly someone would propose to tear it down and would attract many followers to his enterprise.

And then—it is you saying all this—a new economic policy will come into being, absolutely complete and also calculated with mathematical precision so that all conceivable questions will vanish in a flash, for the simple reason that every conceivable answer has been given to them. Then they will erect the Crystal Palace . . . Of course, there is no guarantee (this is me speaking now) that it will not be dreadfully boring . . . For example, I should not be in the least surprised if suddenly, for no reason at all, some gentleman or other with a dishonourable, or shall we say, a reactionary and sarcastic demeanour springs up amidst this future reign of universal good sense and puts his hands on his hips and says to us all: 'Well, gentlemen, why don't we get rid of all this good sense once and for all, give it a kick, throw it to the wind, just in order to send all these logarithms to hell so that we can once again live according to our own foolish will?' And this wouldn't matter either, but it's upsetting that he would undoubtedly find followers: that's the way man is made.

But neither at the beginning nor at the end does the narrator translate his protestations on behalf of the will into a powerful new code of confident action. On the contrary he sinks back into a sense of powerlessness and futility and, as he has constantly told us, he actually comes masochistically to enjoy the contradictions and self-laceration this involves, especially when it occasions some discomfort to other people who otherwise choose to ignore him. One of the most memorable passages in the book contains his reflections on the nineteenth-century man with toothache:

There is pleasure in toothache . . . The person suffering expresses his pleasure in these groans . . . First these groans give vent to the whole consciousness of the humiliating futility of pain; the whole legitimacy of nature about which you probably couldn't give a damn but on account of which you nevertheless suffer, whilst she doesn't . . . Gentlemen, I beg you to listen sometime to the groans of an educated person of the nineteenth century who is suffering toothache, and on the second or third day of the illness, when he is no longer groaning as he did on the first day, that is to say, not simply because he's got toothache . . . His groans turn into something foul, filthy, evil, and go on for days and nights on end. And after all, he himself knows that his groans will not bring him any kind of relief . . . he knows that even the audience for whom he is making his efforts, and his whole family, are by now listening to him with loathing . . . But the sensuousness is indeed composed of all this consciousness and disgrace.

The man from underground has an unattractive personality and his predicament is unenviable. This remains the case when he recalls his youth in the 1840s, when he was 24, and his excruciatingly embarrassing attempts to insinuate himself into the company of his former schoolmates, vulgar men of the world who have no comprehension of his exalted values and romantic fantasies and no respect for his sensitivities. These fantasies are composed of recollections from Pushkin, Lermontov, Byron, George Sand, Nekrasov, and others, particularly the social romanticism of the period. In the 1840s he was a dreamer who preferred romantic fiction and its characters to the vulgarity of the real world and real people and resented their refusal to acknowledge its superiority. Yet when one person, the prostitute Liza, shows an inclination to take his fantasies at face value and accepts his invitation to visit him, he is overcome with confusion and takes his sense of guilt and anger out on her. Liza herself, as she is presented here, echoes a romantic stereotype—the pure prostitute.

To a considerable degree the underground man lives in a world derived from books and books about books (no doubt also conversations and thoughts about books), to the extent that, as he says himself, without them humanity in the modern world would be completely disorientated and without any source of authority for its values. In the 1840s as in the 1860s values derive not from any inner conviction but from the ephemeral authority of cultural fashion. Ironically, the passages in Chapter 10 in which Dostoevsky had intended to express the need for faith in Christ were cut out by the censor. He was upset since he regarded these as crucial, but preferred to accept the ruling than risk delays in publication.

Notes from the Underground is remarkable, however, not simply for its thematic interest. Mikhail Bakhtin has argued persuasively that it is the mode of the narrator's discourse which is truly innovative, for his every word is directed at the anticipated response of the reader, now cringing, now shrill and spiteful, the tone rising at the end of each section in open anticipation of the reader's response. He frequently attributes thoughts to the reader as he does in the above quotation on the future Crystal Palace. He always leaves open the possibility of having the final word in the dialogue himself or altering the final meaning of his own words. Stewart Sutherland has shown that this strategy is fundamental to the plausibility of the narrator's arguments in favour of individual freedom, and that Dostoevsky here anticipated twentieth-century philosophical thinking on the subject. At all events the reader's expected response is vital in determining the form of the confession. Hence, perhaps, the narrator's paradoxical insistence, in his reference to Heine and Rousseau, that he is writing for himself alone and will never have any readers. Most ironic of all is that this man, who yearned for any label, provided it furnished him with a postive identity, and who failed to find it, has become one of the best-known figures in modern European fiction.

The importance of the fact that Dostoevsky had been in prison and exile for virtually a decade cannot be exaggerated in understanding the genesis of this work. Although it must not be read as autobiographical in the crude sense, there is no doubt that it reflects Dostoevsky's anguished wrestling with the new ideas he discovered on his return to the capital, ideas which he found deeply antipathetic and yet virtually irresistible, because endued with the authority of the latest scientific wisdom and intellectual fashion. Moreover the feelings of entrapment the underground man experiences are surely enriched, if that is the word, by Dostoevsky's own experiences of imprisonment. And the narrator's guilt feelings, at a time when Dostoevsky's attention was divided between his dying wife and his imperious young mistress, must surely draw to some degree on the feelings of his creator.

3

The Gambler is also occasioned by a subject of contemporary discussion with which Dostoevsky was closely acquainted: that of Russians abroad, especially those who teemed in the European spas and gambling resorts with which Dostoevsky himself was all too familiar. Between 1863, when he gambled for the first time at the gaming tables at Wiesbaden, and 1871, when his gambling obsession eventually and inexplicably disappeared, he played at Baden-Baden, Homburg, and Saxon-les-Bains on numerous occasions, often beginning by winning and then going on to sustain disastrous losses. His young wife Anna Grigorevna was not spared the misery of having to pawn clothes and other possessions to enable him to try to recoup his losses. The obsession was intermittent. Sometimes Dostoevsky resisted the temptation, but Anna Grigorevna's diaries and reminiscences, no less than Dostoevsky's own correspondence, tell the awful tale of debt, pawnbrokers, outpourings of guilt, and begging letters and pleas to friends. Like his hero,

Dostoevsky had his 'system', which of course kept on failing him at crucial moments. He wrote to Varvara Dmitrievna Konstant from Paris on 20 August 1863, recounting his experiences in Wiesbaden,

Varvara Dmitrievna, I watched those players attentively for four days. There are several hundred gambling here and, to be honest with you, only two of them really know what they're doing. They all lose heavily because they don't know how to gamble. There was a Frenchwoman and an English lord. They knew how to play. Not only didn't they lose but they almost broke the bank. Please don't think that I'm bragging about the fact that I didn't lose in saying that I know the secret of not losing, but winning. I really do know the secret. It's very stupid and simple and amounts to ceaseless self-control at all stages of the game and not getting excited. That's all there is to it. That way you can't lose and are bound to win. But that's not the point. The point is whether, once you know the secret, you are capable of exploiting it.

On 8 September he wrote to his brother Mikhail from Turin,

You write to ask how I could possibly lose absolutely everything while travelling with someone I love. Misha, my friend, in Wiesbaden I invented a system, actually tried it out, and immediately won 1,000 francs. The next day I got excited and departed from the system and immediately lost. In the evening I returned to the strict letter of the system again and soon won 3,000 francs again without difficulty. Tell me, after such an experience, how could I not get carried away and believe that if I followed my system strictly I should be sure to win? And I needed money, for myself, for you, for my wife, for writing my novel. And here people win tens of thousands at a stroke. Moreover, I came here to save you all and to rescue myself from disaster. And I believed in my system as well. And then to cap it all I arrived in Baden, went to the tables, and *within a quarter of an hour* I won 600 francs. This whetted my appetite. Suddenly I started to lose, couldn't control myself and lost everything. After that I wrote to you from Baden, took my *last* money, and went to play. Starting with 4 napoléons I won 35 napoléons in half an hour. I was carried away by this unusual good fortune and I risked all 35 napoléons and lost them all. I had 6 napoléons d'or left to pay the landlady and for the journey. In Geneva I pawned my watch.

Jacques Catteau makes the telling point that Dostoevsky did not confine his gambling to the casinos. His contract with

Stellovsky was itself a gigantic gamble, as was his growing reliance on advance payments for other unwritten works.

The Gambler is told in the first person singular like *Notes from the Underground* but it is not devoted to philosophizing or to reminiscences of the distant past. There are, it is true, passages of reflection on gambling or, for example, on the attitude of Russian women to Frenchmen, but the novel is structured by a tale of passion and intrigue and based on notes which the hero supposedly made as the events themselves unfolded.

The hero himself is, like the underground man, obsessive and emotionally disturbed in his relations with other people. The main objects of his obsessions are gambling and a beautiful and proud young Russian woman. He compulsively tries to reconstruct the motives and the secret thoughts of others about him, on evidence which is palpably partial and inadequate. Moreover, he tends to act and make accusations on the basis of these inadequate reconstructions, thus compounding his difficulties in his personal relationships.

Aleksey Ivanovich, like the man from underground, is the social inferior of those he seeks to mix with on equal terms and he is deeply self-conscious and resentful about this. His vanity causes him to commit social solecisms and even to do so on purpose in order to force himself on the attention of others, even when he himself suffers as a result. His social position is better than that of the underground man, however. Although reduced to working as a tutor (*uchitel*), he claims to be of noble stock and to have a university degree. He speaks French and German tolerably well, especially French. Moreover, since the family he works for is travelling abroad, he has the advantage of accompanying them. Much more significantly, however, he has the opportunity of hoisting himself out of his position of inferiority by winning at roulette.

Mikhail Bakhtin, in his famous book on Dostoevsky, has discussed what he calls the 'carnivalization of literature'. The medieval carnival, according to this view, was an institutionalized occasion when all the normal hierarchical relations in society were temporarily reversed. Kings became paupers and paupers kings, normally impermissible *mésalliances* were allowed, and the rules of social decorum could be breached with impunity—provided everything reverted to normal when the carnival was over. Bakhtin sees *The Gambler* as a particularly striking example of carnivalization within Dostoevsky's fictional world, because the gaming table is the means by which all these social relations can be, if only temporarily, reversed. The rich become poor, the poor rich, the suppliant becomes master, and the master suppliant. Aleksey understands this. One turn of the wheel and everything changes. He will become someone different in relation to Polina once he has money.

When he arrives back in Roulettenburg at the beginning of the novel Aleksey is greeted haughtily by the General, who has acquired some money from somewhere. Consistently with this relationship, the General dismisses him from his service when, responding to a whim of Polina's, Aleksey publicly insults the wife of a German baron. But it is at this point that Aleksey perceives the opportunity of turning the tables. By transforming a trivial indiscretion into a major scandal he can, he realizes, cause enormous damage to the General's relationship with Mademoiselle Blanche, and the very threat gives him a powerful weapon.

The dramatic appearance of the Grandmother, on whose death the General is relying for the restoration of his fortunes, together with the Grandmother's reliance on him for instruction at the gaming tables, gives Aleksey another advantage. At the end of Chapter 11 the members of the General's household are imploring Aleksey to save them. A little later, abandoned by his prospective bride and her retinue, the General is on his knees in his presence. But the ultimate transformation in Aleksey's relations with the other characters, if only temporarily, is brought about by his own staggering success at the gambling table.

Ironically, the two people whose good opinion he most desires refuse to take advantage of or be impressed by this success. The first is Mr Astley and the second is Polina.

Mr Astley is an interesting character in his own right. He is the only Englishman to figure in Dostoevsky's mature works and what is more is a wholly positive and attractive character. His name, it has been speculated, was borrowed from a character in Mrs Gaskell's *Ruth*, a translation of which appeared in *Time* in 1863. In some respects—his wisdom, his shyness—he seems to foreshadow Prince Myshkin, the famous hero of *The Idiot*.

In other respects he prefigures those characters (Razumikhin in *Crime and Punishment* and Radomsky in *The Idiot*) who seem to embody relaxed common sense and realism in a world fraught with tension, in which perceptions and relationships are distorted by obsessional and other forms of neurosis. Considering Dostoevsky's xenophobia and his treatment in the same novel of the Germans, the French, and the Poles, the Englishman cuts a rather satisfactory figure.

Polina's relationship with Aleksey is, by his own account, one of mistress and slave. Polina does not like this 'slave theory' of his, but he is besotted by her and tormented by the thought that she has no affection for him and even despises him, even that she is infatuated with the Frenchman de Grieux. Aleksey constantly protests his willingness to make any sacrifice, even to throw himself off the Schlangenberg, to satisfy her merest whim. He recognizes that she is entirely inaccessible to him and that his obsession is futile. She seems to respond to his confidences with indifference, to mock his passion and manipulate him for her own purposes. Or so he is inclined to think. And he does not hesitate to reveal to her that in the end he may find this treatment intolerable and murder her. She takes this seriously, even saying that if he were really to murder someone for her sake he would kill her next. This love-hate relationship foreshadows that of Rogozhin and Nastasia Filippovna in *The Idiot*. Rogozhin really does kill Nastasia.

From Aleksey's point of view Polina is continually provoking him by her inconsiderate behaviour. She allows him to declare his love but mocks and torments him in return. Indeed, she deploys most of those strategies in her relationship with Aleksey which, I have argued elsewhere, Dostoevsky's characters often deploy in relation to each other and which create that atmosphere of emotional stress and perceptual confusion which is so characteristic of his world. She calls attention to aspects of his personality of which he is dimly aware and which he would rather not acknowledge; she stimulates him (here sexually) in situations in which it would be disastrous for him to seek gratification; she exposes him to rapidly alternating stimulation and frustration; she switches from one topic to the next while maintaining the same emotional wavelength (discussing a matter of life and death to him with the same levity as a trivial happening) or changes emotional wavelength, turning serious things into a joke.

There is no mystery about the origin of the portrayal of Polina, though, as always, it would be wrong to assume that it is copied directly from life. Dostoevsky's relationship with Suslova, which included physical intimacy, was much more complex. But the words which he wrote of her in one of his letters seem to fit his heroine equally well: 'She demands everything from people, every perfection, and she never forgives an imperfection in her respect for other positive characteristics.'

Although Polina's attitude to Aleksey seems to mirror Polina Suslova's to Dostoevsky—and we know how much torment this caused him—it is not clear whether we are justifed in taking Aleksey's view of his Polina literally. For near the end of the novel Mr Astley assures Aleksey that Polina had indeed loved him and clearly believes that Aleksey is entirely unworthy of her. It is open to the reader to draw the conclusion that the distance that Polina interposes between herself and Aleksey is caused in great measure by his impossible behaviour towards her and his obsessive conviction of his social inferiority and her inaccessibility; and that her inconsistency in her attitude to him is in part a response to his own wild and unpredictable conduct. In the beginning their relationship seems to have been less fraught with tension, for Aleksey records that she had seemed to want him to be her friend, her confidant, and had appeared to be testing him out. It is his own obsessions that in large measure give rise to their current peculiar relationship. When the household breaks up and she refuses his offer of part of the money he has just won at roulette, she accuses him of trying to buy her. Perhaps this is not just the crude accusation that he is trying to buy her body, so much as a rejection of his whole way of seeing things in terms of wealth and social standing. It is indeed how others see them, but perhaps she requires better of him.

Such thoughts arise as a consequence of what Bakhtin calls the 'polyphonic' structure of the novel. As in the case of *Notes from the Underground* the narrator interposes his own perception between other people and the reader. But here, Mr Astley, whom the narrator respects, but who disagrees with him, offers a plausible alternative view which forms part of the chorus of independent voices including that of the narrator. Full polyphony, that is to say, the accordance of roughly equal weight to each of the principal voices, requires a greater distancing of the narrator's voice than we have here, but still this is a significant advance on *Notes from the Underground*, where everything is heavily coloured by the narrator's perception, in the direction of *Crime and Punishment*, in which Dostoevsky opted for third-person 'omniscient' narrative while still retaining, for the most part, the focus of the hero. But at least in *The Gambler* the narrator is honest and clear-sighted enough to perceive Mr Astley's good sense and to let him have his say.

Another example of 'carnival' is Aleksey's sojourn in Paris with Mademoiselle Blanche in which he gladly allows her to spend all his money in the space of less than a month and finally funds her marriage to the General. For a while they live a life of pure fantasy, a sort of holiday of unreality in which Aleksey's standing is actually quite uncertain apart from his role as provider. Mademoiselle Blanche and her mother are unmasked; she gives him a small allowance while shamelessly and openly using his money for her own enjoyment and advantage without any offer of return. He will be welcome back when he has more money for her to spend. The whole episode is a kind of carnival holiday from real life, to which Aleksey soon returns with a bump when his money runs out.

But the most dramatic reversals are associated with the Grandmother herself. A supposedly fatally ill old woman makes a long train journey and arrives to show more energy and life than any of them. Instantly she disrupts all their plans and the relationships they have built upon expectations of her demise. A respectable old woman acts like an irresponsible child and turns their whole world upside-down.

Such occurrences are closely related with another characteristic situation in Dostoevsky's fictional world: the public scandal. Dostoevsky was to prove the master of depicting public scandals, situations in which the preservation of public decorum and socially sanctioned illusions is radically threatened. In *Notes from the Underground* the hero causes embarrassment and irritation rather than scandal, for the company he embarrasses has few airs and graces to subvert. But that is not true of the Baron and Baroness, who are easily scandalized, and, realizing that the General's household is also vulnerable, Aleksey weaves a complex plot to compound the embarrassment and catch up the whole entourage in his web. In fact he does not carry his plan through and an even greater threat to decorum in the shape of the Grandmother steals the scene.

It was only in later novels that Dostoevsky showed full mastery of the potential of the scandal scene. In *The Devils* the scandal embraces and lays low the whole of high society in the provincial capital. In *The Brothers Karamazov* it invades even the monastery.

There is no doubt, however, that in this respect as in others, *The Gambler* foreshadows Dostoevsky's later work.

4

Both *Notes from the Underground* and *The Gambler* echo and re-echo literary texts and stereotypes as well as the personal experience of their author, and both prove powerful precursors of literature to come. Some of the echoes and anticipations have already been indicated. *Notes from the Underground* is in considerable measure, as Joseph Frank has shown, not only a philosophical polemic with Chernyshevsky but a parody of his novel *What is to be Done?*. Moreover, the form of the confession calls to mind the tradition of St Augustine and Rousseau, which was well known to Dostoevsky. There are many allusions to Rousseau's confessions in his works. The underground man is part of the Russian tradition of the superfluous man, which itself derives from the tradition of the Romantic outsider. There are numerous significant literary precursors for the gambling theme. Russian literature notably provides Pushkin's *Queen of Spades* and Lermontov's *Masquerade*, while Balzac and Thackeray have been suggested as foreign influences. On a more trivial level the name of de Grieux is clearly taken (parodically?) from Prévost's *Manon Lescaut*.

But whatever voices from the past can be heard echoing in

Dostoevsky's texts, each of these works is a short masterpiece in its own right, revealing different aspects of Dostoevsky's mature genius. The emotional intensity of Dostoevsky's world and his capacity for Dickensian humour, his ability to give expression to the underground 'confession' of a tortured individual consciousness, and his sense of dramatic plot struc-ture—all are to be found in these two works.

It is not surprising that *The Gambler* has been rewritten for the stage numerous times and has, of course, been converted into a well-known opera by Prokofiev.

NOTE ON THE TRANSLATION

THE translations are taken from the Russian texts in an edition of Dostoevsky's collected works published in twelve volumes by 'Pravda', Moscow, 1982.

SELECT BIBLIOGRAPHY

BAKHTIN, M., *Problems of Dostoevsky's Poetics*, tr. from the Russian and ed. C. Emerson, introd. W. Booth (Manchester, 1984).

CATTEAU, J., *Dostoyevsky and the Process of Literary Creation*, tr. from the French by A. Littlewood (Cambridge, 1989).

DOSTOEVSKAYA, A., *Reminiscences*, tr. from the Russian and ed. B. Stillman, introd. H. Muchnic (London, 1975).

FRANK, J., *Dostoevsky: The Seeds of Revolt, 1821–1849* (Princeton, NJ, 1976).

—— *Dostoevsky: The Years of Ordeal, 1985–1859* (Princeton, NJ, and London, 1983).

—— *Dostoevsky: The Stir of Liberation* (Princeton, NJ, and London, 1987).

GROSSMAN, M., *Dostoevsky: A Biography*, tr. from the Russian by M. Mackler (London, 1974).

HINGLEY, R., *Dostoyevsky: His Life and Work* (London, 1978).

HOLQUIST, M., *Dostoevsky and the Novel* (Princeton, NJ, 1977).

JACKSON, R. L., *The Art of Dostoevsky: Deliriums and Nocturnes* (Princeton, NJ, 1981).

JONES, J., *Dostoevsky* (Oxford, 1985).

JONES, M. V., *Dostoyevsky: The Novel of Discord* (London, 1976).

—— and TERRY, G. M. (eds.), *New Essays on Dostoyevsky* (Cambridge, 1983).

JONGE, A. DE, *Dostoevsky and the Age of Intensity* (London, 1975).

KJETSAA, G., *Fyodor Dostoyevsky: A Writer's Life*, tr. from the Norwegian by S. Hustvedt and D. McDuff (London, 1987).

KRAG, E., *Dostoevsky: The Literary Artist*, tr. from the Norwegian by S. Larr (Oslo and New York, 1976).

LEATHERBARROW, W. J., *Fedor Dostoevsky* (Boston, Mass., 1981).

MOCHULSKY, K., *Dostoevsky: His Life and Work*, tr. and introd. M. A. Minihan (Princeton, NJ, 1967).

PEACE, R. A., *Dostoyevsky: An Examination of the Major Novels* (Cambridge, 1971).

SLONIM, M., *Three Loves of Dostoevsky* (New York, 1955).

WASIOLEK, E., *Dostoevsky: The Major Fiction* (Cambridge, Mass., 1964).

CHRONOLOGY OF
FYODOR DOSTOEVSKY

Italicized items are works by Dostoevsky listed by year of first publication. Dates are Old Style, which means that they lag behind those used in nineteenth-century Western Europe by twelve days.

1821	Fyodor Mikhailovich Dostoevsky is born in Moscow, the son of an army doctor (30 October).
1837	His mother dies.
1838	Enters the Chief Engineering Academy in St Petersburg as an army cadet.
1839	His father dies, probably murdered by his serfs.
1842	Is promoted Second Lieutenant.
1843	Translates Balzac's *Eugénie Grandet*.
1844	Resigns his army commission.
1846	*Poor Folk* *The Double*
1849	*Netochka Nezvanova* Is led out for execution in the Semenovsky Square in St Petersburg (22 December); his sentence is commuted at the last moment to penal servitude, to be followed by army service and exile, in Siberia; he is deprived of his army commission.
1850–4	Serves four years at the prison at Omsk in western Siberia.
1854	Is released from prison (March), but is immediately posted as a private soldier to an infantry battalion stationed at Semipalatinsk, in western Siberia.
1855	Is promoted Corporal. Death of Nicholas I; accession of Alexander II.
1856	Is promoted Ensign.
1857	Marries Maria Dmitrievna Isaeva (6 February).
1859	Resigns his army commission with the rank of Second Lieutenant (March), and receives permission to return to European Russia.

Resides in Tver (August–December).
Moves to St Petersburg (December).
Uncle's Dream
Stepanchikovo Village

1861   Begins publication of a new literary monthly, *Vremia*, founded by himself and his brother Mikhail (January).
The Emancipation of the Serfs.
The Insulted and The Injured
A Series of Essays on Literature

1861–2 *Memoirs from the House of the Dead*

1862   His first visit to Western Europe, including England and France.

1863   *Winter Notes on Summer Impressions*
Vremia is banned for political reasons but through a misunderstanding, by the authorities.

1864   Launches a second journal, *Epokha* (March).
His first wife dies (15 April).
His brother Mikhail dies (10 July).
Notes from the Underground

1865   *Epokha* collapses for financial reasons (June).

1866   Attempted assassination of Alexander II by Dmitry Kara-kozov (April).
Crime and Punishment
The Gambler

1867   Marries Anna Grigorevna Snitkina, his stenographer, as his second wife (15 February).
Dostoevsky and his bride leave for Western Europe (April).

1867–71 The Dostoevskys reside abroad, chiefly in Dresden, but also in Geneva, Vevey, Florence, and elsewhere.

1868   *The Idiot*

1870   *The Eternal Husband*

1871   The Dostoevskys return to St Petersburg.

1871–2 *The Devils* (also called *The Possessed*)

1873–4 Edits the weekly journal *Grazhdanin*.

1873–81 *Diary of a Writer*

1875   *An Accidental Family* (also called *A Raw Youth*)

1878   Death of Dostoevsky's beloved three-year-old son Alesha (16 May).

1879–80 *The Karamazov Brothers*

1880   His speech at lavish celebrations held in Moscow in honour
        of Pushkin is received with frenetic enthusiasm on 8 June,
        and marks the peak point attained by his reputation during
        his lifetime.

1881   Dostoevsky dies in St Petersburg (28 January). Alexander II
        is assassinated (1 March).

Notes from the Underground

Both the author of the notes and the *Notes* themselves are, of course, fictional. Nevertheless, types such as the creator of these notes not only could, but are also bound to exist in our society, taking into account the circumstances that have shaped our society. I wanted to present to the public, in a more striking manner than usual, one of the character types belonging to the very recent past. He is one of the representatives of a generation still surviving. In the part entitled 'The Underground', this personage presents himself and his outlook on life, and as it were tries to clarify the reasons that led to his appearance in our midst, and which were bound to lead to it. In the next part follow the actual 'notes' made by this personage, describing various events in his life.

Fyodor Dostoevsky

PART I
THE UNDERGROUND

CHAPTER 1

I AM a sick man . . . I'm a spiteful man. I'm an unattractive man. I think there is something wrong with my liver. But I cannot make head or tail of my illness and I'm not absolutely certain which part of me is sick. I'm not receiving any treatment, nor have I ever done, although I do respect medicine and doctors. Besides, I'm still extremely superstitious, if only in that I respect medicine. (I'm sufficiently well educated not to be superstitious, but I am.) No, it's out of spite that I don't want to be cured. You'll probably not see fit to understand this. But I do understand it. Of course, I won't be able to explain to you precisely whom I will harm in this instance by my spite; I know perfectly well that I cannot in any way 'sully' the doctors by not consulting them. I know better than anyone that in doing this I shall harm no one but myself. Anyway, if I'm not receiving medical treatment it's out of spite. If my liver is hurting, then let it hurt all the more!

I've been living like this for a long time—for about twenty years. I'm now forty. I used to work for the government, but I no longer work. I was a spiteful civil servant. I was rude and I enjoyed being rude. You see, I didn't accept bribes so I had to reward myself in this way. (That's a lousy joke, but I won't delete it. I wrote it thinking that it would come across very wittily; but now that I can see that I only wanted to show off in a vulgar way, I'm deliberately not going to cross it out.) When people used to come with their enquiries to the desk where I sat I would bare my teeth at them and I used to feel an overwhelming sense of pleasure whenever I succeeded in upsetting someone. It nearly always worked. The majority of them were timid folk—we all know what petitioners are like. But amidst the fops there was one particular officer whom I couldn't stand. He simply would not give in and used to rattle his sword loathsomely. He and I waged war over this sword for a year and a half. Finally I won. He stopped the rattling. This, however, took place in my youth. Gentlemen, do you know what lay at the heart of my malice? The main point, and indeed the most sordid thing about it, was that, even during moments of extreme biliousness, I was constantly and shamefully aware that not only was I not spiteful, I was not even embittered. I was simply comforting myself by scaring sparrows in vain. I might be foaming at the mouth, but bring me some kind of toy, give me a cup of sugary tea, and it's more than likely I'd calm down. I might even be spiritually moved, but I'd be certain to snarl at myself afterwards and suffer insomnia for several months out of shame. I've always been like this.

I lied about myself just now when I said I was a spiteful civil servant. I lied out of spite. I was simply being mischievous with these people and their enquiries and with the officer, and in reality could never have been spiteful. I was ever aware of the great number of completely conflicting elements within me. I felt that they were literally swarming around inside me, these conflicting elements. I knew they had been swarming inside me all my life and that they were begging to be released, but I would not let them out, I wouldn't, I deliberately wouldn't let them out. They tormented me shamefully; they brought on convulsions and, well, finally I grew bored of them, goodness how they bored me! Gentlemen, do you think I'm making a confession to you, asking your forgiveness for something? . . . I'm sure that's what you think . . . But I assure you that I couldn't care less even if you do think so . . .

It's not just that I'm not spiteful, but I've never really been able to be anything: neither spiteful nor good, neither a villain nor an honest man, neither a hero nor an insect. I'm now living out my days in my corner, tormenting myself with the spiteful and utterly useless comfort that an intelligent man cannot seriously become anything and that it is only a fool that does. Oh yes! an intelligent man of the nineteenth century must be, and is morally bound to be, primarily a characterless creature; whereas a man of character, a man of action, is primarily a limited creature. This is my forty-year-old opinion. I'm now forty, and after all forty is an entire lifetime, it really is extreme old age. It isn't done to live beyond forty, it's vulgar and immoral. Who lives beyond forty, give me an honest answer? I'll tell you who does: fools and good-for-nothings. And I'm prepared to say this looking all my elders in the face.

I'll say it to all those respectable old men, to all those sweet-smelling, silver-haired old men. I'll say it straight to the face of the whole world! I've got the right to speak thus because I myself will live to be sixty. I'll live to be seventy! I'll live to be eighty! . . . Stop now! Let me get my breath back . . .

Gentlemen, you probably think I'm trying to make you laugh? You're mistaken in that too. I'm not really the cheerful person I seem, or may perhaps seem, to you; however, if all the chatter is irritating you (I can already sense that you are irritated), why don't you ask me who precisely I am? I'll answer like this: I'm just a collegiate assessor.* I used to work in the government service in order to eat (but only for that reason), and when last year a distant relative left me six thousand roubles in her will I gave up working at once and settled down in my corner. This corner used simply to be the place where I lived, but now I've thoroughly settled into it and made it my home. My room is cheap and filthy, on the outskirts of town. My servant, a country peasant woman, is old and spiteful out of stupidity, and on top of it she always gives off a terrible smell. I'm told that the Petersburg climate is becoming bad for me, and that with my negligible means Petersburg is a very expensive place to live. I know all this, I know it better than all those experienced and wise advisers and head-shakers. But I'm going to stay in Petersburg. I won't leave Petersburg! I won't leave because . . . Oof! You see, it doesn't make any difference whether or not I leave.

However: what can a respectable man talk about with the greatest of pleasure?

Answer: About himself

And so I'm going to talk about myself.

CHAPTER 2

GENTLEMEN, I now want to tell you, whether or not you wish to hear it, why I did not even manage to become an insect. I tell you solemnly, that I often wanted to become an insect. But

I wasn't even granted that. I swear to you, gentlemen, that to be too conscious is an illness, a genuine full-blown illness. Normal human consciousness ought to be more than sufficient for man's everyday needs, that is, a half or a quarter less than that portion which falls to the lot of an educated person of our unfortunate nineteenth century, who on top of this has the added misfortune of living in Petersburg, the most abstract and premeditated city on the face of the earth. (Cities tend to be premeditated and unpremeditated.) The sort of consciousness, for example, with which all so-called spontaneous people and men of action live ought to be quite enough. I'll wager you think that I'm writing all this out of bravado in order to make fun of men of action and that it's also out of bravado, in rather poor taste, that I'm rattling my sword like my officer. But really, gentlemen, who can take pride in his illnesses, still more boast about them?

However, what am I saying? Everyone does it; they do take pride in their illnesses, and I perhaps more than most. We won't argue about it; my line of argument is rather awkward. But nevertheless I'm firmly convinced that not just too much consciousness, but even any consciousness at all is an illness. I insist on that. Let's put that aside for a moment. Now tell me this: why has it happened, as if deliberately, that at those very—yes, at precisely those very—moments when I was most capable of comprehending the whole subtlety of 'all that is beautiful and sublime',* as we once used to say, I would not only fail to comprehend it but I would do such unseemly things, the sort of things that . . . well yes, in short, that perhaps everyone does, but which came to me, as if deliberately, precisely when I was most aware that I absolutely ought not to be doing them? The more I became conscious of goodness and of this whole issue of the 'beautiful and sublime' the deeper I sank into my mire and the more I became capable of completely submerging myself in it. But the most important feature of it all was that it seemed as if all this was not there in me by chance, but that it was bound to be so. It was as if it were my normal condition and not at all an illness or a depravity, so that I finally lost interest in battling with this depravity. It ended in my almost believing (and it's possible that in the end I did believe) that perhaps this was indeed my normal condition. But at first, oh, in the beginning what torments I had to suffer in this struggle! I didn't believe that it happened to others and so all my life I kept it to myself as a secret. I was ashamed (maybe I'm still ashamed now); it reached the point where I felt some sort of secret, abnormal, base pleasure when on some revolting Petersburg night I would return to my corner and feel powerfully aware that today I had yet again done something vile, and that what's done is done, and inside myself I would gnaw, gnaw away at myself with my teeth on account of it, nag and consume myself to the point when the bitterness finally turned into some kind of shameful, accursed sweetness and then in the end into definite, serious pleasure! Yes, into pleasure, pleasure! I insist on it. I raised the subject because I want to find out for certain whether other people experience this kind of pleasure. Let me explain: in this instance the pleasure stemmed directly from being too clearly aware of one's own humiliation; from the feeling that you've gone too far; that it's foul but that it can't be otherwise; that you've no way out, that you'll never change yourself into another person; that even if you still had enough time and the faith to change yourself into something else, you probably wouldn't want to change yourself; and that if you did want to you would still do nothing because in the end there's maybe nothing to change yourself into. But chiefly, and finally, because it all stems from normal fundamental laws of heightened consciousness and from the inertia that is a direct result of these laws, and consequently not only would you not change yourself, you would simply do nothing at all. For instance, as a consequence of heightened consciousness it follows that one is justified in being a scoundrel—as if a scoundrel is somehow reassured by his own awareness of really being a scoundrel. But enough . . . Ah, I've been going on so, but what have I explained? . . . How can this pleasure be explained? But I will explain. I'll get to the bottom of it. That's why I took up my pen . . .

I, for instance, am terribly touchy. I'm sensitive and quick to take offence, like a hunchback or a dwarf, but it's true I've had moments when if someone had slapped me I might even have been pleased. I'm talking seriously: most probably, even in this instance I would have been able to derive some sort of pleasure, by which I mean the pleasure of despair; but it's precisely in despair that you find the most intense pleasure, especially if you are already powerfully conscious of the hopelessness of your predicament. And when you get a slap—well then you're simply weighed down by the awareness of the filth you are being rubbed in. And the important thing is that whichever way you look at it it's always the case that I'm the first to be blamed for everything and, what is most hurtful of all, that I'm guilty without guilt, but according to the laws of nature, as they say. I'm guilty, first, on account of being cleverer than others around me. (I've always considered myself cleverer than others around me and—would you believe it?—I've sometimes even felt ashamed of it. At any rate, my whole life I've somehow looked sideways and never been able to look people straight in the eye.) And I'm guilty, finally, for the reason that if I'd had any magnanimity I would only have found it a greater torment because of my consciousness of its utter futility. You see, I would probably have been unable to do anything through magnanimity: neither forgive, because the offender may have struck me in accordance with the laws of nature, and one cannot forgive the laws of nature; nor forget, because even if they are laws of nature, they are nevertheless offensive. And finally because even if I had wished to be wholly unmagnanimous and, on the contrary, had wished to take my revenge on the offender, I would not have been able to revenge myself on anyone for anything because I would, most probably, have been unable to resolve to do anything, even if I could have. Why couldn't I resolve to do anything? I want to say a few words about this in particular.

CHAPTER 3

How, for instance, do people who are able to take revenge and to stand up for themselves in general do this? You see, they are so overwhelmed by, let us suppose, a sense of revenge, that for a time this feeling completely pervades their whole being. This sort of gentleman heads straight for his target, like a maddened bull with his horns lowered, and it is really only the wall* that stops him. (By the way: faced with the wall these gentlemen, that is to say spontaneous people and men of action, sincerely submit. For them the wall is not a diversion, as it is for instance for people like us, who think and consequently do nothing; it is not a pretext for turning back, a pretext in which we lot usually do not believe ourselves, but of which we are always very glad. No, they submit with absolute sincerity. The wall offers them something reassuring, morally decisive, and absolute, perhaps even somewhat mystical . . . But more of the wall later.) Well, sir, it is just this sort of spontaneous man that I regard as the real, normal person, such as tender mother nature herself wanted to see as she lovingly planted him on earth. This sort of man makes me green with envy. He is stupid, I'm not disputing that with you, but perhaps a normal person is supposed to be stupid, how do you know? Perhaps that is even a very fine thing. And I am still further convinced of this, shall we say, suspicion by the fact that if, for instance, you take the antithesis of a normal person, that is, a person of heightened consciousness, who of course has not arisen from the bosom of nature but from a retort (this already borders on mysticism, gentlemen, but I am suspicious of that too), then this retort person sometimes submits before his antithesis to such an extent that he himself, with all his intensified consciousness, duly regards himself as a mouse and not a man. Albeit an intensely aware mouse, but nevertheless a mouse, whilst the other is a man, and consequently, and so on. And the important thing is that he, he himself, regards himself as a mouse; no one has asked him to do so; and this is a crucial point. Let us now take a look at this mouse in action. Let us suppose, for example, that he too is offended (and he would nearly always be offended) and also wishes to take his revenge. There may be even more spite accumulated in him than in *l'homme de la nature et de la vérité*.* The despicable, lowly, petty little desire to repay the offender in kind may gnaw away inside him even more horribly than in *l'homme de la nature et de la vérité*, because *l'homme de la nature et de la vérité*, on account of his innate stupidity, regards his revenge as an act of simple, straightforward justice; whereas the mouse, as a result of his heightened consciousness, denies the justice in it. Finally he arrives at the real thing, the actual act of revenge. Apart from the original disgust, the unfortunate mouse has by now succeeded in piling up around him so much additional disgust in the way of questions and doubts; one question has led to so many other unresolved questions that he has willy-nilly gathered around himself some kind of fatal bog, some sort of stinking filth comprising his doubts, his emotions, and finally the spit showered upon him by spontaneous men of action, who have gathered triumphantly around him, as judges and dictators, and who are laughing at him with all their might. It stands to reason that the only thing left to do is to wash his little paws of the whole thing and with a smile of assumed disdain, in which not even he himself believes, to creep shamefully into his crevice. There in his foul, stinking underground, our offended, downtrodden, and ridiculed mouse quickly submerges himself in cold, venomous, and essentially never-ending spite. For forty years on end he will remember his offence, to the last, to the most shameful detail, and every time he does so he will add details of his own that are still more shameful, maliciously teasing and annoying himself with his own fantasy. He will be ashamed of his own fantasy, but nevertheless he will recall all of it, he will go over it all, concocting fantastic stories under the pretext that they too could take place, and forgiving nothing. Quite likely he will even start taking revenge, but somehow in fits and starts, in a paltry way, from behind the stove, anonymously, believing neither in his own right to revenge nor in the success of his revenge, and knowing in advance that all his attempts at revenge only cause him to suffer a hundred times more than the person he is taking his revenge on, who most probably doesn't even bat an eyelid. He will recall it all again on his deathbed, with the interest that has been accumulating all this time . . . But the essence of that strange pleasure about which I spoke is to be found precisely in this cold, loathsome state of semi-despair, semi-faith, in the conscious burying of oneself alive with grief in the underground for forty years, in the strenuously created but nevertheless partially doubted inevitability of one's situation, in all the poison of unfulfilled wishes that have turned inwards, in the whole delirium of vacillation, of decisions taken once and for all and regretted a minute later. It is so subtle, at times so subconscious, that even very marginally restricted people, or even simply people with strong nerves cannot understand the first thing about it. 'Maybe', you'll interrupt me with a grin, 'those who have never been slapped won't understand it either'—and in this way you politely remind me that perhaps, in the course of my life, I too have experienced a slap and that's why I'm talking like an expert. I'll wager that's what you think. But rest assured, gentlemen, I have never received any slaps, although it's all the same to me whatever you might think about it. I'm perhaps even a little sorry that I have distributed so few slaps in my life. But enough, not another word on this subject that interests you so much.

I will continue calmly about people with strong nerves who fail to understand a certain refinement of pleasure. Although under certain conditions these gentlemen may indeed roar like bulls, at the top of their voices, and although we can assume that this earns them great respect, as I have already said, faced with an impossibility they immediately capitulate. Impossibility—is that the stone wall? What stone wall? Well, the laws of nature, of course, the conclusions of the natural sciences and mathematics. Once they prove to you, for instance, that you are descended from apes there's no point frowning about it, you must accept it as a fact. And once it has been proven to you that in truth one ounce of your own fat must be dearer to you than a hundred thousand of your fellow creatures and that this result settles the whole issue of so-called virtues and duties and other such ravings and prejudices, then you must accept it, there's nothing else to do because, twice two is mathematics. Try and refute it. 'Forgive me', they will scream at you, 'you cannot fight it: twice two is four! Nature doesn't stop to ask; she's not concerned with your wishes, or with whether or not you like her laws. You are obliged to accept her as she is, and consequently all her results. A wall means a wall . . . etc, etc.' God Almighty, what do I care about the laws of nature and about arithmetic when for some reason I don't like these laws or 'twice two is four'? Of course, I won't knock this wall down with my head if in the end I haven't got the strength to do so, but I won't submit to it simply because I'm up against a stone wall and haven't got sufficient strength.

As if such a stone wall really did offer reassurance and really did bear at least some kind of message to the world, even if only that twice two is four. Oh, absurdity of absurdities! Surely the thing to do is to understand everything, to be conscious of everything, of all the impossibilities and stone walls; not to submit to one single one of these impossibilities or stone walls if it disgusts you to do so; to follow the path of the most irrefutable logical combinations to their most revolting conclusions on the eternal theme of how you are somehow to blame for even the stone wall, although once again it is absolutely apparent that you are in no way to blame, and consequently to grit your teeth silently and impotently and sink, voluptuously, into inertia, dreaming about how you haven't even got anyone to be angry against; that you haven't got an object and maybe will never find one, that it's all a deceit, an illusion, a trick, that it's all bunkum—no one knows who, no one knows what, but despite all these uncertainties and illusions you are still in pain, and the more it is unknown to you the more you ache!

CHAPTER 4

'HA, ha, ha! Next you'll be trying to find pleasure in toothache!' you'll shout with a laugh.

'And what if I do? There is pleasure in toothache', I'll reply. 'I had toothache for a whole month, I know what it's like. In this instance, of course, people do not rage in silence, but groan; and they are not candid groans but groans of malice, and this malice is what the whole thing is about. The person suffering expresses his pleasure in these groans; if he didn't enjoy it he wouldn't be groaning. This is a fine example, gentlemen, and I'll develop it. First these groans give vent to the whole consciousness of the humiliating futility of pain; the whole legitimacy of nature about which you probably couldn't give a damn but on account of which you nevertheless suffer, whilst she doesn't. They express an awareness that you cannot find your enemy but that you are in pain; a consciousness that you, together with all the various Waggenheims,* are at the complete mercy of your teeth; that if someone so wants they can stop your teeth aching, and if they don't then they'll go on aching for another three months or so; and, finally, that if you're still not in agreement and are still protesting then the only thing you can do to comfort yourself is flog yourself, or beat harder with your fists against the wall, but nothing more decisive than that. Well, it is these terrible insults, these gibes, made by we don't know whom, that finally give rise to pleasure, at times reaching an extreme degree of sensuousness. Gentlemen, I beg you to listen sometime to the groans of an educated person of the nineteenth century who is suffering toothache, and on the second or third day of the illness, when he is no longer groaning as he did on the first day, that is to say, not simply because he's got toothache; not like a coarse peasant but rather as a person touched by progress and European civilization groans, like a person "torn from the soil and from his native roots", as we say nowadays. His groans turn into something foul, filthy, evil, and go on for days and nights on end. And after all, he himself knows that his groans will not bring him any kind of relief; better than anyone he knows that he is overstraining and irritating himself and others to no avail; he knows that even the audience for whom he is making his efforts, and his whole family, are by now listening to him with loathing, they no longer believe in him in the slightest and know inside themselves that he could groan in a simpler fashion, without the trills and without the affectation, and that he is only indulging himself out of malice and spite. But the sensuousness is indeed composed of all this consciousness and disgrace. "They tell me I'm disturbing you, I'm taxing your heart, that I'm not letting anyone in the house sleep. Then don't sleep, you too can experience each moment of my toothache. I am no longer the hero I used to seem, but just a nasty person, a good-for-nothing. Well, so be it! I'm very glad you've seen through me. Do you find it revolting listening to my degrading groans? Well let it be revolting, I'm now going to give you an even more revolting display . . ." Don't you understand yet, gentlemen? No, clearly one must be highly evolved and highly conscious in order to understand all the nuances of this sensuousness! Are you laughing? I'm very glad. My jokes, gentlemen, are of course in poor taste, uneven, inconsistent, full of self-distrust. But, you see, this is because I do not respect myself. Can a conscious person really have any respect for himself?'

CHAPTER 5

BUT is it really possible, can it really be possible, for a person to feel respect for himself when he has attempted to find pleasure in the actual feeling of self-humiliation? I am not saying this out of some kind of sickly repentance. Indeed, on the whole I could never bear to say: 'Forgive me, papa, I won't do it again'—not because I was not able to say it, but quite the opposite, perhaps it was precisely because I was much too ready to say it, and do you know when? As if on purpose I would get myself into an awkward situation on the very occasions when I was innocent in both thought and deed. This was the nastiest thing of all. On these occasions I would once again be spiritually moved, I would repent, shed tears, and of course fool myself without the slightest pretence. My heart was already somehow defiled . . . I could not even blame the laws of nature, although all my life it is the laws of nature that have offended me, continually, and more than anything else. It is vile to remember it all, and what's more it was vile at the time too. You know, after a few minutes I would be angrily reflecting that the whole thing was a lie, a lie, a loathsome, hypocritical lie, that is to say all this repentance, all this emotion, all these promises of regeneration. Are you asking why I twisted and tortured myself so? The answer: for the reason that I was already bored of sitting with my arms folded; and so I lapsed into affectation. It is true. Observe yourselves more closely, gentlemen, and then you'll see that it's true. I thought up adventures for myself, I concocted a life for myself so that at least I could live somehow. How many times did it happen that—well, for example, that I took offence just like that, for no reason, deliberately! and after all, I used to know very well that I'd taken offence for no reason, that I was making a show of myself; but you carry on to such an extent that by the end, it's true, you really are offended. Somehow all my life I've been so attracted by this sort of game-playing that by the end I was no longer in control of myself. Another time I wanted desperately to fall in love, it even happened twice. I suffered, you know, gentlemen, I can assure you. In the depth of my soul I don't believe in my suffering, there's a flicker of derision, but all the same I do suffer, in a real, all-out fashion; I feel jealous, I feel quite beside myself . . . And all out of boredom, gentlemen, all out of boredom; crushed by inertia. You see the direct, legitimate, spontaneous result of consciousness is inertia, that is to say consciously sitting with folded arms. I have mentioned this earlier. I repeat, I emphatically repeat: all spontaneous people and men of action are active because they are dull-witted and limited. How can this be explained? This is how: as a result of their limitations they take immediate and secondary causes for primary ones, and in this way they are more quickly and easily convinced than others that they have discovered an indisputable basis for their activity, and so they rest assured; and this is important. You see, in order to begin to act one must be completely assured beforehand that there are absolutely no remaining doubts. But how am I, for instance, to reassure myself? Where are the primary causes that I am to take my stance upon, where are my bases? Where am I to take them from? I practise thinking, and as a result any primary cause I have immediately drags another one in tow, one that is even more primary, and so on *ad infinitum*. And this is precisely the essence of any kind of consciousness or thought process. Again this must be a law of nature. And what, finally, is the result? Always the same thing. Remember, I was talking earlier on about revenge. (You probably didn't take it in very well.) It was said: man takes his revenge because he finds justice in it. This means that he has found his primary cause, he has found a basis for his action, namely: justice. Therefore, he is assured on all fronts, and consequently seeks his revenge calmly and successfully, being convinced that what he is doing is honourable and just. But, you see, I fail to see the justice here, neither can I find anything virtuous about it, and so, if I start to seek revenge then it's really only out of spite. Spite could of course overcome everything, all my doubts, and therefore it could serve quite successfully in place of a primary cause for the very reason that it is not a cause. But what can I do if I lack even spite (after all, this is what I began with earlier)? Once again, as a consequence of these damned laws of consciousness, my spite is subject to chemical decomposition. Look—and the subject evaporates, the basis vanishes into thin air, the culprit is nowhere to be found, the offence is no longer an offence, but fate, something in the nature of a toothache, for which no one is guilty, and consequently one is left once again with the same way out—that is, to beat harder against the wall. And to give it up as a bad job because no primary cause has been found. But just try letting yourself be carried along blindly by your feelings, without reason, without first principles, banishing consciousness at least for the time being; hate or love, anything rather than sit with folded arms. The day after tomorrow, at the very latest, you will begin to despise yourself because you have knowingly fooled yourself. The result: a soap bubble and inertia. Oh, gentlemen, you know perhaps I only consider myself to be an intelligent person because all my life I've never been able to start or finish anything. Very well, very well, I'm a chatterbox, a harmless, annoying chatterbox, like we all are. But what can be done about it if the direct and single purpose of any intelligent person is to chatter, that is to say the deliberate pouring of emptiness into the void?

CHAPTER 6

OH! if only it were out of laziness that I've done nothing. Good heavens, I should have had so much self-respect. I should have respected myself precisely because I was at any rate capable of being lazy; there would at least have been one seemingly positive characteristic in which I myself could have believed. Question: who is he? Answer: a lazy fellow. Oh yes, you know it really would be extremely pleasant to hear that said of oneself. It implies a positive definition, it means that there is something that can be said about me. 'A lazy fellow.' Why, that's a rank and title, that's a career! Don't laugh, it's true. Then by rights I should be a member of the leading club and do nothing other than continually take care of my self-esteem. I knew a gentleman who spent his entire life priding himself on the fact that he knew everything there is to know about Château-Lafite. He considered this to be his own positive merit and never doubted himself. He died not so much with a peaceful as with a triumphant conscience, and he was absolutely right. And I should have chosen a career for myself; I would have been lazy and a glutton, but not a straightforward one, rather one who, let us say, feels for all that is beautiful and sublime. How do you like that? I used to dream about that a long time ago. This 'beautiful and sublime' has been troubling me no end now that I'm forty. But that's now that I'm forty, whereas at that time—oh! then it would have been different. I would instantly have sought out the appropriate thing for me to do—namely, drinking the health of all that is beautiful and sublime. I would have seized at every opportunity of first dropping a tear into my glass and then drinking it in honour of all that is beautiful and sublime. At that time I would have turned everything in the world into the beautiful and sublime. I would have discovered it even in the most repulsive, unquestionable filth. And I would have done it with tears in my eyes, like a wet sponge. For instance, the artist Gey* paints a picture and I at once drink the health of the artist responsible for the painting, because I love all that is 'beautiful and sublime'. An author writes 'To one's Satisfaction'* and I immediately drink the health of 'whomever it satisfies', because I love all that is 'beautiful and sublime'. And I should have insisted that others respect me for this and tormented anyone who failed to show me this respect. To live peacefully, to die majestically—why that's delight, sheer delight! And I should have developed such a paunch, put up such a triple chin, fashioned myself such a purple nose that anyone meeting me would have said, looking at me: 'What an outstanding fellow! He's positively got something about him.' And, you see, gentlemen, whether you like it or not, it's extremely pleasant to hear this sort of comment in this negative age of ours.

CHAPTER 7

BUT these are all golden dreams. Oh, tell me, who was it who first announced, who first proclaimed that man only does vile things when he does not know where his real interests lie? and that if he were enlightened, if his eyes were opened to his real, normal interests, he would at once cease doing vile things and would immediately become good and honourable, because being enlightened and understanding where his real advantage lay, he would indeed see his own personal advantage in goodness, and because it is well known that no one can knowingly act against his own personal advantage, he would find himself as it were obliged to do good. Oh, you child! You sweet, innocent babe! To start with, when in all these thousands of years has man ever acted solely to his own advantage? What about all the millions of facts that bear witness to people *knowingly*, that is to say fully understanding their real advantages, putting them into the background and flinging themselves onto another path, at risks, at chances, and not because anyone or anything has forced them to do so, but as if not wishing to follow the appointed path they stubbornly and wilfully thrust their way along another, difficult, absurd one, barely able to make it out in the darkness? Well, it means that man really finds this obstinacy and wilfulness more pleasant than any kind of advantage to himself . . . Advantage! What is an advantage? And would you take it upon yourselves to give a completely accurate definition of what it is that human advantage consists of? And what if it so happens that *sometimes* human advantage not only can, but even must, lie precisely in the fact that under certain circumstances man desires what is bad for himself and not what is advantageous? And if this is so, if this circumstance is even possible, then the whole rule is blown to the wind. What do you think, can this event arise? You are laughing; laugh away, gentlemen, only tell me: are human advantages calculated altogether reliably? Are there not some that not only do not fit in, but cannot fit into any form of classification? After all, gentlemen, as far as I can see, you

have taken your whole register of human advantages from
averages derived from statistical data and scientific and economic formulae. And since your advantages are prosperity,
wealth, freedom, peace, etc., etc., a person who might, for
instance, act overtly and knowingly against this whole register
would in your opinion, and yes, in mine as well of course, be
an obscurantist, or completely mad, wouldn't he? But the
really astonishing thing is how it has come about that all these
statisticians, sages, and lovers of the human race in their
enumeration of human advantages always omit one of them.
They don't even take it properly into account in their numera-
tions, and the whole calculation depends on that. It would be
no great misfortune to take this advantage and add it to the
list. But that's where the snag lies, that this abstruse advantage
does not fall into any classification, it doesn't fit into any one
of the lists. For example, I've got a friend . . . Ah, gentlemen!
The fact is, he's your friend too; and indeed, he's everyone's
friend! When he's about to do something this gentleman at
once informs you, grandiloquently and clearly, exactly how he
must proceed according to the laws of reason and truth. Not
only that: he will talk to you with excitement and fervour
about real, normal human interests; he will scornfully reproach
those short-sighted fools who understand neither what's to
their advantage, nor the real meaning of virtue; and then—
exactly a quarter of an hour later, without any sudden external
cause, but rather at the dictate of something inside him that is
stronger than any of his interests—he will about turn, in other
words manifestly go against what he has just said: against the
laws of reason, and against his own personal advantage; well,
in short, against everything . . . I am warning you that my
friend is a collective type and so it is rather difficult to blame
him alone. But that's just it, gentlemen; surely there does in
fact exist something of this kind, something which to almost
everyone is dearer than his own very best advantage, or (not to
destroy the logic) there is one such most advantageous advantage (namely, the omitted one about which we were just
speaking) that is more important and more advantageous than
all other advantages and on account of which man, if he is so
required, is prepared to go against all the laws, that is to say
against reason, honour, peace, prosperity—in a word, against

all these appealing and useful things, if only to achieve this primary, most advantageous advantage which is the dearest thing to him.

'But all the same, it's still an advantage', you interrupt me. Allow us, sir, let us explain a bit further, we're not talking about a play on words, but the fact that this advantage is astonishing because it destroys all our classifications and continually defeats all the systems devised by lovers of humanity for the happiness of the human race. In short, it interferes with everything. But before I name this advantage to you, I want to compromise myself personally and therefore I boldly declare that all these attractive systems—all these theories explaining man's real, normal interests by saying that in striving to achieve them he inevitably at once becomes good and honourable—are in my opinion, for the time being, nothing but sophistry! Yes, sir, sophistry! You see, to advance even this theory of the reform of the whole human race by means of the system of its personal advantages is, if you ask me, almost the same thing as . . . well, as asserting Buckle's* theory that civilization mollifies man, and he consequently becomes less bloodthirsty and less inclined to war. Logically it appears that this should be so. But man is so partial to systems and abstract conclusions that he is prepared to distort the truth intentionally, he is prepared not to see what he sees, not to hear what he hears, simply in order to justify his logic. The reason I choose this example is that it is such a striking one. Just look around yourselves: blood is flowing in rivers, and in such a merry way too, like champagne. There's the whole of our nineteenth century for you, the one which Buckle too lived in. There's Napoleon for you—both the great one and the contemporary one.* There's North America for you—the everlasting union. And finally, there's the grotesque Schleswig-Holstein* for you . . . And what then is it that civilization is mollifying in us? Civilization only develops in man the many-sidedness of his sensations and . . . absolutely nothing else. And in the course of the development of this many-sidedness man progresses still further to the point where he finds pleasure in bloodshed. You see, it's already happened to him. Have you never noticed that the most refined bloodshedders have almost invariably been the most highly civilized gentlemen, to whom all the various Attilas and Stenka Razins* could not even have held a candle, and if they don't strike you as much as Attila or Stenka Razin then it's precisely because you meet them too often, they are too commonplace, too familiar? At any rate, as a result of civilization man has become, if not more blood-thirsty, then undoubtedly more horribly, more revoltingly bloodthirsty than before. Before, he saw justice in bloodshed and, with an easy conscience, he destroyed anyone he needed to; nowadays, although we regard bloodshed as something vile, we nevertheless involve ourselves in this bloodshed even more than before. What is worse?—decide for yourselves. We are told that Cleopatra (excuse me for using an example from Roman history) loved to stick gold pins into the bosoms of her slaves and took pleasure in their shrieks and convulsions of pain. You will say that this was during relatively barbaric times; that today is still a barbaric period because (also relatively speaking) people today still stick pins in people; that even if man has now learnt at times to see more clearly than in barbaric periods, then he is still far from *accustomed* to behaving according to the dictates of science and reason. But you are nevertheless absolutely convinced that he undoubtedly will grow accustomed to it when he completely discards various old, bad habits and when human nature is completely re-educated and generally governed by common sense and sci-ence. You are convinced that man will then *of his own accord* cease to err, and will, as it were willy-nilly, not wish to separate his will from his normal interests. Moreover, you say, science itself will then teach man (although it's really a luxury, in my opinion) that in actual fact he has neither will, nor caprice, nor did he ever have them, and that he is nothing more than something in the nature of a piano-key or an organ-stop; and that, besides, there are still the laws of nature in the world, so that whatever he does is done not through his own volition, but automatically, following the laws of nature. Consequently these laws of nature only have to be revealed and man will no longer be responsible for his own actions and life will become extremely easy for him. All human action will automatically be computed according to these laws, mathematically, like a table of logarithms, reaching to 108,000 and compiled in a directory; or still better there will appear various loyal publications, like our contemporary encyclopedias, in which everything will be so accurately calculated and designated that there will no longer be any actions or adventures in the world.

And then—it is you saying all this—a new economic policy will come into being, absolutely complete and also calculated with mathematical precision so that all conceivable questions will vanish in a flash, for the simple reason that every conceivable answer has been given to them. Then they will erect the Crystal Palace.* Then . . . well, in short, the bird of Kagan* will appear. Of course, there is no guarantee (this is me speaking now) that it will not be dreadfully boring, for instance (because what will there be to do when everything is worked out according to tables?); on the other hand, everything will be extremely reasonable. Of course, you'd think up all sorts of things out of boredom! Indeed, gold pins get stuck into people out of boredom, but all this would not matter. The vile thing (this is me speaking again) is that, I dare say, they may well be glad even of gold pins then. You see, man is stupid, phenomenally stupid. That is to say, even if he's not totally stupid then he's so ungrateful that one shouldn't expect anything else of him. For example, I should not be in the least surprised if suddenly, for no reason at all, some gentleman or other with a dishonourable, or shall we say, a reactionary and sarcastic demeanour springs up amidst this future reign of universal good sense and puts his hands on his hips and says to us all: 'Well, gentlemen, why don't we get rid of all this good sense once and for all, give it a kick, throw it to the wind, just in order to send all these logarithms to hell so that we can once again live according to our own foolish will?' And this wouldn't matter either, but it's upsetting that he would undoubtedly find followers: that's the way man is made. And all this for the most trifling reasons, which one would think were hardly worth mentioning: namely, because man has always and everywhere, whoever he was, loved to act as he wants and not in the least as his reason and personal advantage dictates; it is possible to desire against one's own best interest, and sometimes one *positively should* (this is my idea). One's own, independent, and free desire, one's own, albeit wild, caprice, one's fantasy, sometimes provoked to the point of madness—it is indeed all of this that comprises that omitted, that most advantageous advantage, which does not fall into any category, and which continually results in all systems and theories being sent to the devil. And from where did all these sages get the idea that man needs some kind of normal, some kind of virtuous desire? Why have they unfailingly imagined that man definitely needs sensible, advantageous desire? Man needs one thing only: *independent* desire, whatever that independence costs and wherever it may lead him. But the devil only knows what desire . . .

CHAPTER 8

'HA, ha, ha! You see, as a matter of fact, if you want, this desire doesn't exist!' you interrupt with a guffaw. 'By now science has succeeded so far in its dissection of man that we know that desire and this so-called free will are nothing other than . . .'

'Stop there a moment, gentlemen, I was just about to say that myself. I confess I took fright. I was just about to shout out that the devil only knows what desire depends on and that perhaps we should thank God for that, and then I remembered about science and . . . I subsided. And then you began talking. In actual fact, if they really do discover some day a formula for all our desires and caprices, that is to say on what they depend, from exactly which laws they originate, exactly how they diffuse themselves, what their aims are in this situation and in that, and so on and so on, in other words a real mathematical formula—then, you see, man would very likely immediately cease to desire, in fact he'd more than probably cease altogether. What is it to want if it means wanting by tables? Moreover: he would at once change from a man into an organ-stop or something of the kind; because what is a man without his wants, without will, without desire, if not a stop on a barrel-organ? What do you think? Weigh up the possibilities, could this happen or not?'

'Hmm . . .', you decide, 'on the whole our desires are

mistakes that have resulted from a mistaken attitude towards what is to our advantage. The very reason why we sometimes desire sheer nonsense is that, in our stupidity, we see in this nonsense the simplest method of achieving some sort of presupposed advantage. And when all this is explained and calculated on paper (which is very probable because it is vile and senseless to believe beforehand that there are various laws of nature that man will never discover), then, we can suppose, there will not be any of these so-called desires. If desire should at some time completely coincide with reason, we would reason and not desire precisely because it is impossible, for example, whilst safeguarding reason to *desire* nonsense and thus act knowingly against reason and wish to harm oneself . . . And since all desire and reasoning can really be calculated, because at some time they will discover the laws of our so-called free will, they will therefore, quite seriously, be able to establish something in the nature of tables in order that we really will desire according to this tabulation. You see, if at some stage it were calculated and proven to me that if I made an aggressive gesture at someone then it was for the very reason that I could not help making it, and that I was absolutely bound to make that particular gesture at him, what kind of *freedom* would I have left, especially if I'm learned and have studied science somewhere? You know I'd then be able to calculate the next thirty years of my life; in short, if they do work this out, there will be nothing we can do about it—we'll have to accept it anyway. And indeed we must tirelessly repeat to ourselves that without doubt in certain moments and in certain situations nature does not stop to ask us; that we must accept her as she is, and not as we fantasize, and if we are genuinely striving towards the tables and the directory, well . . . and possibly even towards the retort, then what else can we do but accept the retort as well? Otherwise the retort will become accepted by itself, without us . . .'

Yes, sir, but that's just where I see the snag. Gentlemen, forgive me for philosophizing so; that's what forty years in the underground does! Allow me to fantasize a bit. Don't you see, gentlemen? Reason is a fine thing, there's no question about it, but reason is only reason and only satisfies man's rational faculties, whereas desire is a manifestation of the whole of life,

that is of the whole of human life, along with reason and all
our head-scratching. And even if in this manifestation our life
frequently turns out to be rubbishy, it's nevertheless life and
not just the extraction of a square root. I, for instance, quite
naturally want to live in order to satisfy the whole of my
capacity for living and not just in order to satisfy my rational
capacity, which is about one-twentieth of my capacity for
living. What does reason know? Reason knows only what it
has managed to find out (the rest, perhaps, it will never
discover; that's no comfort, but why not say it?), whereas
human nature acts as a whole, by everything that is in it,
consciously and unconsciously; and even if it lies, it still lives.
I suspect, gentlemen, that you're looking at me with pity; you
will tell me again that an enlightened and educated person, in
short, the sort of person man will be in the future, cannot
knowingly desire something disadvantageous to himself, and
that's mathematics. I'm in complete agreement, it really is
mathematics. But I repeat to you for the hundredth time, there
is only one instance, just one, when man may deliberately,
consciously desire something injurious, foolish, even extremely
foolish, namely: in order to *have the right* to desire even
something very foolish, and not to be bound by an obligation
to desire only what is intelligent. You see, this very foolish
thing is your caprice, and in actual fact, gentlemen, it can be
more advantageous to us all than anything else on earth,
especially on certain occasions. But in particular it can be more
advantageous than any other advantage in a situation where it
leads us to obvious harm and contradicts the soundest conclusions of our reason on the subject of advantages—because in
any case it preserves the thing that is most important and
precious to us, which is our personality and our individuality.
Some people assert that this is the most precious thing of all to
man. Desire may, of course, if it wants, coincide with reason,
especially if it is not misused but used in moderation; that's
useful and at times even laudable. But very often, perhaps
more often than not, desire completely and obstinately disagrees with reason and . . . and . . . and do you know that this
too is useful and sometimes even very laudable? Gentlemen,
let us suppose that man is not stupid. (Really, you know, it's
quite impossible to say this about him, even if only because, if

he is stupid, then who is intelligent?) But even if he's not stupid, he's nevertheless astonishingly ungrateful! Phenomenally ungrateful. I even think that the very best description of man is this: a creature on two legs and ungrateful. But that's not all yet, that's not even his chief shortcoming; his most important shortcoming is his continual impropriety, continual from the time of the Flood to the Schleswig-Holstein period of human destiny. Impropriety and consequently irrationality; for it has been known for a long time that irrationality stems from nothing other than impropriety. Just take a look at the history of mankind—and what do you see? Majesty? Perhaps even majesty; how much is the Colossus of Rhodes* alone worth, for instance?! It is not for nothing that Mr Anaevsky* testifies that while some people say it must be the work of human hands, others insist that it is a creation of nature herself. Variety? Perhaps even variety; one need only collect the ceremonial uniforms, both military and civilian, of all nations, of all ages, and just think what that's worth, and if you include the uniforms of the Civil Service then you really will get lost; not a single historian would be able to cope. Monotony? Well, perhaps monotony too: fighting and fighting, they are fighting now, they fought before, and they fought after—you'll agree this is already too monotonous. In short, anything can be said about world history, things that might enter the head of only the most disordered imagination. The only thing that cannot be said is that it's rational. You'd choke on the first word. And then there's another snag you keep coming across: such decent and sensible people keep appearing in life, such wise men, and such lovers of the human race who, throughout their lives, set themselves the very task of conducting themselves as properly and sensibly as possible, as it were to enlighten their neighbours for the very purpose of proving to them that it really is possible to live decently and sensibly on this earth. And so? It is well known that, sooner or later, towards the end of their lives, many of these people have betrayed themselves by committing some ludicrous act or another, at times even of the most indecent sort. Now I'm going to ask you: what can one expect from man as a creature endowed with such strange qualities? Indeed, you can shower him with every earthly blessing, drown him in happiness from head to toe so that only bubbles jump about the surface of his happiness, like on water; give him such economic prosperity that he has absolutely nothing left to do except sleep, eat gingerbread, and fuss about the never-ending history of the world—and he's still just a man, and still out of ingratitude alone, out of plain lampoonery will commit abominations. He will even jeopardize his gingerbread and deliberately wish for the most ruinous rubbish, the most uneconomical nonsense, simply in order to print his own disastrous, fantastic element onto all this positive good sense. It is just his fantastic dreams, his abject foolishness that he wants to cling on to, solely in order that he can convince himself (as if it were absolutely necessary) that people are still people and not piano-keys, on which the laws of nature themselves are playing with their own hands, but are threatening to go on playing to the point when they would no longer be able to want anything beyond the directory. And besides: even in that case, even if he did turn out to be a piano-key, if that were proven to him by even the natural sciences and mathematically, he would still not come to his senses, and would deliberately do something to contradict it, simply out of ingratitude; just in order to assert himself. And in a situation where he did not have the means to do it, he would invent chaos and destruction, he would think up various forms of suffering, and—my goodness!—he'd assert himself. He would unleash his curse on the world, and since it is only man that can swear (this is a privilege that to a large extent differentiates him from the other animals) he might achieve his aim through his curse alone, that is he would really convince himself that he is a man and not a piano-key. If you say that even all this can be calculated on tables, the chaos, the gloom, and the curses, so that the possibility alone of a preliminary calculation would put a stop to everything and reason would hold sway—well, in that case man would deliberately go mad in order to escape his reason and assert himself. I believe this, I will vouch for it because this whole human business seems really only to consist of the fact that man has been continually proving to himself that he's a man and not an organ-stop. He'll prove it, whatever the way; he'll prove it even by becoming a troglodyte . . . And after that, how can you fail to transgress, to applaud the fact that this is not yet the case and that as yet the devil only knows on what desire depends? . . .

You will shriek at me (if you still find me worthy of your shrieks) that it is not as if someone is trying to take my will away from me; that all that's happening is that they're fussing about how so to arrange things that my own will itself should of its own accord coincide with my normal interests, with the laws of nature, and with arithmetic.

Eh, gentlemen, what will have become of your will when the whole thing has ended up with tables and arithmetic, when there is only twice two is four in demand? Twice two will be four without my will. That's what will become of your will!

CHAPTER 9

GENTLEMEN, I'm joking of course, and I myself know that I'm not joking very successfully, but you see you mustn't take it all for a joke. Maybe I'm joking through clenched teeth. Gentlemen, I'm tormented with questions; resolve them for me. For example, here are you, wanting to wean man from his old habits, and to correct his will in line with the demands of science and common sense. But how do you know that man not only could but *ought* to adapt himself in this way? What has led you to conclude that it is absolutely *necessary* for human desire to be altered? In a few words, how do you know that this reform will really be to man's advantage? And, to say it all, why are you so *certain* in your conviction that not going against real, normal advantages that are guaranteed by the deductions of reason and arithmetic is really always to a man's advantage and is a law that applies to all humanity? And yet these are just your suppositions. Let us suppose that they are rules of logic, but not at all of humanity. You may well think, gentlemen, that I'm mad! Let me be more specific. I agree: man is a predominately creative creature, condemned to strive consciously after aims and to engage himself in the art of engineering, that is to say to building himself a path eternally and incessantly *wherever it may lead to*. But the reason why at times he wants to swerve to the side may be precisely that he is *condemned* to make his way along this path, and furthermore, perhaps, because however foolish a spontaneous man of action is in general, he nevertheless sometimes gets the idea that, as it turns out, this path almost always leads *wherever it's going to lead* and that the important thing is not where it leads to, but that it should go somewhere and that a well-behaved child abandoning the art of engineering should not give in to pernicious idleness, which as is well known is the mother of all vice. Man loves to create and to lay paths, that's beyond doubt. But why is he also so passionately fond of destruction and chaos? Now tell me that! But I should like to say a few words about that in particular. Is he not perhaps so fond of destruction and chaos (and it's indisputable that he is sometimes terribly fond of it, that's absolutely so) because he is instinctively afraid of achieving his aim and completing the building he is erecting? How do you know?—maybe he only likes the building from a distance and not in the least from nearby; perhaps he only likes building it and not living in it, handing it over afterwards *aux animaux domestiques*,* like ants, sheep, and so on and so on. These ants have a completely different taste. They have one incredible building of this kind, forever indestructible—the anthill.

The respectable ants began with the anthill and they will no doubt finish with the anthill, which does great credit to their steadfastness and optimism. But man is a superficial and unseemly creature and perhaps, like a chess-player, he only loves the process of achieving his end and not the actual end in itself. And—who knows? (it's impossible to be certain)—perhaps the whole aim after which man strives on this earth consists simply in this uninterrupted process of achievement, or to put it another way—in life itself and not strictly in the aim, which, it goes without saying, can be none other than twice two's four, that is to say a formula, and, you see, twice two's four is no longer life, gentlemen, but the onset of death. At least man has always been so afraid of this twice two's four, and I'm still afraid of now. Let us suppose that man does nothing but search for this twice two's four, he crosses oceans, he sacrifices his life in this quest, but to find it, really to find it—good God, he's somehow afraid. You see he feels that, when he finds it, there won't be anything left to look for. At least when workmen finish their work they receive money, go down to the tavern, and then end up in the police station—and that keeps them busy for a week. But where can man go? At any rate one notices something awkward about a person whenever he has achieved such an aim. He loves the process of achievement, but not so much the achievement itself, and of course this is terribly amusing. In a word, man is comically constructed; and obviously there is a joke in all this. But twice two's four—it's nevertheless an intolerable thing. Twice two's four, well in my opinion it's a cheek. Twice two's four watches smugly, stands in the middle of your road with his arms akimbo, and spits. I agree that twice two's four is a marvellous thing; but to give everything its due praise, twice two is five can also be a very nice little thing.

And why are you so staunchly, so solemnly convinced that only normal and positive—in short, that only prosperity is advantageous to man? Doesn't reason make mistakes about what is advantageous? I mean, perhaps man doesn't only love prosperity. Maybe he loves suffering just as much? Maybe suffering is just as much of an advantage to him as prosperity? And at times man is terribly fond of suffering, he loves it to the point of passion, and that's a fact. In this instance it's no use asking world history; ask yourselves if you've had any experience of life. As for my own personal opinion, I think that to love only prosperity is even rather unseemly. Whether it's a good thing or a bad thing it is sometimes very pleasant to smash something. I am not advocating suffering, nor prosperity either. I'm advocating . . . caprice, and that it be guaranteed to me when I need it. For example, suffering isn't allowed in vaudeville, I know that. It's inconceivable in the Crystal Palace; suffering is doubt, it's negation, and what's a Crystal Palace where you can doubt? And besides, I'm sure that man will never give up real suffering, that is, destruction and chaos. Suffering is indeed the sole cause of consciousness. Even if I declared at the beginning that in my opinion consciousness is man's greatest misfortune, I know that man loves it and will not exchange it for any other form of satisfaction. Consciousness is, for instance, endlessly superior to twice two. After twice two, it goes without saying, there's nothing left, not only nothing to do but nothing to discover either. The only thing that will then be possible will be to dismiss your five senses and bury yourself in contemplation. But even though the very same result arises in a state of consciousness, that is to say, there is also nothing to do, at least one could sometimes beat oneself and that, at least, is stimulating. Albeit retrogressive, but it's still better than nothing.

CHAPTER 10

YOU believe in the Crystal Palace, eternally indestructible, that is, in something at which you cannot secretly stick out your tongue, or make gestures of defiance. But perhaps the reason I fear this Crystal Palace is that it is crystal and that it is eternally indestructible and that you cannot even stick your tongue out at it.

Don't you see?—if instead of the palace there were a chicken-coop and it was raining I might even climb into the chicken-coop in order not to get drenched, but I would nevertheless not take the chicken-coop for a palace out of gratitude for the fact that it had saved me from the rain. You're laughing, you're even saying that it doesn't make any difference if it's a chicken-coop or a mansion. True, I answer, if one only lived in order not to get drenched.

But what if I took it into my head that that isn't the only reason for living and that if we have to live it might as well be in mansions? That is my desire, that is my wish. You can only rid me of that by changing my desires. Well, change them, tempt me with something else, give me another ideal. But in the meanwhile I still won't take a chicken-coop for a mansion. Granted it might even be true that the Crystal Palace is a hoax, that the laws of nature do not provide for it, and that I invented it all simply on account of my own stupidity, and on account of certain outdated irrational habits of our generation. But what does it matter to me if it's not provided for? Isn't it all the same if it exists in my desires, or better still it exists so long as my desires exist? Perhaps you are laughing again? Go on, laugh; I will put up with all the derision but I still won't say that I'm full when I'm still hungry; still I know that I won't settle for a compromise, for a constantly recurring zero, simply because it exists according to the laws of nature and *really* does exist. I won't accept as the crown of my desire a tenement block divided into flats for impoverished tenants on thousand-year leases, with the dentist Waggenheim's name on the signboard in case of need. Suppress my desires, erase my ideals, show me something better, and I will follow you. You will probably say that it's not worth getting tied up with me; but in that case I can give you the same answer. We are having a serious discussion; if you don't want to honour me with your attention then I'm not going to beg for it. I've got the underground.

In the meantime I go on living and desiring—and, I'd sooner cut off my right hand than take one brick to that block of flats! Don't take any notice that just now I rejected the Crystal Palace for the sole reason that it's impossible to stick one's tongue out at it. It is not the case at all that I said this because I am so fond of sticking my tongue out. Perhaps I only got angry because, of all your buildings, there is so far not one at which you wouldn't stick your tongue out. On the other hand I would cut my tongue out with gratitude if only it could be arranged that I would never again wish to stick my tongue out. What does it matter to me that such a building is impossible and that we must be content with flats? Why then am I created with these sort of desires? Am I really created simply to reach the conclusion that my whole creation is nothing but a swindle? Is that really the whole aim? I don't believe it.

However, do you know what? I'm convinced that our friend in the underground needs to be kept in check. He might be able to sit silently in the underground for forty years, but if he once emerges into the light of day and breaks his silence, how he talks, talks, talks . . .

CHAPTER 11

THE end of it all, gentlemen, is this: it's better to do nothing at all! Better conscious inertia. And so, long live the underground! I might have said that I'm green with envy of the normal person, but in the circumstances in which I see him I would not like to be in his place (although I will nevertheless not stop envying him. No, no, whatever the case the underground is more advantageous!) There at least it is possible . . . Ah! but here again I'm lying! I'm lying because I know myself, as well as I know that twice two is four, that it's not the underground that's any better, but something else, something quite different, after which I thirst, but which I will never find! To hell with the underground!

It would even be better if at least I could believe something of what I have written here. I swear to you, gentlemen, I do not believe one, not one single word of what I have scribbled down here! That is, perhaps I do believe, but at the same time, for some unknown reason I feel and suspect that I'm lying like a bootmaker.

'What have you written it all for then?' you will say to me.

'Well I'd like to sit you down for forty years or so without any occupation, then come and see you after forty years, in the underground, to see how you're getting on. Is it really possible to leave a man alone for forty years with nothing to do?'

'But isn't this a disgrace, isn't this humiliating!' you might say to me, shaking your heads disdainfully. 'You thirst after life and yet you try to solve life's questions with tangled logic. And how importunate, how daring your pranks are, and at the same time, how frightened you are! You talk rubbish and are satisfied with it; you talk daringly but then you are always afraid, and beg forgiveness for it. You assure us that you are not afraid of anything, and at the same time cringe after our approval. You assure us that you're clenching your teeth, and at the same time you make jokes in order to make us laugh. You know that your jokes are not very witty, but you are obviously very pleased with your literary merit. Perhaps you have really had cause to suffer, but you have no respect whatsoever for your suffering. There is even some truth in you, but no virtue; out of the most petty vanity you put your truth on display, you put it to shame, you take it to the market-place . . . You really want to say something, but out of fear you never say the last word because you do not have the resolution to say it, but only cowardly impertinence. You boast about consciousness, but you merely vacillate, because although your mind is working, your heart is darkened by corruption, and without a pure heart there is no overall, true consciousness. And how importunate you are, how querulous, how affected you are! Lies, lies, and more lies!'

Of course, I myself have invented all your words. They're also from the underground. It is now forty years that I've been there listening to your words through a chink. I thought them up myself, you see that's all there was to think up. It's no wonder they've been learnt by heart and have adopted a literary form . . .

But surely, surely you aren't really so gullible as to imagine that I would publish all this, let alone give it to you to read? And I've got another problem: why in fact do I call you 'gentlemen', why do I address you as if I were addressing readers? The sort of confessions that I intend to expound do not get published or given to others to read. At any rate I am not sure enough of myself, neither do I think it necessary. But don't you see?—it is just a fantasy that has entered my head, and whatever happens I want to make it come alive. This is what the whole thing's about:

In every man's memory there are things which he does not divulge to everyone, but really only to friends. And there are those things which he doesn't even divulge to friends, but really only to himself, and then as a secret. And, finally, there are those which a man is afraid to divulge even to himself, and every respectable person has accumulated quite a few of these. One might even say: the more respectable the person, the more of these he has. At any rate, not long ago I myself decided to recall various of my former adventures, which up until then I had always shirked, indeed rather nervously. Now, however, that I have not only resolved to remember them but even to note them down, I really do wish to discover: is it really possible to be absolutely open with oneself and not be frightened of the whole truth? Incidentally, I note: Heine* asserts that true autobiographies are almost impossible and that a person is bound to lie about himself. In his opinion, Rousseau,* for example, undoubtedly lied about himself in his confession and even lied intentionally, through vanity. I am certain that Heine is right: I understand very well how at times out of sheer vanity it is possible to pin entire crimes on oneself, and I can also well grasp the nature of this vanity. But Heine was passing judgement on a person making a public confession. I, however, am writing for myself alone and declare once and for all that if I'm writing as if I'm addressing readers then it's quite simply for show, because it makes it easier to write. This is mere form, empty form; as for readers, I'll never have any of them. I've already stated that.

I do not want to be restricted in any way in the editing of my notes. I don't want to introduce any system or order. I'll note down whatever I remember.

But at this point, for instance, people could start quibbling and ask me: if you are really not counting on readers, then why are you now making such agreements with yourself (and on paper, at that)?—that is to say, that you won't introduce any order or system, that you'll only write what you remember, etc.? To what purpose are you explaining this? What's the point of excusing yourself?

'Just imagine', I answer.

Here, however, lies an entire psychology. Maybe it's that I'm a simple coward. Or maybe it's that I'm deliberately imagining an audience in front of me in order that I might behave better when the time comes to write. There are a thousand possible reasons.

But there's something else too: why, why exactly do I wish to write? If it's not for the public, then wouldn't it be possible to remember it all in my head without transferring it to paper?

Quite so; but on paper it comes across somehow more majestically. There's something inspirational about it, one's a stricter judge of oneself, it adds to the style. Moreover: perhaps I genuinely get comfort from writing. Just today, for instance, I am particularly oppressed by one very old memory. It came to my mind very clearly just the other day and since then it hasn't left me, like an irritating musical motif that gets stuck. But none the less you must get rid of it. I've got hundreds of memories of this sort; but from time to time, one or other of them stands out from the hundreds and weighs on me. For some reason I believe that if I write it down I'll get rid of it. Why not try?

Finally: I'm bored, but I never do anything. Writing is really some sort of work. They say that work makes a man good and honest. There's a chance, at any rate.

Today it's snowing, almost wet, yellowish, dull snow. Yesterday it snowed as well, and the day before. It seems to me that it was the wet snow that caused me to recall this anecdote which I can't get out of my head. So, let this be a tale concerning the wet snow.

PART II
CONCERNING THE WET SNOW

When out of the darkness of delusion
Using an ardent word of persuasion
I rescued your fallen soul,
And full of profound torment,
Wringing your hands, you cursed
The vice which had ensnared you;
When your forgetful conscience
Was being punished by memories,
You told me the story of
All that came before me,
And suddenly, covering your face with your hands,
Full of shame and fear,
You let your tears flow,
Troubled, shaken . . .
etc., etc., etc.

From the poetry of N. A. Nekrasov*

CHAPTER 1

At that time I was only twenty-four years old. Even then my life was gloomy, disordered, and insanely lonely. I did not associate with anyone, even avoided talking, and retreated further and further into my corner. At work, at the office, I even tried not to look at anyone and I was well aware that my colleagues not only considered me an odd fellow but—this is how it aways seemed to me—looked on me as if with a kind of loathing. The thought came to me: why is it that it's only me that feels he's being regarded with loathing? One of the office clerks had a repulsive, spotty face, he even looked a bit like a criminal. I felt that if I'd had such an ugly face I would never have dared to look at anyone. Another one had a uniform that was so worn out that there was a nasty smell all around him. None the less neither one of these gentlemen felt embarrassed—either on account of his clothes, or on account of his face, or about any of the moral issues involved. Neither one of them imagined that he was being regarded with loathing; or if he did, then he did not mind so long as his superiors did not take it upon themselves to stare. It is now quite apparent to me that because of my boundless vanity and the strict demands I thereby made of myself, I very often looked on myself with a violent dissatisfaction, which reached the point of loathing, and therefore I mentally attributed my own outlook to others. For instance, I hated my face, I found it disgusting and I even suspected that it had a rather mean expression, and therefore each time I appeared at work I desperately tried to behave as independently as possible, in order not to be suspected of cringing, and to make my face look as dignified as possible. 'Well, all right, so my face is unattractive', I thought, 'but on the other hand nothing will prevent it from having a noble, significant, and more importantly, an *extremely* intelligent expression.' But I knew with certainty, and suffered deeply over the fact, that my face would never express any of these perfections. But what was still worse was that I found it decidedly stupid. And I would have been quite happy to settle for intelligence. Even to the extent that I would have accepted a mean expression on the one condition that at the same time people found my face frightfully intelligent.

Needless to say, I detested all our office clerks, from the first to the last, and I despised them all, although I was somehow afraid of them as well. All of a sudden I would regard them as superior to myself. It would somehow happen so suddenly that one minute I would find myself despising them and the next esteeming them superior to myself. A cultured and respectable person cannot be vain without making boundless demands on himself and without at various moments despising himself to the point of hatred. But whether or not I despised them or looked on them as superior to myself, at practically every encounter I lowered my eyes. I even made some experiments: I would try to out-stare someone who was looking at me, but I was always the first to give in. This drove me wild with annoyance. I also made myself ill with fear of seeming ridiculous and therefore I slavishly followed a routine in everything that concerned me outwardly. I enthusiastically followed the general trend and with my whole being feared any eccentricity within myself. But how was I to keep it up? I was morbidly cultured, in the way that it befits a man to be cultured in our times. Whereas they were all dull-witted and one just like the next, like a flock of sheep. Maybe I was the only person in the whole office who constantly thought I was a coward and a slave; that's precisely why it seemed to me that I was cultured. But it wasn't just that this seemed to be so, in actual fact it really was the case: I was a coward and a slave. I say this without a trace of embarrassment. Every respectable man of our times is, and is bound to be, a coward and a slave. This is his normal condition. I am deeply convinced of this. That is how he is created and what he is made for. And it is not just in our times owing to a certain set of circumstances, but in general, at all times a decent person is bound to be a coward and a slave. This is a natural law pertaining to every respectable person in the world. Even if it so happens that one of them makes a show of bravery over something, he still won't comfort or distract himself with this: he'll still cower before others. Such is the only and the eternal solution. Only asses and their cross-breeds put up this show of bravery, and then only until they come up against something. It's not worth paying any attention to them because they really aren't worth mentioning.

At the time I was tormented by one other circumstance: namely, that no one else was like me, nor was I like anyone else. 'I am alone, and they are *everybody*', I thought, and became pensive.

From this it is clear that I was still a complete child.

Contradictory things occurred. Sometimes I found going to the office quite appalling: it reached the point where I was very frequently ill when I returned from work. And then all of a sudden out of the blue a bout of scepticism and indifference would emerge (with me everything happened in bouts) and I myself would laugh at my own intolerance and fastidiousness, and reproach myself for *romanticism*. At times I did not want to talk to anyone, and then I would find myself not just chatting but even contemplating making friends with people. All at once, just like that, all my fastidiousness would suddenly vanish. Who knows, perhaps it never existed, but was put on, borrowed from books? I still haven't resolved this question. At one time I got so friendly with them I started visiting them at home and playing preference, drinking vodka, discussing promotion . . . But here allow me to make a digression.

Generally speaking we Russians have never had romantics of the foolish star-gazing German kind, or especially the French kind, who are not influenced by anything and even if the earth were trembling beneath them, even if the whole of France were perishing at the barricades, would still do nothing, would change nothing, not even for the sake of decency, but would carry on singing their other-worldly songs, as it were until their dying day, because they are fools. But we, who live on Russian soil, know no fools; that's well known; and that is how we are distinguished from other Germanic peoples. Other-worldly natures are not found here in their pure form. It was those 'positive' contemporary publicists and critics of ours who were hunting out the Kostanzhoglos* and the Uncle Petr Ivanoviches* and stupidly taking them as our ideal, who invented all this about our romantics, making out that they are as other-worldly as those in Germany or France. Quite the contrary, the characteristics of our romantics are completely and utterly opposite to the super-celestial European type and not a single European standard can be applied over here. (Allow me to use this word 'romantic'; it is ancient, respected, time-honoured, and familiar to everyone.) The characteristics of our romantic type are: to understand everything, *to see everything, and frequently to see it incomparably more clearly than our most distinguished intellects*; not to be reconciled to anyone or anything, but at the same time not to balk at anything; to get round everything, to concede to everyone, to behave expediently towards everyone; never to lose sight of his useful, practical aim (some state apartments or other, pensions, medals), to keep his eye on this aim throughout all his enthusiasms and little volumes of lyrical verses, and at the same time to preserve inviolate the 'beautiful and sublime' within himself to his dying day, and incidentally to preserve himself completely, wrapped in cotton wool like some little piece of jewellery, which might for instance be for the benefit of this very same 'beautiful and sublime'. He's a person of breadth, our romantic, and the greatest of all our swindlers, I assure you of that . . . indeed, from experience. Obviously this is only if the romantic is intelligent. Now what am I saying? A romantic is always intelligent. I only wanted to point out that even if we did have stupid romantics among us they don't count, simply because when they were at the height of their strength they all degenerated into Germans, and in order to preserve their precious jewel more suitably they settled somewhere over there, for the most part in Weimar or Schwarzwald. I, for example, sincerely detested my office job and the only reason I did not spit in disgust was through necessity, because I sat there and got paid for it. The outcome though—note this—I still did not spit. Our romantic would sooner go crazy (which happens very seldom, however) than spit unless he has another career in mind, and he will never be thrown out, unless he's carried off to the madhouse as the 'king of Spain', and that's only if he really has gone completely crazy. But, you see, amongst us only the insipid, bloodless types go mad. We have an absolutely countless number of romantics—and they subsequently achieve distinguished posts. An astonishing versatility! And what a capacity for the most contradictory feelings! At that time I was comforted by it, and I still share the same thoughts. That is why we have so many people of 'breadth' who, even at the very last fall, never lose sight of their ideal; and even if they wouldn't lift a finger on behalf of this ideal, even if they are confessed crooks and thieves, they still respect their foremost ideal to the point of tears, and are unusually pure of heart. Yes, sir, it's only amongst us that a declared villain can be utterly, and even eminently, pure of heart whilst in no way ceasing to be a villain. I repeat, businesslike scoundrels of this sort (I'm using the word 'scoundrels' fondly) very often emerge from amidst our romantics, and they suddenly display such a sense of reality and practical ability that the astonished authorities and the public simply click their tongues at them, utterly dumbfounded.

The versatility is truly astounding, and God knows what it will turn into and how it will develop in subsequent circumstances and what it promises us in the future. But the material is not bad! I'm not speaking out of some sort of ridiculous or jingoistic patriotism. However, I'm sure that once again you're thinking that I'm being funny. Or, who knows, perhaps it's the other way round and you're convinced that I do indeed think this? In any case, gentlemen, I will accept either one of your opinions as an honour and as a particular pleasure. But forgive me for my digression.

I did not, of course, sustain a friendship with my companions and I very soon turned up my nose at them, and owing to my then youthful inexperience I even stopped greeting them, as though severing relations. However, this only ever happened once. In general I was always alone.

At home, to begin with, I mostly read. I wanted to stifle all that had swelled up inside me with external sensations. The only external sensation I found possible was reading. Naturally, reading helped a lot—it excited, delighted, and tormented me. But from time to time I grew terribly bored. I felt that I wanted to do something, and would suddenly plunge myself into dark, subterranean, vile—not so much depravity as petty dissipations. My little passions were keen and red-hot, from my customary, morbid irritability. The outbursts were hysterical with tears and convulsions. Apart from reading I had nowhere to turn—that is to say, there was at the time nothing in my surroundings that I could respect, or that appealed to me. Besides, I was seething inside with ennui; a hysterical thirst for contradictions and contrasts used to appear and then I would lapse into debauchery. I haven't just said all this in order to excuse myself . . . However, no . . . That was a lie. To excuse myself was just what I wanted. I'm making this note for my own sake, gentlemen. I don't want to lie. I've given my word.

I led a solitary life of dissipation, by night, furtive, timid, sordid, and with a sense of shame that stayed with me at the most dreadful times; it even used to become a curse at such moments. Even then, at that time I carried the underground inside me. I was dreadfully afraid that I would somehow be seen, or meet someone, or be recognized. I frequented various utterly gloomy places.

On one occasion, walking past a little tavern in the night I caught sight in an illuminated window of some gentlemen standing by a billiard-table fighting with their cues, and then I saw one of them being thrown out of the window. Another time I would have found this quite disgusting; but that time I was taken by surprise and felt very envious of this gentleman who had been hurled out. I envied him so much that I even walked into the tavern, into the billiard-room: 'Perhaps', I said, 'I too will get into a fight, and I'll also get thrown out of the window.'

I was not drunk, but what was I supposed to do?—one can fall into the depths of misery to the point of hysteria. But nothing happened in the end. As it turned out, I wasn't even able to jump out of the window and I was leaving without having a fight.

As soon as I moved I was accosted by an officer. I was standing by the billiard-table and was unaware that I was blocking the way of this fellow who wanted to get by; he took me by the shoulders and without a word—without any advance warning, or explanation—moved me from the place where I was standing to another, and then passed by as if I didn't exist. I would have forgiven even a blow, but under no circumstances could I forgive the fact that he had moved me and so utterly failed to notice me.

The devil only knows what I would have given at that moment for a real, more correct quarrel, a more becoming, more, as it were, *literary* one! I had been treated like a fly. This officer was about six feet tall, whereas I was a short, emaciated man. However, it was in my power to start an argument; I only need to protest and, of course, I would be thrown out of the window. But I changed my mind and preferred . . . to withdraw bitterly into the background.

I walked out of the tavern confused and agitated and went straight home, but the following day I continued my debauchery—more timidly, I was more downtrodden and gloomier than before, almost with tears in my eyes—but all the same I carried on. Don't imagine, however, that I backed away from the officer through cowardice: I have never been a coward at heart, although I constantly behaved like one, but—wait a bit before laughing, there's an explanation for this; there's an explanation for everything that concerns me, rest assured.

Oh, if only that officer had been one of those types that would agree to a duel! But no, he was one of those gentlemen (alas, long since vanished) who prefer to act with billiard-cues, or like Gogol's Lieutenant Pirogov*—through the authorities. They would absolutely never fight a duel, and in any case would have considered a duel with me, with an office-worker, very unpleasant—indeed, on the whole they have regarded a duel as something inconceivable, free-thinking, French, whereas they have caused enough offence, especially if they are six feet tall.

On this occasion I backed out not through cowardice but through boundless vanity. I was not afraid of his height of six feet, or of the fact that I would be badly beaten and thrown out of the window; truly, I had quite sufficient physical courage; but I lacked moral courage. I was afraid that everyone there, from the cheeky marker to the last rotten, pimply little clerk hanging around with his greasy collar, would fail to understand and would ridicule me when I started protesting and talking to them in literary language. Because up until now it has been impossible for us to discuss a point of honour, that is, not honour but a point of honour (*point d'honneur*), in anything but literary language. In ordinary language 'point of honour' doesn't mean anything. I was utterly convinced (this flair for reality despite all the romanticism!) that they would all simply split their sides laughing, and that the officer would not simply, that is inoffensively, have flattened me, but he would have been bound to kick me with his knees, dragging me in this manner around the whole billiard-table and would only then have taken pity on me and hurled me out of the window. Of course, I couldn't let this wretched little episode end there. Subsequently I frequently bumped into this officer in the street and observed him very carefully. The only thing is that I don't know whether he recognized me. He can't have done; various indications led me to this conclusion. But I, well I—I looked at him with malice and loathing and this went on . . . well quite a few years. My hatred even grew stronger and firmer over the years. In the beginning I started, furtively, to find out more about this officer. I found it very difficult because I had no acquaintances. But one day someone called him by his surname on the street while I was following him at a distance, as though I were on a lead, and thus I learnt his surname. Another time I followed him right up to his flat and for a few copecks I learnt from the caretaker where he lived, on what floor, alone or with someone, etc., etc.—in short, everything that can be learnt from a caretaker. One morning, although I have never engaged in literary activities, I suddenly got the idea of describing this officer in the form of a denunciation, making a caricature of him in a kind of story. I delighted in writing this story. I exposed him, I even slandered him; to begin with I modified the name in such a way that it could still be immediately recognized, but then on mature reflection I changed it altogether and sent it to *Fatherland Notes*.* But at that time there was still no nefarious literature and my story was not published. I found this extemely annoying. At times I was simply choking with anger. In the end I decided to challenge him to a duel. I composed a delightful, charming letter to him, imploring him to apologize to me; I made heavy references to a duel in the event of refusal. The letter was composed in such a way that if the officer had had the slightest notion of the 'beautiful and sublime', he would have been bound to come running to me, in order to throw his arms around my shoulders and offer his friendship. And how wonderful that would have been! What a life we would have begun, what a life! 'He would have protected me with his exalted rank; I would have ennobled him with my culture, and well, with my ideas—and who knows what might have happened!' But you can imagine, two years had now passed since he had offended me and my summons was an extremely impolite anachronism, despite the cunningness of my letter in explaining and covering up the anachronism. But thank God (to this day I thank the Almighty with tears in my eyes), I did not send my letter. It makes my blood run cold to remember what might have happened if I had sent it. And then suddenly, suddenly I took my revenge in the most simple, most ingenious fashion! A brilliant idea suddenly dawned on me. Sometimes on holidays between three and four o'clock I used to hang around the Nevsky Prospect, strolling along the sunny side. That is to say, I did not really stroll but rather experienced countless torments, disparagements, and outbursts of spleen; but to be honest there was something about it that I needed. I darted about like a rabbit, in the most unattractive way, amidst the passers-by, continually making way for generals, or horse-guards officers or hussars, or fine ladies; at these moments I would feel a convulsive pain in my heart and a burning sensation in my back at the mere thought of the misery of my outfit, of the misery and puniness of my little figure darting about. It was an excruciating torment, the uninterrupted, intolerable humiliation of my thoughts, that at times turned into an incessant and spontaneous feeling that I was a fly in the eyes of the whole world, a repulsive, obscene fly—more intelligent than anyone else, more cultured than anyone else, more virtuous than anyone else—that need hardly be said— but a fly that was constantly giving in to others, humiliated and offended by all. Why I brought this torment on myself, why I walked along the Nevsky Prospect I do not know. But I was literally *drawn* there at every opportunity.

It was then that I started experiencing surges of that pleasure about which I spoke in the first part. After the incident with the officer I was even more powerfully drawn there—to the Nevsky Prospect, where I met him most often, where I feasted my eyes on him. He too tended to go there mostly on holidays. He also stepped off the road to make way for generals and high-ranking personages and he also wormed about between them, but he simply trod upon people of my sort, and even those of a higher rank than me; he walked straight over them as if there was an empty space in front of him and under no circumstance did he step back. I revelled in my own anger as I watched him . . . and resentfully I made way for him each time. I was tormented by the fact that not even on the street could I stand on an equal footing with him. 'Why is it you are invariably the first to make way?' I asked myself in wild hysterics, having woken up as I sometimes did, at three in the morning. 'Why should it be you and not him? You know there's no law for that, it's not laid down anywhere in writing. Why can't it be divided in equal parts, as normally happens when refined people meet?—he steps back half-way and you half-way, and you both walk on in mutual respect.' But that was not what happened and I still stepped aside and he didn't even notice that I was making way for him. And then a marvellous idea suddenly struck me. 'What would happen', I thought, 'if we were to meet and . . . and I didn't step aside? Deliberately not to step aside, even if it meant bumping into him: how would that be?' Bit by bit this daring idea so overwhelmed me that it would not leave me in peace. I dreamt about it incessantly, horribly, and I deliberately went to the Nevsky more frequently so that I could visualize more clearly how I would act when I came to do it. I was in ecstasy. More and more it seemed to me that the intention was probable and possible. 'Of course, I won't give him a proper shove,' I thought, already mellowing in advance out of sheer joy, 'I'll simply not move aside, I'll bump into him not so that it hurts, but shoulder to shoulder, in exact accordance with propriety; I'll bump into him no harder than he bumps into me.' Finally I was completely resolved. But the preparations took up a lot of time. The first thing was that at the time of doing it it was necessary to look more attractive and take some trouble over my attire. 'To be on the safe side—if for instance it should give rise to a public scandal (and here the public are very refined: a countess walks here, Prince D. walks here, the whole of literature walks here)—one needs to be well dressed; this creates a good impression and in a number of respects puts you at once on an equal footing in the eyes of high society.' With this in mind I asked for my salary in advance and purchased a pair of black gloves and a respectable hat from Churkin's. I thought the black gloves both more respectable and more in *bon ton* than the lemon ones that I made for at first. 'The colour's too sharp, it gives too much of an impression of a person wanting to make a show of himself', and I didn't take the lemon ones. A good shirt with white bone cuff-links I had already prepared long before; but I was very much delayed by the overcoat. In itself my overcoat really wasn't bad, it was warm; but it was wadded and the collar was made out of racoon, which constituted the height of servility. Whatever happened I had to change the collar and put on a beaver one, the kind officers had. I started going round the arcades in search of this and after several attempts determined on a cheap German beaver collar. These German beaver collars might wear out very quickly and start to look extremely wretched, but at first, when they are newly acquired, they can even look very attractive; and you see I only needed it for one occasion. I asked the price; all things considered it was too expensive. After profound deliberation I decided to sell my racoon collar. The remaining, and for me quite considerable, sum I decided to try and borrow from Anton Antonych Setochkin, the head of my section at work, a meek but serious and respectable man who had never lent money to anyone but to whom I had been especially recommended when I started work, by the distinguished person who had appointed me the post. I was dreadfully anxious. It seemed to me that to borrow money from Anton Antonych was monstrous and shameful. I even had two or three sleepless nights; actually, on the whole I didn't sleep much at the time, I was delirious; my heart used to stop somehow in confusion or would suddenly begin to pound, pound . . . At first Anton Antonych was taken aback, then he knitted his brows, then he considered it, and in the end made the loan, after receiving a note from me giving him the right to repayment of the loaned moneys in two weeks' time out of my salary. And thus everything was finally ready; the lovely beaver collar reigned in place of the filthy racoon one, and I gradually started getting ready for action. It was impossible to decide on the spur of the moment, it would be useless; the thing needed to be managed skilfully, bit by bit. But I confess that after several repeated attempts I had come to the point of despair: we'll never bump into each other and that's that! Either I wasn't quite ready, or I hadn't quite made up my mind: it would appear that we were about to collide, then I would look and—once again I had stepped aside, and he had walked past without noticing me. I even said prayers, as I approached him, that God would inspire me with resolve. On one occasion I had my mind completely made up, but it ended in my simply getting in his way, because at the very last moment, at a distance of some three or four inches, I lost heart. He walked past me very quietly whilst I flew to the side like a little ball. That night I was again feverishly ill and delirious. And then everything suddenly came to a head in the best possible way. The day before, during the night, I finally agreed not to fulfil my fatal intention and to give it all up as hopeless, and with this in mind I went for the last time to the Nevsky Prospect just to reflect on how it was that I was giving it all up as hopeless. All of a sudden, at three paces from my enemy, I unexpectedly decided to screw up my eyes and—we bumped squarely into each other, shoulder to shoulder! I didn't step back a single inch and walked by on an exactly equal footing! He didn't even look round and even gave the impression of not noticing; but he only gave that appearance, I'm sure of that. To this day I'm sure of it. Of course, I had come off the worse; he was stronger, but that wasn't the point. The point was that I had achieved my aim, upheld my worth, not moved aside a single step, and publicly put myself on the same social footing as him. I returned home completely avenged. I was ecstatic. I celebrated and sang Italian arias. Of course, I shan't describe to you what happened to me three days later; if you have read the first part of my story, 'The Underground', then you might be able to guess for yourself. After that the officer was posted somewhere else; it's about fourteen years since I've seen him. What of him now, my dear friend? Who is he trampling on?

CHAPTER 2

BUT my bout of dissipation was coming to an end and I was becoming dreadfully sick of it. I was struck by remorse, but I drove it away: I was already too sickened. None the less, little by little I grew accustomed to it. I grew accustomed to everything, that is I didn't exactly grow accustomed but I sort of agreed, of my own accord, to put up with it. But I had one outlet that reconciled everything, which was to escape into all that is 'beautiful and sublime', dreaming, of course. It's dreadful the way I dreamt, I dreamt for three months on end, hidden away in my corner, and I can assure you that in those moments I bore no resemblance to that gentleman who in his chicken-hearted confusion had sewn a German beaver collar onto his overcoat. I suddenly became a hero. I would not even have admitted my six-foot lieutenant into my house. In those moments I couldn't even have visualized him. What exactly my dreams were about and in what way they satisfied me it is hard to say now, but at that time they satisfied me. Even now they partially satisfy me. Especially sweet and powerful dreams came to me after some act of dissipation, leading to repentance and tears, together with swearing and ecstasy. There were moments of such positive rapture, of such happiness, that I swear I did not feel even the slightest sense of absurdity. There was faith, hope, love. But that's just the point: I blindly believed at that time that by some sort of miracle, through some external circumstance, all this would suddenly slide apart, opening up a wide horizon of appropriate activity, wholesome, beautiful, and more importantly *completely ready* (precisely what kind, I never understood, but the important thing was that it should be completely ready), and thus I would suddenly step into the light of God, practically on a white steed wearing a laurel wreath. I could not understand secondary roles and that was the reason why in reality I very often took the most insignificant one. Either a hero, or mud, and there was nothing in between. This was my very downfall because in the filth I comforted myself with the thought that the rest of the time I was a hero, but that the hero had disguised himself in the filth: for an ordinary person, I said, it is shameful to wallow in filth, but a hero is too great to filthy himself completely, therefore he can wallow in it. It is remarkable that these outbursts of 'the beautiful and sublime' came to me both at moments of dissipation and at precisely those moments when I had reached rock-bottom. They came in separate outbursts, as if to remind me of their existence, but their appearances did not destroy the debauchery; on the contrary, they enlivened it by contrast and came in exactly the right quantity for a good sauce. In this instance the sauce consisted of contradiction and suffering, of a tormented inner analysis, and all the resulting agony and little torments added a sort of piquancy, even meaning, to my depravity—in short, entirely fulfilled the duties of a good sauce. None of this was without a certain profundity. Indeed, how could I have accepted a simple, vulgar, plain, clerkish, petty depravity and borne that filth? What would there have been in it to attract me and lure me out onto the streets in the night? No, sir, I had a respectable loophole for everything . . .

But how much love, Lord, how much love I experienced in those dreams of mine, in these escapes into all that is 'beautiful and sublime'! It may have been fantasized love, it may never, in reality, have been applied to anything human, but there was so much of it, of this love, that later on, in truth, I never felt the need to project it onto anything: that would have been a superfluous luxury. However, luckily everything always ended in a lazy and intoxicating transition into art, that is to say into beautiful forms of existence, completely ready, forcibly stolen from poets and novelists and adapted to every possible use and requirement. For instance, I triumph over everyone; needless to say, all have crumbled to nothing and are forced to recognize voluntarily all my perfections, and I offer forgiveness to them all. I fall in love as a famous poet and chamberlain. I inherit countless millions and immediately donate them to the human race, at the same time confessing all my vices to the whole nation, vices which are of course not just simple vices but include a great deal of 'the beautiful and the sublime', something rather Manfredian.* They all weep and kiss me (otherwise what sort of blockheads would they be?) and I go forth barefooted and hungry to preach new ideas and rout the reactionaries at Austerlitz.* Next there's a march being played, they call an amnesty, the Pope agrees to leave Rome for Brazil; next there's a ball for the whole of Italy held in the Villa Borghese,* which is on the banks of Lake Como, because Lake Como has been deliberately transferred to Rome for the occasion; next a scene in the bushes, etc., etc.—you must know it. You'll say that it's vulgar and mean to bring all this out into the open now after all the rapture and tears I've admitted to. Why should it be ignoble? Surely you don't think that I'm embarrassed by it all and that it is all far more stupid than anything in your own lives, gentlemen? Besides, I can assure you that some of it was not at all badly presented . . . Not everything took place on Lake Como. But, you're still right; it really is base and vulgar. But the most vulgar thing of all is that I'm now trying to justify it before all of you. And the most vulgar thing of the lot is making this remark. Well, enough, otherwise it will never end: the next thing will be worse than the thing before . . .

I was not up to dreaming for more than three months in a row without starting to feel an indefinable need to plunge into society. To me plunging into society meant going to visit my head of department, Anton Antonych Setochkin. He was the one and only constant acquaintance I had in my life; even now I am quite surprised at this circumstance. But I only went to see him when one of these bouts came on and my dreams had become so incredibly happy that I felt an absolute need to embrace people instantly, to embrace the whole of mankind; and for this purpose I needed at least one person at hand, someone who really existed. However, I had to go to Anton Antonych's on a Tuesday (the day he received people) and consequently I had to adapt this need to embrace the whole of mankind so that it always happened on a Tuesday. This Anton Antonych lived near Five Corners Square, on the third floor with four rooms, all low-ceilinged, and each one smaller than the next, all very austere and yellowish in appearance. He had two daughters and their aunt, who poured out the tea. The daughters—one thirteen and the other fourteen—both had little snub noses, and I was dreadfully embarrassed by them because they spent the whole time whispering and giggling to each other. The host usually sat in his study on a leather sofa in front of the table, together with some grey-haired guest, an official from our department or from some other one. I never saw more than two or three guests there, and then always the same ones. They discussed excise duty, the haggling going on in the Senate, salaries, promotion, his Excellency, ways of gaining approval, etc., etc. Like a fool, I had the patience to sit it out for four hours at a time next to these people, listening to them, feeling afraid and unable to discuss anything with them. I grew dumb, and on quite a few occasions I went into a profound sweat, paralysis hovering over me; but it was useful and good for me. Returning home I used to put aside, for a time, my desire to embrace the whole of mankind.

I had, however, another alleged friend, Simonov, who used to be one of my school-fellows. There were probably a number of my school-fellows in Petersburg, but I never associated with them and even stopped greeting them in the street. Perhaps the reason that I had changed to a different department at work was in order not to be together with them, and to cut myself off with a stroke from everything to do with my hateful boyhood. Curse that school and those dreadful years of imprisonment! In a word, I immediately broke off with my school-fellows once I stepped into freedom. There remained just two or three people whom I greeted when I met them. Amongst them was Simonov, who had not stood out in any way at school; he was even-tempered and quiet, but in him I could discern a certain independence of character and integrity. I don't even think that he was a particularly narrow-minded person. At times I spent some rather joyful moments with him, but they didn't last long and would somehow suddenly cloud over. He obviously found these memories oppressive and was always afraid that I would lapse into my old tone. I suspected that I was quite repulsive to him, but nevertheless not being certain of this I carried on seeing him.

Then one day, on a Thursday, unable to contain my loneliness and knowing that Anton Antonych was not at home on a Thursday, I remembered Simonov. Climbing up to him on the third floor I was just thinking about how this man found me oppressive and how pointless it was to go. But since it always happened that considerations of this sort, as luck would have it, incited me all the more to get into an ambiguous situation, I carried on. It was almost a year since I had last seen Simonov.

CHAPTER 3

I FOUND two more of my school-fellows with him. They seemed to be discussing some important matter. None of them paid much attention at all to my arrival, which was actually a bit odd, because I hadn't seen them for years. Obviously they considered me some kind of common house-fly. They hadn't even treated me like that at school, although everyone there hated me. Of course, I realized that they were bound to despise me on account of my failed career, and because I had gone so badly to pieces and was walking around in dreadful clothes and so forth—which in their eyes pointed to my lack of ability and insignificance. But I had nevertheless not anticipated such a level of contempt. Simonov even seemed astonished by my arrival. Actually he had always seemed surprised when I came. All of this puzzled me; I sat down somewhat dejected and began listening to their discussion.

A serious, indeed heated, conversation was going on about a farewell dinner which these gentlemen wished to arrange jointly the very next day for their friend Zverkov,* an army officer who had been posted to a distant province. Monsieur Zverkov had been at school with me all the way through. I came especially to loathe him when I was in the upper classes. In the lower classes he was just a pretty little playful chap, whom everyone loved. I, however, loathed him even in the lower classes precisely because he was a pretty little playful chap. He was always a consistently bad pupil, and the further he got the worse he became; but he left school having passed his exams, because he had connections. In his last year at our school he was left two hundred serfs, and since almost all of us were poor he began to brag in front of us. He was an extremely vulgar person but he was a fine lad, even when he was bragging. Despite our outwardly fantastic and rhetorical forms of honour and arrogance, all of us, with a few exceptions, actually curried Zverkov's favour the more he bragged. And we didn't ingratiate ourselves with the hope of gaining any-thing, but simply because he was a person blessed with the gifts of nature. Moreover, it had somehow been accepted among us that Zverkov was an expert in adroitness and good manners. It was the latter point that particularly enraged me. I loathed the piercing, self-assured sound of his voice, his delight in his own witticisms, which always came across as terribly stupid although he had a bold tongue; I loathed his good-looking, but silly, face (which I would nevertheless have willingly exchanged for my own *intelligent* one) and his carefree manner typical of an officer of the forties. I hated the fact that he used to talk about his future successes with women (he had decided not to start womanizing until he had his officer's epaulettes and awaited them impatiently), and how he would be continually fighting duels. I remember how on one occasion, although I was usually a taciturn person, I suddenly went for Zverkov whilst he was chatting with his friends during his free time about his forthcoming philandering. Finally, carried away like a puppy playing in the sun, he had suddenly declared that not a single country lass on his estate would be spared his attention, that this was his droit de seigneur, that if the peasants dared to protest he would have them all flogged and he would demand double dues from them all, the bearded rogues. Our louts applauded him, whereas I grappled with him, and it was not in the least because I felt sorry for his lasses or their fathers, but simply because they were applauding such an insect. On that occasion I came out the winner, but Zverkov, although he was stupid, was cheerful and impudent and therefore laughed it off, and indeed in such a way that in truth I did not completely beat him: he had the last laugh. After that he got the better of me quite a few times, but without malice, jokingly, in passing, laughing. Angry and contemptuous I did not answer him. After we left school he started making a move towards me; I did not particularly object because I was very flattered; but we quickly and naturally went our own ways. Then I used to hear about his successes as a barrack-room lieutenant, and about how he *boozed*. Later other rumours circulated about how *well* he was doing in his job. He no longer greeted me in the street and I suspected that he was afraid of compromising himself by exchanging bows with such an insignificant person as myself. I also saw him once in the theatre, in the third circle, already wearing aiguillettes. He was paying court, stooping over the daughters of a very ancient general. In the three years since I'd seen him he had gone dreadfully to seed, although he was still fairly good-looking and agile; he seemed to have become swollen, and had grown stout; you could tell that by the time he was thirty he would be completely flabby. It was this same Zverkov who was finally departing and our friends wanted to give him a dinner. They had kept up with him throughout the three years, although in their hearts they did not feel his equal, I'm sure of that.

Of Simonov's two guests one was Ferfichkin, one of the Russo-Germans, a small man with an ape-like face, a fool who derided everyone, and my most hated enemy since the lowest classes. He was a mean, cheeky little show-off, posing as a person with extremely delicate pretensions although he was of course a coward at heart. He was one of those admirers of Zverkov who played up to him for the sake of appearances and often borrowed money from him. Simonov's other guest, Trudoliubov,* was not a very remarkable person, a military chap, tall with a cold demeanour, fairly honest but bowing to every kind of success and capable of discussing nothing other than promotion. He was some sort of distant relative of Zverkov's and this, stupidly enough, gave him a certain importance amongst us. He never thought me worth mentioning; he behaved, if not altogether politely, tolerably.

'Well then, if we put up seven roubles each,' said Trudoliubov, 'that's three of us, makes twenty-one roubles, we can dine pretty well. Zverkov, of course, won't pay.'

'Of course not, if we're inviting him', Simonov decided.

'Surely you don't really think,' joined in Ferfichkin, haughtily and with the ardour of an impudent lackey boasting about his master the General's decorations, 'surely you don't think that Zverkov will allow us to foot the whole bill? Out of propriety he'll accept, but then he'll stand us half a dozen bottles.'

'But what will the four of us do with half a dozen bottles?' commented Trudoliubov, thinking only of the half-dozen bottles.

'All right then, three of us, with Zverkov four, twenty-one roubles at the Hôtel de Paris, tomorrow at five o'clock', decisively concluded Simonov, who had been chosen as master of the ceremony.

'What do you mean, twenty-one?' I said rather agitatedly, even seemingly offended; 'if you include me then it won't be twenty-one but twenty-eight roubles.'

It had seemed to me that to propose myself suddenly and so unexpectedly would be really rather beautiful, and they would all be conquered at once and look upon me with respect.

'You don't really want to come?' remarked Simonov, annoyed and somehow avoiding meeting my eyes. He knew me through and through.

I was infuriated that he knew me through and through.

'Why ever not? After all, I believe I'm also his friend, and I confess I even find it offensive that I've been left out', I spluttered forth again.

'And where were we supposed to look for you?' said Ferfichkin, joining in again rather rudely.

'You were always at odds with Zverkov', added Trudoliubov, frowning. But I had already seized on the idea and would not give up.

'It seems to me that no one has the right to judge that', I answered in a shaking voice, as if God knows what had happened. 'Maybe it's precisely because we weren't on good terms that I want to be now.'

'Well who on earth can make sense of you? . . . all this loftiness . . .', grinned Trudoliubov.

'We'll make a note of your name,' decided Simonov, turning to me; 'tomorrow at five o'clock at the Hôtel de Paris; don't get it wrong.'

'And what about the money?' Ferfichkin began in a half-whisper to Simonov, nodding towards me, but he stopped short because even Simonov was embarrassed.

'Enough', said Trudoliubov, getting up. 'If he wants to so badly, then let him come.'

'But after all we make up our own little group, we're all friends', raged Ferfichkin, also picking up his hat. 'It isn't an official gathering. Perhaps, we don't want you at all . . .'

They left. On leaving, Ferfichkin didn't bow to me at all, Trudoliubov gave a slight nod, without looking. Simonov, with whom I was left face to face, seemed to be in a state of vexed bewilderment and gave me a strange look. He did not sit down, nor did he invite me to.

'Hm . . . Yes . . . So it's tomorrow. The money, are you going to hand it over now? I'm saying that in order to be certain', he muttered in embarrassment.

I flared up, but blushing I remembered that from time immemorial I had owed Simonov fifteen roubles, which although I had never forgotten, I had never given back.

'You must agree, Simonov, that coming here I couldn't have known . . . and I'm very annoyed at having forgotten . . .'

'All right, all right, it doesn't matter. Pay tomorrow at dinner. You see I just wanted to know . . . Would you please . . . ?'

He stopped short and started pacing up and down the room with even greater annoyance. As he did so he started coming down on his heels, which made him stamp even more loudly.

'I'm not holding you up, am I?' I asked after a two-minute silence.

'Oh no!' he suddenly started; 'well, that is to say, in truth— yes. You see, I still need to go to . . . Somewhere nearby . . .', he added in a sort of apologetic voice, partly ashamed.

'Ah, my God! Why didn't you sa-a-ay?' I shouted, grabbing my peaked cap in a surprised but casual manner. God only knows where I got that from.

'It's really not far away . . . A couple of steps . . .', repeated Simonov, accompanying me to the hall in a bustling fashion, which didn't suit him at all. 'So tomorrow at five o'clock sharp', he shouted to me on the stairs; he was really very pleased that I was leaving. I, however, was in a wild rage.

'Whatever came over me, whatever came over me to burst forth like that?' I gnashed my teeth as I strode along the street. 'And on behalf of that vulgar little swine Zverkov! Of course I shouldn't go, of course I should wash my hands of it; I'm not bound, am I? Tomorrow I'll inform Simonov through the town post . . .'

But I was furious because I knew for certain I would go; that I would deliberately go; and the more tactless, the more inappropriate it would be to go, the more certain I would be to go.

There was even one positive obstacle to my going: I had no money. All I had in the world was nine roubles. And out of them tomorrow I had to give seven, as his monthly wage, to Apollon, my servant, who lived with me for seven roubles, without keep.

Judging by Apollon's character it would be impossible not to pay them. But of this rogue, of this curse of mine I will speak sometime later.

However, I knew that I would nevertheless not hand them over, and that I would be bound to go.

That night I had the most disturbing dreams. It was no wonder: the entire evening I was oppressed by memories of the punitive years of my school life, and I could not get rid of them. I was sent to that school by my distant relatives, on whom I depended and of whom I have not heard since. I was sent as an orphan, already downtrodden by their reproaches, already pensive, taciturn, and looking distrustfully at everything around me. My school-fellows met me with spiteful and merciless ridicule because I was not like any of them. But I could not bear the derision; I could not get on with them as easily as they could with one another. I instantly loathed them and shut myself away from them all in my timorous, wounded, but excessive pride. I was revolted by their rudeness. They made cynical fun of my face, of my awkward figure; and yet what stupid faces they themselves had! In our school people's expressions seemed somehow to degenerate and become particularly stupid. So many nice-looking children entered the school. After a few years they became repulsive even to look at. By the time I was sixteen I was sullenly amazed by them; even at that time I was astonished by the triviality of their ideas, the stupidity of their pursuits, their games, their conversations. They failed to understand even the most essential things, the most strikingly inspired subjects failed to interest them, so I inevitably came to regard them as inferior to myself. It was not wounded vanity that urged me to do so, and please God do not come out with such nauseatingly banal retorts as that I was 'simply dreaming and even then they understood real life'. They understood nothing, nothing at all of real life, and I swear this is what most angered me about them. Quite the opposite, they understood the most obvious, glaring truths of reality in a fantastically stupid way and even at that time were accustomed to worshipping nothing but success. Cold-heartedly and disgracefully they ridiculed everything that was just, but oppressed and downtrodden. They rated rank as intelligence; at sixteen they were already discussing snug little jobs. Of course a great deal of all this was a result of the stupidity and poor example that continually surrounded them in their childhood and youth. They were odiously depraved. Of course, it was mostly a façade, mostly feigned cynicism; naturally youth and a certain freshness could be fleetingly glimpsed in them beneath the depravity; but even the freshness was unattractive in them and manifested itself as some kind of prankishness. I absolutely hated them, although I was perhaps even worse than them. They repaid me in kind and did not conceal their loathing for me. But I no longer wanted them to like me; on the contrary, I constantly longed for them to be humiliated. In order to spare myself their sneers, I deliberately started to study as hard as I could and made my way towards the top of the class. This impressed them. Moreover, they all gradually came to realize that I had already read the sort of books that were still well beyond them, and understood all sorts of things about which they had never even heard (and that did not enter the curriculum of our specialized course). They regarded this with wild derision, but they were morally subordinated, still more because on this account even the teachers paid me attention. The sneers ceased, but a hostility remained and a cold, strained relationship was established. By the end I myself could no longer keep it up: with the years I had developed a need for people and friends. I tried to get close to some of them, but this intimacy always came about unnaturally and came to an end of its own accord. I did once make a sort of friend. But I was already a despot at heart and I wanted to have unlimited power over his soul; I wanted to inculcate a contempt for his surroundings in his heart; I demanded that he make an arrogant and final break with his milieu. I frightened him with my passionate friendship; I reduced him to tears, to convulsions; he was a naïve, submissive soul but when he gave himself up entirely to me I immediately began to hate him and pushed him away—it was as if I had needed him simply in order to gain my victory over him, simply for his submission. But I could not conquer everyone; my friend was also quite different from all the others and constituted an extremely rare exception. The first thing I did after leaving school was to leave the special job that I was destined for so that I could break every link, cursing the past and scattering it to the wind . . . And the devil only knows why after that I began to hang around this Simonov! . . .

In the morning I got out of bed early, leaping up in excitement as if it was all about to begin there and then. I believed that some radical turning-point in my life was approaching, and was bound to take place that day. Through lack of experience maybe, but throughout my life, whenever anything external happens, however trivial the event, I've always thought that I was about to reach some radical turning-point in my life. However, I set off for work as usual, but I slipped off home two hours early in order to get ready. The important thing, I thought, is not to be the first to arrive or they will think I'm terribly eager. But there were thousands of important things of this kind, and they were all worrying me into a state of impotence. I had personally polished my boots again; not for anything in the world could Apollon have been made to clean them twice in a day, because he would have found it out of order. So I cleaned them, stealing the brushes from the hallway so that there was no way of him noticing and then starting to despise me for it. Then I inspected my clothes in detail and found them all old, threadbare, and worn out. I really had become too slovenly. My office coat, however, wasn't too bad, but I wasn't going to dinner in my office coat. And the main thing was that on the very knee of the trousers there was a huge yellow spot. I foresaw that this spot alone would detract nine-tenths of my personal dignity. I also knew that it was very low to think like that. 'But this isn't to do with thinking, this is to do with reality', I thought, my spirit flagging. I also knew perfectly well, even at that time, that I was exaggerating all these facts incredibly; but what on earth could I do? I could no longer control myself and I was shaking with fever. In despair I imagined how patronizingly and coldly that 'vulgar chap' Zverkov would greet me; with what stupid, irresistible contempt that blockhead Trudoliubov would look at me; how horridly and impertinently that little insect

Ferfichkin would snigger at my expense, in order to worm himself into Zverkov's favour; how perfectly Simonov would understand everything and how he would despise me for the meanness of my vanity and my faint-heartedness, and—chiefly—how it would all be wretched, *unliterary*, ordinary. Of course, it would be far better not to go. But by now this was even more impossible: once I had been gripped by the idea, I was already in it up to my neck. I would have teased myself for the rest of my life: 'And so, you took fright, you took fright at *reality*!' On the other hand, I terribly badly wanted to show this 'riff-raff' that I was not the coward I imagined myself to be. Besides, in the most extreme moments of my paroxysm of cowardly delirium I dreamt of gaining the upper hand, of defeating them, of alluring them, of forcing them to love me—if only for 'the loftiness of my thought, and my unquestionable wit'. They would abandon Zverkov, he would sit at one side, silent and ashamed, and I would crush him. Later on I might make it up with him and drink, using the familiar form of address, but what was most cruel and hurtful of all to me was that even then I knew, I knew full well and without any doubts, that in reality none of this was necessary to me, that in reality I had no wish at all to crush them, subdue them, or attract them, and that even if I did achieve it all I would be the first not to give a halfpenny for the results. Oh, how I implored God that the day would pass quickly! In inexpressible anguish I walked over to the window, opened the ventilating pane, and looked out at the turbid haze of the densely falling wet snow . . .

Finally my rotten old wall-clock sputtered out five o'clock. I grabbed my hat, and trying not to look at Apollon—who had been waiting since morning for me to hand over his salary, but out of pride had not wanted to be the first to speak—I crept past him through the door and drove like a lord to the Hôtel de Paris, in a cab that I hired with my last fifty copecks.

CHAPTER 4

EVEN the day before, I had known that I would be the first to arrive. But it was not a question of who got there first.

Not only was none of them there, but I was barely able to find our room. The table was still not fully laid. What did this imply? After a lot of questioning I eventually learnt from the servants that the dinner had been ordered for six o'clock, not for five. This was confirmed once again in the refreshment room. I even felt ashamed to ask. It was still only twenty-five minutes past five. If they had altered the time they should at any rate have informed me; that is what the town post is for, and they should not have subjected me to this 'disgrace' in my own eyes and . . . and . . . in front of the servants too. I sat down; a servant started laying the table; I somehow felt even more humiliated in his presence. Towards six, in addition to the lamps already burning, candles were brought into the room. It had not, however, occurred to the servant to bring them the moment I arrived. In the adjoining room, two somewhat gloomy, angry-looking guests were dining in silence at separate tables. There was a lot of noise coming from one of the rooms further away; there was even shouting; one could hear the loud laughter of a whole gang of people; one could hear some nasty French shrieks: they were dining with women. In a word, it was quite sickening. I have seldom experienced worse moments, so that when, at exactly six o'clock, they all arrived at once, for a few seconds I was so delighted to see my liberators that I almost forgot that I was supposed to look offended.

Zverkov entered at the head of them, evidently in charge. Both he and all the others were laughing, but on seeing me Zverkov assumed an air of dignity, came towards me without hurrying, and bending over slightly from the waist, really flaunting himself, he gave me his hand, affectionately, but not overly so, rather with a somewhat restrained, almost military courtesy, as if while giving me his hand he were protecting himself from something. I had imagined that, to the contrary, the moment he entered he would laugh his former weak, squeaky laugh, and start his feeble jokes and witticisms right from the beginning. I had prepared myself for this since the day before, but I had not in the least expected such condescension, such stupendous kindness. It must have meant that he now regarded himself as immeasurably superior to me in all respects. If he had only wanted to offend me by behaving like a general, then that would have been fine, I thought; I would have shrugged it off somehow. But what if, in actual fact, without any wish to offend, the idea had seriously crept into his mutton head that he was immeasurably superior to me and he couldn't help looking at me patronizingly? This presumption alone was making me gasp.

'I learnt with surprise of your wish to join us', he began, lisping slightly and emphasizing his consonants, and drawling in a way he never used to. 'We somehow never seem to meet. You avoid us. No need. We are not as frightening as you think. Well, at any rate I'm pleased to renew the acquaintance . . .'

And he turned carelessly away to put his hat on the window.

'Have you been waiting long?' asked Trudoliubov.

'I arrived at five sharp, as I was instructed yesterday', I answered loudly, with irritation that was threatening to burst forth at any moment.

'Surely you let him know that we'd changed the time?' said Trudoliubov, turning to Simonov.

'I didn't. I forgot', replied the latter, but without a hint of remorse, and without even apologizing to me he went off to see about the hors-d'œuvre.

'So you've already been here an hour, you poor thing!' Zverkov exclaimed jokingly, because from his point of view it really must be terribly funny. That whelp Ferfichkin followed suit, in a vulgar, whining voice, like a dog's. He also found my situation very amusing and awkward.

'It's not in the least funny!' I shouted at Ferfichkin, getting more and more irritated. 'It's the others' fault, not mine. Nobody bothered to tell me. It's, it's, it's . . . simply absurd.'

'It's not just absurd, it's something else as well', muttered Trudoliubov, naïvely backing me up. 'That's putting it too mildly. It's quite simply rude. Of course, unintentional. And how could Simonov . . . hm!'

'If I'd been treated like that,' remarked Ferfichkin, 'I would have . . .'

'You'd have ordered something for yourself,' interrupted Zverkov, 'or simply asked for your dinner without waiting.'

'You'll agree, I could have done that without anyone's permission', I snapped. 'If I waited, it's because . . .'

'Be seated, gentlemen,' cried Simonov, coming in, 'it's all ready; I myself will vouch that the champagne is chilled to perfection . . . Anyway, I didn't know your flat, didn't know where to look for you, did I?' he said, suddenly turning to me, but once again somehow not looking at me. He obviously had something against me. He must have thought again since yesterday.

Everyone sat down, and so did I. It was a round table. On my left I had Trudoliubov, on my right Simonov. Zverkov sat opposite, and Ferfichkin beside him, between him and Trudoliubov.

'Te-e-ell me-e, are you . . . in the department?' Zverkov said, contining to pay me attention. Noticing my embarrassment, he seriously imagined that I needed to be shown some kindness and, as it were, to be cheered up. 'What does he want, does he want to me to fling a bottle at him?' I thought, in a fury. I had somehow got irritated, unnaturally quickly, through lack of experience.

'In the—— section', I answered abruptly, looking at my soup-plate.

'And . . . are you, are you satisfied? Tell me, what persuaded you to leave your former job?'

'I was persuaded by the fact that I wanted to leave my former job', I drawled three times worse than him, already almost out of control. Ferfichkin snorted. Simonov looked at me ironically; Trudoliubov stopped eating and began looking me over with curiosity.

Zverkov winced at this, but he did not want to admit to it.

'We-e-ell, and what's your allowance?'

'What do you mean, allowance?'

'I mean, s-salary?'

'What a cross-examination!'

However I went and told him what my salary was. I blushed terribly.

'Not enormous', commented Zverkov, importantly.

'Quite, not enough to dine in smart restaurants with!' put in Ferfichkin insolently.

'If you ask me, even rather beggarly', remarked Trudoliubov earnestly.

'How thin you've become, how changed you are . . . from that time . . .', added Zverkov, not without venom, looking with some kind of brazen pity at my suit.

'Stop embarrasing him', cried Ferfichkin with a snigger.

'My dear sir, I can tell you I'm not embarrassed', I finally burst forth. 'Now listen. I'm dining here in a "smart restaurant" at my own expense, and not that of others; note that, Monsieur Ferfichkin.'

'What's that? Which of us isn't here at his own expense? It's as if you . . .', Ferfichkin latched on, blushing like a lobster, and looking me in the eye frenziedly.

'So-o', I replied, feeling that I had gone far enough, 'I suggest it would be better if we pursued a more intelligent conversation.'

'It seems you're determined to show us your intelligence?'

'Don't worry, it would be quite superfluous here.'

'But my dear sir, why did you start cackling, eh? You haven't lost your wits, have you, in your lepartment?'

'Enough, gentlemen, enough!' cried the almighty Zverkov.

'How stupid it is!' muttered Simonov.

'Absolutely stupid, we've gathered together as a friendly group in order to see a dear friend off on a journey, and you are considering the cost', Trudoliubov said, turning rudely to me alone. 'It was you who thrust yourself at us yesterday, so don't go and destroy the general harmony . . .'

'That's enough, enough!' shouted Zverkov. 'Stop it, gentlemen, it's not the thing. You'd better let me tell you how I nearly got married the day before yesterday . . .'

And so some sort of pasquinade began about how this gentleman had almost got married two days before. However, there was no mention of a marriage, rather the whole story glittered with generals, colonels, and even gentlemen of the bedchamber, and Zverkov right there in the thick of it all. They started to laugh approvingly; Ferfichkin even let out a yelp. They all deserted me, and I sat crushed and broken.

'Lord, is this the sort of company I want to keep?' I thought.
'And what a fool I've made of myself before them. However,
I let Ferfichkin get away with a bit much. The boobies think
they have paid me an honour by giving me a place at their
table, whereas they don't understand that it's me, me, that's
paying them the honour and not they me. "Grown thinner!
My suit!" Oh, damn the trousers! Zverkov had noticed the
yellow spot on the knee ages ago . . . Well so what? Any
moment now I'll get up from the table, take my hat, and
simply leave, without a word . . . Out of contempt! Even if
there's a duel tomorrow. The rotters. As if I grudge the seven
roubles. Perhaps they'll think . . . The devil take them! I don't
grudge seven roubles! I'm leaving this instant! . . .'

Needless to say, I stayed.

Aggrieved, I drank Château-Lafite and sherry by the glass-
ful. Because I was not accustomed to it I soon got tipsy, and
the more tipsy the more annoyed. I suddenly wanted to offend
them all in the most audacious fashion and only then to leave.
To seize the moment and prove myself—let them at least say:
even if he's ridiculous he's clever . . . and . . . and . . . in
short, to hell with them!

I insolently scanned them all with bleary eyes. But it was as if
they had completely forgotten about me. *They* were noisy,
bawdy, cheerful. Zverkov was doing all the talking. I began to
listen in. Zverkov was telling a story about some luxurious lady
whom he had egged on until she finally declared her love (of
course, he was lying like a trooper), and that he was greatly
helped in this affair by an intimate friend of his, a certain young
prince, Kolia, a hussar, who owned three thousand serfs.

'But nevertheless this Kolia with his three thousand serfs is
plainly not here to see you off', I said, suddenly drawing
myself into the conversation. They all fell silent for a moment.

'You're already drunk', said Trudoliubov, finally consenting
to acknowledge my presence, and casting a disdainful glance
in my direction. Zverkov was silently eyeing me as if I were a
little insect. I lowered my eyes. Simonov hastily started
pouring the champagne.

Trudoliubov raised his glass, and the others followed suit,
apart from myself.

'Your good health, and successful journey,' he yelled at

Zverkov; 'for old times' sake, gentlemen, and to our future, hurrah!'

They all emptied their glasses and got up to exchange kisses with Zverkov. I did not budge; the full glass was standing in front of me, untouched.

'Surely you're not going to refuse to drink his health?' roared Trudoliubov, losing his patience, and addressing me threateningly.

'I wish to make a speech of my own, separately . . . then I'll drink, Mr Trudoliubov.'

'You bad-tempered old grouse', muttered Simonov.

I sat up in my chair, and in a state of delirium I grabbed the glass, preparing myself for something out of the ordinary, and still really not knowing what I was going to say.

'Silence!' shouted Ferfichkin. 'It's bound to be something intelligent!' Zverkov was waiting very earnestly, realizing what was at hand.

'My good Lieutenant Zverkov,' I began, 'do you know that I hate big talk, word-mongers, and tight waists? . . . that's the first point, and from that follows the second.'

They all stirred noisily.

'The second point: I hate philandering and philanderers. Especially philanderers!'

'The third point: I love truth, sincerity, and honesty', I continued almost mechanically, because I was already beginning to freeze up through fright, and I didn't understand how I came to be saying all this . . . 'I love ideas, Monsieur Zverkov; I love real friendship, on an equal footing, and not . . . hm . . . I love . . . Anyway what's the point of all this? And I'll drink to your health, Monsieur Zverkov. May you fall in love with the Circassian girls, may you shoot the enemies of the fatherland, and . . . and . . . To your health, Monsieur Zverkov!'

Zverkov got up from the table, bowed to me, and said: 'I'm most grateful to you.'

He had gone white and was dreadfully offended.

'The devil be with you', roared Trudoliubov, banging the table with his fist.

'Oh no, sir! You're asking to be punched in the face!' yelped Ferfichkin.

'He ought to be thrown out!' muttered Simonov.

'Not a word, gentlemen, don't do anything!' shouted Zverkov triumphantly, putting a stop to the general indignation. 'I thank you all, but I myself am capable of showing him how much I value his words.'

'Mr Ferfichkin, tomorrow you will give me satisfaction for what you have just said!' I said loudly, addressing Ferfichkin with an air of importance.

'Do you mean a duel, sir? Allow me!' he answered. I probably looked so funny, challenging him, and cut such an unlikely figure that all of them, Ferfichkin following suit, just fell over laughing.

'Yes, of course, throw him out! After all, he's completely drunk', said Trudoliubov with loathing.

'I'll never forgive myself for asking him!' muttered Simonov once again.

'Well, now I could fling a bottle at them all', I thought, and picked up a bottle and . . . poured myself a full glass.

'. . . No, it's better to sit it out to the end!' I carried on thinking to myself; 'you'd be only too pleased, gentlemen, if I were to leave. Not for anything. I'll deliberately sit here and drink to the end, as a mark of the fact that I don't have the slightest bit of respect for you. I will sit and drink, because this is a tavern and I've paid my entrance fee. I'll sit and drink because I consider you my pawns, my non-existent pawns. I'll sit and drink . . . and sing, if I want, yes I will, and sing, because I've got the right . . . to sing . . . hmm.'

But I didn't sing. I only tried not to look at any of them; I adopted an extremely detached pose and waited impatiently for them to speak to me *first*. But, alas, they did not speak. And how, oh how I should have liked to make it all up with them at that moment! It struck eight o'clock, then at last nine. They moved from the table to the divan. Zverkov stretched himself out on the sofa, resting one leg on a small round table. They took the wine over there too. He had indeed put forward three bottles of his own. Of course, I was not invited. They were all sitting around him on the divan. They were listening to him, almost reverentially. It was clear that they were fond of him. 'Why, why?' I thought to myself. Every now and then they went into a drunken rapture and embraced each other.

They talked about the Caucasus, about what constituted true passion, about card-games, about the most advantageous jobs in the army; about how much was earned by Podkharzhevsky of the Hussars, whom none of them knew personally, and they delighted in the fact that he earned a great deal; and about the unusual beauty and grace of Princess D—— , who had also never been seen by any of them; and finally they went so far as to say that Shakespeare was immortal.

I smiled contemptuously, and walked along the other side of the room, straight opposite the sofa, alongside the wall, back and forth between the stove and the table. I wanted, with all my might, to show them that I did not need them; meanwhile I deliberately stamped my feet, coming down on my heels. But it was all in vain. *They* didn't pay me any attention. I had the patience to walk up and down like that, right in front of them, from eight o'clock to eleven o'clock, keeping always to the same spot, from the table to the stove, and from the stove back to the table. 'I'm doing it because I want to, and no one can stop me.' On several occasions the servant stopped to look at me when he entered the room; my head was spinning from the frequent turns; at moments I thought I was delirious. During those three hours I broke into a sweat and dried out again three times. At times a profound, poisonous pain pierced my heart at the thought that ten years would go by, twenty years, forty and I would still, even after forty years, remember with loathing and humiliation these most filthy, most ridiculous, most dreadful minutes of my entire life. It would have been quite impossible to humiliate myself more shamelessly and more wilfully, and I fully, fully understood this and yet I still continued walking from the table to the stove and back again. 'Oh, if only you knew what thought and feeling I am capable of and how cultured I am!' I thought momentarily, mentally addressing the divan where my enemies were seated. But my enemies were carrying on as if I were not in the room. Once, only once, did they turn to me; to be precise, it was when Zverkov started talking about Shakespeare, and I suddenly burst out with a scornful laugh. I made such a contrived and revolting chuckle that they all stopped talking at once, and for a couple of minutes they watched gravely, without laughing, as I walked along the wall from the table to the stove *paying them no attention at all*. But nothing happened: they said nothing and after two minutes they abandoned me again. It struck eleven.

'Gentlemen,' shouted Zverkov, getting up from the divan, 'let's all go *there* now.'

'Of course, of course!' the others said.

I turned abruptly to Zverkov. I was so worn out, so shattered, that even if it meant cutting my throat I had to bring it to an end! I was in a fever; my hair was now so damp it stuck to my forehead and temples.

'Zverkov! I beg your forgiveness,' I said sharply and decisively; 'Ferfichkin, and yours too, everyone's, everyone's. I have offended everyone!'

'Aha! So you're no longer for the duel!' hissed Ferfichkin venomously.

I felt as if I'd been stabbed in the heart.

'No, I'm not frightened of a duel, Ferfichkin! I'm prepared to fight with you tomorrow, even after a reconciliation. Actually I insist on it, and you can't refuse. I want to show you that I'm not afraid of duels. You'll fire first and I'll fire into the air.'

'You are the only one to believe it', remarked Simonov.

'He's simply putting up a show of bravery!' answered Trudoliubov.

'Well, allow me to pass, you're standing in the way . . . What do you want anyway?' answered Zverkov contemptuously. They were all red-faced, they all had glowing eyes: they had drunk a lot.

'I ask for your friendship, Zverkov, I offended you, but . . .'

'Offended me? Y-o-u! M-e-e! Let me tell you, dear sir, that you could never, under any circumstance, offend *me*!'

'Enough with you. Be off!' said Trudoliubov in support. 'Let's go!'

'Bags I Olympia, gentlemen, agreed?' yelled Zverkov.

'We won't contest it! We won't contest it!' answered the others, laughing.

I stood there, disgraced. The gang left the room noisily, Trudoliubov drawling some stupid song. Simonov stopped for a second to give the servants a tip. I went up to him at once.

'Simonov! Give me six roubles!' I said resolutely and desperately.

He looked around at me in total amazement, with sort of bleary eyes. He too was drunk.

'Don't tell me you're going *there* with us?'

'Yes!'

'I haven't got any money!' he snapped, laughing disdainfully, and he left the room.

I grabbed him by his overcoat. It was a nightmare.

'Simonov! I saw your money, why are you refusing me? Am I really so dreadful? Watch out if you refuse me: if only you knew, if you only knew what I want it for! Everything depends on it, my whole future, all my plans . . .'

Simonov pulled out some money and practically hurled it at me.

'Take it if you're so shameless!' he said mercilessly and ran off to catch up with the others.

For a moment I was left on my own. Disorder, left-over food, a broken glass on the floor, spilled wine, cigarette butts, tipsy and feverish in the head, tormenting despair in my heart, and finally the servant who had seen it all and heard everything, staring curiously into my eyes.

'*There*!' I yelled. 'Either they'll all be down on their knees, clasping my legs and begging my friendship, or . . . or . . . I'll slap Zverkov in the face.'

CHAPTER 5

'So this is it, this is it, this is an encounter with reality', I muttered, rushing headlong down the stairs. 'This, you know, is no longer the Pope leaving Rome and setting off for Brazil; this is not a ball on Lake Como!'

'You rotter!' went through my head, 'if you're going to laugh at this now.'

'Very well!' I screamed, answering myself. 'Anyway, it's all over now!'

There was not a trace of them; but never mind: I knew where they were going.

A solitary cabby was standing by the porch, a night driver in a coarse peasant coat completely powdered in the ever-falling, wet, almost warm snow. It was steamy and stuffy outside. His shaggy little skewbald horse was also covered in snow and was coughing; I remember this very well. I threw myself towards the sleigh, but no sooner had I raised a leg to get in when I was suddenly so struck by the memory of the way in which Simonov had just given me six roubles that I flopped into the sledge like a sack.

'No. It'll take a lot to redeem all this,' I burst out in a shout; 'but I'll redeem it or I'll perish this very night, right on the spot. Let's go!'

We moved off. There was a veritable whirlwind raging in my head: 'Going down on their knees and begging for my friendship, that they won't do. That's a mirage, a vulgar mirage, disgusting, romantic, and fantastic; just like the ball on Lake Como. And therefore I *must* slap Zverkov on the face! I'm obliged to do so. And so it's decided. I'm rushing off to give him a slap on the face.'

'Come on!'

The driver jerked the reins.

'The moment I go in I'll do it. Ought I to say a few words before the slap by way of an introduction? No! I'll simply walk in and do it. They'll all be sitting in the hall, and he'll be on the sofa with Olympia. Damn Olympia! Once she laughed at my face and refused me. I'll tug Olympia aside by the hair, and Zverkov by the ears. No, better still by one ear, and I'll drag him around the whole room by the ear. They might all begin hitting me and throw me out. That's even a certainty. Well let them! I'll still have slapped him first: my initiative; and according to the code of honour that's enough; he's thereby branded and no amount of blows will wash that slap away, apart from a duel. He'll have to fight. So let them all thrash me now. Let them, the ignoble lot! Trudoliubov will hit especially hard: he's so strong; Ferfichkin will pounce on me from the side, and he's almost certain to go for my hair. But let them, let them! That's why I'm going. The enormous tragedy of it all must get through to their mutton heads in the end. When they drag me to the door, I'll shout out that in reality they aren't worth so much as my little finger.'

'Push on, driver, go on!' I shouted at the cabby. He jumped in fright and brandished his whip. I had shouted extremely wildly.

'We'll fight at dawn, that's already settled. I'm finished with the department. Ferfichkin said lepartment instead of department earlier on. But where can I get hold of some pistols? Rubbish. I'll get my salary advanced and buy them. What about gunpowder and bullets? That's up to the second. And how can I get all this done before dawn? And where can I find a second? I haven't got any friends . . .'

'Rubbish!' I cried, getting into even more of a frenzy. 'Rubbish!'

'The first person I meet on the street and ask has to be my second, just as if he were dragging a drowning man out of the water. The most eccentric circumstances must be permitted. Yes, even if tomorrow I were to ask the director himself to be a second, then he too would have to agree, simply as a matter of chivalry, and he'd have to keep the secret! Anton Antonych . . .'

The fact was that at that very moment I could see more clearly and more vividly than anyone else in the world the utterly vile absurdity of my assumptions, the reverse side of the coin.

'Come on driver, come on you rascal, come on!'

'Oh master!' muttered he, the salt of the earth.

I was suddenly overwhelmed by the cold.

'Wouldn't it be better . . . wouldn't it be better . . . to go straight home? Oh, good Lord! Why, why did I go to that dinner yesterday?! But no, it's not possible! And then walking up and down for three hours between the table and the stove. No, no, they and absolutely no one else must pay for that walking up and down! They must wipe out that disgrace!'

'Hurry!'

'And what if they hand me over to the police! Would they dare? They'd be afraid of the scandal. And what if Zverkov declines the duel, out of contempt? That's even quite likely; but I'll show them then . . . I'll rush to the posting station from where he'll depart tomorrow, grab hold of him by the legs, rip off his overcoat as he's climbing into the carriage. Then I'll plunge my teeth into his arm, I'll bite him. "Just look, all of you, at what despair can do to a man!" Let him hit me on the head, and all the rest of them from behind. I'll shout to all the onlookers: "Just look at this young puppy who's off to capture Circassian girls, with my spit on his face!"'

Of course, after this it would all be over! The department vanishes from the face of the earth. I'm arrested, they'll try me, they'll throw me out of my job, put me in prison, send me to Siberia, into exile. Never mind! Fifteen years later after my release from prison, dressed in rags, a beggar, I shall drag myself after him. I shall find him in some provincial town. He'll be married and happy. He'll have a grown-up daughter . . . I shall say: 'Look, you monster, look at my hollow cheeks, look at my rags! I've lost everything—my career, my happiness, culture, science, *the woman I loved*, and all on your account. Here are the pistols. I've come to discharge my pistol, and . . . forgive you.' Then I shall fire into the air, and that is the last that's heard of me . . .

I was on the verge of tears, although I knew perfectly well, even then, that this was all borrowed from Silvio* and Lermontov's *Masquerade*.* And I suddenly felt terribly ashamed, so ashamed that I stopped the horse, got out of the sledge, and stood in the snow in the middle of the road. The cabby watched me in amazement, gasping.

What was I to do? I couldn't go there, it had turned into a nonsense; nor could I set the matter aside, that too would lead to a . . . 'Lord! How could it just be forgotten?! After such offence!'

'No!' I shouted, flinging myself into the sledge once again, 'it's predestined! it's fate, drive on, let's go!'

And I impatiently struck the driver a blow on his neck.

'What's up, why are you going for me?' cried the poor old peasant; nevertheless he whipped the nag, and it began kicking its hind legs.

The wet snow was coming down in huge flakes; I uncovered myself, I was unconcerned about it. I forgot everything else because I had finally resolved on the slap and fearfully I felt that it was *absolutely bound* to happen now and that *nothing at all could prevent it.* The deserted street-lamps were flickering sullenly like burial torches in the snowy haze. The snow was getting under my coat, under my frock-coat, under my tie and then melting there; I did not cover myself up: after all it was all already lost anyhow. Finally we arrived. I leapt out, almost out of my mind, ran up the steps, and started hammering at the door with my hands and feet. My legs in particular were terribly weak at the knees. The door seemed somehow to open very quickly; it was as if they knew about my arrival. (And indeed, Simonov had warned that there still might be someone else, for here one had to give prior notice and to take precautions in general. It was one of those 'fashionable shops' of the day, which the police have long since done away with. By day it was indeed a shop; but in the evenings those with a recommendation could go there as guests.) I walked with hurried steps across the dark shop into the familiar hall where a single lamp was burning, and stopped in bewilderment: there was no one there.

'Where are they then?' I asked someone.

But of course they had already managed to disperse . . .

Standing in front of me was this character with a silly smile, the mistress of the house herself, whom I knew slightly. A minute or two later the door opened and another character appeared.

Not paying any attention to this either, I strode about the room, talking to myself. It was as if I had been saved from death and my whole being was joyfully aware of this: after all, I would have slapped his face, without a doubt, for certain I would have slapped him! But now they weren't here . . . and it had all disappeared, it had all changed . . . I looked around. I still could not believe my eyes. Mechanically I glanced at the young girl who had come in: before me I caught a fleeting glimpse of a fresh, young, slightly pale face, with straight, dark eyebrows and a serious, as it were slightly bewildered, expression. I immediately liked it; I would have hated her if she had smiled. I started to stare at her more attentively, with a bit of effort, shall we say: I still hadn't collected my thoughts. There was something simple-hearted and good in that face, but somehow serious to the point of being strange. I was sure that this didn't help her here, and that none of the idiots noticed her. Moreover, she could not be called a beauty, although she was tall, strong, well built. She was dressed extremely simply. Something horrible overcame me; I walked straight up to her . . .

I accidentally glanced into the mirror. My agitated face seemed utterly revolting: pale, spiteful, mean, my hair dishevelled. 'Well, I'm even quite pleased about that,' I thought, 'I'm really pleased that I shall appear revolting to her; it appeals to me . . .'

CHAPTER 6

. . . SOMEWHERE behind the partition a clock began wheezing, as if under some kind of strong pressure, as if someone were suffocating it. After an unnaturally long wheeze there followed a thin, nasty, and rather unexpectedly rapid chime— just as if someone had suddenly leapt forward. It struck two o'clock. I came to, although I hadn't been asleep but just lying in a state of semi-consciousness.

In the narrow, cramped, low-ceilinged room, crammed with a huge wardrobe, scattered with cardboard boxes, rags, and every conceivable sort of article of clothing, it was almost completely dark. A candle-end burning on a table at the end of the room had almost gone right out, giving only an occasional flicker. In a few moments it was bound to be totally dark.

It didn't take me long to regain consciousness; all at once, without effort, everything instantly came back to me, as if it had been keeping watch over me in order to strike again. Indeed, even in the state of semi-consciousness there had always remained a kind of focal point in my mind that had not been blotted out at all and around which my sleepy daydreams painfully revolved. But it was odd: everything that had happened to me that day seemed to me now, on waking, to have already happened a long time ago, as if I had lived through it all long, long ago.

My head felt very fuzzy. Something seemed to be hovering

over me, brushing against me, rousing and disturbing me. Sorrow and spleen were building up again and seeking an outlet. All at once I saw alongside me two wide-open eyes, staring at me with a curious, intent expression. It was a cold, apathetic, morose look, like something completely alien; it made me feel uneasy.

A depressing thought developed in my brain and passed through my entire body with a vile sensation, similar to when one descends into the damp and mouldy underground. It was somehow unnatural that literally only now did these two eyes decide to start looking me over. I also recalled that in the course of two hours I had not spoken a single word to this creature and had considered it quite unnecessary; until a moment before I had for some reason even felt quite pleased about it. But now I was suddenly filled with a vivid vision, as ridiculous and revolting as a spider, of debauchery, which without love begins crudely and brazenly at exactly the point where true love culminates. We looked at each other for a long time but she neither lowered her eyes under my gaze, nor altered her look, so that in the end for some reason I felt terrified.

'What's your name?' I asked abruptly, in order to get it over as quickly as possible.

'Liza', she answered, almost in a whisper, but somehow in a very unfriendly manner and averted her eyes.

I remained silent for a while.

'The weather today . . . snow . . . filthy!' I mumbled almost to myself, putting my hand behind my head in a melancholy fashion and staring up at the ceiling.

She did not answer. It was all preposterous.

'Are you local?' I asked her a moment later, almost in a fit of temper, turning my head slightly in her direction.

'No.'

'Where are you from?'

'From Riga', she said reluctantly.

'Are you German?'

'Russian.'

'Have you been here long?'

'Where?'

'In this house?'

'Two weeks.' She was speaking more and more abruptly. The candle had completely gone out; I could no longer distinguish her face.

'Have you a mother and father?'

'Yes . . . no . . . I have.'

'Where are they?'

'There . . . in Riga.'

'What are they?'

'Just . . .'

'What do you mean, "just"? Who, what do they do?'

'Tradesmen.'

'Have you always lived with them?'

'Yes.'

'How old are you?'

'Twenty.'

'Why did you leave them?'

'It just . . .'

That *just* meant: leave it, I'm sick of it. We said nothing. God knows why I didn't leave. I myself was getting increasingly sick and bored of it. Images of all that had happened the previous day had started filling my mind in a disordered fashion, as if of their own accord, without my volition. I suddenly remembered a particular scene that I had witnessed in the morning on the street, whilst I was anxiously trotting along to work.

'They were carrying a coffin today and almost dropped it', I suddenly said aloud, not really intending to start a conversation, but almost unintentionally.

'A coffin?'

'Yes, in the Haymarket; they were lifting it out of a cellar.'

'Out of a cellar?'

'Not a cellar but from the basement . . . you know . . . down below . . . from a house of ill fame . . . There was such filth all around . . . Eggshells, litter . . . it all smelt . . . it was quite horrible.'

Silence.

'It's a dreadful day to be buried', I began again, simply in order to avoid the silence.

'Why's it dreadful?'

'The snow, the damp . . .' (I yawned.)

'It doesn't matter', she suddenly said after a short silence.

'No, it's awful . . .' (I yawned again.) 'You can be sure the grave-diggers were swearing because the snow was making them wet. No doubt there was water in the grave.'

'Why should there be water in the grave?' she asked with some curiosity, but speaking even more rudely and abruptly than before. Something suddenly began egging me on.

'Of course, water in the bottom, about a foot. There in the Volkovy cemetery there's not a single grave that's been dug dry.'

'Why?'

'What do you mean, "why"? It's a wet area. It's all marsh around here. So they just put them down in the water. I've seen it myself . . . lots of times . . .'

(I had never once seen it, neither had I ever been to the Volkovy cemetery, but had simply heard others talking about it.)

'Do you really not mind if you die like that?'

'And why should I die?' she answered, rather defensively.

'Well, sometime you'll die, and you'll die in just the same way as that corpse I just told you about. She was . . . also still a girl . . . She died of consumption.'

'A whore ought to die in hospital . . .'

('She already knows about it,' I thought, 'and she said "whore", not "young girl".')

'She was in debt to her mistress,' I retorted, continuing to provoke the argument, 'and she served her practically up till the very end even though she was consumptive. The cab-drivers round about were talking to the soldiers, they told them that. They were probably former acquaintances. They were laughing. They were planning to pray for her in the tavern. (At this point I was making a lot of it up.)

Silence, a profound silence. She did not even stir.

'You mean it's better to die in a hospital?'

'Isn't it much the same? . . . And what am I going to die of?' she added, annoyed.

'If not now, then later on?'

'Well then, later on . . .'

'It's not like that. At the moment you're young, pretty,

fresh, you're worth quite a bit to them. But after a year of this life you won't be the same, you'll fade away.'

'After a year?'

'At any rate, after a year you'll be worth less', I continued maliciously. 'You'll be transferred from here to somewhere inferior, in another house. After another year, to a third house, always inferior, and after seven years or so you'll arrive in a cellar in the Haymarket. That would still be all right. But the misfortune arises if on top of that you contract some kind of illness, some weakness of the chest, catch a cold or something like that. In that sort of life it's difficult to get rid of an illness. It latches on and won't go away. And then you die.'

'So I'll die', she replied, now with real malice, and quickly changed position.

'But after all I feel sorry.'

'Who for?'

'Sorry about the life.'

Silence.

'Have you ever had a young man? eh?'

'What's it got to do with you?'

'It's all right, I won't press you. I don't care. What's making you so angry? Of course you may well have had your troubles. What does it matter to me? I'm just sorry, that's all.'

'Who for?'

'I'm sorry for you.'

'Don't bother . . .', she whispered barely audibly and shifted about again.

This immediately made me more angry. So! I was being so sweet to her, but she . . .

'Do you ever stop and think? Are you following a good path, eh?'

'I never think about anything.'

'That's bad, not to think. Open your eyes, whilst there's still time. And there is still time. You're still young, you're good-looking; you could fall in love, get married, be happy . . .'

'Not all marriages are happy', she broke in sharply in her former rude patter.

'Not all, of course, but nevertheless it's much better than being here. It's incomparably better. And when there is love you can carry on living without happiness. Even in grief life is good, it's good to be alive in the world however you live. But here, what is there apart from . . . filth? Phew!'

I turned away in disgust; I was no longer coldly philosophizing. I myself had begun to feel what I was saying, and I was getting heated. I was thirsting to expound those cherished 'little ideas' conceived in my little corner. Something suddenly flared up inside me, some sort of aim 'presented itself'.

'Don't look at me, I'm here, I'm no example. Maybe I'm even worse than you. However, I was drunk when I came here', I nevertheless hastened to excuse myself. 'Besides, a man is no example to a woman. It's a different thing; although I might degrade and sully myself I'm still not a slave to anyone; I come and go and that's it. I can shake it off and I'm no longer the same person. But let's take the fact that fundamentally you're a slave. Yes, a slave! You have surrendered everything, your whole will. And later you'll wish to break these chains and it'll be too late: you'll be more and more firmly ensnared. And what a cursed chain it is. I know it. I'm not going to mention anything else, you probably won't understand, so please tell me: you must already be indebted to your mistress? There, you see!' I went on, although she hadn't answered me, but simply remained silent, listening with her entire being; 'that's your chain! You'll never pay her back. That's how they do it. It's like being sold to the devil . . .

'. . . And besides . . . for all you know I might be another such miserable wretch, deliberately wallowing in the mud in despair. After all, sorrow makes some people turn to drink: and I come here—out of sorrow. But tell me, what good does it do? You and I . . . we came together . . . just now, and during all the time we didn't exchange a single word, and afterwards you started looking at me like a wild animal; and I did the same to you. Is that really the way to love? Is that really the way that two people ought to make love? It's simply repugnant, that's what!'

'Yes!' she agreed sharply and hastily. I was even surprised by the hastiness of that 'yes'. Did it mean that perhaps the same thought had been running through her mind when she looked at me just now? Did it mean that she too was capable of some thought? . . . 'Heavens, this is very interesting, this—

similarity', I thought, almost rubbing my hands together with joy. 'And how can one fail to cope with such a young spirit? . . .'

Above all I found the game appealing.

She had turned her head closer to me and in the darkness it seemed to me that she was leaning on her elbow. Perhaps she was staring at me. I was sorry that I couldn't distinguish her eyes. I could hear her breathing heavily.

'Why did you come here?' I began, already with a certain sense of authority.

'Because . . .'

'But after all it must be so nice to live in a family home. Warm, free and easy; one's own little nest.'

'And supposing it was worse than this?'

The thought flashed through my mind that I must hit the right note; she didn't seem to like sentimentality very much.

However, it was just a passing thought. I swear she did actually interest me. Besides, I was feeling sort of relaxed and well disposed. After all, knavery gets along very well with sentiment.

'Who can say?' I hastened to reply. 'Anything is possible. But I'm convinced that someone has offended you and you were certainly more wronged than guilty before *them*. After all, I know nothing at all about your background, but a young girl like yourself certainly didn't end up here of her own accord . . .'

'What kind of a girl am I?' she whispered, barely audibly; but I heard.

'Damn it, but I'm flattering her. That's revolting. Or maybe it's all right . . .' She remaind silent.

'Look here, Liza, I'll talk about myself! If I'd had a family during my childhood I wouldn't be as I am now. I often think about it. You see, however bad a family is they're nevertheless a father and mother and not enemies, not strangers. Even if they only show their love for you once a year. All the same you know you're at home. I grew up without a family; that's doubtless why I turned out like this . . . unfeeling.'

I waited again.

'Maybe she doesn't understand,' I thought, 'and she finds it amusing, this moralizing.

'If I were a father, and I had a daughter, I think I would love her more than a son, truly', I began obliquely, as if on a different subject, so as to divert her attention. I admit I was blushing.

'Why's that?' she asked.

Ah, she must be listening!

'I just would; I don't know why, Liza. You see, I knew one father who was a strict, stern man but who used to kneel before his daughter kissing her arms and legs, truly he couldn't take his eyes off her. She would be dancing at a party and he would stand on the same spot for five hours without taking his eyes off her. He was crazy about her; I can understand this. At night-time she would get tired and fall asleep and he would wake up and go in to kiss her in her sleep and make the sign of the cross over her. He used to wear a greasy old frock-coat; he was stingy towards everyone else, but for her he would spend his last penny, making gifts of expensive presents, and oh what joy it gave him if she liked the present! A father always loves his daughters more than a mother does. For some girls home is a very happy place! I don't think I would even allow my daughter to get married.'

'What do you mean?' she asked, with a slight laugh.

'Good God I would be jealous. How could she start kissing someone else? love a stranger more than her father? It's painful to imagine. Of course, it's all nonsense; of course, everyone has to come to his senses in the end. But I think that before letting her marry I would have worn myself out with one anxiety: I would have found each of her suitors in turn to be wanting. But nevertheless it would end with her marrying the one she loved. But the one the daughter herself loves always seems to the father to be the worst of them all. That's always been the case. It causes a lot of trouble in families.'

'Others are happy to sell their daughters, rather than give them away decently', she suddenly said.

Ah, so that's it.

'That happens, Liza, in those cursed families where there is neither God nor love,' I threw in heatedly, 'and where there's no love there's no reason. True, families of that sort exist, but I'm not talking about them. Clearly, from the way you speak, you didn't experience kindness in your family. You are very unfortunate. Hm . . . It's almost always the result of poverty.'

'Is it better among gentlefolk then? Honest folk can live decently even in poverty.'

'Hmm, yes. Perhaps. And then again, Liza, people only like counting their unhappinesses, they don't count their happiness. But were they to count as they should then they'd see that everyone gets his fair share. Well, suppose everything goes well in a family, God bestows his blessing on it, the husband turns out to be a good person, he loves you, he flatters you, he doesn't leave you. It would be a fine family. Sometimes half of it may be spent in sorrow, but that's fine; is there anywhere without sorrow? Maybe if you yourself got married *you'd find out for yourself*. But take the first period of marriage to the one you love: what happiness, what happiness it sometimes brings! And it nearly always does. During the first period arguments between husband and wife end well. In some instances the more a woman loves her husband the more she stirs up quarrels with him. It's true; I knew one like that: "You know I love you", she would say, "very much, and it's out of love that I torment you, so you can feel it." Do you know that a person can deliberately torment someone through love? It's usually women. And the woman thinks to herself: "But afterwards I'll be so sweet and loving that it's really not a sin to torment him now." And everyone in the house is delighted with you, and there's goodness and happiness and peace and honesty . . . And then there are others that can be jealous. He goes out—I knew one such type—and she can't stand it, and leaps up in the middle of the night and runs out furtively to see if he's there, in that house, with that woman. It's really dreadful. And she herself knows it's dreadful and her heart freezes and she blames herself, but she loves him; its all out of love. And how good it feels to make peace after an argument, to admit her fault before him or to forgive him. And how good they both feel, how marvellous everything suddenly becomes—it's just as if they've met each other anew, married anew, found love again. And no one, absolutely no one, need know what takes place between husband and wife, if they love each other. And whatever sort of quarrels they get into the mother ought never to be summoned as arbitrator, while they tell tales about each other. They are their own judges. Love is one of God's secrets and must be kept hidden from the eyes of everyone else, no matter what goes on. In that way it's more sacred, and better. They respect each other more, and a great deal is based on respect. And if there once was love, if they married through love, why should love go away? Is it really impossible to sustain it? It very seldom happens that it's impossible. Well, if a husband succeeds in being a good and honest man, how can love then pass away? The first conjugal love passes, that's true, and then an even better love emerges. Then they unite spiritually, and everything is done jointly; they hold no secrets from one another. And when children come, then every moment, even the most difficult, seems a happiness; it is enough to love and be steadfast. Then the work is joyous, then even if you sometimes sacrifice your own bread for your children, it is joyous. After all, later on they'll love you for it; you're storing it up, you see, for yourself. The children grow up—and you feel that you are setting them an example, that you lend them support; that were you to die they would carry your thoughts and feelings for the rest of their lives, since they have taken their image and likeness from you. It means it's a stupendous duty. How can it fail to bring father and mother even closer together? Some people say that having children is a heavy burden. Who is it that says this? It is an unbelievable joy! Do you love small children, Liza? I love them terribly. Imagine, a little rosy baby sucking at your breast, every man's heart must turn to his wife when he watches her sitting there with his little baby! A rosy little chubby baby, stretching itself and cuddling up; juicy little arms and legs, clean nails, small, so tiny that they look funny, eyes that look as if they already understand everything. And it sucks away, the tiny hand fiddling and playing with your breast. The father walks up, it tears itself away from the breast, leans over backwards and looks up at the father, laughing—as if it's something terribly funny—and then it resumes its sucking. Or it might suddenly go and bite the mother's breast, if its teeth have already started coming through, squinting its little eyes at her: "You see, I've bitten you!" Surely it's utter happiness, when the three of them, husband, wife, and baby are together? Much can be forgiven for those moments. No, Liza, you know one must learn how to live oneself before blaming other people!'

'Little images, you need to go on making these little images', I thought to myself, although, my God, I was speaking with feeling, and I suddenly blushed. 'What if she suddenly bursts out laughing, what can I do with myself then?' This thought had been driving me crazy. Towards the end of the speech I was genuinely heated, and now my vanity was somehow being wounded. The silence dragged on. I even felt like giving her a nudge.

'For some reason you . . .', she suddenly began, and then stopped.

But I already understood everything: there was already something different in her trembling voice, it wasn't sharp or rude, or defiant as it had been not long ago, but somehow soft and bashful, in fact so bashful that I suddenly felt ashamed before her, I felt guilty.

'What?' I asked with tender curiosity.

'Well, you . . .'

'What?'

'For some reason you . . . it's just like in books', she said, and there suddenly seemed again to be a hint of derision in her voice.

This remark stung me painfully. I hadn't expected that.

And I did not realize that this derision was a deliberate camouflage, that it is the typical final subterfuge of people with shy and chaste hearts who have been submitted to vulgar and persistent probing and who, out of pride, refrain from succumbing until the very last minute, and are afraid of speaking their thoughts before you. From the timidity with which she made these several attempts at mockery, and only finally managed to utter the words, I should have been able to guess. But I did not guess, and an angry feeling overwhelmed me.

'Just wait', I thought.

CHAPTER 7

'OH, that's enough, Liza, what can there be that's bookish about it when I myself find it horribly alien? Or maybe it isn't alien. All this has only just awoken in my heart . . . Surely, surely you yourself find it revolting here? No, obviously habit counts for a lot! The devil only knows what habit can do to a person. Come on, surely you don't seriously think that you'll never grow old, that you'll be attractive for ever and that they'll keep you here till kingdom come? Not to mention the fact that it's sordid here . . . However, I'll say this to you, about your present existence: at the moment you're young, comely, attractive, you've got spirit and feeling; but do you know that just now when I came to I felt disgusted at being here with you?! One can only make it to this place in a drunken state. But were you somewhere else, living a decent person's life, I might do more than chase after you, I would quite simply fall in love with you, delight in a look from you, let alone a word; I would be waiting for you by the gate, go down on my knees before you; look on you as my bride-to-be, and consider myself honoured. I would not even be so bold as to harbour an impure thought about you. But here I know that after all I only have to whistle and, like it or not, you will come with me, since I am not answerable to your will but you to mine. Even the lowest peasant can hire himself out to work, but he's still not bound his whole self into slavery, and he knows that it's only for a fixed term. But where's your fixed term? Just think: what is it you're surrendering here? What are you enslaving? Your soul, your soul over which you are not the mistress, and along with it your body! You permit your love to be desecrated by any old drunkard. Love!—why that's everything, yes, really, it's an uncut diamond, a young virgin's treasure, this love! Some men are ready to sacrifice their souls, to risk their lives to attain this love. But what is your love worth now? You are completely sold, every bit of you, and why on earth should anyone seek to attain love when the whole thing's feasible without love? Really, a young woman can suffer no greater insult, do you understand that? So, I've heard it said that they keep you idiots quiet by letting you have your lovers here. You know it's just a trick, a deceit, nothing but a joke at your expense, and you're taken in. In all truth, this lover, does he really love you? I don't believe he does. How can he love you when he knows that at any moment you might be summoned away from him? He'd be a pretty nasty piece of work if he did. Could he have even a drop of respect for you? What do you have in common with him? He laughs at you and steals from you and that's the sum total of his love! And you're lucky if he doesn't beat you. But perhaps he does beat you. And then, if you've got one of these fellows, you'll go and ask him if he'll marry you. He'll laugh straight in your face, that is if he doesn't spit at you or knock you down—and perhaps he's not worth more than a couple of brass farthings. And for what, tell me, have you ruined your life here? In order to have someone pour the coffee out for you and keep you well fed? But why is it they keep you well fed? Another sort of person, an honest person, wouldn't allow one crumb of it to pass her lips, because she'd know why they were feeding her. You're under an obligation here, and you'll always be under an obligation, right up to the very end, right up until the moment when your customers begin to balk at you. And that moment will come soon, don't count on youth. Because in this sort of place all that goes in a flash. You'll be thrown out. Indeed, not just thrown out, because for a long time before that they'll start picking on you, they'll start reproaching you, cursing you, as if, instead of having sacrificed your health and youth to her, and having allowed your soul to perish for nothing on her behalf—as if, instead of that, you'd brought about her ruin, abandoned her to the world, robbed her. And don't expect any support: others, your friends too, will pounce on you in order to worm their way into her favour, because everyone here is in slavery and they've long since lost any sense of conscience or compassion. They are contaminated and there is nothing on this earth more revolting, more obscene, more offensive than their abuse. But nevertheless you'll sacrifice everything, everything, selflessly—your health and youth, your beauty, your hopes, and at twenty-two you'll look like a thirty-five-year-old, and you'll be lucky if you're in health, you'll pray to God for that. More than likely at the moment you think that yours is not really work, that it's revelry! But indeed there is no other work in the world that is more difficult and gruelling, nor has there ever been. One would think it would make your heart dissolve in tears. And you won't dare utter a word, not a single word, when you're driven out of here, you'll go as if you were guilty. You'll move to another place, then to a third, then to somewhere else, and you'll end up, finally, in the Haymarket. There they'll beat you as a matter of routine; that's the speciality of the house; the customers don't know how to fondle a woman unless they've beaten her. You don't believe that it's so unpleasant there? Go over, take a look sometime, and perhaps you'll see it with your own eyes. Once at New Year I saw one of them over there standing by the door. She had been thrown out in ridicule by her own people to cool off a bit because she was howling dreadfully, and they'd shut the door on her. At nine o'clock in the morning she was already completely drunk, dishevelled, half-naked, bruised all over. Her face was powdered but she had black eyes; blood was flowing from her nose and her lips: some cabby or other had just had a go at her. She sat down on the stone doorstep, holding some kind of salted fish in her hands; she was bellowing, sort of lamenting her "lot", thumping the fish against the doorsteps. The doorway was crowded with cab-drivers and drunken soldiers who were taunting her. You don't believe that you'll end up like that? Nor would I wish to think so; but who knows?—maybe ten years, or even eight years ago, that same woman with the salted fish arrived here from somewhere, all fresh like a cherub, innocent, pure, knowing no evil and blushing at every word. Maybe she was like you, proud, sensitive, unlike the others, and maybe she looked around like a princess and was aware that perfect happiness awaited him who loved her and whom she loved. You see how it ended up? And what if at that very moment when she was thrashing the fish against the dirty steps, drunk and dishevelled, what if at that very moment she had remembered all her former, innocent years spent in her parents' home, when she still went to school and a neighbour's son lay in wait for her on the road, and assured her that he would love her for the rest of his life, give her everything he had, and then the two of them had proposed to love one another for ever and marry just as soon as they were grown up?! No, Liza, it would be a blessing if you were to die of consumption as quickly as possible, in some little corner or basement, like that girl I just told you about. In a hospital, you say. Fine if they'll take you there, but what if your mistress still needs you? Consumption is a peculiar kind of illness, it's not a fever. A person who has it hopes, right up until the last moment, and says she's well. You reassure your own self. And that suits the mistress. Don't worry, it's true; it means you've sold your soul, and moreover you owe money, which means you can't utter a word. But you'll die, they'll all abandon you, they'll all turn their backs on you, because what use are you to them then? And what's more you'll be reproached for taking up space for nothing, for not getting on and dying. You'll have to implore them for a drink and then they'll give it to you with a curse: "When", they'll say, "are you going to snuff it, you slut? You don't let us sleep, you keep moaning, the guests are disgusted." It's true, I myself have overheard things like this being said. They'll shove you, as you are dying, into the most filthy corner of the cellar, where it's dark and damp. And what, as you lie there all alone, will you think then? Then you'll die, you'll be collected hastily, by strangers, grumbling, impatient; absolutely no one will bless you, no one will grieve for you, all they'll want will be to get you off their backs as quickly as possible. They'll buy a sort of cheap wooden coffin and then they'll carry you off, like that wretched girl was carried off today, and they'll say their prayers for you in the tavern. The grave will be slushy, full of dregs, wet snow—they won't stand on ceremony for you, will they? "Lower her in here, Vaniushka. Look, if she isn't in luck, she's going in with her legs in the air, that's the sort she is. Shorten the ropes now, you fool." "It's fine like this." "What do you mean, it's fine? Come on, it's lying on its side. That was a human being too, wasn't it? Oh well, all right, fill it up." They won't bother to quarrel for long on your account. They'll rapidly shovel in the wet blue clay and then go off to the tavern . . . And that's the last that'll be remembered of you on this earth; children, fathers, husbands come to the graves of other women, but for you— not a tear, not a sigh, nor a prayer of remembrance, and nobody, nobody in the whole world will ever come to visit you; your name will vanish from the face of the earth, just like that, as if you'd never existed and never been born. Mud and marsh, but still at night-time, when the dead awaken, you'll knock on the lid of your coffin: "Allow me, good people, to live in the world again! I was alive, but I didn't see life, my life was frittered away, it was swallowed up in the tavern in the Haymarket; allow me, good people, to live in the world again! . . ."'

I went into such pathos that I had a lump in my throat, and . . . suddenly I stopped, sat up a little in fright, bowed my head timidly, and with a thumping heart began listening. I had reason to feel embarrassed.

For some time I had been feeling that I had stirred up her whole soul, broken her heart, and the more I felt sure of this the more I wanted to achieve my aim as quickly and powerfully as possible. The game, the game attracted me; however, it was not only a game . . .

I knew that I was speaking in a rigid, contrived, even bookish manner; in a word, I did not know any other way than 'as happened in books'. But that didn't trouble me; after all, I knew, I could feel, that I would be understood and that this very bookishness might perhaps still further enhance the matter. But at this point, having made an impact, I suddenly lost courage. No, never, never before had I witnessed such despair! She was lying there prone, with her face firmly buried in her pillow and both arms clutching it. Her breast was heaving. The whole of her young body seemed to be writhing in convulsions. The stifled sobs filled her chest, tore it asunder, and suddenly broke out with shrieks and wails. Then she pressed herself even more firmly against the pillow: she didn't want anyone here, not a single living soul to know about her suffering and tears. She bit the pillow, bit her hand until she drew blood (I saw that later), then clutching her unravelled plait she collapsed with the effort, holding her breath and clenching her teeth. I was about to say something to her, to implore her to calm down, but I felt that I didn't dare, and then suddenly in some sort of violent tremor, almost in terror, I threw myself around, groping, trying to get ready to go. It was dark: however hard I tried I couldn't get it over quickly enough. Suddenly I found a box of matches and a candlestick with a completely untouched candle. The moment the room was lit up Liza jumped up at once, sat down, and with a kind of distorted face, a half-crazed smile, started looking at me almost vacantly. I sat down beside her and took her hand; she came to her senses, threw herself at me, wanting to grab hold of me, but did not dare and hung her head quietly in front of me.

'Liza, my friend, I didn't mean . . . Forgive me', I began, but her fingers squeezed my hand with such force that I guessed that it was the wrong thing to say and stopped.

'Here's my address, Liza, come and see me.'

'I'll come . . .', she whispered emphatically, still without raising her head.

'And now I'm going; goodbye . . . until we meet again.'

I stood up; so did she, and then suddenly blushed all over, started, grabbed the shawl on the chair, and flung it over her shoulders, covering herself up to her chin. Having done this, once again she smiled somewhat painfully, blushed, and looked at me strangely. I found it upsetting. I hastened to leave, to get away from it all.

'Wait a moment', she said all of a sudden, when we were already right by the doors of the entrance hall, putting a hand on my overcoat to stop me, and then she hastily put down the candle and ran off—she had clearly remembered something, or wanted to fetch something to show me. As she ran off she went all red, her eyes were gleaming, there seemed to be a smile on her lips— what could it be? Against my will I waited. She returned after a moment with a look that seemed to be begging forgiveness for something. By and large it was no longer the same face, or the same look as earlier on—sullen, distrustful, and obstinate. Now her look was imploring, tender, and at the same time trusting, gentle, meek. It was like the way in which children look at those whom they love very much and from whom they are asking something. She had lovely light-brown eyes, alive, capable of expressing both love and sullen hatred.

Without explaining anything to me—as if I were some kind of superior being who must be able to understand everything without explanations—she handed me a piece of paper. At that moment her entire face was wonderfuly illuminated with the most naïve, almost childlike exultation. I unfolded it. It was a letter to her from some medical student or something like that—a very high-flown, flowery, but excruciatingly polite declaration of love. I don't recall the terminology now but I can well remember that through the elevated style one could detect the sort of sincere feeling that cannot be feigned. When I had read it through, I encountered her fervid, curious, and childishly impatient gaze. She glued her eyes to my face and waited impatiently—what would I say? In a few words, hurriedly but somehow joyfully and almost boasting, she explained to me that she had gone to a ball in some family house, belonging to some very, very, nice people, *family people*, where they *still knew nothing*, absolutely nothing, because she was just new here and only just . . . and had certainly not yet resolved to stay but would be leaving very shortly, the moment she had repaid her debt . . . Well, and this student had been there and danced with her the whole evening. He talked to her and it turned out that he had already known her as a child in Riga, that they'd played together—but that was a long time ago now—and he'd known her parents. However, he knew nothing, nothing at all about *this*, and didn't suspect anything. And then the day after the ball (three days ago) he'd sent this letter through the friend who had accompanied her to the party . . . and . . . well, that was all!

When she had finished telling the story she lowered her sparkling eyes rather bashfully.

Poor little thing, she was preserving the letter from this student like a treasure, and had run off for this, her only precious thing, not wishing me to go without knowing that even she was loved honestly and sincerely, that even she was spoken to respectfully. Most probably this letter was destined to lie in a casket without further consequences. But never mind; I am certain that she would preserve it all her life as a treasure, as her pride, and her justification, and now at this moment she had remembered the letter and fetched it in order, naïvely, to show off in front of me, resurrect herself in my eyes, in order that I too would see it and that I would praise her. I said nothing, squeezed her hand, and left. I wanted to go so badly . . . I walked the whole way on foot, despite the fact that the wet snow was still coming down in huge flakes. I was exhausted, crushed, bewildered. But the truth was already shining through the bewilderment. The awful truth!

CHAPTER 8

HOWEVER, it took me some time until I was prepared to admit this truth. On waking up the following morning after a few hours of deep, leaden sleep and instantly putting my mind to all that had happened the previous day, I was really astonished at my *sentimentality* with Liza and at all the 'horror and misery of yesterday'. 'What a womanish attack of nerves, phew!' I decreed. 'And why did I go and foist my address on her? What if she comes? Oh well, let her come, what's it matter . . .' But *obviously* that was not the chief or most important consideration at that moment: I had to make haste at all costs to save my reputation in the eyes of Zverkov and Simonov as quickly as possible. That was the most important thing. And I was so flustered that morning that I completely forgot about Liza.

First of all I needed to repay quickly yesterday's debt to Simonov. I resolved on a desperate measure: to borrow the entire fifteen roubles from Anton Antonych. As luck would have it, he was in an extremely pleasant mood that morning and lent them immediately, at the first request. I was so delighted by this that, as I signed the loan note with a rather dashing air, I *casually* informed him that the day before 'I was out boozing with some friends at the Hôtel de Paris; we were seeing off an old friend, one might even say a childhood friend, and, you know, he's a real playboy, a spoilt chap, but of course from a good family, of considerable fortune, and a brilliant career, quick-witted, kind, always intriguing with the ladies, you know what I mean; we drank an extra " half-dozen" and . . .'. Well nothing; the whole thing was delivered with great ease, familiarity and smugness.

Arriving home I wrote at once to Simonov.

To this day I feel pleased with myself when I remember the truly gentlemanly, good-natured, open tone of my letter.

Skilfully, nobly, and—most importantly—without any superfluous words, I blamed myself for everything. I excused
myself, 'if I may be permitted to excuse myself at all', with the
fact that I was completely unused to wine and had got drunk
after the first glass, which I had (allegedly) drunk before their
arrival, whilst I was waiting for them at the Hôtel de Paris
between five and six o'clock. I begged Simonov's forgiveness
in particular; I asked him to relay my excuses to all the others,
especially to Zverkov, whom 'I remember as if in a dream',
and whom I must have offended. I added that I would have
called on each of them, but that my head, and still more my
conscience, ached. I was particularly pleased with the 'rather
light', almost casual touch (very polite, however) which suddenly found expression through my pen and, better than all
possible arguments, instantly forced them to understand that I
looked on 'all of yesterday's nastiness' in a rather detached
way; that I was not in the least, no, in no sense at all, was I
finished outright, as you, gentlemen, no doubt think, but on
the contrary I looked on the thing as a calmly self-respecting
gentleman ought. 'Water under the bridge', I said.

'Isn't there even a certain marquis-like playfulness?' I said
admiringly as I reread the letter. 'And all on account of my
being a cultured and educated man! Other people in my shoes
wouldn't know how to get round it, but look how I've
extricated myself, and I'll be off having fun again and all
because I'm an "educated and cultured person of our times".'
And indeed, maybe it was all a result of the alcohol yesterday.
Hm . . . well, no, not of the alcohol. I didn't drink any vodka
at all between five and six, when I was waiting for them. I lied
to Simonov; I lied unscrupulously; and even now I'm not
ashamed . . .

Anyway, damn it! What mattered was that I'd got round it.

I put six roubles into the letter, sealed it, and asked Apollon
to take it to Simonov. Discovering that there was money inside
the letter Apollon became more respectful and agreed to go.
Towards evening I went out for a walk. My head was still
aching and in a whirl from the day before. But the closer the
evening drew in and the denser the twilight, the more my
impressions altered and got tangled up, and my thoughts with
them. Something inside me would not die down, something in

the depth of my heart and conscience did not want to give up and was proclaiming itself with burning despair. For the most part I pushed my way along the most crowded shopping streets, along the Meshchansky, the Sadovaia, near the Iusupov Gardens. I have always been particularly fond of walking along these streets in the twilight, just when the crowd is thickening and the various passers-by, tradesmen and artisans, their faces preoccupied to the point of anger, are going home from their daily work. It was precisely this shoddy hubbub that I liked, the blatant prosaicness of it all. On this occasion the jostling in the street only irritated me still further. I simply couldn't come to terms with myself, find a solution. Something was rising up, something kept on rising up painfully in my soul, and it wouldn't calm down. Utterly distraught I returned home. It was just as if there were some crime weighing on my soul.

I was continually tormented by the thought that Liza might come. I found it strange that of all the memories of the day before it was her memory that tormented me in particular, as it were completely separately. Towards evening I was able to forget about almost everything else; I brushed it all aside and still remained very pleased with my letter to Simonov. But on this issue I really didn't feel very happy. It was as if Liza alone were tormenting me. 'What if she comes?' I kept thinking. 'Well, so what, let her come. Hm. The thing that's awful is that she'll see how I live, for instance. Yesterday I presented myself to her as such a . . . a hero . . . and now, hm! It's dreadful that I've let myself go so badly. The flat is simply destitute. And yesterday I resolved to go out to dinner in such an outfit! And that oilskin sofa of mine with the stuffing sticking out! And that dressing-gown of mine which won't even cover me up! All in tatters . . . And she'll see it all; and she'll see Apollon too. That swine, he's bound to insult her. He'll have a go at her in order to be rude to me. And of course I'll turn cowardly as usual, and start shuffling around before her, wrapping myself up in the folds of my dressing-gown, I'll start smiling, I'll start lying. Oh, how frightful! And what's more, that's not the most frightful thing yet! There's something even more important, even worse, even more despicable, yes, despicable! Once again, yes, once again I'll put on that dishonest, lying mask! . . .'

On reaching this thought I flared up: 'Why dishonest? What's dishonest? I was talking sincerely yesterday. I remember feeling quite genuine about it. I just wanted to arouse some noble emotions in her . . . if she cried a bit, it was no bad thing, it will have a beneficial effect . . .'

But all the same I couldn't relax.

All that evening, well after I had returned home, which was already past nine o'clock, and according to my calculations there was no chance that Liza would come, she still continued to haunt me, and significantly I remembered her always in the same attitude. There was one particular moment in all that had taken place the previous day which stood out very clearly in my memory: it was when I lit the room up with a match and saw her pale, distorted face, with its excruciatingly tormented look. And how pitiful, how unnatural, how distorted her smile was at that moment! But at that time I was not yet to know that fifteen years later I would still recall Liza with the same pitiful, distorted, superfluous smile she had at that instant.

The next day I was once again prepared to accept that it was all nonsense, the result of nervous exhaustion and, most importantly, of *exaggeration*. I had always recognized that as my weak point and sometimes feared it greatly: 'I keep on exaggerating, that's where I fall down', I repeated to myself by the hour. But still it was this refrain, 'however, Liza may perhaps still come', that concluded all my rationalizing at that time. I was so worried that at moments I went into a rage. 'She'll come! she's bound to come!' I exclaimed, darting about the room, 'if not today then she'll come tomorrow and she'll find me! Such is the damned romanticism of all these "pure hearts"! Oh, the wretchedness, the stupidity, oh, the narrow-mindedness of these "impure sentimental souls"! But why doesn't she understand, how is it she seems not to understand? . . .' But at this point I would stop, greatly confused.

'And how few,' I thought in passing, 'how few words were needed, how little of the idyllic was needed (and an artificial, bookish, contrived idyll at that) in order to turn a person's whole soul round instantly the way I wanted. So much for virginity! So much for the untouched soil!'

At times I thought of going to see her myself, 'to tell her everything', and beg her not to come and see me. But when this thought came over me such anger would rise up within me that I believe I would have crushed that 'damned' Liza, if she had happened to appear suddenly beside me, I would have insulted her, humiliated her, chased her away, I would have hit her!

However, one day passed, another, a third, and she didn't come, and I started to calm down. I became especially cheerful and alert after nine o'clock and at times I would even start having rather sweet dreams: 'For instance, I am saving Liza simply by virtue of her coming to see me and my talking to her . . . I am developing her, educating her. Finally I notice that she loves me, loves me passionately. I pretend that I don't understand (I don't know, however, quite why I'm pretending; I just am, for effect probably). Finally, all embarrassed, beautiful, trembling, and sobbing she throws herself at my feet and tells me that I'm her saviour and that she loves me more than anything else in the world. I'm astonished, but . . . "Liza," I say, "surely you don't think that I haven't noticed your love? I've seen it all, I've guessed everything, but I have not been so bold as to encroach upon your heart first, because I have had an influence on you and I was afraid that out of gratitude you would deliberately force yourself to respond to my love, trying to force emotions that might not be there, and I did not wish for that because it's . . . despotism . . . It's indelicate (well, in a word, at this point my tongue got carried away with some sort of European, George-Sandish,* indescribably noble subtleties . . .). But now, now you are mine, my creation, you are pure and beautiful, you are my lovely wife.

> And into my house, boldly and freely,
> Enter as mistress of it all!"

After that we start living happily ever after, go abroad, etc., etc.' In a word, it would become foul to me, and I would finish up by sticking my tongue out at myself.

'Anyway, they won't allow her, the slut!' I thought. 'After all, they don't let them go out for walks very much, least of all in the evenings' (for some reason I felt certain that she would come in the evening, precisely at seven o'clock). 'However, she said she wasn't yet completely tied down there, and enjoyed special rights; that means, hm! Damn it, she'll come, she's bound to come!'

It was a good thing that during this time Apollon was there to distract me with his vulgarity. He drove me to the end of my tether! He was a curse, a scourge, sent to me by providence. He and I had been continually crossing swords for years on end, and I detested him. My God, how I loathed him! I don't think that ever in my life have I loathed anyone as much as I loathed him, especially at certain moments. He was a middle-aged, pretentious man who spent some of his time doing tailoring. But for some unknown reason he despised me, really beyond all measure, and he regarded me with intolerable condescension. However, he was patronizing to everyone. You had only to look at that flaxen-haired, smoothly brushed head, at that quiff which he fluffed up over his forehead and greased with some sort of vegetable oil, at that solid mouth with pursed lips, and you felt the presence before you of a creature who never ever doubted himself. He was a pedant in the highest degree, and the most gigantic pedant of all those I've come across on this earth; and on top of this with a self-esteem appropriate only to Alexander of Macedon.* He was infatuated with each and every one of his buttons, every one of his fingernails—absolutely infatuated, that's how he was! He treated me in a totally despotic fashion, said extremely little to me, and if he had to look at me then it was with a firm, majestically self-assured, and constantly sneering look that sometimes drove me mad. He performed his duties with such an air that it made it seem that he was doing me an enormous favour. Besides, he practically never did anything at all for me, neither did he consider it his duty to do anything. There can be no doubt that he considered me the greatest fool in the world, and if 'he retained me', then it was for the singular reason that he could receive a monthly salary from me. He consented to 'do nothing' for me for seven roubles a month. I will be forgiven many of my sins because of him. At times it reached such a point of hatred that his gait alone almost threw me into convulsions. But I found his lisp the most revolting thing of all. He had a rather long tongue, or something of the sort, which meant that he always lisped and hissed and he seemed to be extremely proud of it, imagining that this lent him great distinction. He spoke softly, evenly, putting his hands behind his back and lowering his eyes to the floor. He particularly infuriated me when he used to start reciting the Psalter from behind the partition. A lot of battles were waged on account of these recitals. He particularly liked to recite in the evenings, in a quiet, even voice, intoning as if over a corpse. It's interesting that that's how he ended up: he's now employed to read the Psalms over the dead, and he also exterminates rats and makes shoe wax. But at that time I couldn't dismiss him, he was quite literally chemically fused to my existence. Moreover, on no account would he ever have agreed to leave. I couldn't live in furnished rooms: my flat was my private residence, my shell, my wrapper in which I hid myself from the rest of humanity, and Apollon, goodness knows why, seemed to me to belong to that flat, and for seven whole years I couldn't get rid of him.

Anyway, to withhold his salary for two, or even three, days was impossible. He would have made such a to-do that I wouldn't have known what to do with myself. But during those days I was so embittered with everyone that I resolved, for some reason and purpose, to *punish* Apollon and not to give him his salary for another two weeks. For a long time, for about two years, I'd been intending to do this—just to show him that he shouldn't be so bold as to lord it over me in such a way, and that if I felt so inclined I could always not give him his salary. I proposed not to speak to him about it and deliberately to remain silent in order to conquer his pride and force him to be the first to broach the subject of the salary. Then I would pull all seven roubles out of a drawer, show him that I had them and that I'd deliberately put them aside, but that 'I didn't want, didn't want, simply didn't want to give him his salary, and I didn't want to because *I just didn't want to*', because that was 'my will as his master', because he was disrespectful, because he was boorish; but that if he asked me for it respectfully I might perhaps relent and give it to him; otherwise he'd wait two weeks, three weeks, he'd wait a whole month . . .

But for all my anger, he still won. I didn't even hold out for four days. He began in the way he always began in similar circumstances, because similar instances had already occurred, and been tested (and let me remark that I knew it all beforehand, I knew his mean tactics by heart), namely: he would begin by directing an extremely stern look at me, without dropping it for several minutes on end, especially if he was letting me in or out of the house. If, for instance, I stood up to it and gave the appearance of not noticing these looks he would, whilst remaining as silent as ever, embark on further tortures. Suddenly, for no reason at all he would glide quietly into my room, whilst I was walking around or reading, stop by the door, put one hand behind his back, move his legs slightly apart, and fix on me a gaze that was not so much stern as contemptuous. If I were suddenly to ask him what he wanted, he would not answer but would continue staring at me for a few more seconds and then, pursing his lips together in a very special way, with a very telling look he would slowly turn around on the spot and slowly retire to his room. After a couple of hours he would suddenly come out and make exactly the same appearance before me. It sometimes happened that I was in too much of a temper to ask him what he wanted, but simply raised my head sharply and imperiously, and then I too would start staring at him. We would look at each other in this way for about two minutes; in the end he would turn around, slowly and importantly, and retreat for another two hours.

If even this failed to bring me to reason and I carried on with the rebellion, he would then suddenly begin sighing; looking at me he would give these long, deep sighs, as if with these sighs alone he were measuring the whole depth of my moral decline, and of course, it would end with his complete success: I raged and screamed but I would nevertheless be obliged to grant him whatever it was all about.

On this occasion the usual manœuvres of 'stern looks' had only just begun when I immediately lost my temper and threw myself at him in a fury. I was already too annoyed as it was.

'Stop!' I shouted at him frenziedly, when he slowly and silently, with one hand behind his back, turned to retire to his room, 'Stop! turn back, turn back I say.'

And I must have bellowed so unnaturally that he did turn round and began looking at me with some amazement. However, he still wouldn't say a word and it was this that made me furious.

'How dare you come into my room without asking and look at me like that! Answer me!'

But after looking at me calmly for half a minute or so he once again started turning away.

'Stop!' I roared, running up to him. 'Don't move! There. Answer me now: what have you come in here to gawp for?'

'If you have any little requests, then it is my duty to fulfil them', he answered, after a further silence, lisping softly and evenly, raising his eyebrows and gently shifting his head from one shoulder to the other, and all of it done with the most dreadful calm.

'It's not that, I'm not asking you about that, you torturer!' I shrieked, shaking with anger. 'I'll tell you myself, torturer, why you came here: you can see I'm not giving you your wages, and out of pride you, don't want to cringe and ask for them, and that's why you come in with your stupid stare to punish me, to torment me, and you have *no i-dea*, torturer, how stupid it is, stupid, stupid, stupid, stupid!'

He was about to turn away again in silence but I grabbed hold of him.

'Listen!' I shouted at him. 'Here's the money, look! here it is!' (I pulled it out of the little desk.) 'All seven roubles, but you won't get them, you *shan't* get them until you come up to me respectfully with your head bowed in repentance, to implore my forgiveness. Do you hear?!'

'That will never happen!' he replied with somewhat unnatural self-assurance.

'It will!' I screamed, 'I give you my word it will!'

'And there is no reason for me to ask your forgiveness,' he went on, as if completely oblivious to my shouts, 'because you have called me a "torturer", and I can always go and file a complaint against you with the local warden.'

'Go! Go and tell him!', I roared. 'Go now, this minute, this second! But you're still a torturer! A torturer! A torturer!' But he simply looked at me, and then he turned round and, still not listening as I shouted my summons to him, he glided off to his room, without looking back.

'If it wasn't for Liza, none of this would have happened!' I said to myself. And then, after standing still for a moment, solemnly, and with dignity, but with my heart beating slowly and strongly, I went off in pursuit of him behind the screen.

'Apollon!' I said quietly and without hurrying, although I was panting, 'go straight away, without a moment's delay, for the local warden!'

He had already sat down at his table, put on his spectacles, and picked up some sewing. But on hearing my order he suddenly chuckled with laughter.

'Now, this minute, go! Go, or I can't tell you what will happen!'

'You're literally out of your mind', he remarked, without even raising his head, with the same slow lisp and continuing to thread his needle. 'When have you ever heard of a person reporting himself to the authorities? And as for scaring me, it's pointless over-exerting yourself, because nothing will come of it.'

'Go on!' I shrieked, grabbing him by the shoulder. I felt I was on the verge of hitting him.

But I had not noticed the door from the entrance hall suddenly opening at that very moment, quietly and slowly, and a figure entering, stopping, and beginning to stare at us in amazement. I cast a glance, froze with shame, and rushed off to my room. There, clutching my hair with both hands, I leaned my head against the wall and stopped dead in that position.

After about two minutes I heard Apollon's slow steps.

'There's *someone* to see you', he said, looking at me particularly severely, and then he stepped back and made way for—Liza. He was not eager to leave and was looking at us with derision.

'Off you go! Off you go!' I ordered him, losing my grip. At that moment my clock gathered its strength, wheezed, and struck seven.

CHAPTER 9

And into my house, boldly and freely,
Enter as mistress of it all.

(Nekrasov)

I STOOD before her, crushed, discredited, sickeningly ashamed, and I think I smiled, trying with all my might to wrap the folds of my shaggy old quilted dressing-gown round me: to the last detail, it was as I had imagined just now in my depression. After standing in front of us for a couple of minutes Apollon left the room, but I didn't feel any easier. And what made it worst of all was that she too had suddenly grown embarrassed, to an extent I had never anticipated. Of course, it was from looking at me.

'Sit down', I said mechanically, bringing a chair over to the table for her, and myself sitting down on the sofa. She sat down at once, obediently, all eyes, and was evidently expecting something from me. This naïve expectation made me furious but I controlled myself.

In this situation one ought to pretend not to notice anything, as if everything were normal, whereas she . . . And I vaguely sensed that she would pay me dearly *for all this*.

'You've found me in a peculiar situation, Liza', I began, stammering and knowing that this was exactly how not to begin.

'No, no, what are you thinking?!' I shouted, seeing that she had suddenly blushed. 'I'm not ashamed of my poverty . . . Quite the opposite, I look upon it with pride. I am poor but honourable. It is possible to be poor and honourable', I muttered. 'However . . . would you like some tea?'

'No . . .', she started to say.

'Wait a minute!'

I jumped up and ran off to find Apollon. I felt the need to disappear somewhere.

'Apollon,' I whispered, feverishly, tongue-tied, and I tossed him the seven roubles that had been in my fist all the time, 'here are your wages; see, I'm giving them to you; but for that you must save me: go at once and fetch some tea and ten plain biscuits from the tavern. If you don't want to go you'll make me a very unhappy man! You've no idea what sort of woman she is . . . That's all! Perhaps you're thinking something . . . But you don't know what sort of a woman she is! . . .'

Apollon, who had already sat down to work and put on his spectacles, at first squinted at the money without putting down his needle; then, without paying any attention to me and without giving me any answer, he continued to fiddle around with the needle, which he was still trying to thread. I waited about three minutes, standing in front of him with my arms folded *à la Napoléon*. My brow was moist, I was pale, and I could feel it. But, thank God, he must have felt sorry for me as he looked at me. Having finished with his needle he slowly stood up, slowly moved away from the table, slowly took off his spectacles, slowly counted the money, and, finally, having asked me over his shoulder whether he should fetch a whole portion, he slowly walked out of the room. As I went back to Liza a way out crossed my mind: couldn't I just run out as I was, in my dressing-gown, go wherever my eyes took me and take what came?

I sat down again. She looked at me anxiously. We remained silent for several minutes.

'I'll kill him!' I suddenly screamed, slamming the table forcefully with my fists, splashing ink out of the inkstand.

'Ah, what do you mean?' she shouted, trembling.

'I'll kill him, kill him!' I screamed, thumping on the table in a total frenzy and, at the same time, fully understanding how stupid it was to get so worked up.

'You don't know, Liza, what a torment he is to me. He's my torturer . . . At the moment he's gone off for some biscuits; he . . .'

And I suddenly burst into tears. It was a downpour. Between sobs I felt so ashamed, but I couldn't hold them back any longer.

She took fright. 'What's the matter with you? What's the matter with you?' she cried, fussing over me.

'Water, give me some water, over there!' I muttered in a weak voice, realizing, however, that I had no real need of water, nor did I need to mutter in a feeble voice. But I was *putting it on*, as you say, in order to save face, although the downpour was genuine.

She passed me the water, looking at me like a lost soul. At that moment Apollon came back with the tea. I suddenly felt that this commonplace and prosaic tea was dreadfully unseemly and wretched after all that had happened, and I blushed. Liza looked at Apollon in terror. He went out without looking at us.

'Liza, do you despise me?' I said, staring at her, trembling with impatience to discover what she was thinking.

She became embarrassed and could not manage any reply.

'Drink the tea!' I said spitefully. I was angry with myself but of course I had to take it out on her. My heart was suddenly boiling with a terrible spite directed at her; I think I could have killed her. In order to take my revenge on her I silently vowed not to speak a word to her all the time she was there. 'She's the cause of it all', I thought.

Our silence had already lasted about five minutes. The tea stood on the table; we didn't touch it: I had reached the point where I deliberately did not wish to start drinking, in order to burden her still further with that; it was awkward for her to start by herself. She looked at me several times with sad perplexity. I remained stubbornly silent. Of course, I myself was the main person to suffer, because I was fully aware of how horribly mean my spiteful stupidity was, and at the same time I could not restrain myself.

'I want . . . to go away from . . . that place altogether', she began, in order somehow to break the silence, but—the poor thing!—that was precisely the wrong thing to start talking about at such an utterly stupid moment and to such an utterly stupid person as myself. My heart even sank in pity at her clumsiness and uncalled-for bluntness. But something outrageous instantly suppressed all my pity and even egged me on still further: to hell with it all! Another five minutes went by.

'Am I disturbing you?' she began timidly, barely audibly, and started getting up.

But the moment I saw this first outburst of offended dignity, I shook so badly from anger that I instantly exploded.

'Why have you come to me, tell me please?' I began, gasping

and without even retaining any logical sequence to my words. I wanted to tell her everything, in one breath; I didn't even worry about where to begin.

'Why did you come? Answer me! Answer!' I shouted, barely in control of myself. 'I'll tell you, woman, why you came. You came because I once spoke words of *compassion* to you. And then you grew soft and wanted some more "words of compassion". But let me, let me tell you, that I was laughing at you. And I'm laughing at you now. Why are you trembling? Yes, I was laughing. I had been insulted, at dinner, by that lot who arrived before me. I came over to your place in order to give one of them a thrashing, an officer; but I didn't succeed, I didn't find him; since I had to get revenge on someone for the insult, you showed up and I unleashed my anger on you, and laughed. I was humiliated and so I wanted to humiliate someone else; I had had my face rubbed in the mud, and so I wanted to show my power . . . That was what it was, and you thought that I had come on purpose to save you. Is that what you thought? Is that what you thought?'

I knew that she would, perhaps, get lost and miss the finer points of what I was saying; but I also knew that she would understand the essence of it perfectly well. And what's what happened. She turned as pale as a handkerchief, tried to say something, her lips were painfully distorted; but she collapsed back in her chair as if she had been struck with an axe. And after that she listened to me all the while with her mouth open, her eyes open, and shaking dreadfully with terror. The cynicism, the cynicism of my words crushed her . . .

'To save you!' I went on, jumping up from my chair and running up and down the room before her. 'Save you from what? I may be worse than you. Why didn't you throw it back in my face when I read you that sermon and say: "And why, pray, did *you* come here? To preach morality?" It was power, power that I needed at that moment, I needed a game, I needed to reduce you to tears, I needed your humiliation, your hysterics—that's what I was after then! Anyway, I couldn't carry it off because I'm a good-for-nothing, I got afraid and, the devil knows why, without thinking I went and gave you my address. And then, even before I got home I was already cursing you for all I was worth on account of that address. I already hated you because I'd lied to you. Because I only play with words, fill my head with dreams, and in reality do you know what I want? For you to disappear, that's what! I need peace of mind. Indeed, just in order to be left in peace, right now I would sell the whole world for a copeck. Shall we let the whole world go, or shall I always go without my tea? I say, let the world go so long as I can always drink my tea. Did you know that, or not? Well, I know that I'm a scoundrel, a villain, an egoist, a lazy-bones. I've been shaking so much these last three days through fear that you would come. And do you know what it was that especially troubled me during these three days? It was that I had presented myself to you as such a hero on that occasion and then you'd suddenly see me in this tatty old dressing-gown, beggarly, repulsive. I've just told you that I'm not ashamed of my poverty; well, let me tell you that I *am* ashamed of it! I'm ashamed of it more than of anything else, I'm afraid of it more than of anything else, I'm more afraid of it than if I were a thief, because I'm so vain that it's as if I'd been skinned alive and found even plain air painful. Surely by now you must have guessed that I'll never forgive you for having found me in this dressing-gown, throwing myself like an angry little dog at Apollon. The saviour, the former hero throwing himself like a mangy, tousled little dog at his flunkey, who laughs at him! And those tears which I couldn't hold back just now, like some old woman who's been put to shame, I'll never forgive you! Neither will I ever forgive you for the fact that I'm confessing all this now! Yes, you— you alone must answer for it all because you just turned up, and because I'm a scoundrel, because I'm the most revolting, the most ridiculous, the most small-minded, the most stupid, the most jealous of all the worms in this world, none of whom are in any way better than me, but who, the devil only knows why, are never embarrassed; and there's me, who all his life will be insulted by any old nit—and that's what typifies me! And what does it matter to me that you won't understand any of this? And what does it matter to me if you're rotting in that place or not? And do you realize how much, having told you this, I will detest you for having been here and listened? After all, a man only talks like this once in his life, and then it's when he's in hysterics! . . . What more do you want? Why after all this are you still hanging around me, tormenting me, why don't you go?'

But at this point there was a very strange occurrence.

I was so accustomed to thinking and imagining everything as it happened in books, and to regarding everything in the world as I had already created it in my dreams, that at first I didn't even understand the meaning of this strange occurrence. This is what happened: Liza, whom I had crushed and humiliated, had understood a great deal more than I had imagined. She understood from it all the thing that a sincerely loving woman always understands first, namely: that I myself was unhappy.

The terrified and outraged feeling in her face changed at first into pitiful bewilderment. When I started calling myself a rogue and a scoundrel and my tears began to flow (I uttered this whole tirade in tears), her whole face went into a sort of grimace. She wanted to stand up, to stop me; when I had finished she paid no attention to my yells—'Why are you here? why don't you go away?'—but only to the fact that it must be extremely painful for me to be saying all this. And she was so crushed, the poor thing; she thought of herself as infinitely beneath me; how could she be angry or offended? Suddenly, on some sort of irresistible impulse she leapt out of her chair, and striving towards me, but still feeling too timid and not daring to move from the spot, she stretched out her arms to me . . . At this point my heart turned over. Then she suddenly threw herself at me, flung her arms around my neck, and burst into tears. I, too, could hold back no longer and sobbed as never before . . .

'I don't get a chance to . . . I can't be . . . good!' I just about got out, and then walked over to the sofa, collapsed onto it with my face down, and for a quarter of an hour sobbed really hysterically. She pressed herself close to me, embraced me, and seemed to freeze in that embrace.

But nevertheless, the fact of the matter was that the hysterics had to come to an end. And so (I'm telling the sickening truth), as I lay with my face down on the sofa, burying my head tightly in my tatty, leather cushion, I began, little by little, from afar, unwillingly but irrepressibly, to sense that after all it would be awkward to raise my head and look Liza straight in the eyes now. What was I ashamed of? I don't know, but I was ashamed. The thought also entered my agitated head that now the roles had definitely been reversed, that she was now the heroine and I was just the oppressed and crushed creature she had been that night with me—four days ago . . . And all this occurred to me whilst I lay face-down on the sofa!

My God! Surely I wasn't jealous of her?

I don't know, to this day I still can't decide, and of course at the time I was even less able to comprehend it than I am now. After all, I cannot live without power and tyranny over someone . . . But . . . but, you see, rationalizing doesn't explain anything, so it's useless to rationalize.

I did, however, overcome myself and raised my head a bit; I had to raise it sometime . . . And then, I'm convinced to this day that, precisely because I was ashamed to look at her, another feeling was suddenly kindled and flared up in my heart . . . it was a feeling of supremacy and possession. My eyes shone with passion and I clasped her hands firmly. How I detested her and yet how I felt drawn to her at that moment! The one feeling reinforced the other. It was verging on revenge . . . At first her face expressed what might have been perplexity, what might even have been fear, but only for a second. She embraced me rapturously and fervently.

CHAPTER 10

A QUARTER of an hour later I was running up and down the room in a state of wild impatience, time and again going up to the screen and peering through the crack at Liza. She was sitting on the floor, leaning her head against the bed, and she must have been crying. But she didn't leave, and it was this that was irritating me. By now she already knew everything. I had thoroughly insulted her, but . . . there's no need to go into that. She had guessed that my fit of passion was simply revenge, a new humiliation for her, and that to my recent, almost aimless hatred, was now added a *personal, jealous* hatred of her . . . However, I do not maintain that she grasped this very precisely; but on the other hand she fully understood that I was a vile person, and more importantly, that I was not in a condition to love her.

I know that I shall be told that it is unbelievable, unbelievable that anyone could be as spiteful and stupid as me, and no doubt in addition that it is unbelievable that I didn't fall in love with her, or at any rate appreciate that love. What makes it so unbelievable? In the first place I was no longer capable of falling in love because, let me repeat, in my terms love meant tyranny and moral superiority. All my life I've been unable even to imagine any other kind of love and I've reached the point where at times I think that love consists of the right to tyrannize that the loved one freely gives the lover. Even in my underground dreams I have not been able to conceive of love other than as a struggle; I always began it with hatred and ended it with moral subjugation, and then I could never think what to do with the submissive object. And besides, what is there that's unbelievable about it, given that I had already become so morally corrupt, so unaccustomed to 'living life' that just a little while before I had taken it upon myself to reproach and shame her for coming to me to listen to 'words of compassion'? and I hadn't guessed that she had not in the least come to hear words of compassion, but to love me, because for women love comprises a whole resurrection, an entire salvation from whatever sort of ruin, a whole regeneration, and it cannot manifest itself in any other way. However, as I charged around the room, peering through a crack in the screen, I no longer hated her so much. It was just that her presence here was unbearably painful to me. I wanted her to disappear. I yearned for 'tranquility', I longed to be left alone in the underground. Because I was so out of the habit, 'living life' oppressed me to the extent that I found it difficult to breathe.

But several more minutes went by and she still did not get up; it was as if she was in a coma. I was unscrupulous enough to knock gently on the screen in order to remind her . . . All at once she roused herself, leapt up from her place, and began hurriedly searching for her shawl, her hat, her fur coat, just as if she were escaping from me . . . After a couple of minutes she slowly walked out from behind the screen and gave me a distressing look. I grinned at her maliciously; however, it was a forced grin, *for the sake of appearances*, and I turned away from her gaze.

'Farewell', she said, heading for the door.

I suddenly rushed up to her, grabbed her hand, unfolded it, put in . . . and then closed it again. After that I instantly turned away and ran off as fast as I could to the opposite corner of the room, so that at least I couldn't see . . .

I was on the point of lying just now—of writing that I did it unintentionally, without thinking, because I was flustered, out of stupidity. But I do not want to lie so I'll tell you straight out that I unclasped her hand and placed in it . . . out of malice. The idea came to me while I was running up and down the room and she was sitting behind the screen. But I can say with certainty that even if I committed this act of cruelty deliberately, it came not from my heart but from my foolish head. This act of cruelty was so artificial, so cerebral, so contrived, so *bookish*, that I couldn't keep it up even for a minute. First I dashed into the corner in order not to see, and then full of shame and despair I threw myself after Liza. I opened the door leading to the hallway and began to listen.

'Liza! Liza!' I shouted down the stairs, but without courage, in a weak voice . . .

There was no reply; I thought I could hear her tread on the bottom steps.

'Liza!' I shouted louder.

No answer. But at that moment I heard a noise below as the close-fitting glazed entrance door creaked open and then slammed shut. The boom reverberated up the staircase.

She had left. I went back to my room, immersed in thought. I found it horribly distressing.

I stopped beside the table near the chair where she had sat and looked vacantly in front of me. About a minute went by and then I suddenly trembled: right in front of me on the table I saw . . . in a word, I saw a crumpled, dark-blue five-rouble note, the very one I had put in her hand a moment ago. It was *that* note; it couldn't have been any other, there wasn't another in the house. She must have managed to throw it onto the

table at that moment when I dashe͏̸ ͏
of the room.

And what of it? I might have known
Might I have expected it? No. I was suc͏
have so little respect for other people, t͏
have imagined that even she would do tha͏
A second later, like a madman I hurri͏
throwing on whatever clothes I could lay m͏
tearing hurry, and then I rushed headlong a͏
not yet managed to go two hundred paces whe͏. . .   ͏.͏.to
the street.

It was quiet, it was snowing, falling almost perpendicularly,
forming a blanket over the pavement and the empty road.
There were no passers-by, there was not a sound to be heard.
The street-lamps were flickering despondently and uselessly. I
ran about two hundred paces to the crossroads and stopped.

'Where has she gone and what am I running after her for?'
What for? To fall in front of her, to start sobbing with
repentance, to kiss her feet, to beg her forgiveness! And that
was what I wanted; my heart was being torn apart, and never,
never will I be able to recall that moment with indifference.
But the thought came to me: 'Why? Surely I'll start hating
her, perhaps even tomorrow, precisely because I kissed her
feet today? Could I really make her happy? Surely today for
the hundredth time I have once again recognized my own true
worth? Surely I'll plague the life out of her!'

I stood in the snow, staring into the dull mist, and thought
about it.

'And isn't it better, won't it be better?' I romanticized to
myself later on at home, stifling the sharp pain in my heart
with fantasies, 'won't it be better if she bears the insult for
ever? Insult—after all, it's a purification; it's the most caustic,
painful consciousness! Only tomorrow I would have defiled
her soul and wearied her heart. But now the insult will never
ever die within her, and however repulsive the filth that awaits
her, the insult will elevate her, it will cleanse her . . . with
hatred . . . hm . . . perhaps, and with forgiveness . . . However, will all this make things easier for her?'

And indeed, now I'll pose an empty question on my own

s better—cheap happiness, or sublime suffering?
, which is better?

d thus I dwelt on things, as I sat at home that evening,
half dead with mental pain. I have never ever experienced such
suffering or repentance; but could there really be even the
slightest doubt, when I ran out of the flat, that I would get
half-way and turn back home? I never met Liza again, nor did
I hear of her. I might add that for a long time I remained very
pleased with the *expression* about the usefulness of insults and
hatred, despite the fact that I almost fell ill with grief.

Even now, after so many years, I find it somehow too
unpleasant to remember all this. I remember a lot of unpleasant
things but . . . shouldn't I finish the 'Notes' here? It seems to
me that I made a mistake in starting to write them. At any rate
I felt ashamed the whole time I was writing this *tale*: it must
mean that it is not so much literature as corrective punishment.
After all, to tell a long story about how, for instance, I wasted
my life in my little corner through moral corruption, lack of
means, lack of contact with life, and vain malice in the
underground—good God, it's not very interesting. A novel
needs a hero, and here I've *deliberately* gathered together all the
features of an anti-hero, and what's more important, it all
produces the most unpleasant impression because we have all
grown detached from life, we all limp along, each one of us,
more or less. We have grown so out of the habit of even living
that we sometimes feel a sort of loathing for 'living life', and
therefore we cannot bear to be reminded of it. You see, we
have reached the point where we look upon real 'living life'
almost as a burden, almost as servitude, and we are all agreed
amongst ourselves that it is much better to live life according
to books. And what are we rummaging about for, what makes
us so capricious, what is it we're asking for? We ourselves
don't know what. It would be worse for us if our capricious
whims were fulfilled. Just try, for example, giving us a bit
more independence, untie the hands of any one of us, expand
our field of activity, relax the surveillance, and we . . . yes, I
assure you: we would immediately ask to be put back under
surveillance. I know that perhaps you'll be angry with me
about this, you'll cry out, and stamp your feet: 'You,' you'll
say, 'are only speaking for yourself and your own miseries in

the underground, so don't be so bold as to say "all of us".'
Excuse me, gentlemen, after all I'm not trying to justify myself
with this *allness*. As for what applies to me in particular, during
my life I have after all only carried to an extreme things that
you don't have the courage to do even in half measure, and
what's more you have taken your cowardice to be good sense,
and thereby comfort yourselves by deceiving yourselves. And
so I'll most likely prove to be more 'alive' than you. Yes
indeed! Look more carefully! After all, we don't even know
where this life is at the moment, or what it is, what it's called.
Leave us alone, without books, and we'd instantly trip up, get
lost—we don't know where to place our allegiance, what to
hang on to; what to love and what to hate, what to respect and
what to despise. We even find it difficult to be human beings—
human beings with our *own* real flesh and blood; we're
ashamed of it, we consider it a disgrace and strive to be some
kind of imaginary general type. We are stillborn, and for a
long time we have not been begotten of living fathers and this
pleases us more and more. We are acquiring the taste. Before
long we'll think up a way of being somehow begotten by an
idea. But enough; I don't want to write any more 'from the
underground' . . .

The notes of this paradoxical writer are still not finished. He
could not resist and continued further. But it also seems to us
that we might stop here.

The Gambler

A NOVEL

(From the Notes of a Young Man)

CHAPTER 1

I HAVE at last returned after my two-week absence. Our group has already been in Roulettenburg for three days. Goodness me, I thought they would be awaiting my return with impatience, but I was mistaken. The General looked at me with an independent air, spoke to me condescendingly, and sent me off to see his sister. It was clear that they had borrowed some money from somewhere. I even felt that the General was a bit ashamed to look at me. Maria Filippovna was terribly busy and hardly said a word to me; she did, however, accept the money. She counted it and then listened to all I had to report. We were expecting Mezentsov, and the little Frenchman, as well as some Englishman to dinner; as is the way, when there is some money there is a banquet: Moscow-style. When she saw me, Polina Aleksandrovna asked why I had been away so long, and then without waiting for a reply she went off somewhere. Of course, she did this deliberately. Nevertheless we need to sort a few things out. A lot of things have been building up.

I had been allocated a small room on the third floor of the hotel. Everyone here knows that I belong to the *General's suite*. It is quite apparent that they have somehow succeeded in making their mark. The General is regarded by everyone here as a very wealthy Russian grandee. Before dinner he managed, among other tasks, to give me two thousand-franc notes to change. I changed them at the hotel bureau. Now, for at least a week, they will think we are millionaires. I was planning to fetch Misha and Nadia and take them out for a walk, but as I was coming downstairs I was summoned to the General: he thought fit to enquire where I was taking them. This man certainly cannot look me straight in the eyes; he would very much like to, but every time I reply with such an intent look, that is to say such a disrespectful look, that he seems to get embarrassed. In an utterly pompous speech, piling one sentence on top of the other, and finally getting completely tangled up, he gave me to understand that I ought to take the children for their walk in the park, as far as possible from the casino. In the end he lost his temper completely and added, abruptly: 'Otherwise, you might, perhaps, take them to play roulette in the casino. Forgive me,' he added, 'but I know that you're still rather frivolous and may be capable of gambling. In any case, even if I'm not your mentor, and I have no wish to adopt such a role, I do at least have the right to express the wish that you do not, so to speak, compromise me . . .'

'Actually, I haven't got any money,' I replied calmly; 'in order to lose it one first has to have it.'

'You'll have some straight away', replied the General, blushing a little. He rummaged through his desk, consulted a notebook, and it turned out that he owed me about a hundred and twenty roubles.

'How are we going to work it out?' he began. 'We need to convert it into thalers. Well, anyway, take a hundred thalers, it's a round figure; of course, the rest won't be forgotten.'

I took the money without saying a word.

'Please don't be offended by what I say, you're so sensitive . . . If I spoke reprovingly to you, I was only, so to speak, giving you a warning, and of course I have a certain right to do that . . .'

As I was returning home with the children before dinner, I met a whole cavalcade. Our party were going off to see some ruins or other. Two magnificent carriages, superb horses. Mademoiselle Blanche in one carriage with Maria Filippovna and Polina; the Frenchman, the Englishman, and our General on horseback. The passers-by were stopping to look; there was quite a stir; only it will not change matters for the General. I calculated that with the four thousand francs that I had brought, added to what they had evidently managed to borrow, they now had seven or eight thousand francs, which is not enough for Mademoiselle Blanche.

Mademoiselle Blanche is also staying in our hotel, together with her mother; and our Frenchman is there too, somewhere. The servants call him 'Monsieur le comte', and they call Mademoiselle Blanche's mother 'Madame la comtesse', and indeed perhaps they really are a count and countess.

I knew perfectly well that Monsieur le comte would not recognize me when we gathered for dinner. Of course, the

General would not think of presenting me to him, or even of introducing us; but Monsieur le comte has been to Russia himself and is aware that what they call an 'outchitel'* is a very small fry. However, he knows me very well. But I admit I showed up at dinner uninvited; it appeared that the General had forgotten to make the arrangements, or else he would most certainly have sent me to the table d'hôte. I appeared of my own accord and the General looked at me with disapproval. Kind Maria Filippovna immediately found me a seat; but the meeting with Mr Astley saved the day and I became a member of the party, willy-nilly.

I first met this strange Englishman in Prussia, in a railway carriage, where we were seated opposite each other, while I was catching up with the rest of our group; then I bumped into him on my way to France, and finally in Switzerland; that was twice during those two weeks—and now I have suddenly encountered him again in Roulettenburg. Never in my life have I met such a shy person; he is shy to the point of being ridiculous, and of course he knows it because he is not stupid in the least. However, he is very gentle and quiet. I forced him into conversation the first time we met in Prussia. He told me he had been to the North Cape that summer and that he very much wanted to go to the fair at Nizhny Novgorod. I do not know how he made the General's acquaintance; I think that he is head over heels in love with Polina. When she came in he turned bright red. He was very pleased that I was sitting next to him at the table and, it appears, he already regards me as his bosom friend.

During the meal the Frenchman droned on uncommonly; he is offhand and arrogant with everyone. I remember in Moscow he used to blow a lot of hot air. He went on and on about economics and about Russian politics. At times the General found the courage to disagree with him—but modestly, only going as far as he could without causing undue harm to his own sense of importance.

I was in a peculiar mood; of course, even before dinner was half-way through I had managed to ask myself my habitual question: 'Why do I hang around this General, and why haven't I left them ages ago?' From time to time I looked at Polina Aleksandrovna; she completely ignored me. In the end I got very angry and decided to be offensive.

It started when I suddenly, for no reason at all, butted loudly into someone else's conversation. The main thing I wanted was to quarrel with the miserable little Frenchman. I turned to the General and suddenly, very loudly and distinctly, interrupting him, I believe, I remarked that it was almost completely impossible for Russians to dine at the table d'hôte in hotels this summer. The General directed a look of astonishment at me.

'If you are a self-respecting person,' I went on, 'you're bound to invite abuse and have to put up with appalling insults. In Paris, on the Rhine, and even in Switzerland there are so many of these wretched Poles and their French sympathizers that there's not a chance of getting a word in if you're just a Russian.'

I said this in French. The General watched me in disbelief, not knowing whether to be angry or just surprised that I had forgotten myself to such an extent.

'It means that somebody, somewhere has taught you a lesson', said the Frenchman, nonchalantly and scornfully.

'In Paris I started by quarrelling with a Pole,' I replied, 'then with a French officer who was siding with the Pole. But afterwards a contingent of Frenchmen came over to my side, when I told them how I had wanted to spit in the Monsignore's coffee.'

'Spit?' asked the General with pompous disbelief, looking round the table. The Frenchman glanced at me mistrustfully.

'Just so', I replied. 'Since for two whole days I had been convinced that I might have to set off on a brief trip to Rome in connection with our business, I went to the office of the Holy Father's embassy in Paris to get a visa for my passport. There I was met by some little abbé, about fifty years old, a withered man with frosty features, who after listening to me in a polite but extremely chilly manner, asked me to wait. Despite the fact that I was in a hurry I did, of course, sit down to wait, and took out my copy of *Opinion Nationale** and began reading a frightfully abusive article about Russia. Meanwhile I heard someone in the room next door going in to see the Monsignore; I watched my abbé bowing to him. I addressed him once again with my earlier request; in an even colder tone he again asked me to wait. A little bit later a stranger went in, but on business—some Austrian, who was given an audience and then immediately led upstairs. At that point I got very annoyed; I rose, went up to the abbé, and told him determinedly that since the Monsignore was receiving people he could deal with me too. The abbé suddenly recoiled from me in total amazement. He simply could not comprehend how an insignifcant little Russian dared to put himself on a par with the Monsignore's guests in such a way. In the most impertinent tone of voice, as if delighting in the fact that he could offend me, he looked me over from head to toe and shouted: "You don't really think the Monsignore is going to abandon his coffee for you?" At that point I too started shouting, but even louder than he did: "Let me tell you, I could spit in your Monsignore's coffee! If you don't deal with my passport right now, I'll go in to see him myself."

'"What! While the Cardinal is in with him?" shouted the wretched abbé, and withdrawing from me in terror he threw himself at the door and spread his arms out to barricade it, as if to say that he would sooner die than let me past.

'Then I replied that I was a heretic and a barbarian—"que je suis hérétique et barbare"—and that all these archbishops, cardinals, monsignores, and so on didn't mean a thing to me. In short, I let him know that I wasn't going to give in. The abbé glanced at me with profound malice, then he snatched my passport and took it upstairs. A minute later I had my visa. Would you care to see?'

I took out my passport and displayed the visa for Rome.

'However, you . . .', the General began.

'You were saved by the fact that you declared yourself a barbarian and a heretic', remarked the Frenchman, grinning. 'Cela n'était pas si bête.'*

'Surely one doesn't need to follow the example of our Russians? They sit here not daring to utter a word and may even be prepared to deny that they are Russian. At least in my hotel in Paris they began paying much more attention to me after I told them about my scuffle with the abbé. The fat Polish fellow, who was the person most hostile to me at the table d'hôte, faded into the background. The French even put up with it when I told them that a couple of years ago I saw a person who had been shot by a French chasseur in 1812 for the sole reason that he had wanted to discharge his rifle. At the time this person was still only a ten-year-old child whose family had not managed to get out of Moscow.'

'That cannot be true,' the Frenchman flared up, 'a Frenchman wouldn't shoot at a child!'

'Nevertheless he did', I answered. 'I was told this by a respectable retired captain, and I myself saw the scar on his cheek from the bullet.'

The Frenchman started talking rapidly, and at length. The General was about to support him but I recommended that as an example he read some excerpts from the *Memoirs* of General Perovsky,* who had been a prisoner of the French in 1812. Finally, Maria Filippovna started talking about something else in order to change the subject. The General was very displeased with me, because the Frenchman and I had been practically screaming. But Mr Astley seemed quite delighted by my argument with the Frenchman; getting up from the table he proposed that we have a glass of wine together. That evening, I duly managed to have a quarter of an hour's conversation with Polina Aleksandrovna. It took place while we were having a stroll. Everyone had gone off to the park, heading for the casino. Polina sat down on a bench opposite the fountain and let Nadenka go off and play with some children nearby. I also allowed Misha to go off to the fountain and, at last, we found ourselves alone.

First of all, of course, we started discussing business. Polina was simply infuriated when I handed her only seven hundred gulden. She had been sure that I would bring her back at the very least two thousand gulden from Paris, after pawning her diamonds, or perhaps even more.

'I need money at all costs,' she said, 'and it must be got hold of, otherwise I'm simply done for.'

I began asking her what had happened during my absence.

'Nothing except two bits of news from Petersburg; first that Grandmother was very poorly, and two days later that she had, apparently, already died. This news came from Timofey Petrovich,' added Polina, 'and he's a very precise man. We are waiting for the final, definitive news.'

'And so everyone here is in a state of anticipation?' I asked.

'Of course: all and everyone; that's been the only hope for six months now.'

'And are you hoping too?' I asked.

'After all, I'm not related to her at all, I'm only the General's stepdaughter. But I know for certain that she'll remember me in her will.'

'I should think you'll receive a great deal', I said confidently.

'Yes, she loved me; but what makes *you* think so?'

'Tell me,' I replied with a question, 'is our marquis also a party to the family secrets?'

'But what makes you interested in all this?' asked Polina, glancing at me sternly and coldly.

'I should think I am. If I'm not mistaken, the General has already succeeded in borrowing some money from him.'

'You've guessed quite correctly.'

'Well, would he have given him the money if he didn't know about Granny? Did you notice at dinner that on three occasions he said something about Grandmother, calling her "Granny"— la baboulinka?* What very friendly and familiar terms!'

'Yes, you're right. As soon as he finds out that I too have inherited something, he'll instantly start courting me. Is that what you wanted to find out then?'

'Start? Only start courting? I thought he'd been courting you for ages.'

'You know perfectly well he hasn't!' said Polina, with feeling. 'Where did you meet that Englishman?' she added after a moment's silence.

'I just knew that you were going to ask about him.'

I told her about my previous encounters with Mr Astley while travelling. 'He's shy and amorous, and of course he's already in love with you, isn't he?'

'Yes, he is in love with me', replied Polina.

'And also, he is of course ten times richer than the Frenchman. What do you think, has the Frenchman really got anything? Is there reason to doubt it?'

'No, there's no reason to doubt. He's got some sort of château. Only yesterday the General spoke to me about it with certainty. Well, is that enough for you?'

'If I were you I would certainly marry the Englishman.'

'Why?' asked Polina.

'The Frenchman is better-looking, but he's a less reputable person; whilst the Englishman, apart from being honest, is ten times richer', I snapped.

'Yes, but then the Frenchman is a marquis and he's more intelligent', she replied in the most serene voice.

'Is that so?' I went on as before.

'Absolutely.'

Polina thoroughly disliked my questions and I could tell that she wanted to annoy me by the tone and the absurdity of her replies. I told her this straight away.

'I must say I find it really entertaining when you get in a rage. You ought to pay me just for allowing you the privilege of asking such questions and making these suppositions.'

'I do indeed consider that I have a right to ask you all sorts of questions,' I answered calmly, 'precisely because I am prepared to pay for them in any way you like, and because my life is worthless to me now.'

Polina burst into laughter.

'The last time we were on the Schlangenberg you told me you were prepared, as soon as I said the word, to throw yourself down head first, and I should think it's a thousand-foot drop there. Some day I shall say the word, simply in order to see how you settle your debts, and you can be quite sure I'll stick to my word. I loathe you, precisely because I've let you get away with so much, and I loathe you even more because I need you. But so long as I need you I must spare you.'

She began to get up. She had spoken with annoyance. Recently she always ended a conversation with me full of malice and irritation, absolute malice.

'Permit me to ask, what of Mademoiselle Blanche?' I asked, not wishing to let her go without an explanation.

'You know about Mademoiselle Blanche yourself. There's nothing more to add since then. Mademoiselle Blanche will probably become the General's wife—if of course the rumour about the death of Grandmother is confirmed, because Mademoiselle Blanche, her mother, and her third cousin the marquis all know perfectly well that we are ruined.'

'And is the General desperately in love?'

'That's beside the point at this moment. Listen and remember: take these seven hundred florins and go and gamble, try and win as much as you can for me at roulette; come what may I need some money now.'

Having said this she called for Nadenka and set off for the casino, where she joined the rest of our party. I took the first little path I came to on the left, lost in thought and stunned. After that order to go and play roulette I felt just as if I'd been hit on the head. It was odd: I had lots to think about, but instead of doing so I was absorbed in analysing my feelings for Polina. It was true it had been easier for me during my two weeks away than it was for me now, on the day of my return, although during my travels I had pined like a madman, rushed around like a cat on hot coals, and even in my sleep I saw her before me at every moment. Once (it was in Switzerland), falling asleep in a railway carriage, I think I started talking aloud to Polina, to the amusement of all the other passengers in the compartment. And now once again I asked myself the question: do I love her? And once more I could not answer, that is to say, again, for the hundredth time, I answered that I hated her. Yes, I found her detestable. There were moments (whenever we concluded a conversation, as a matter of fact), when I would have given half my life to strangle her. I swear, if it had been possible to plunge a sharp knife slowly into her bosom, I believe I would have grabbed the chance with delight. And yet, I swear by all that is sacred that if on that fashionable peak of the Schlangenberg she really were to say to me 'throw yourself over', I would do so immediately, and even with pleasure. That I knew. One way or another this thing must be resolved. She understands it all surprisingly well, and the thought that I am quite clearly and distinctly aware of how completely inaccessible she is to me, and of the utter imposs- ibility of fulfilling my fantasies—this thought, I am sure, gives her extreme pleasure; otherwise how could she, so careful and clever, be on such intimate and open terms with me? It seems to me that up until now she has looked on me in the manner of the ancient empress who began to undress before her slave, considering him less than a man. Yes, she has frequently considered me less than a man . . .

All the same I had her commission—to win at roulette at all costs. I had no time to ponder why or how soon I must win, and what new ideas had arisen in that ever-scheming head.

Besides, clearly during those two weeks a multitude of new facts had accrued of which I still knew nothing. I had to guess it all, to fathom it all, and as quickly as possible. But for the moment there was no time: I had to set off to play roulette.

CHAPTER 2

I ADMIT I found it disagreeable; although I had made up my mind that I would play, I was not at all disposed to start playing for others. It even threw me a bit off course and I entered the gaming halls with a feeling of extreme annoyance. Once there, from the first glance, I disliked everything. I cannot tolerate the flunkeyism one finds in feuilletons all over the world, above all in our Russian newspapers, where almost every spring our feuilletonists write stories about two things: first, the exceptional magnificence and luxury of the gaming halls in the towns on the Rhine where roulette is played, and secondly, about the piles of gold that are alleged to lie on the tables. It is not as if they are paid for this; it is simply said out of gratuitous obsequiousness. There is absolutely nothing magnificent about these squalid rooms, and far from there being piles of gold on the tables, there is rarely any at all. Naturally, every now and then during the course of the season some eccentric will show up, an Englishman, or some Asiatic, or a Turk, as happened this summer, and suddenly win or lose a great deal; but all the rest play with trifling sums, and on average there is very little money on the table. When I walked into the gaming hall (for the first time in my life), it took me some time before I made up my mind to play. In addition there was a dense crowd. But even if I had been alone, I think I would still rather have left than begun playing. I confess my heart was thumping and I was not composed; I knew for certain and had already resolved long before that I would not leave Roulettenburg in my present state. Something was undoubtedly going to alter my destiny, radically and irreversibly. So it must be, so it will be. However amusing it may seem that I am banking on so much from roulette, I find the standard opinion, accepted by everyone, that it is stupid and absurd to expect anything from gambling, even more ridiculous. And why is it that gambling is worse than any other method of making money, than trading, for example? It is true that out of a hundred only one wins. But—what do I care about that?

In any case, I determined to watch in the beginning and not to start anything serious that evening. If something were to happen that evening, it would be accidental and insignificant— that is what I assumed. Besides, I needed to study the actual game, because, despite the thousands of descriptions of roulette that I had always read so avidly, I certainly understood nothing about its principles until I saw it for myself.

In the first place, it all seemed so sordid—somehow morally obscene and nasty. I am not talking at all about those eager and troubled faces which cluster round the gaming tables in tens, and even hundreds. I certainly do not see anything sordid in the desire to win as much as possible as quickly as possible; the idea put forward by a certain well-to-do and well-fed moralist—who answered somebody's excuse that 'after all, they play for very small stakes' by saying 'so much the worse, because it's petty greed'—has always seemed to me to be very silly. As if petty greed and greed on a grand scale don't come to the same thing! It is a relative matter. What is nothing to a Rothschild is great wealth to me, and as for profits and winnings, not just at roulette but everywhere, people are always taking or winning something from someone else. Whether profit and gain are always bad is another question. I am not going to resolve that here. Since I myself was thoroughly gripped by the desire to win I found all this covetousness, and all this mercenary grossness, if you like, somehow very convenient and familiar as I entered the hall. It is so pleasant when people do not stand on ceremony but behave openly and informally together. And why deceive oneself? It is the most futile and wasteful occupation! What was particularly unpleasant, at first sight, about all that roulette-playing riff-raff was their respect for the occupation, the seriousness, even reverence with which they all clustered round the tables. That is why there is a sharp distinction here between the sort of game called *mauvais genre* and the kind acceptable to an honourable gentleman. There are two games—one gentlemanly, and the other plebeian, mercenary, the game for any sort of riff-raff. Here there is a strict distinction, and yet how essentially base this distinction is! For instance, a gentlemen may stake five or ten louis d'or, seldom more, although if he is very rich he may even stake a thousand francs, but simply for the sake of the game itself, only for the amusement, just in order to watch the process of winning or losing; but he is not in the least obliged to be interested in the actual winnings. After he has won he may, for instance, laugh aloud, or make a remark to one of those gathered nearby, he may even stake again, and double his money once more, but solely out of curiosity, to observe the chances, to make calculations, and not out of a plebeian desire to win. In short, he must look upon all these gaming tables, be it roulette or trente-et-quarante, as nothing other than an amusement, organized solely for his pleasure. He must have no suspicion of the mercenary greed and the snares upon which the bank is founded and run. It would not really be such a bad thing at all if, for instance, he were to think that all the other players, all that rabble, trembling over a gulden, were just as rich and gentlemanly as he himself, and were playing for nothing other than their own entertainment and amusement. This complete ignorance of reality and innocent view of other people would, of course, be extremely aristocratic. I have seen many mothers push forward naïve and elegant fifteen- or sixteen-year-old misses, their own daughters, and, handing them a few gold coins, teach them how to play. The young dames used to win or lose, but always with a smile, and they would leave feeling very satisfied. Our General approached the table, with a respectable, dignified air; a lackey made as if to dash forward to give him a chair but he failed to notice him; he took a long time getting out his purse, then took a long time taking out three hundred francs in gold, staked them on the black, and won. He did not take his winnings but left them on the table. It landed on black again; once again he did not take it, and when on the third time it landed on the red he lost twelve hundred francs in one go. He left smiling and did not lose face. I am sure he felt heavy-hearted, and had the stake been two or three times as much he would not have been able to retain his composure and would have shown his agitation. However, I witnessed some Frenchman winning and then losing something approaching thirty thousand francs quite happily and without any display of emotion. A true gentleman, even if he were to lose his entire fortune, must not show emotion. Money must be so far beneath a gentleman that it is almost not worth bothering about. Of course it would be wholly aristocratic not to pay any attention at all to the obscenity of this whole rabble and the entire surroundings. However, sometimes it is no less aristocratic to adopt the opposite approach and to take notice of all the rabble, that is to say to gaze at them, or even examine them through a lorgnette, for instance; but it can only be done by accepting this whole crowd and the ugliness of it all as a form of entertainment, as though it were a spectacle organized for the amusement of gentlemen. You can mill about in this crowd, and yet look around with the complete conviction that you yourself are a spectator and in no way a part of it. However, it would not be correct to pay too much heed: once again this would not be fitting for a gentleman, because in any case the show does not warrant undue or over-careful observation. Indeed, in general there are few public events which are worth the close attention of a gentleman. But for the time being I personally thought it was all worth watching very carefully, especially for one who had come not just to observe, and I, sincerely and honestly, classed myself with the rabble. As for my innermost moral convictions, in my present reasoning there is, of course, no place for them. Be that as it may; I am saying this in order to clear my conscience. But let me make this observation: recently I have somehow found it dreadfully objectionable to apply any kind of moral standard to my thoughts and actions. I have been driven by another . . .

The rabble really do play a very dirty game. I would even go as far as to say that a great deal of very straightforward thieving goes on at the table. The croupiers, who sit at the ends of the tables, watching the stakes and handing out the money, have a tremendous amount to do. And what rabble they are too! On the whole they are French. However, I am not making these observations and noting all this here in order to describe roulette; I am taking my bearings in order to know how to behave on a future occasion. I have noticed, for instance, that there is nothing more usual than for someone to stretch their hand out from the other side of the table and take your winnings. An argument begins, not seldom shouting, and—'I beg you kindly to prove, to produce witnesses, that it was your stake.'

To start with this whole business was double Dutch to me; I was only guessing and somehow discerned that stakes were placed on numbers, on odds and evens, and on colours. I decided to experiment with a hundred gulden of Polina Aleksandrovna's money that evening. The thought that I was not going to gamble for myself somehow distracted me. It was an extremely unpleasant sensation, and I wanted to rid myself of it as quickly as possible. I kept thinking that by starting to play for Polina I was undermining my own luck. Is it really not possible to touch the gaming table without being instantly infected with superstition? I started by taking out five gold friedrichs, that is fifty gulden, and placed them on evens. The wheel spun and landed on thirteen—I had lost. With a kind of morbid sensation, solely in order to get it over with somehow and leave, I placed another five gold friedrichs on red. It landed on red. I put on another ten gold friedrichs—once again it landed on red. Again I staked the whole lot, and again it was red. After receiving forty gold friedrichs I staked twenty on the twelve middle numbers, not knowing what to expect. I was paid thrice over. And thus, out of the ten gold friedrichs, I had suddenly acquired eighty. I was so overwhelmed by such an intolerably unusual and strange sensation that I decided to leave. It seemed to me that I would not have played like that at all if I had been playing for myself. However, I staked all eighty gold friedrichs on evens once again. This time it landed on four; I was dealt out another eighty gold friedrichs and, grabbing the whole pile of one hundred and sixty gold fried-richs, I set off to look for Polina Aleksandrovna.

They were all having a walk somewhere in the park, and I did not manage to see her until supper. On this occasion the Frenchman was absent and the General let himself go; incident-ally, he deemed it necessary to remark to me once again that he would rather not see me at the gambling table. In his opinion he would be greatly compromised if at some time I lost too much;

'but even if you were to win a lot, I would still be compromised', he added significantly. 'Of course, I do not have the right to dictate your behaviour, but you yourself will agree . . .' As usual, he did not finish what he was saying. I answered drily that I had very little money and that consequently I could not lose too conspicuously, even if I were to play. Going upstairs to my room I managed to hand Polina the winnings and informed her that I really would not play for her again.

'Why not?' she asked uneasily.

'Because I want to play for myself,' I replied, looking at her in surprise, 'and this prevents me.'

'And so you continue to be absolutely convinced that roulette is your only hope and salvation?' she asked sarcastically. Once again I answered her very seriously, 'yes'; and as for my certainty of winning I agreed it might be comical, but 'do leave me in peace'.

Polina Aleksandrovna insisted that I must split today's winnings in half, and handed me eighty gold friedrichs, proposing that we continue to play on that basis in the future. I refused my half, resolutely and finally, and declared that the reason I could not play for others was not that I did not want to, but because I was sure to lose.

'None the less, however silly it may seem, I myself have practically pinned all my hopes on roulette', she said thoughtfully. 'And so you absolutely must continue playing on a fifty-fifty basis with me, and, of course, you will.' At that point she left me, without listening to my further objections.

CHAPTER 3

HOWEVER, yesterday she did not say a word to me all day long about gambling. Indeed, she avoided talking to me altogether yesterday. Her former manner to me has not altered. The same completely offhand behaviour when we meet, even something contemptuous and hostile about it. She has no wish to conceal her loathing for me; I can see that. In spite of this, neither does she hide from me the fact that she needs me for something and that she is sparing me for some reason. A peculiar kind of relationship has developed between us, much of which is incomprehensible to me—taking into account her pride and arrogance towards everyone. She knows, for instance, that I love her to distraction, and even allows me to talk about my passion—and of course she could not make her contempt for me more apparent than by allowing me to talk freely and without censorship of my love. It is like saying, 'I have so little regard for your feeling that I really couldn't care what you talk to me about and what your feelings for me are.' As for her own affairs, she used to talk to me about them a lot before, but was never entirely open. And what is more, her indifference to me bore certain subtleties, like this, for example: she knows, let us suppose, that I am aware of some circumstance of her life, or something that worries her greatly; she will even tell me something about her circumstances if she needs to use me in some way for her purposes, like a slave, or an errand-boy; but she only tells me as much as someone who is employed to run errands need know, and—if I still do not know the whole chain of events, if she herself can see how tormented and worried I am by her torments and worries, she never favours me with the full reassurance of her open friendship, although by using me on frequent errands that are not only a nuisance but also dangerous, she is, in my opinion, obliged to be open with me. But is it worth troubling about my feelings, about the fact that I am also worried, and may be three times as anxious and concerned about her troubles and misfortunes as she is herself?!

For three weeks I have known of her intention to play roulette. She even warned me that I would have to play on her behalf because it would be unseemly for her to do so. It was then that I noticed, from the tone of her speech, that she had some kind of serious worry, and not just a desire to win some money. What does she care about money in itself? There is a purpose here, there are some circumstances about which I can guess, but which I do not yet know. Of course, this position of humiliation and slavery in which she keeps me can offer me (and very often does) the possibility of questioning her candidly and directly. Since I am her slave and utterly insignificant in her eyes, she finds nothing offensive in my brazen curiosity. But the fact of the matter is, while she allows me to ask questions she does not answer them. Sometimes she completely fails to notice them. That is how things are between us!

Yesterday there was a lot of talk among us about a telegram dispatched to Petersburg four days ago, and to which there had been no reply. The General is clearly upset and preoccupied. It is about Grandmother, of course. Even the Frenchman is upset. Yesterday, for instance, they had a long and serious discussion after dinner. The Frenchman's tone with all of us is unusually haughty and offhand. As the saying goes: sit a swine down to eat and he'll put his feet on the table. Even with Polina he is offhand to the point of rudeness; however, he participates quite happily in the communal walks in the grounds of the casino, and the excursions into the country, on horseback or by carriage. For a long time I have known about some of the circumstances linking the Frenchman and the General: in Russia they were setting up a factory together; I do not know whether their project has fallen through, or whether they are still discussing it. Apart from which, I happen to know part of a family secret: last year the Frenchman actually came to the rescue of the General and gave him thirty thousand to replenish a deficit in a government fund when he gave up his job. And of course the General really is in his clutches; but now, right now, the main role in this whole thing is still being played by Mademoiselle Blanche, and I am sure I am not mistaken here.

Who is Mademoiselle Blanche? Here they say that she is a distinguished Frenchwoman, who has her mother with her and a colossal fortune. It is also known that she is related in some way to our Marquis, only very distantly, a sort of cousin, or second cousin. It is said that before my trip to Paris the Frenchman and Mademoiselle Blanche behaved much more formally together, apparently on a far more subtle and delicate footing; but now their acquaintance, their friendship and kinship somehow look more coarse and intimate. Maybe they think our affairs are already so bad that they do not even consider it necessary to stand on too much ceremony with us, or behave more discreetly. The day before yesterday I noticed the way Mr Astley was watching Mademoiselle Blanche and her mother. It seemed to me that he knew them. It also seemed to me that our Frenchman, too, has met Mr Astley before. However, Mr Astley is so shy, withdrawn, and reticent that one can just about depend on him not to wash dirty linen in public. At any rate the Frenchman barely greets him and almost never looks at him—presumably he is not afraid of him. That is quite understandable; but why is it that Mademoiselle Blanche almost never looks at him either? Especially as the Marquis let something out yesterday: he suddenly said in the middle of a general discussion, I do not remember in what connection, that Mr Astley is immensely wealthy and that he knows that for a fact. You would think Mademoiselle Blanche would have looked at Mr Astley at this point! The General is in an altogether anxious position. One can understand what a telegram about his aunt's death might mean to him now!

Although I felt certain that Polina was avoiding a conversation with me, as if on purpose, I too assumed a cold and indifferent air; but I kept thinking that in time she would approach me. On the other hand, yesterday and today I have mainly paid attention to Mademoiselle Blanche. The poor General is absolutely done for. To fall in love at fifty-five with such intense passion is, of course, a misfortune. Add to that his widowhood, his children, his completely ruined estate, his debts, and lastly the woman he came to fall in love with. Mademoiselle Blanche is beautiful. But I do not know whether I shall be understood correctly if I say that she has one of those faces that can be frightening. At least I have always been frightened of this sort of woman. She is probably about twenty-five. She is tall, with broad, sloping shoulders; her neck and her bosom are splendid; her skin is a swarthy yellowy colour, her hair is jet black, and she has a terrific amount of it, enough for two *coiffures*. Her eyes are black with yellowish whites, she has an impudent look, very white teeth, and her lips are always painted; she uses a musk perfume. She dresses to create an effect, expensively, with chic, and with great taste. Her hands and feet are astonishing. Her voice—a husky contralto. She sometimes bursts into laughter, showing all her teeth, but she usually looks around silently and insolently, at least in the presence of Polina and Maria Filippovna. (There is a strange rumour: Maria Filippovna is leaving for Russia.) I think

Mademoiselle Blanche is altogether without education, and perhaps she is not even intelligent, but on the other hand she is suspicious and cunning. I have the feeling her life has not been without its adventures. To tell the truth, the Marquis may not be in any way related to her, and her mother not be her mother at all. But there is information that in Berlin, where we met them, she and her mother have a certain number of respectable acquaintances. As for the Marquis himself, although I still doubt that he is really a marquis, there seems to be no question that he belongs to a respectable social circle, like ours for instance in Moscow, and in some places in Germany as well. I do not know how he is accepted in France. They say he has six châteaux. I thought that a lot of water would have flowed under the bridge in these two weeks; however, I still do not know for certain if anything definite has been said between Mademoiselle Blanche and the General. Everything is now completely dependent on our fortune, that is to say on whether the General can produce a lot of money. If, for instance, news were to arrive that Grandmother had not died, then I am sure Mademoiselle Blanche would disappear immediately. I myself find it surprising and amusing that I have become such a gossip-monger. Oh, how objectionable it all is! With what delight I would discard everybody and everything! But can I really leave Polina, can I really give up spying on her? Of course espionage is a lowly occupation, but—what do I care!

I was also very curious about Mr Astley, yesterday and today. Yes, I am convinced he is in love with Polina. It is curious and ridiculous that so much can sometimes be expressed by the glance of a shy and painfully chaste man, touched by love, and particularly at that moment when, quite naturally, the man would rather sink through the floor than say or express anything through a word or a look. We very frequently meet Mr Astley on our walks. He takes off his hat and walks past, dying, of course, to join us. But if he is invited to, he immediately refuses. At the resting-points, the casino, the bandstand, or in front of the fountain, he is bound to stop somewhere not far from our bench; and wherever we are, be it in the park, the woods, or on the Schlangenberg, we only need to raise our eyes, look round, and somewhere, whether on a nearby path, or behind a bush, there will be a small fragment of Mr Astley visible. It seems to me that he is seeking a chance to speak to me in particular. This morning we met and exchanged a couple of words. At times his conversation is extremely curt. Before he had even said 'good morning', he began saying: 'Ah, Mademoiselle Blanche! . . . I have seen a lot of women like Mademoiselle Blanche.'

He stopped talking and looked at me significantly. What he meant to say by that I do not know, because to my question, 'what does that mean?' he nodded his head with a sly smile and added: 'Indeed it is so. Is Mademoiselle Pauline very fond of flowers?'

'I don't know, I really don't know', I answered.

'So! You don't even know that!' he exclaimed, utterly amazed.

'I don't know, I've never noticed', I repeated, laughing.

'Hm, that gives me a very good idea.' And then he nodded and walked on. He looked pleased, however. We talk in appalling French.

CHAPTER 4

TODAY has been a ridiculous, shocking, absurd day. It is now eleven o'clock at night. I am sitting in my tiny little room recollecting it. It began in the morning when I had to go and play roulette for Polina Aleksandrovna. I took her entire sixty gold friedrichs, but on two conditions: first, that I did not want to play for equal shares, that is to say that if I won I would not take anything for myself, and, secondly, that Polina should explain to me this evening why it is that she so badly needs to win some money, and exactly how much it is that she needs. I am still unable to suppose that it is simply for money. It is apparent that money is essential, and as soon as possible, for some particular purpose. She promised to explain, and I set off. There was a frightful crowd in the gaming halls. How brazen they are, and how greedy they all are! I squeezed my way towards the middle and stood next to the croupier himself; then I started timidly testing the game, staking two or three coins at a time. In the meanwhile I watched and took note; it seemed to me that calculation in itself means little enough and has none of the importance many gamblers give it. They sit there with bits of paper all ruled out, noting down the wins, counting up, working out the chances, making calculations, finally placing a bet, and—losing in exactly the same way as we simple mortals, who play without any calculations. On the other hand, I did reach one conclusion which, it seems, is correct: in a random series of spins there really is, if not a system, then some sort of order—which is, of course, extremely odd. For instance, it tends to happen that after the twelve middle numbers, the last twelve come up; twice, shall we say, the ball lands on the last twelve and then changes to the first twelve. Having landed on the first twelve it moves again to the middle twelve, falls there three or four times in a row, and then moves again to the last twelve, from where after two goes it moves on to the first twelve, lands there once and then again falls three times on the middle numbers, and it continues like this for an hour and a half or two hours. One, three, and two; one, three, two. It is most amusing. One day, or one morning, it can go like this, for example: the red and the black alternate, changing every minute with no order, so that it does not land on either red or black for more than two or three goes in succession. The next day, or the next evening, it will keep landing on red, as many as twenty-two times in a row, and carry on doing so without fail for some length of time, for an entire day for instance. Much of this was explained to me by Mr Astley, who stood by the gaming tables for a whole morning, without betting once. As for me, I lost everything, and very quickly. Straight away I staked twenty gold friedrichs on evens and won, staked five, won again, and so it went on for another two or three turns. I think about four hundred gold friedrichs must have come into my hands in some five minutes. That was when I should have left, but a strange sort of sensation came over me, a kind of challenge to fate, a sort of desire to give it a fillip, to stick my tongue out at it. I staked the largest bet allowed, four thousand gulden, and lost. Then, getting heated, I took out all I had left, staked in the same way, and lost again, after which I left the table, stunned. I did not even comprehend what had happened to me, and only told Polina Aleksandrovna about my losses just before dinner. Until then I wandered aimlessly around the park.

Once again at dinner I was in a state of agitation, just as I had been three days ago. The Frenchman and Mademoiselle Blanche dined with us again. It turned out that Mademoiselle Blanche had been in the gaming halls in the morning and saw my exploits. On this occasion she spoke to me somewhat more attentively. The Frenchman was more direct, and simply asked me whether I had indeed lost my own money. I think he suspects Polina. In short, there is something up. I lied at once and said it was mine.

The General was extremely surprised: where had I got that sort of money from? I explained that I had begun with ten gold friedrichs, that six or seven wins in a row, on doubles, had brought me up to five or six thousand gulden, and that I had then lost it all in two turns.

Of course, all this was plausible. As I was giving this explanation I watched Polina, but could make out nothing from her face. However, she had let me lie and had not corrected me; from this I concluded that I ought to lie and hide the fact that I was gambling on her behalf. In any case, I thought to myself, she owes me an explanation and she has promised, not long ago, to disclose something to me.

I thought the General would make some comment to me, but he remained silent; I did, however, notice that agitation and worry were written all over his face. Perhaps in his drastic circumstances he simply found it painful to hear how such a respectable heap of gold passed in and out of the hands of such an improvident fool as myself, in the course of a quarter of an hour.

I suspect that he and the Frenchman had some kind of fierce disagreement yesterday evening. They spent a long time talking heatedly about something behind closed doors. The Frenchman came out looking as if he was very irritated about something, and early this morning he went to see the General again—presumably to continue yesterday's conversation.

Hearing about my losses, the Frenchman remarked

caustically, and even spitefully, that one ought to be more prudent. I do not know why, but he added that, although many Russians gamble, in his opinion they have no flair for it.

'In my opinion roulette is simply made for Russians', I said, and when the Frenchman grinned scornfully at my retort, I pointed out to him that of course the truth must be on my side, because when I talk about the Russians as gamblers I am criticizing them far more than praising them, and consequently I can be trusted.

'And on what do you base your opinion?' asked the Frenchman.

'On the fact that the ability to acquire capital has, historically, emerged as practically the most important item in the catechism of the merits and values of civilized man in the West. On the other hand, a Russian is not only incapable of acquiring capital, but he even squanders it disgracefully, and to no purpose. Nevertheless, we Russians also need money,' I added, 'consequently we are very glad to have, and very susceptible to, methods like roulette, for example, where one can make money on the spot, in a couple of hours, with no effort. It's very attractive to us; and since we gamble to no purpose, with no effort, we lose!'

'That is partially correct', remarked the Frenchman smugly.

'No, it's wrong, and you ought to be ashamed of talking about your own native country like that', remarked the General sternly and imposingly.

'Forgive me,' I answered; 'after all, it's true that we haven't yet made up our minds which is worse: the disgraceful things done by Russians, or the German ability to amass money through honest toil.'

'What a shocking thought!' exclaimed the General.

'What a Russian thought!' exclaimed the Frenchman.

I laughed, I desperately wanted to provoke them.

'And I'd rather spend my life roaming around in a Kirghiz tent', I cried, 'than bow down to the German idol.'

'To what idol?' cried the General, now beginning to get truly angry.

'To the German method of accumulating wealth. I haven't been here long, but nevertheless what I've managed to notice and to verify since I've been here makes my Tatar blood boil.

Good God, I don't want those virtues! Yesterday I managed to cover the ground for six or seven miles all round. Well, its just like in those edifying little German picture-books: here everyone, everywhere has a Vater* in their house, terribly virtuous and exceptionally honest. So honest one dare not approach him. I can't stand honest people who are too frightening to approach. Every one of these Vaters has a family, and in the evening they all read instructive books aloud. Above the little houses the elm-trees and chestnuts are rustling. It's sunset, there's a stork on the roof, and the whole thing is extraordinarily poetic and moving . . .

'Now don't get angry, General, allow me to speak with a bit of sentiment. I can remember myself how my father, now deceased, also used to sit under the linden-trees in the front garden in the evenings and read similar books to my mother and me . . . You see, I'm in a proper position to judge this. But here every family is in a state of complete servitude and submission to the Vater. They all work like asses and they all save money like Jews. Let us suppose the Vater has already put away a certain sum of gulden and is counting on handing over his trade or plot of land to his eldest son; to this purpose his daughter is not given a dowry, and she remains a spinster. To this purpose the younger son is sold into bondage, or the army, and the money is added to the household capital. It's true, that's what they do here; I've asked people. It's all done out of sheer honesty, honesty intensified to the point where the younger son who has been sold believes that he was sold out of nothing other than honesty—and it's truly ideal when the victim himself rejoices at being led to the slaughter. And what else? The fact that things aren't easy for the older son either: there he is with his Amalchen, with whom his heart is united—but they can't get married because there still aren't enough gulden stored away. They too wait decently and faithfully, and go to the slaughter with a smile. Amalchen's cheeks have already become hollow, she's wasting away. Finally, about twenty years later the fortune has increased; the gulden have been piled up honestly and virtuously. The Vater blesses his forty-year-old elder son and the thirty-five-year-old Amalchen, with her withered breasts and her red nose . . . As he does so he weeps, reads a moral, and then dies. The elder son himself turns into a virtuous Vater, and the same story starts again. And thus after fifty years, or after seventy years, the grandson of the first Vater has indeed realized a significant capital and he hands it on to his son, as he does to his, and he to his, and after five or six generations we get Baron Rothschild himself, or Hoppe & Co.,* or the devil knows whom. Well, sir, what a majestic spectacle: a hundred, or two hundred years of continuous work, patience, intelligence, honesty, strength of character, endurance, reckoning, the stork on the roof. What more could you ask for? After all, beyond this you can't go, and from this stance they start passing judgement on the whole world, and instantly punishing the guilty, that is those who differ, even slightly, from themselves. Well, sir, this is the point: I would far rather create an uproar, Russian-style, or get rich at roulette. I don't want to be Hoppe & Co. after five generations. I need money for myself, and I don't consider myself in any way as something necessary and subordinate to making capital. I know I've been romancing dreadfully, but let that be as it is. Such are my convictions.'

'I don't know that there's much truth in what you've been saying,' remarked the General thoughtfully, 'but I know for certain that you start being unbearably theatrical if you are allowed to forget yourself for even a second . . .'

As was his custom he did not finish what he was saying. If our General started talking about something even the tiniest bit more significant than the usual everyday conversation, he never finished what he was saying. The Frenchman, gawping, was listening scornfully. He had understood almost nothing of what I had said. Polina was looking on with a kind of haughty indifference. It appeared that she had heard neither what I, nor what anyone else, had said over dinner on this occasion.

CHAPTER 5

SHE was unusually lost in thought, but the moment we left the table she told me to accompany her on a walk. We took the children and set off towards the fountain in the park.

Because I was in a particularly excited state, I stupidly and rudely blurted out the question why nowadays our Marquis de Grieux, the Frenchman, not only did not accompany her when she went out somewhere, but had not even spoken to her for days.'

'Because he's a scoundrel', she replied strangely. I had never before heard her refer to de Grieux in this way and I remained silent, afraid of interpreting this irritability.

'And did you notice that he's out of favour with the General today?'

'You want to know what it's about', she answered me drily and irritably. 'You know that the General has mortgaged everything to him; his whole estate is his, and if Grandmother doesn't die the Frenchman will instantly take possession of everything that is mortgaged to him.'

'And so it really is true that everything has been mortgaged? I heard about it, but didn't know that it was absolutely everything.'

'What else then?'

'In that case it's goodbye to Mademoiselle Blanche', I remarked. 'She won't be the General's wife then! Do you know what? I think the General is so in love that he might well shoot himself if Mademoiselle Blanche gives him up. At his age it's dangerous to fall in love like that.'

'I myself feel that something will happen to him', said Polina Aleksandrovna thoughtfully.

'And how splendid it is!' I exclaimed, 'it couldn't be more crudely revealed that she has only consented to marry him for his money. In this instance not even the rules of propriety have been observed, it's all been done entirely without etiquette. Amazing! And as for Grandmother, what could be more comical and nasty than sending telegram after telegram asking:

has she died? has she died? Eh? How do you like it, Polina Aleksandrovna?'

'That's all rubbish', she said with revulsion, interrupting me. 'What surprises *me* is that you're in such a cheerful mood. What are you so pleased about? Surely it isn't because you have lost my money?'

'Why did you give it to me to lose? I told you that I can't play for other people, least of all for you. I obey whatever you order me to do; but the outcome doesn't depend on me. After all, I warned you that nothing would come of it. Tell me, are you very despondent at losing so much money? Why do you need so much?'

'Why are you asking all these questions?'

'After all, you yourself promised to explain to me . . . Listen: I'm absolutely convinced that when I start playing for myself (and I've got twelve gold friedrichs), I'll win. Then you can take as much as you need of mine.'

She made a scornful face.

'You aren't angry with me', I continued, 'for making such a suggestion. I'm so well aware of the fact that I'm nothing to you, I mean in your eyes, that you could as well accept money from me. You couldn't be offended by a gift from me. And besides, I've lost yours.'

She quickly glanced at me, and having noticed that I was speaking irritably and sarcastically, she interrupted my conversation again: 'There is nothing in my circumstances of interest to you. If you want to know, I'm simply in debt. I've borrowed some money and I'd like to give it back. I had a crazy and peculiar idea that I was bound to win here, at the gaming table. Why I had such an idea, I don't know, but I believed it. Who knows? Perhaps I believed it because with the options left to me I had no other chance.'

'Or because it really was so very *necessary* to win. It's exactly like a drowning man clutching at a straw. You must agree that if he wasn't drowning he wouldn't take a straw for the bough of a tree?'

Polina was astonished.

'How is it, then,' she asked, 'that you yourself are relying on the same thing? Once, two weeks ago, you too spoke to me at great length about how you were completely certain of winning at roulette here, and you tried to persuade me not to think you were crazy; or were you joking then? But I can remember you were talking so seriously that it couldn't possibly have been taken for a joke.'

'That's true,' I answered thoughtfully; 'I'm still convinced that I'll win. I'll even admit that you've now led me to the question why today's senseless and disgraceful losses have not left me with any doubts. I am still fully convinced that the moment I start playing for myself I'm bound to win.'

'Why are you so absolutely certain?'

'If you like—I don't know. I only know that I *need* to win, that it is also my only escape. Well, maybe that's why I feel that I'm absolutely bound to win.'

'Consequently, you also desperately *need* to win, if you're so fanatically certain?'

'I'll wager you think that I'm incapable of experiencing a serious need?'

'That doesn't matter to me?' Polina replied, softly and indifferently. 'If you like—*yes*, I do doubt that you could be seriously troubled by anything. You may be troubled, but not seriously. You're a disorderly person, and are not settled down. What do you need money for? I found nothing serious in any of the reasons you gave me then.'

'By the way,' I interrupted, 'you said that you needed to repay a debt. It must be a fine debt! It's not the Frenchman, is it?'

'What sort of questions are these? You're particularly biting today. You aren't drunk, are you?'

'You know I don't mind what I say and sometimes ask very direct questions. I repeat, I'm your slave, and people aren't embarrassed by slaves, and a slave cannot give offence.'

'That's nonsense. And I can't stand this "slave" theory of yours.'

'Take note, I don't talk about my slavery because I want to be your slave, but I simply speak about it as a fact that doesn't depend on me at all.'

'Tell me straight out: why do you need money?'

'And why do you need to know?'

'As you like', she answered, with a proud toss of her head.

'You can't bear the "slave" theory, but you demand

servitude: "Answer and don't argue!" All right, so be it. Money for what, you ask? How can you say, for what? Money is everything!'

'That I understand, but not falling into such a state of madness through wanting it! After all, you too are approaching a state of frenzy, of fatalism. There is something going on here, some special sort of purpose. Tell me without beating about the bush, that's what I want.'

She seemed to be getting angry, and I was terribly pleased that she was questioning me so crossly.

'Of course there's a purpose,' I said, 'but I don't know how to explain what it is. It's no more than that with money I'll become a different person, even to you, and not a slave.'

'How? How will you achieve that?'

'How will I achieve it? How is it that you can't even understand that I could succeed in making you look at me as something other than a slave?! But this is what I don't want, this surprise and bewilderment.'

'You said that you found this slavery a pleasure. And that's what I thought myself.'

'That's what you thought!' I exclaimed with a sort of strange enjoyment. 'Well, that's a fine sort of naïvety coming from you! Well, yes, yes, I find being a slave to you a pleasure. There is, yes, there is enjoyment in the highest degree of submission and insignificance!' I rambled on. 'The devil knows, perhaps there is in the knout as well, when it lands on the back and tears the flesh to shreds . . . But maybe I want to try other pleasures as well. Just recently in your presence at the table the General gave me a warning about the seven hundred roubles a year which I still may not receive from him. And the Marquis de Grieux, with his eyebrows raised, is staring at me, and at the same time not taking any notice. Whereas maybe I, for my part, am desperately longing to take the Marquis de Grieux by the nose in your presence?'

'Juvenile talk. Whatever the situation, one can behave with dignity. If there's conflict involved then it ennobles, not degrades.'

'Straight out of the copy-book. You just assume that perhaps I do not know how to behave with dignity. That is to say, I'm most probably a dignified person, but I don't know how to behave with dignity. Do you understand that this may be the case? Indeed, all Russians are like that, and do you know why? Because Russians are too richly and variously gifted to be able to find the appropriate form straight away. In this instance it's all got to do with form. The majority of us Russians are so richly endowed that it takes genius to find the appropriate form. Well, more often than not this genius doesn't exist, because on the whole it is seldom found. It is only among the French, and perhaps certain other Europeans, that form has been so well defined that they can look extremely dignified, whilst being quite undistinguished. That is why form means so much to them. A Frenchman can put up with an insult, a real, deep insult, without a frown, but a fillip on the nose he won't put up with on any account, because it's an infringement of the accepted and time-honoured form of propriety. The reason why our young ladies have such a penchant for Frenchmen is that they have good form. In my opinion, however, they don't have any form at all, but only the cockerel, "le coq gaulois".* However, that is something I am unable to understand, I'm not a woman. Perhaps the cockerels are indeed good-looking. Anyway, I've been talking a lot of nonsense and you don't stop me. Stop me more often; when I talk to you I want to say everything, everything, everything. I lose any kind of form. I'll even agree that not only do I have no form, but I have no virtues at all. I'm stating this to you. I don't even worry about virtues. Everything has now come to a halt within me. You know yourself why. I haven't got a single human thought in my head. It's a long time now since I've known what's going on in the world, either in Russia or here. I passed through Dresden and yet I can't remember what Dresden was like. You yourself know what it is that's devoured me. And since I have no hope at all, and am worth nothing in your eyes, I'll say straight out: I see only you everywhere, and I don't care about the rest. Why and how I love you, I don't know. Do you know that perhaps you are not beautiful at all? Imagine, I don't even know whether you're beautiful or not, not even your face. Your heart is probably bad; your mind is ignoble; that's very likely.'

'Maybe it's because you don't believe in my nobility that you're counting on buying me with money?' she said.

'When have I hoped to buy you with money?' I exclaimed.

'Your tongue has run away with you and you've lost your thread. If it's not me you think you can buy, then you think you can buy my respect with money.'

'But no, that's not entirely so. I told you it's difficult for me to explain. You overwhelm me. Don't let my prattle anger you. You know why it's impossible to get angry with me; I'm simply crazy. However, it's all the same to me if you do get angry. Upstairs in my little room I only have to remember and imagine the rustle of your dress, and I'm ready to chew my fingers to the bone. And why are you angry with me? Because I call myself your slave? Make use of it, make use of my slavery, use it. Do you know that one day I'll kill you? I won't do it because I'm no longer in love with you, or because I'm jealous but—I'll just kill you for no better reason that I sometimes long to devour you. You're laughing . . .'

'I'm certainly not laughing', she said in a fury. 'I order you to be silent.'

She stopped, breathless with rage. My God, I do not know whether she was beautiful, but I always loved looking at her when she stopped like that before me, and that's why I frequently liked to provoke her anger. Perhaps she noticed this and got angry deliberately. I told her this.

'How nasty!' she exclaimed with revulsion.

'It's all the same to me', I went on. 'Do you also realize that it's dangerous for us to go about together? On many occasions I've felt an irresistible urge to knock you down, to disfigure you, to strangle you. And don't think I wouldn't go that far. You'll drive me crazy. I couldn't be afraid of the scandal, could I? Or your anger? What do I care about your anger? I love without hope and I know that I'll love you a thousand times more after this. If I kill you sometime, then you know I'll have to kill myself as well; so, there we are—I'll wait for as long as I can before killing myself, so that I can experience the unbearable pain of being without you. Do you know an improbable thing? Every day I love you *more*, and you know that's almost impossible. And after that how can I help being a fatalist? Remember the day before yesterday on the Schlangenberg, I whispered to you, provoked by you: "Say the word and I'll leap into that abyss." If you'd said that word I would have jumped then. You believe that I would have jumped, don't you?'

'What stupid talk!' she exclaimed.

'It's nothing to do with me whether it's stupid or not', I cried. 'I know that in your presence I need to talk, talk, talk—and so I do talk. I lose all my self-esteem in your presence, and I don't care.'

'Why would I want to make you jump off the Schlangen-berg?' she said drily, and somehow particularly offensively. 'It would be completely useless to me.'

'Tremendous!' I exclaimed. 'You deliberately said that magnificent "useless" in order to crush me. I can see through you. Useless, you say? But after all, pleasure is always useful, and savage, unlimited power, even if it's only over a fly, is also a pleasure of its own kind. Man is a despot by nature and loves being a torturer. You love it terribly.'

I remember she looked at me with a kind of particularly intent expression. My face must have expressed all my incoher-ent and ridiculous feelings. I can now remember that our conversation really did run, almost word for word, like the conversation I have described here. My eyes were bloodshot. The edges of my lips were caked in foam. As for the Schlangen-berg, I swear on my honour, even now: if at that moment she had ordered me to throw myself down, I would have thrown myself! If she had simply said it as a joke, or with contempt, or if she'd spat the words at me—I would still have flung myself off.

'No, why on earth, I believe you', she articulated, but she said it in a way that only she is capable of at times, with such disdain and malice, with such haughtiness that, by God, I could have killed her at that moment. She was taking a risk. I hadn't lied about that either when I spoke to her.

'You aren't a coward?' she suddenly asked me.

'I don't know, maybe I am a coward. I don't know . . . I haven't thought about it for a long time.'

'If I were to say to you, "kill that man", would you kill him?'

'Who?'

'Whoever I wanted.'

'The Frenchman?'

'Don't ask questions, but answer me—whoever I instructed you to kill. I want to know whether you were speaking seriously just now.' She waited so earnestly and impatiently for an answer that I felt rather odd.

'Come on, won't you for heaven's sake tell me what's going on here?' I cried. 'What is it, are you afraid of me? I can see for myself what a mess everything is in here. You are the stepdaughter of a ruined madman who is stricken with passion for that devil—Blanche; then there's that Frenchman with his mysterious influence over you, and—now you're asking me so seriously . . . such a question. At least let me know; otherwise I'll go crazy and I'll do something. Or are you ashamed of honouring me with your candour? But surely you can't be embarrassed in front of me?'

'That's not what I'm talking to you about at all. I asked you a question and I'm waiting for an answer.'

'Of course I'd kill him,' I exclaimed, 'anyone you ordered me to, but surely you couldn't . . . You won't really ask that?'

'And what do you think, I'll feel pity for you? I'll tell you to do it, but I'll keep out of it myself. Could you bear it? No, how could you? You might well kill at my command, but then you'd come and kill me because I dared to make you do it.'

On hearing these words I felt as if something had hit me on the head. Of course, even then I considered that she asked the question half-jokingly, as a challenge; but all the same, she spoke too seriously. Nevertheless, I was stunned that she had spoken in this way, that she kept such a hold over me, that she was willing to have such power over me, and could say so directly: 'Go to your ruin and I will keep out of it.' There was something so cynical and candid in these words that, in my opinion, it really went too far. And so, how did she look on me after that? It had already gone beyond the confines of slavery and insignificance. Looking at a person like that raises him to your own level. And however absurd, however implausible our entire conversation had been, my heart was trembling.

She suddenly burst out laughing. At the time we were sitting on a bench, facing some children who were playing, right opposite the place where the carriages stopped and let out the passengers in the avenue in front of the casino.

'Can you see that fat baroness?' she exclaimed. 'It's Baroness Wurmerhelm. She arrived just three days ago. Do you see her husband?—the tall, withered Prussian holding a stick in his hand. Do you remember how he looked us over the day before yesterday? Off you go now, straight up to the Baroness, take off your hat, and say something to her in French.'

'What for?'

'You swore that you would have jumped off the Schlangen-berg; you swear that you are prepared to murder, if I tell you to. Instead of all these murders and tragedies, I just want to have a good laugh. Go on without making excuses. I want to watch the Baron hitting you with his stick.'

'You're challenging me; you think I won't do it?'

'Yes, I'm challenging you, go on, I want you to!'

'All right, I'll go, although it's a wild fantasy. The only thing is: there won't be any unpleasantness to the General and through him to you? My God, I'm not bothered about myself, but about you, well—and about the General. And what sort of a whim is it to go and insult a woman?'

'I can see you're just a talker,' she said scornfully. 'Only just now your eyes were bloodshot—but perhaps it was because you drank a lot of wine at dinner. As if I myself don't know that it's stupid, and trite, and that the General will be angry? I simply want to have a good laugh. Well, I want to, and that's all there is to it. And why should you insult a woman? You'll most likely get beaten with a stick.'

I turned round and without a word set off to carry out her assignment. Of course it was stupid, and of course I was unable to get out of it, but when I started approaching the Baroness, I remember, I seemed to be egged on by something; to be precise, it was the schoolboyish aspect of it that was egging me on. And I really was dreadfully exasperated, like being drunk.

CHAPTER 6

Two days have already passed since that stupid day. And what a fuss and palaver, what noise and commotion! And how confused, disordered, stupid, and vulgar the whole thing is, and I am the cause of it all. However, it can be funny at times, to me at any rate. I cannot realize what has happened to me, whether in actual fact I am in a state of frenzy, or whether I have gone off the rails and am creating havoc while I am at large. At times I think my mind is disturbed. And then at times I think that I am still not far from childhood, from the school bench, and I am simply fooling around in a rude schoolboyish way.

It is Polina, it is all Polina! Perhaps there would not have been this schoolboyish episode if it were not for her. Who knows, perhaps I did it all out of despair (however stupid it may be to reason in this way)? And I do not understand, I simply do not understand, what there is that is good about her! She is beautiful, however, beautiful; it seems that she is. After all, she drives other men out of their minds as well. Tall and shapely. Very slim though. I think you could tie her into a knot or bend her in two. Her footprints are very long and narrow—tormenting. Really tormenting. Her hair has a hint of red. Her eyes are truly feline, but how proudly and arrogantly she can use them. About four months ago, when I had just arrived, she had a long and heated discussion with de Grieux one evening in the hall. And she was looking at him in such a way that . . . later on when I went upstairs to go to bed, I imagined that she had slapped him—had just done it and was standing in front of him, looking at him . . . It was that evening that I fell in love with her.

However, to the point.

I walked along the path to the avenue, stopped in the middle of it, and waited for the Baroness and the Baron. When they were five paces away I took off my hat and bowed.

I remember, the Baroness was wearing a silk dress with an immense circumference, light-grey-coloured with frills, a crinoline, and a train. She is small and exceptionally fat, with a horribly fat, sagging chin, which makes it impossible to see her neck at all. A crimson face. Small eyes, spiteful and impudent. She moves as if she were conferring an honour on everyone. The Baron is tall and withered. The usual kind of German face, wry, with thousands of fine wrinkles; wears spectacles; about forty-five years old. His legs practically start from his chest; that indicates good breeding. Proud as a peacock. A little clumsy. Something sheeplike in his expression, a substitute in its own way for profundity.

All this flashed before my eyes in three seconds.

At first, my bow and the hat in my hands only barely caught their attention. Only the Baron knitted his brows slightly. The Baroness just sailed straight on at me.

'Madame la Baronne,' I said aloud distinctly, articulating each word, 'j'ai l'honneur d'être votre esclave.'*

Then I bowed, put my hat back on, and walked past the Baron, politely turning my face to him and smiling.

She had told me to take my hat off, but the bow and the schoolboy prank were of my own accord. Heaven knows what it was that prompted me. It was as if I was flying off a mountain.

'Hein!'* the Baron cried, or rather grunted, turning to me in angry surprise.

I turned round and stopped, in polite anticipation, continuing to look at him and smile. He was evidently perplexed and raised his eyebrows to a position *ne plus ultra*. His face grew darker and darker. The Baroness also turned in my direction and she, too, watched me in angry bewilderment. Some of the passers-by were starting to stare. Others even stopped in their tracks.

'Hein!' the Baron grunted again, twice as gutturally and twice as furiously.

'Jawohl!'* I drawled, continuing to look him straight in the eye.

'Sind Sie rasend?'* he shouted, waving his stick and, apparently, beginning to get slightly cold feet. Perhaps he was confused by my attire. I was very respectably dressed, even foppishly, like a person who fully belongs to the very best society.

'Jawo-o-ohl!' I suddenly shouted as hard as I could, dragging out the 'o', like the Berliners, who use the expression 'jawohl' all the time in their conversation, drawling the 'o' to a greater or lesser extent, to express various shades of thought and feeling.

The Baron and Baroness quickly turned round and almost ran away from me in fright. Some members of the public were starting to talk, others were looking at me in astonishment. I do not remember very well, however.

I turned away and started walking at my usual pace towards Polina Aleksandrovna. But before I had got within a hundred paces of her bench I saw that she had got up and set off for the hotel with the children.

I caught up with her by the front entrance.

'I've done it . . . the folly', I said, drawing level with her.

'Well, so what? Now you had better sort it out', she replied, not even looking at me, and went upstairs.

I spent the whole of that evening walking in the park. Across the park and then across the wood; I even walked into the neighbouring principality. In one of the peasant cottages I ate an omelette and drank some wine: they stung me for one and a half thalers for that idyll.

I did not return home until eleven o'clock. I was immediately sent for by the General.

One group occupies two of the hotel room-numbers; there are four rooms. The first—a large one—is the drawing-room, with a grand piano. Next to it is another large room—the General's study. He was waiting for me there, standing in the middle of the study in an extremely majestic pose. De Grieux was sitting, sprawled out on the sofa.

'My dear sir, allow me to ask what you have been doing', the General began, addressing me.

'I would prefer it, General, if you would come straight to the point', I said. 'You doubtless wish to speak about my encounter today with a certain German?'

'A certain German! That German is the Baron Wurmerhelm, and he's an important person, sir! You were rude to him and the Baroness.'

'Not at all.'

'You frightened them, dear sir', cried the General.

'No, not in the least. Whilst I was still in Berlin my ears were continually bombarded with this "jawohl" they keep repeating every other word, and which they drawl out so revoltingly. When I met them in the avenue, I don't know why, but this "jawohl" suddenly sprang to mind, and had an irritating effect on me . . . And besides, on the three occasions that I have met the Baroness, she has had the habit of walking straight at me, as if I were a worm that could be trampled underfoot. You must agree that I, too, can have my self-esteem. I took off my hat and politely (I assure you, politely) said: "Madame, j'ai l'honneur d'être votre esclave." When the Baron turned round and started shouting, "Hein!"—I was suddenly prompted to shout back: "Jawohl!" I shouted it twice: the first time in an ordinary manner, and the second— drawling as hard as I could. And that's all.'

I admit I was exceedingly pleased with this utterly school-boyish explanation. I was surprisingly keen to pad the whole story out, making it as absurd as possible.

The further I went the more I got the taste of it.

'You're making fun of me, aren't you?' shouted the General. He turned to the Frenchman and told him in French that I was definitely asking for trouble. De Grieux grinned contemptuously and shrugged his shoulders.

'Oh, don't get that idea, that's not it at all!' I exclaimed to the General. 'Of course I was wrong to behave like that, I sincerely and openly admit that. One might even say that what I did was a stupid and unpleasant schoolboy prank, but no more than that. And I must say, General, that I entirely regret it. But there is one circumstance which, in my eyes, practically absolves me from regret. Recently, for about two weeks now, even three, I haven't felt very well: ill, nervous, irritable, whimsical, and on certain occasions I completely lose control of myself. It's true, sometimes I felt terribly like suddenly turning to the Marquis de Grieux and . . . However, there's no point in going on; it might be offensive to him. In short, these are symptoms of an illness. I don't know whether Baroness Wurmerhelm will take this circumstance into account when I beg her forgiveness (because I intend to ask her forgiveness). I expect she won't, especially since, as far as I know, of late this circumstance has started to be abused in the legal world: frequently in criminal cases lawyers have begun trying to justify their clients, criminals, by saying that at the moment of the crime they couldn't remember anything and this is, supposedly, a kind of illness. "He killed," they say, "but remembers nothing about it." And can you imagine, General, the medical world agrees with them?—it actually confirms that such an illness exists, a temporary insanity, when a person remembers almost nothing, or half-remembers, or a quarter remembers. But the Baron and Baroness are people of an older generation; besides, they are Prussian Junkers and landowners. This advance in the legal and medical world must still be unknown to them, and therefore they won't accept my explanations. What do you think, General?'

'Enough, sir!' pronounced the General sharply and with restrained indignation, 'enough! I will try once and for all to rid myself of your juvenile behaviour. You will not apologize to the Baroness and Baron. Any communication with you, even were it to consist solely of your begging forgiveness, would be too degrading for them. The Baron, on learning that you belong to my household, has already had this out with me, in the casino, and I can tell you that had you gone just the tiniest bit further he would have demanded satisfaction from me. Do you understand what you have subjected me to, me, sir? I, I have been compelled to beg the Baron's forgiveness and to give him my word that shortly, as from this very day even, you will cease to belong to my household . . .'

'Allow me, allow me, General; so he himself absolutely demanded that I cease to belong to your household, as you are pleased to put it?'

'No; but I considered myself obliged to grant him this satisfaction, and of course the Baron was pleased. We are parting, good sir. You are owed another four gold friedrichs and three florins in local currency. Here's the money, and here's the piece of paper with the accounts; you can check it. Goodbye. From now on we are strangers. I've had nothing but trouble and unpleasantness from you. I will ring for the waiter and tell him that as from tomorrow I will no longer be responsible for your expenses in the hotel. I have the honour of remaining your servant.'

I took the money, the scrap of paper on which the account

was written in pencil, bowed to the General, and said to him, quite sincerely: 'General, we cannot conclude the matter in this way. I am very sorry that you've been subjected to unpleasantness from the Baron, but—if you'll excuse me—it's your own fault. Why did you take it upon yourself to answer to the Baron for me? What is the meaning of this expression, that I belong to your household? I'm just a tutor in your house, and that's all. I'm neither your son, nor under your guardianship, and you cannot answer for my behaviour. In the eyes of the law I myself am competent to do so. I'm twenty-five, I'm a university graduate, I'm a nobleman, I'm a complete stranger to you. It is only my boundless respect for your merits that stops me from demanding satisfaction from you right now, as well as a further account of why you took upon yourself the right to answer on my behalf.'

The General was so stunned that he spread his arms in disbelief, and then suddenly turned to the Frenchman and hurriedly informed him that I had practically summoned him to a duel there and then. The Frenchman started laughing loudly.

'But I don't intend to let the Baron get away with it,' I went on with utter composure, not in the least embarrassed by Monsieur de Grieux's laughter, 'and since you, General, by agreeing today to listen to the Baron's complaint and thereby siding with him, have made yourself a party to the whole affair, I have the honour to inform you that no later than tomorrow morning I will demand from the Baron, in my own name, a formal explanation of why, when the matter concerned me, he addressed himself over my head to some other person—as though I couldn't answer or was unworthy of answering him for myself.'

The thing I predicted happened. On hearing this new stupidity, the General lost his nerve dreadfully.

'Why, surely you don't intend to drag this confounded affair out any further!' he shouted. 'But what are you doing to me, oh good Lord?! Don't you dare, don't you dare, sir, or, I swear to you! . . . there are authorities here as well, and I . . . I, in short, with my rank . . . and the Baron's too . . . in short, you'll be arrested and sent away from here under police escort, so you won't create a disturbance! Do you understand, sir?!'

And although he was breathless with rage, he was still terribly scared.

'General,' I replied with a composure he found insufferable, 'it is impossible to arrest someone for creating a disturbance before the disturbance has been created. I haven't as yet started making my explanations to the Baron, and you still have no idea in what way, or on what basis, I intend to proceed with the matter. I only wish to clarify the offensive supposition that I am under the guardianship of a person who allegedly has some power over my free will. You are worrying and alarming yourself in vain.'

'For God's sake, for God's sake, Aleksey Ivanovich, give up this senseless plan!' the General muttered, suddenly switching from an angry tone to an imploring one, and even seizing my hands. 'Can you imagine what this will lead to? Further trouble. You must agree that I have to keep up a certain image here, especially now! . . . especially now! . . . Oh, you don't know, you don't know the whole of my circumstances! . . . When we leave here I'm prepared to take you back again. It's just for now, but, in short—after all, you know the reasons!' he exclaimed in desperation. 'Aleksey Ivanovich, Aleksey Ivanovich! . . .'

Retreating to the door, I once again asked him emphatically not to worry himself, I promised that it would all turn out well and respectably, and I hurried off.

At times Russians abroad are too timorous and are dreadfully afraid of what people will say, and what they will think of them, whether it would be appropriate to do this, or that; in a word, they behave as if they were wearing corsets, especially those with pretensions to importance. What they love most is any kind of preconceived, established form, which they can follow slavishly—in hotels, on walks, at meetings, on their travels . . . But the General had let slip that on top of all this he had certain special circumstances that made it necessary for him to 'keep up an appearance'. That was why he had so suddenly become faint-hearted and cowardly, and changed his tone with me. I took this into consideration and made a note of it. And of course the next day he might be stupid enough to go to some authority, so in actual fact I did need to be careful.

However, I had no wish to anger the General in particular;

but now I wanted to make Polina cross. Polina had treated me
so cruelly, and it was she who had pushed me in such a stupid
direction, that I very much wanted to get her to the point
where she herself begged me to stop. My schoolboyish pranks
might finally compromise her too. Besides, certain other
feelings and desires were taking shape inside me: if, for
example, of my own accord I shrink to nothing in her esteem,
that after all in no way means that other people must think me
a milksop; and of course there's no chance of the Baron
'beating me with a stick'. I felt like laughing at them all and
coming out the hero myself. Let them watch. I dare say, she'll
be afraid of the scandal and call me back again. And even if
she doesn't call me back, she'll still see that I'm not a
milksop . . .

(Astonishing news: I've just this moment heard from our
nanny, whom I met on the stairs, that Maria Filippovna has
today set off on the evening train, completely alone, for
Carlsbad, to see her cousin. What does this news mean? Nurse
says that she's been meaning to go for a long time; but how
was it that no one knew? However, it may have been only
I who did not know. Nurse also let slip to me that Maria
Filippovna and the General had a serious discussion the day
before yesterday. I understand. This probably means Mademoiselle
Blanche. Yes, something decisive is about to happen
here.)

CHAPTER 7

THE next morning I called for the waiter and told him to make
my bill out separately. My room was not really expensive
enough to give me cause for great alarm, or to leave the hotel
altogether. I had sixteen gold friedrichs and there . . . there
. . . perhaps, wealth! It is a strange thing, I have not won yet
but I am acting, feeling, and thinking like a rich man, and
I cannot envisage anything else.

I was getting ready, despite the early hour, to set off immediately to see Mr Astley in the Hôtel d'Angleterre, not far away from ours, when de Grieux suddenly came to see me. This had never happened before, and besides, relations of late between this gentleman and me have been extremely distant and strained. He has obviously not even been trying to conceal his contempt for me, and has even made a point of not concealing it; but I—I have had my own personal reasons for not regarding him favourably. In short, I loathe him. His arrival surprised me greatly. I immediately grasped that something out of the ordinary was brewing.

He walked in very courteously and complimented me on my room. When he saw that I had my hat in my hand he enquired whether I was really going out for a walk so early. On hearing that I was going to see Mr Astley on business, he stopped for a moment and thought, took it in, and his face assumed an extremely troubled expression.

De Grieux was like all Frenchmen, that is to say cheerful and courteous when it is necessary and advantageous, and insufferably boring when being cheerful and courteous has ceased to be a necessity. A Frenchman is seldom instinctively courteous; he is always courteous at the opportune moment, as if to order. For example, if he can see the necessity of being eccentric, original, unusual, then his utterly silly and unnatural fantasy takes its shape from previously adopted and long since vulgarized forms. The natural Frenchman is made up of the most bourgeois, petty-minded, commonplace staidness—in short, he is the most boring creature in the world. In my opinion only those with little experience, and especially young Russian ladies, are charmed by the French. Any decent creature instantly notices the conventionality of well-established forms of drawing-room courtesy, familiarity, and gaiety, and finds it insufferable.

'I've come to see you on business,' he began, extremely aloofly, albeit politely, 'and I will not conceal the fact that I have come to you as an ambassador, or should we say a mediator, from the General. Having a very poor knowledge of Russian I understood almost nothing yesterday; but the General has carefully explained, and I admit . . .'

'But, listen, Monsieur de Grieux,' I interrupted him, 'since you've undertaken to be a mediator in this affair. Of course I am an "outchitel" and have never pretended to have the honour of being a close friend of this family or of being on any kind of particularly intimate terms, and therefore do not know all the circumstances; but do explain to me: surely by now you are fully a member of this family? Because, in the final analysis, you have shown so much concern, that now, inevitably you mediate in everything . . .'

My question did not please him. It was too transparent for him and he did not want to give any secrets away.

'I am involved with the General, partly through business, and partly through *certain special* circumstances', he said coldly. 'The General has sent me to ask you to drop your intentions of yesterday. Of course everything you devised was very witty; but he has particularly requested me to impress upon you that you're bound to fail; what is more—the Baron will not receive you, and, lastly, he has in any case the means of sparing himself further unpleasantnesses on your part. You yourself must admit that. So tell me, what's the use in continuing? The General himself has certainly promised to accept you into his house again at the first convenient opportunity, and until then to honour your salary, "vos appointements". After all, that is pretty much to your advantage, is it not?'

I retorted with complete calm that he was somewhat mistaken; that it may well be that the Baron would not throw me out but on the contrary would listen to me, and I asked him to admit that, more than probably, he had come in order to try and discover precisely how I intended to take the whole thing in hand.

'Oh, goodness! if the General is so interested, of course he would be pleased to learn what you are going to do and how you are going to do it. That's quite natural!'

I started to explain, and he began to listen, sprawled out, with his head inclined slightly to one side, in my direction, and with a blatantly unconcealed hint of irony in his face. On the whole he behaved extremely condescendingly. I tried with all my might to pretend that I was regarding the matter from the most serious point of view. I explained that since the Baron had addressed the General with his complaint about me, as if

I were the General's servant, he had, first, deprived me thereby
of my post, and secondly, treated me as a person who is not in
a position to answer for himself, and whom it is not even worth
speaking to. Naturally I had considered myself justifiably
offended; however, appreciating the difference in age, and in
our positions in society, and so on and so forth (I could barely
hold back my laughter at this point), I had not wished to
commit yet another fresh folly, that is, by directly confronting
the Baron, or even by merely proposing that he give me
satisfaction. Nevertheless I had considered myself completely
entitled to offer him, and more especially the Baroness, my
apologies, particularly since of late I really had been feeling
unwell, out of sorts, one might say whimsical, etc., etc.
However, the offence the Baron caused me yesterday by
talking to the General and his insistence that I be deprived of
my post had put me in a position whereby I was now unable to
offer my apologies to him or the Baroness, because both of
them, and the rest of the world, would probably think that I
had gone to make my apologies through fear, in order to get
back my post. From all this it followed that I now found
myself compelled to ask the Baron to apologize to me first, in
the most modest terms—for example to say that he had not
wished to offend me in any way. And once the Baron had said
this I would feel myself free to offer him my own apologies
candidly and sincerely. In short, I concluded, all I asked was
that the Baron untie my hands.

'Phew, what punctiliousness, and what refinement! And
why should you apologize? Well, you'll agree, monsieur . . .
monsieur . . . that you are setting this all up on purpose, to
annoy the General . . . and perhaps you have some especial
purpose . . . mon cher monsieur, pardon, j'ai oublié votre
nom, monsieur Alexis? . . . n'est ce pas?'*

'But allow me, mon cher marquis, but what has it to do with
you?'

'Mais le général . . .'

'What about the General? Yesterday he said something about
needing to maintain a certain status . . . and he was so worried
. . . but I didn't understand any of it.'

'In this instance there is—in this instance a special circumstance definitely exists', de Grieux put in, using a pleading

tone which sounded more and more like vexation. 'Do you know Mademoiselle de Cominges?'

'That is, Mademoiselle Blanche?'

'Well yes, Mademoiselle Blanche de Cominges . . . et madame sa mère . . . you must agree, the General . . . in short, the General is in love and even . . . the marriage may even take place here. And just imagine the various scandals and stories about it . . .'

'I do not see any scandal or story concerning the marriage.'

'But le baron est si irascible, un caractère prussien, vous savez, enfin il fera une querelle d'Allemand.'*

'With me then, not with you, because I am no longer a part of the family . . .' (I deliberately tried to be as incoherent as possible). 'But excuse me, is it settled that Mademoiselle Blanche is to marry the General? What are they waiting for? What I mean is, what is there to conceal about this, at any rate from us, the staff?'

'I cannot . . . however, it is not all absolutely . . . still . . . you know they are awaiting news from Russia; the General needs to settle his affairs . . .'

'Ah, ah! la baboulinka!'

De Grieux looked at me with loathing.

'In short,' he interrupted, 'I have complete trust in your innate courtesy, your intelligence, your tact . . . of course you will do it on behalf of the family which accepted you as one of their own, loved and respected . . .'

'I beg your pardon, I was thrown out! And now you're insisting that it was done for appearances; but you'd agree, if they said to you: "Of course I have no wish to pull your ears, but, for the sake of appearances, allow your ears to be pulled . . ." So, after all, isn't it almost the same thing?'

'If this is how things stand, if no request can influence you,' he began, sternly and arrogantly, 'then let me assure you that steps will be taken. There are authorities here, you will be deported this very day—que diable! un blanc-bec comme vous* wants to summon a personage like the Baron to a duel! And you imagine that you'll be left in peace? Let me assure you, nobody here is afraid of you! If I made a request to you it was more of my own accord, because you are troubling the General. And surely, surely you don't believe that the Baron would do anything other than simply order a lackey to chase you away?'

'But you see I won't go myself,' I replied with utmost composure; 'you are mistaken, Monsieur de Grieux, all this will be handled far more decently than you think. This very moment I am setting off to see Mr Astley and I will ask him to be my mediator, in short, to be my second. This man likes me and will probably not refuse. He will go to the Baron, and the Baron will receive him. If I am only an "outchitel" and appear to be some sort of "subalterne", and of course defenceless, then Mr Astley is a nephew of a lord, a real lord, as everybody knows Lord Peabrook, and this lord is here. I assure you the Baron will be polite to Mr Astley and he will listen to him. And if he will not listen to him Mr Astley will consider it a personal insult (you know how insistent the English are) and send one of his friends to the Baron, and he has some very fine friends. Now you can see that things may not turn out the way you presumed.'

The Frenchman definitely lost his nerve; in fact all this was very close to the truth, and so, as it turned out, I did in fact have the power to stir up a scandal.

'But I beg you,' he began in an extremely pleading voice, 'forget the whole thing! You seem quite delighted that it will give rise to a scandal! It is not satisfaction that you want, but a scandal! I said the whole thing would turn out to be amusing and witty, which might even be what you are trying to achieve, but to put it in short,' he concluded, having seen that I had stood up and was putting on my hat, 'I have come in order to hand you this brief note from a certain person; read it—I was told to wait for the answer.'

Having said this he took out of his pocket and handed to me a little note, folded and closed with a paper seal.

Written in Polina's hand, it said:

It has seemed to me that you intend to continue this saga. You have become very angry and are beginning to play the fool. But there are special circumstances here and, perhaps, I will explain them to you later; but please, will you stop and calm down? How silly it all is! I need you, and you yourself promised to obey. Remember the Schlangenberg. I beg you to be obedient, if need be I order you. Yours, P.

PS If you are angry with me for yesterday, then forgive me.

Reading these lines, I felt as if everything were swimming before my eyes. My lips went white and I began to tremble. The damned Frenchman looked at me with an air of exaggerated discretion, his eyes turned away from me as if to avoid seeing my confusion. It would have been better if he had burst out laughing at me.

'Very well,' I replied, 'tell Mademoiselle to rest assured. However, permit me to ask you', I interrupted sharply, 'why you waited so long before handing me this note. It seems to me that instead of chattering away about nothing you should have begun with this . . . if that is what you were specifically instructed to come and do.'

'Oh, I wanted . . . it is altogether so strange, that you must forgive my natural impatience. I wanted to find out as quickly as possible for myself, and from you personally, what your intentions are. I did not, however, know what was in the note, and thought that there would always be time to give it to you.'

'I see, you were ordered, very simply, to give it to me only in the last resort, and if you could settle it verbally, then not to give it to me. Isn't that so? Tell me straight, Monsieur de Grieux!'

'Peut-être',* he said, adopting an air of particular restraint, and looking at me rather oddly.

I took my hat; he nodded and left. I thought he had an ironic smile on his lips. And how could it be otherwise?

'You and I will square things up later, little Frenchman, I'll settle things with you yet', I muttered, going downstairs. I still could not understand anything; it was as if I had been hit on the head. The air revived me a little.

A couple of minutes later, when I was only just beginning to grasp things clearly, I was vividly confronted by two thoughts: *first*, that such trifles, just a few improbable, schoolboyish threats, hurriedly spoken yesterday, had produced such *general* panic. And my *second* thought: what sort of influence does the Frenchman have over Polina? Just a word from him—and she does anything he wants, writes notes, even *begs* me. Of course, their relationship has always been a mystery to me, from the very beginning, ever since I first knew them; however, in the last few days I have noticed a definite loathing, even contempt for him, and he has not even looked at her, has even been downright rude to her. I have noticed this. Polina herself has spoken to me of her loathing for him; she has already come out with some extremely significant admissions . . . It means that she is simply in his power, he has some kind of hold over her . . .

CHAPTER 8

ON the promenade, as they call it here, that is to say in the chestnut avenue, I met my Englishman.

'Oh, oh!' he began, catching sight of me, 'I'm on my way to you, and you to me. Have you already left your party?'

'First of all, tell me how you know all this?' I asked with surprise. 'Does everyone know all about it?'

'Oh no, no one knows about it; anyway, it's not worth knowing about. Nobody is saying anything.'

'Then how do you know?'

'I know, that is to say, I happened to hear about it. Where will you go after leaving here? I am fond of you and that's why I've come to see you.'

'You're a splendid person, Mr Astley,' I said (I was, however, very taken aback: where did he find out?), 'and since I have not yet had a coffee, and yours was probably not very good, let's go to the casino café, sit down, have a smoke, and I'll tell you everything, and . . . you can tell me as well.'

The café was only about a hundred yards away. They brought us some coffee, we sat down, I lit a cigarette; Mr Astley did not smoke anything, but giving me his attention, he prepared to listen.

'I'm not going anywhere, I'm staying here', I began.

'And I felt certain you would stay', said Mr Astley, approvingly.

On my way to see Mr Astley, I had no intention at all of telling him, and even deliberately did not want to tell him, anything about my love for Polina. In all these days I had hardly said a word to him about it. Moreoever, he was very

shy. From the start I had noticed that Polina made a tremendous impression on him, but he never mentioned her name. But
for some strange reason, now, all of a sudden, as soon as
he had sat down and fixed his intense, steely gaze on me, I do
not know why, but I was filled with a desire to tell him
everything, that is all about my love, with all its nuances. I
spent a full half-hour telling the story, and I found it extremely
pleasant to be talking about it for the first time! Noticing that
at certain particularly ardent junctures he became embarrassed, I deliberately exaggerated the fervour of my tale. One
thing I regret is that maybe I said too much about the
Frenchman . . .

Mr Astley listened, as he sat opposite me, motionless,
without uttering so much as a word, looking me straight in the
eye; but when I started talking about the Frenchman, he
suddenly checked me and asked, sternly, whether I really had
the right to mention this irrelevant circumstance. Mr Astley
has always put his questions very strangely.

'You are right: I fear I do not', I replied.

'Have you anything precise to say about this Marquis and
Polina, or is it all only conjecture?'

I was once again surprised by such a categorical question,
coming from a person as shy as Mr Astley.

'No, nothing precise,' I replied, 'nothing, of course.'

'If that is so, you have done wrong not only in talking about
it to me, but even in imagining it.'

'All right, all right! I admit that; but that is not the point
now', I interrupted, wondering to myself. And then I told him
all about what had happened yesterday, in full detail; the fiasco
with Polina, my adventure with the Baron, my dismissal, the
General's extraordinary cowardice, and, finally, I gave him a
detailed account of today's visit from de Grieux, and all its
niceties; I ended by showing him the note.

'What do you conclude from this?' I asked; 'I came expressly
to find out what you think of it. As far as I'm concerned I
could kill that wretched Frenchman, and perhaps I shall do.'

'Me too', said Mr Astley. 'As for Miss Polina, well . . . you
know, we enter into relationships even with people whom we
detest, if necessity compels us to. Here there may be factors
you do not know about, and which depend on extraneous

circumstances. I think you may rest assured—partially, of course. As for her behaviour yesterday, well of course it's peculiar—not because she wanted to get rid of you, and sent you to face the Baron's club (and I cannot understand why he did not use it, since it was in his hand), but because that sort of fiasco, for such a young lady . . . for such a wonderful young lady is unbecoming. Of course, she could not have foreseen that you would carry out her whim so literally . . .'

'Do you know what?' I suddenly exclaimed, looking intently at Mr Astley. 'It seems to me that you have already heard all about this, you know from whom—from Miss Polina herself.'

Mr Astley looked at me in astonishment.

'Your eyes are flashing and I detect suspicion in them,' he went on, instantly regaining his former composure, 'but you do not have the least right to unveil your suspicions. I cannot acknowledge this right and I completely refuse to answer your question.'

'Now enough! There is no need!' I cried, getting strangely agitated and unable to understand why this thought had suddenly sprung to my mind! And when, where, and how could Mr Astley have been chosen by Polina as a confidant? Recently, however, I have not always paid a great deal of heed to Mr Astley, and Polina has always been an enigma to me— so much of an enigma that now, for instance, having launched into a narrative of the whole saga of my love to Mr Astley, I was suddenly struck, even while I was telling the story, by the fact that I was almost unable to say anything precise or positive about my relations with her. On the contrary, everything was fantastical, strange, frivolous, unlike anything else.

'Well, all right, all right; I'm confused and at the moment there is much that I cannot understand', I replied, literally gasping. 'However, you're a fine person. Now to another matter, and I ask not for your advice but for your opinion.'

I remained silent for a moment and then began: 'Why do you think the General was so scared? Why have they all got so worked up by my silly capers? There's such a to-do that even de Grieux himself has found it necessary to intervene (and he only intervenes in the most important cases); he paid me a visit (goodness me!), begged me, implored me—he, de Grieux, implored *me*! Last, but not least—take note of this!—he came at nine o'clock, even before nine, and Miss Polina's note was already in his hands. When then, one might ask, was it written? Perhaps Miss Polina was woken up to do it. Apart from the fact that I can see from all this that Miss Polina is his slave (because she has even asked my forgiveness!)—apart from that, what has she got to do with all this, she personally? What makes her so interested? Why are they afraid of some baron or other? And what are we to make of the General marrying Mademoiselle Blanche de Cominges? They say that because of this they must "keep up a *certain appearance*", but this, after all, is too much, you'll agree. What do you think? From your eyes I am convinced that here too you know more than I do!'

Mr Astley grinned and nodded his head.

'Indeed, here too I do seem to know a lot more than you', he said. 'The whole thing concerns Mademoiselle Blanche alone, and I'm certain that is the absolute truth.'

'Well, what about Mademoiselle Blanche then?' I cried impatiently (I suddenly felt hopeful that something would now be revealed about Mademoiselle Polina).

'It seems to me that at the present moment Mademoiselle Blanche is particularly concerned to avoid any encounter with the Baron or Baroness—still less an unpleasant encounter, or worse still a scandalous one.'

'Well! well!'

'Two years ago Mademoiselle Blanche was here in Roulettenburg during the season. I was also here. At that time Mademoiselle Blanche was not called Mademoiselle de Cominges, and likewise her mother Madame veuve Cominges did not exist. At any rate there was never any mention of her. De Grieux—there was no de Grieux either. I have a deep conviction that they are not only unrelated but also that they have only recently become acquainted. It was also only recently that de Grieux became a marquis—there is one particular circumstance that makes me sure of this. One may also assume that he has only recently started to call himself de Grieux. I know one person here who has met him under another name.'

'But after all, doesn't he have a circle of genuinely respectable friends?'

'Oh, that may be so. Even Mademoiselle Blanche may have

as well. But two years ago, Mademoiselle Blanche, because of a complaint from this same Baroness, was invited by the local police to leave the town, and she left.'

'How did that happen?'

'At that time she had arrived here first with an Italian, some prince with a historical name, something like "Barberini",* or something of that sort. He was a person covered in rings and diamonds, and not imitation ones either. They used to go out in a marvellous carriage. Mademoiselle Blanche used to play trente-et-quarante, at first very well, and then her luck began to change drastically, as I remember. I can remember that one evening she lost an enormous sum. But worst of all, *un beau matin** her prince vanished, nobody knew where, and the horses and carriage vanished too—everything disappeared. The hotel bill was frightful. Mademoiselle Zelma (instead of Barberini, she had suddenly changed to Mademoiselle Zelma) was in utter despair. She wailed and howled to everyone in the hotel and tore her dress in a rage. There in the hotel was a certain Polish count (all Polish travellers are counts) and Mademoiselle Zelma, ripping up her clothes and scratching her face like a cat, with her lovely hands washed in scent, made a certain impression on him. They discussed things and by dinner-time she had calmed down. In the evening he appeared at the casino with her on his arm. As was her custom, Mademoiselle Zelma laughed very loudly, and her manner was somewhat more relaxed. She had stepped straight into the ranks of those female roulette-players who, as they approach the roulette table, push as hard as they can against other players, in order to clear a space for themselves. This is a particular style of the ladies here. You have, of course, noticed them?'

'Oh yes.'

'They are not worth it. To the annoyance of the respectable public, they do not remove them here, at any rate those of them who change thousand-franc notes at the table every day. But, the moment they cease changing notes, they are instantly asked to withdraw. Mademoiselle was still continuing to change notes; but her gambling was going even less fortunately than before. Take good note that these ladies very frequently gamble successfully; they have astonishing self-control.

However, my story is coming to an end. One day, just as the Prince had done, the Count disappeared. Mademoiselle Zelma now showed up in the evening to gamble on her own; this time no one appeared to offer her an arm. In two days she lost once and for all. After staking her last louis d'or and losing it, she looked around and saw beside her Baron Wurmerhelm, who was watching her intently and with deep indignation. But Mademoiselle did not notice the indignation and, addressing the Baron with her famous smile, she asked him to put ten louis d'or on the red for her. As a result of this, that evening, following a complaint from the Baroness, she received an invitation not to appear at the casino again. If it surprises you that I am familiar with all these petty and thoroughly unseemly details, it is because I heard them conclusively from Mr Feder, one of my relatives, who that very night carried Mademoiselle Zelma off in his carriage to Spa. Now, listen to this: Mademoiselle Blanche wishes to marry the General probably so that in the future she will not receive any more invitations such as she received from the casino police two years ago. Now she no longer gambles; but this is because, to all appearances, she has some capital, which she loans to the gamblers here at interest. That is far more prudent. I even suspect that the unfortunate General is in debt to her. It is possible that even de Grieux is in her debt. Or perhaps de Grieux is in partnership with her. You yourself will admit that, at least until the wedding, she would not wish to attract the Baron and Baroness's attention for any reason. In a word, in her situation, the last thing she needs is a scandal. Now, you are connected with the household and your behaviour could provoke a scandal, especially since she appears every day in public arm in arm with the General, or Miss Polina. Do you understand now?'

'No, I don't understand!' I shouted, thumping the table as hard as I could, so that the *garçon* came running in alarm.

'Tell me, Mr Astley,' I repeated in a frenzy, 'if you already knew this whole story and consequently knew Mademoiselle Blanche de Cominges inside out, why did you not warn me, at least—and the General himself, and most importantly, Polina, who has appeared here in public in the casino arm in arm with Mademoiselle Blanche? I can't believe it.'

'There was no point in my warning you because there was

nothing you could have done', Mr Astley answered calmly. 'And anyway, what is there to warn you about? The General, possibly, knows even more about Mademoiselle Blanche than I do, and he carries on taking walks with her and with Miss Polina. The General is an unfortunate man. Yesterday I saw Mademoiselle Blanche galloping along on a lovely horse with Monsieur de Grieux and that little Russian prince, while the General galloped along behind them on a chestnut. In the morning he said his legs were aching, but he sat very well in the saddle. And it was at precisely that moment that it suddenly occurred to me that he was a completely ruined man. Moreover, none of this is my business and I have only recently had the honour of getting to know Miss Polina. However,' Mr Astley suddenly remembered, 'I have already told you that I cannot acknowledge your right to ask certain questions, despite the fact that I am sincerely fond of you . . .'

'Enough,' I said, standing up; 'it is now as clear as day to me that Miss Polina also knows everything about Mademoiselle Blanche, but that she cannot break away from that Frenchman and therefore has resolved to carry on going out for walks with Mademoiselle Blanche. Believe me, nothing else could have persuaded her to go out walking with Mademoiselle Blanche and to beg me in a note not to touch the Baron. This determining factor, before which everything is subordinated, simply must be at work here! And yet, it was she, after all, who made me go for the Baron! The devil take it, I cannot understand anything!'

'First of all you're forgetting that this Mademoiselle de Cominges is the General's fiancée, and secondly that Miss Polina, the General's stepdaughter, has a little brother and sister, the General's own children, completely abandoned by this madman and, it seems, robbed by him as well.'

'Yes, yes! That's right! to leave the children means to abandon them altogether, to stay means to protect their interests, and perhaps to save a scrap of the estate. Yes, yes, all that is true! But still, still. Oh, I understand why they are all so interested in Grandma at the moment!'

'In whom?' asked Mr Astley.

'That old witch in Moscow, who won't die and about whom they are awaiting a telegram to say she's dying.'

'Well, yes, of course, all interest is concentrated on her. The whole thing is to do with the inheritance. Once the inheritance is announced the General will get married; Miss Polina will also be freed, and de Grieux . . .'

'Well, what about de Grieux?'

'De Grieux will also receive his money; that's all he's waiting here for.'

'All! Do you think that's all he wants?'

'I don't know of anything else', said Mr Astley, stubbornly refusing to go on.

'But I know, I do,' I repeated furiously; 'he's also awaiting the inheritance because Polina will receive a dowry, and after receiving the money, she will immediately throw herself round his neck. All women are the same! And those that are the proudest turn out to be the most low-grade slaves. Polina is capable of passionate love and nothing else! That's my opinion of her! Just take a look at her, especially when she is sitting by herself, lost in thought: there is something pre-ordained, fated, damned! She is capable of all the horrors of life and passion . . . she . . . she . . . but who is that calling for me?' I suddenly exclaimed. 'Who is shouting? I heard someone shout in Russian: "Aleksey Ivanovich!" A woman's voice, listen, listen!'

By now we were approaching our hotel. We had left the café a long time ago, hardly even noticing it.

'I heard a woman shouting, but I don't know who she's calling; it's in Russian. Now I can see where the shouting is coming from,' Mr Astley was pointing; 'it's that woman sitting in the big armchair who has just been carried up the front steps by all those lackeys. They are carrying the luggage behind, which means the train must have just arrived.'

'But why is she calling me? She's shouting again; look, she's waving to us.'

'I can see her waving', said Mr Astley.

'Aleksey Ivanovich! Aleksey Ivanovich! Oh Lord, what a blockhead!' the desperate cries resounded from the hotel porch.

We almost ran to the doorway. I walked into the porch, my arms fell in amazement, and my feet were rooted to the spot.

CHAPTER 9

On the upper level of the hotel's broad porch, seated regally in the armchair in which she had been carried up, surrounded by servants, maids, and a host of fawning retainers belonging to the hotel, in the presence of the head waiter himself, who had come out to meet the distinguished guest who had arrived with such fuss and bustle, together with her own personal servants and so many trunks and suitcases, was—*Grandmother*! Yes, it was she herself, the formidable, rich seventy-five-year-old Antonida Vasilevna Tarasevicheva, landowner and grand dame of Moscow, la baboulinka about whom telegrams had been sent and received, who was dying and not dying, and who had suddenly appeared before us in the flesh, like a bolt from the blue. Although she did not have the use of her legs and was carried about, as she had been for the last five years, in an armchair, she appeared as usual, lively, impassioned, smug, sitting up straight, shouting loudly and imperiously, scolding everybody—well, exactly as she had been on the two or three occasions when I had the honour of seeing her, after I had taken up the position of tutor in the General's house. Naturally, I stood before her speechless with surprise. She had spotted me with her lynx-eyes when I was a hundred paces away and they were still carrying her up the steps in the armchair, she had recognized me and called to me using my name and patronymic—which she had learnt once and never forgotten, as was her custom. 'And this is the woman they were expecting to see in her coffin, buried and leaving a legacy,' flashed through my thoughts; 'why, she'll outlive all of us, and everyone else in the hotel! But, goodness, whatever's going to happen to us all now, what will become of the General now?! She's going to turn the entire hotel upside down!'

'Well, my dear fellow, what are you standing there for with your eyes popping out of your head?' Grandmother went on shouting at me. 'Don't you know how to bow, or greet a person, eh? Or have you grown too proud for that? Or maybe you didn't recognize me? Do you hear that, Potapych?' she turned to a grey-haired, elderly man with a pink bald patch, wearing a tailcoat and white tie, her butler who accompanied her on her travels, 'do you hear, he doesn't recognize me! I've been buried! They sent telegram after telegram: has she died, or hasn't she? You see, I know everything! And as you can see, I'm alive and kicking.'

'Forgive me, Antonida Vasilevna, why should I wish you any harm?' I replied cheerfully, coming to my senses. 'I was simply surprised . . . Well, how can one help being surprised at such an unexpected . . .?'

'Why should you be surprised? I jumped on a train and came. It was very peaceful in the railway carriage, no jolting. Have you been out for a walk or something?'

'Yes, I went over to the casino.'

'It's lovely here', said Grandmother looking around. 'It's warm and the trees are lush. I love that! Are the family at home? The General?'

'Oh yes! At this time of day they're certainly all at home.'

'They have fixed hours here too then, and all the formalities? Setting the tone. I hear they keep a carriage, les seigneurs russes! They squander everything and then they're off abroad! Is Praskovia with them?'

'Yes, Polina Aleksandrovna is here too.'

'And the wretched Frenchman? Well, I'll see them all for myself; Aleksey Ivanovich, show me the way, straight to him. Do you like it here?'

'So-so, Antonida Vasilevna.'

'And you, Potapych, tell that idiot of a waiter to find me a comfortable suite, a nice one not too high up, and take all my things up there at once. Why is everyone rushing to carry me? Why are they all creeping around? Damned servants! Who is that with you?' she turned to me once again.

'It's Mr Astley', I replied.

'Who's Mr Astley?'

'A traveller, my good friend; he knows the General as well.'

'An Englishman. There he is staring at me, with his jaw set. However, I love Englishmen. Well, haul me upstairs, straight to their apartments; whereabouts are they?'

They carried Grandmother up; I led the way up the broad staircase of the hotel. Our procession was very striking.

Everyone we came across stopped and stared. Our hotel was considered the very best, the most expensive, and the most aristocratic in the resort. One always bumps into magnificent women and distinguished Englishmen in the corridors and on the stairs. Many people downstairs were asking the head waiter about her, and he for his part was deeply impressed. Of course, he told all the enquirers that this was a distinguished foreigner, a Russian, a countess, a *grande dame*, and that she was occupying the same rooms as those occupied by 'la grande duchesse de N.' a week ago. The chief cause of the sensation was Grandmother's imperious and authoritarian outward appearance, as she was carried up in her chair. At each new face we met she instantly sized the person up with her inquisitive look and questioned me loudly about them all. Grandmother came from solid stock and although she never got out of her armchair, from looking at her one got the feeling that she was very tall. She held her back straight as a board, and she did not lean back in the chair. Her large, grey head, with its prominent and sharply delineated features, was held erect; she looked somewhat arrogant and challenging; and it was evident that her expression and gestures were entirely natural. Despite her seventy-five years, her face was fairly fresh and her teeth were not completely ruined. She was wearing a black silk dress and a white cap.

'I find her most interesting', Mr Astley whispered to me as he climbed up the stairs beside me.

'She knows about the telegrams', I thought. 'She knows de Grieux as well, but it seems that she knows little about Mademoiselle Blanche as yet.' I immediately passed this on to Mr Astley.

Sinful person that I am! I had no sooner recovered from my first surprise, when I started getting very excited about the crushing blow we were about to deliver to the General. I felt as if I were being egged on, and I led the way extremely cheerfully.

Our party were staying on the second floor; I did not announce our presence, nor did I even knock on the door, but simply flung it wide open, and Grandmother was carried through in triumph. As if on purpose they were all gathered together in the General's study. It was midday and they seemed to be planning some excursion—some were to go by carriage, others on horseback, as a group; apart from which, there were also other friends whom they had invited. Besides the General, Polina, and the children, with their nannies, present in the study were: de Grieux, Mademoiselle Blanche, once again dressed in a riding habit, her mother Madame veuve Cominges, the little Prince, and some other learned traveller, a German whom I had never seen with them before. Grandmother's armchair was lowered in the middle of the study, three paces away from the General. Goodness, I shall never forget the sensation! Just before we entered, the General was telling them about something and de Grieux was correcting him. It ought to be mentioned that during the last two or three days Mademoiselle Blanche and de Grieux had, for some reason, been paying court to the little Prince—*à la barbe du pauvre général**—and the mood of the party, although perhaps artificial, was that of a very jolly and happy family. When he saw Grandmother the General suddenly froze, his mouth wide open, breaking off in mid sentence. He looked at her, his eyes bulging as though bewitched by a look from a basilisk. Grandmother was also watching him in silence, without moving—but what a triumphant, challenging, sarcastic look it was! They carried on gazing at each other for a good ten seconds, amidst a profound silence from all the others. At first de Grieux froze, but an expression of extraordinary agitation soon flickered across his face. Mademoiselle Blanche raised her eyebrows, opened her mouth, and looked wildly at Grandmother. The Prince and the scholar were contemplating the whole scene in utter bewilderment. Polina's look expressed extreme surprise and bewilderment, but then she suddenly turned as white as a sheet; a moment later the blood quickly rushed to her face and flooded into her cheeks. Yes, it was a catastrophe for them all! All I could do was to turn my eyes from Grandmother to the others around her and then back again. Mr Astley stood to one side, calmly and sedately, as was his custom.

'Well, here I am! Instead of a telegram!' Grandmother finally burst out, breaking the silence. 'Well, weren't you expecting me?'

'Antonida Vasilevna . . . auntie . . . but how on earth . . .?'

muttered the unfortunate General. If Grandmother had waited just a few more seconds before starting to speak, he might well have had a seizure.

'What do you mean, "how on earth"? I jumped on a train and came. What do you think the railway is for? And you were all thinking: ah! she's turned up her toes and left us her legacy. You see I know all about the telegrams that you've been sending from here. You must have spent a good many pennies on them. It's not cheap from here. So I packed my bags and here I am. Is that the Frenchman? Monsieur de Grieux, I believe?'

'Oui Madame,' de Grieux put in, 'et croyez, je suis si enchanté . . . votre santé . . . c'est un miracle . . . vous voir ici, une surprise charmante. . . .'*

'Quite right, "charmante"; I know what a poseur you are, and I'd trust you as much as this!' and she showed him her little finger. 'Who is this?' she turned round and pointed to Mademoiselle Blanche. The spectacular Frenchwoman in her riding habit, holding a whip, evidently impressed her. 'She lives here, does she?'

'It's Mademoiselle Blanche de Cominges, and this is her mama, Madame de Cominges; they are staying here in the hotel', I announced.

'Is her daughter married?' enquired Grandmother without ceremony.

'Mademoiselle de Cominges is a single lady', I replied as respectfully as I could, deliberately in an undertone.

'Jolly?'

I pretended not to understand the question.

'Do you find her boring? Does she know Russian? Now de Grieux here became a master of higgledy-piggledy Russian when he was in Moscow.'

I explained to her that Mademoiselle de Cominges had never been to Russia.

'Bonjour', said Grandmother, suddenly turning abruptly to Mademoiselle Blanche.

'Bonjour, madame', said Mademoiselle Blanche, curtsying ceremoniously and gracefully, hastening, under the cover of exceptional modesty and politeness, to indicate through every gesture of her face and body her extreme surprise at such a strange question and manner of address.

'Oh, she's casting her eyes down, putting on airs and graces; she gives herself away immediately; some sort of actress. I am staying downstairs here in the hotel,' she said, suddenly addressing the General; 'I'll be your neighbour; are you pleased or not?'

'Oh, auntie! Trust my sincere feelings of . . . My delight', the General put in. He had already to some extent regained his self-possession, and since at times he could speak quite aptly, with dignity, and pretensions to being somewhat impressive, he now proceeded to enlarge. 'We were so alarmed and taken aback by the news of your illness . . . We received such despairing telegrams, and then suddenly . . .'

'You're lying! lying!' Grandmother interrupted at once.

'But how could you?' the General, in his turn, quickly interrupted, raising his voice in an attempt not to notice this 'you're lying'; 'what made you decide to undertake such a journey? You must agree that at your age and with your health . . . at any rate, it's all so unexpected that our surprise is understandable. But I'm so pleased . . . and we will all'—he started smiling in an ingratiating, ecstatic way—'do our best to ensure that your stay here this season is as enjoyable as possible . . .'

'Come on, that's enough; empty talk; talking a lot of nonsense as usual; I know how to live myself. However, I have no objection to your being here; I don't bear grudges. You were asking how I came to be here. What's so astonishing about it? The simplest thing in the world. And why is everyone so astonished? Greetings, Praskovia. What are you doing here?'

'Good morning, Grandmother,' said Polina, going up to her, 'was it a long journey?'

'Well, that's the most intelligent question that's been asked yet: so far it's only been oohs and ahs! Now, you see, I lay in bed and lay in bed, and I was given treatment after treatment, so in the end I chased the doctors away and summoned the sacristan from St Nicholas. He had cured an old peasant woman of a similar illness with hay dust. Well, he helped me too; on the third day I sweated the whole thing out and got up. Then my Germans all gathered round again, put on their spectacles, and started laying down the rules: "If you were to go abroad now to a spa", they said, "and take a course of treatment, your blockage would go completely." And why not then, I thought? The silly old Zazhigins made a fuss: "How would you ever get there?" they said. Well what do you think! I arranged everything in a single day, and then last Friday I took a maid, Potapych, Fedor the footman as well, but then I sent Fedor home from Berlin because I could see that I didn't need him at all, and I could get here all on my own . . . I took a special carriage and they have porters at all the stations who'll carry your things wherever you want for twenty copecks. Goodness, what splendid rooms you've taken!' she concluded, looking around. 'Where did you get the money from, old chap? After all, everything you have is mortgaged. You owe a fair bit of money to that Frenchman alone! You see I know everything, I know everything!'

'Auntie, I . . .', the General began, thoroughly embarrassed. 'I'm surprised, auntie . . . I feel I can do without anyone else keeping check on me; besides, my outgoings are not in excess of my means, and here we are . . .'

'Not in excess, did you say?! Then you must have robbed your children of the last copeck held in trust for them!'

'After that, after those words . . .', the General began indignantly. 'I no longer know . . .'

'Quite right, you don't know! No doubt you never leave the roulette table here? Have you squandered it all yet?'

The General was so taken aback that he almost choked on a surge of turbulent feelings.

'Roulette! Me? In my position? . . . Me? Think what you're saying, auntie, you must still be unwell . . .'

'Well, you're lying, lying, lying; I dare say they can't drag you away; it's all lies! I shall go and have a look at this roulette, this very day. You, Praskovia, tell me what there is to look at here, and then Aleksey Ivanovich will show me round, and you, Potapych, write down the names of all the places there are to go to. What is there to look at here?' she suddenly addressed Polina again.

'There are some castle ruins quite nearby, and then there's the Schlangenberg.'

'What's the Schlangenberg? A wood or something?'

'No, it's not a wood, its a mountain, there's a peak there . . .'

'What sort of peak?'

'The highest tip of the mountain, it's an enclosed area. You get a superb view from there.'

'So I'd have to haul my armchair up a mountain? Could you get it up, or not?'

'Oh, one could find porters', I replied.

At that moment Fedosia, the children's nurse, came up to greet Grandmother, taking the General's children with her.

'Come on, there's no need to kiss me! I don't like kissing children; all children have snotty noses. Anyway, how do you find it here, Fedosia?'

'It's terribly, terribly nice here, mama Antonida Vasilevna', answered Fedosia. 'And how are you, mama? We've been worried sick about you.'

'I know, you're such a simple soul. Who've you got with you here, they're all guests are they?' she addressed Polina again. 'Who's that shabby old thing in glasses?'

'Prince Nilsky, Grandmother', Polina whispered to her.

'Russian then? And I thought he wouldn't understand! Perhaps he didn't hear! I've already seen Mr Astley. Oh, here he is again', said Grandmother spotting him. 'Good morning!' she suddenly addressed him.

Mr Astley bowed to her, without saying a word.

'Well, are you going to say something nice to me? Say something! Polina, translate for him.'

Polina translated.

'That it gives me very great pleasure to see you here, and I am delighted to find you in good health', replied Mr Astley gravely, but with complete readiness. It was translated for Grandmother and it clearly pleased her.

'How pleasantly Englishmen always reply', she remarked. 'For some reason I've always been fond of Englishmen, and there's no comparison with the wretched French. Come and see me', she addressed Mr Astley once again. 'I will try not to trouble you too much. Translate that for him, and tell him that I'm staying downstairs here, downstairs here; do you hear? downstairs, downstairs', she repeated to Mr Astley, pointing her finger downstairs.

The invitation pleased Mr Astley very much.

Looking attentive and satisfied, Grandmother examined Polina from head to foot.

'I might come to like you, Praskovia,' she suddenly said, 'you're a superb young lady, the best of them all, you're full of character, phew! Anyway, I've got character too; turn round a moment, that's not a hair-piece you're wearing, is it?'

'No, Grandmother, it's my own.'

'Quite right, I don't like today's silly fashion. You're very pretty. I would fall in love with you if I were a young cavalier. Why aren't you married? However, it's time for me to go. I'd like to go out, it's been nothing but railway carriage after railway carriage . . . Now what's the matter with you, are you still angry?' she addressed the General.

'Please, auntie, think nothing of it!' said the General, heartened by this and suddenly collecting himself, 'I can understand that at your age . . .'

'Cette vieille est tombée en enfance',* de Grieux whispered to me.

'Now, I want to see everything here. You'll let me have Aleksey Ivanovich?' Grandmother went on to the General.

'Oh, as much as you want, but I myself . . . and Polina and Monsieur de Grieux . . . we would all consider it a pleasure to accompany you on your outings . . .'

'Mais, madame, cela sera un plaisir',* de Grieux chimed in with a charming smile.

'Quite right, a pleasure. You amuse me, old chap. However, I'm not giving you any money', she suddenly added to the General. 'Now to my rooms: I need to inspect them, and then we'll set off round all the sights. Come on, lift me up!'

Grandmother was raised up again and everyone flocked downstairs, behind the armchair. The General walked in stupefaction like a person who had just been struck on the head with a club. De Grieux was pondering over something. Mademoiselle Blanche was about to stay behind, but then for some reason she too decided to go along with the rest. The Prince instantly set off behind her, and the only people to remain upstairs in the General's suite were the German and Madame de Cominges.

CHAPTER 10

AT spas—and all over Europe, it seems—when it comes to assigning rooms to their guests, hotel managers and head waiters are guided not so much by the demands and wishes of the guests as by their own personal opinion of them; and one should point out that they seldom get it wrong. However, for no known reason, Grandmother was allocated such a luxurious apartment that it even went too far: four magnificently decorated rooms, with a bathroom, servants' quarters, a special room for her maid, and so on and so forth. Indeed, some *grande duchesse* had stayed in them the week before, and of course the new occupants were immediately informed of this, in order to enhance the value of the suite. Grandmother was carried, or rather wheeled, around all the rooms, and she looked them over attentively and sternly. The heat waiter, a middle-aged man with a bald head, respectfully accompanied her on this preliminary inspection.

I do not know whom they all took Grandmother for, but it would seem that it was for an extremely eminent and, more importantly, enormously wealthy individual. They immediately put in the guest book: 'Madame la générale princesse de Tarassevitcheva', although Grandmother had never been a princess. The servants, the special compartment on the train, the endless unncessary trunks, suitcases, and even chests that arrived with Grandmother probably served as the basis of her prestige; and then the armchair, Grandmother's sharp tone of voice, her eccentric questions, asked in the most uninhibited manner and permitting of no contradictions, in a word, the overall figure Grandmother cut—upright, sharp, imperious—completed the unanimous reverence for her. At times during the inspection Grandmother would suddenly give an order for the armchair to be stopped, point to some aspect of the furnishings, and address some unexpected questions to the head waiter, who was still smiling respectfully but who was already beginning to lose his nerve. Grandmother presented her questions in French, which she spoke rather badly, however, for which reason I tended to translate for her. On the whole she disliked the head waiter's replies and they seemed unsatisfactory. But then she kept asking questions that were somewhat beside the point, goodness knows what about. For instance, she suddenly stopped before a picture—a rather feeble copy of some well-known original with a mythological subject.

'Whose portrait is that?'

The head waiter explained that it was probably some countess.

'How is it you don't know? You live here and don't know. Why is it here? Why are the eyes squinting?'

The head waiter was unable to give satisfactory answers to these questions, and even got flustered.

'What an idiot!' Grandmother said, in Russian.

They took her further on. The same story was repeated with a certain Dresden figurine, which Grandmother spent a long time looking at and then ordered to be removed, for some unknown reason. Finally she badgered the head waiter over what the bedroom carpets had cost and where they had been woven. He promised to find out.

'What an ass!' Grandmother growled, and then she turned her full attention to the bed.

'That's a very lavish canopy. Turn it down.'

The bed was turned down.

'More, more, turn it right down. Take off the pillows, the pillowcases, lift up the feather bed.'

Everything was turned down and Grandmother scrutinized it with great care.

'It's a good thing there aren't any bedbugs. Take off all the linen. Put on my own sheets and pillows. But all this is too luxurious; what need have I, an old lady, of such rooms? It's boring for one. Aleksey Ivanovich, you must spend a lot of time with me, when you aren't tutoring the children.'

'As from yesterday I am no longer working for the General,' I replied, 'I'm staying in the hotel quite by myself.'

'Why is that?'

'A few days ago, a distinguished German Baron arrived here from Berlin, with his wife the Baroness. Whilst I was having a walk yesterday, I started talking to him in German, without adhering to the Berlin accent.'

'Well, so what?'

'He considered this impertinent and complained to the General, and the General dismissed me that same day.'

'What, did you swear at this Baron or something? (Even if you had it wouldn't have mattered!)'

'Oh, no! On the contrary, the Baron raised his stick at me.'

'And you allowed your tutor to be treated in this way, you swine,' she addressed the General abruptly, 'and drove him away from the place too! You simpletons—I can see you're all simpletons.'

'Don't worry, auntie,' the General replied with a slight hint of arrogant familiarity, 'I can handle my own affairs. Moreover, Aleksey Ivanovich has not given you a very accurate account.'

'And you put up with it?' she turned to me.

'I was going to challenge the Baron to a duel,' I replied as modestly and calmly as possible, 'but the General was opposed to it.'

'And why were you opposed to it?' Grandmother once again addressed the General. 'As for you, my good fellow, you may go; come back when I call you,' she said to the head waiter, 'no use just standing there gaping. I can't stand that awful Nuremberg face of yours!' The man bowed and walked out without, of course, understanding Grandmother's compliment.

'I beg your pardon, auntie, surely duels aren't allowed?' the General answered with a grin.

'And why shouldn't they be allowed? All men are cockerels; so they might as well fight. From what I can see you're simpletons, the lot of you, can't defend your own country. Come on, lift me up! Potapych, make arrangements for two porters to be ready at all times, hire them and settle the finances. I don't need any more than two. They only have to carry me up and down the stairs, where its level and in the street they can wheel me, that's what you must tell them. Yes, and pay them in advance, they'll be more courteous. You yourself must stay with me at all times, and you, Aleksey Ivanovich, point this Baron out to me on our walk; I might as

well have a look at this von Baron, see what he's like. Now,
where's the roulette?'

I explained that the roulette tables were situated in the halls
inside the casino. Next came the questions: are there many of
them? do many people gamble? do they play all day long? how
were they arranged? In the end I replied that it was best to see
it with one's own eyes, since it was rather difficult to describe.

'Well then, take me straight there! Lead the way, Aleksey
Ivanovich!'

'Why, auntie, surely you're going to have a rest after your
journey?' the General said, solicitously. He seemed to be
getting rather fussed, indeed they were all getting somewhat
edgy and were exchanging glances. No doubt they all felt a bit
twitchy, even embarrassed, at the idea of accompanying
Grandmother straight to the casino, where of course she might
do something eccentric, and in public too; nevertheless they
all volunteered to go with her.

'What do I need to rest for? I'm not tired; and besides I've
spent five days sitting down. And then we'll go and see what
these springs and healing waters are like and where they are.
And then . . . what this—what did you say, Praskovia, the
peak was it?'

'The peak, Grandmother.'

'Well, the peak then, the peak. And what else is there?'

'There are lot of things here, Grandmother', Polina began
with difficulty.

'Well, you don't know yourself. Marfa, you will come with
me as well', she said to her maid.

'What on earth do you need her for, auntie?' the General
suddenly began to fuss; 'and anyway, it's not allowed; I don't
know whether they'll even let Potapych right into the actual
casino.'

'Oh, nonsense! Because she's a servant I have to leave her
behind! She's a human being as well, you know; we've been
bumping about on the road for a whole week and she'd also
like to have a look around. Who else can she go with but me?
She wouldn't even dare show her nose on the streets by
herself.'

'But, Grandmother . . .'

'What is it, are you ashamed to be seen with me? Stay at

home then, I didn't ask you to come. Look what sort of a general he is; I myself was the wife of a general. And anyway, why do you all want to trail along behind me? Aleksey Ivanovich and I can look at everything together. . . .'

But de Grieux absolutely insisted that everyone should accompany her, and launched into the most courteous phrases about what a pleasure it would be to accompany her, and so on. Everyone set off.

'Elle est tombée en enfance,' de Grieux repeated to the General, 'seule elle fera des bêtises . . .',* after which I could not hear what he said, but it was apparent that he had some plan and that, perhaps, he was regaining hope.

It was less than half a mile to the casino. Our route followed the chestnut-tree avenue to the square, around that, and straight to the casino. The General was somewhat calmer because our procession, despite being rather eccentric, was nevertheless seemly and orderly. And there was nothing astonishing in the fact that a person who was ill and feeble, and unable to walk, had come to the spa. But it was apparent that the General was afraid of the casino: why should a person who was ill, and unable to walk, and an old woman at that, go and play roulette? Polina and Mademoiselle Blanche walked either side of the chair as it was wheeled along. Mademoiselle Blanche was laughing, she was modestly cheerful and at times even flirted politely with Grandmother, so that in the end the latter paid tribute to her. Polina, on the other side, was obliged to answer Grandmother's incessant and countless questions, such as: 'Who was that that went by? Who was that woman that went past in a carriage? Is this a big town? Are the gardens big? What sort of trees are those? What are those mountains? Are there any eagles here? What's that funny-looking roof?' Mr Astley was walking beside me and told me in a whisper that he was anticipating a great deal that morning. Potapych and Marfa were walking directly behind the chair—Potapych in his tailcoat and white tie but wearing a cap, and Marfa, a forty-year-old, red-cheeked woman, already beginning to go grey, wearing a bonnet, a calico dress, and squeaking goatskin boots. Grandmother kept turning round to say something to them. De Grieux and the General were further behind, having a tremendously heated conversation about something. The

General was very depressed; de Grieux was speaking with a decisive air. Perhaps he was reassuring the General; clearly he was giving him some sort of advice. But Grandmother had just uttered the fatal words: 'I shall not give you any money.' Perhaps de Grieux found this news improbable, but the General knew his aunt. I noticed that de Grieux and Mademoiselle Blanche kept winking at each other. I could make out the Prince and the German traveller at the very end of the avenue: they had fallen behind and were going somewhere else.

We arrived at the casino in triumph. The doorman and the footmen displayed the same respect as the hotel servants. However, they watched us with curiosity. First of all Grandmother issued instructions to be carried around all the halls; some she praised, while she remained completely indifferent to others; she asked questions about all of them. Finally we reached the gaming halls. The footman standing guard by the closed door, as if stunned, suddenly flung the door wide open.

Grandmother's appearance in the roulette room produced a profound impression on the public. Clustered round the roulette tables, and at the other end of the hall where the trente-et-quarante table was situated, were a hundred and fifty to two hundred players, several rows deep. Those who had managed to push their way up to the actual table stood there firmly, as usual, and did not give up their place until they had lost; for it is not allowed for those who are only spectators to occupy the gambling positions without playing. Despite the fact that there are chairs placed around the table, only a few players sit down, particularly when there is a large confluence of people—because standing they can squeeze more tightly together and so make more room, and anyway it's more convenient for placing one's bet. The second and third rows press against the first, waiting and watching for their turn; but at times a hand will impatiently push through the first row in order to stake a large sum. People have even contrived to push their stake through from the third row in this manner; before ten or perhaps even five minutes had passed, this would lead to some sort of 'scene' over disputed stakes at one end of the table. The casino police are fairly good, however. It is, of course, impossible to avoid crowding; on the contrary, they are delighted by influxes of people, because it is profitable; but the eight croupiers, seated around the tables, watch the stakes with eager eyes, and it is they who work out the figures, and when arguments erupt it is they who settle them. In extreme instances they summon the police and the matter is settled in a second. The police are present there in the actual hall, dressed in plain clothes, mingling with the crowd, so that it is impossible to recognize them. They are particularly on the look-out for petty thieves and full-timers, who are especially numerous at roulette, because it is exceptionally convenient to their trade. In fact, anywhere else one must pick pockets or break locks in order to steal—and if it proves unsuccessful it can lead to a lot of trouble. But here it could not be easier: all you have to do is walk up to the roulette table, start playing, and then suddenly, publicly and openly, take someone else's winnings and put them in your pocket; if an argument starts, the swindler insists loudly and clearly that the bet was his own. If the thing was done skilfully and the witnesses waver, the thief very often succeeds in getting away with the money—if the sum is not a particularly significant one, of course. If it is a large sum, it will more than likely have already been noticed by the croupiers or one of the players. But if it is not a large sum, it can even happen that the true owner, ashamed of a scandal, simply refuses to prolong the argument, and walks away. But if they manage to expose a thief, he is instantly taken away amidst a furore.

Grandmother was watching all this from a distance, with savage curiosity. She was very pleased that thieves were removed. Trente-et-quarante aroused little interest in her; she far preferred roulette and the little rolling ball. In the end she expressed a wish to get a closer look at the game. I do not know how it happened but the footmen and one or two other bustling agents (for the most part little Poles, who after losing were thrusting their services onto more fortunate players and all foreigners) immediately found and cleared a place for Grandmother, despite the crowding, near the very middle of the table, beside the chief croupier, and her chair was wheeled over there. The many visitors who were not playing, but who were observing the game from one side (mostly Englishmen with their families), instantly pushed their way towards the table, in order to catch a glimpse of Grandmother from behind the players. There were a great many lorgnettes turned in her direction. The croupiers' hopes were rising: such an eccentric player really seemed to promise something out of the ordinary. A seventy-year-old woman, unable to walk, who wanted to gamble was not, of course, an everyday event. I also pushed my way towards the table and settled myself down beside Grandmother. Potapych and Marfa stayed somewhere far behind at the side, among the crowd. The General, Polina, de Grieux, and Mademoiselle Blanche also found some room for themselves at the side, amongst the onlookers.

Grandmother began by looking the players over. She asked me some sharp, abrupt questions in a half-whisper: 'Who is that man? Who is that woman?' She particularly liked a certain young man who was standing at the end of the table gambling on a large scale, staking in thousands, and who had already, so everyone was whispering, won about forty thousand francs, which lay in front of him in a heap of gold coins and banknotes. He was pale; his eyes were sparkling and his hands trembling; he was betting at random, by the handful, and yet he kept on winning and winning, raking it in and raking it in. The footmen were fussing over him, they put an armchair behind him, they cleared a space around him so that he was more comfortable, so that he was not cramped—all in anticipation of a large tip. Some players occasionally tip them from their winnings without counting; out of sheer delight, they just grab from their pockets, also by the handful. Some Pole or other had already established himself at the young man's side, bustling around as much as he could, and whispering things to him respectfully but without interruption, probably showing him how to place his bets, giving him advice, and directing the play—and of course he too was anticipating the fruits of his service. But the player barely looked at him, betted at random, and raked it all in. He was evidently getting overwrought.

Grandmother watched him for a few minutes.

'Tell him,' said Grandmother, suddenly getting very worked up, and prodding me, 'tell him to give it up, to grab his money as quickly as he can and go. He's going to lose now, he's going to lose it all!' she fussed, almost breathless with agitation. 'Where's Potapych? Send Potapych over to him! Go on, tell

him, tell him!' she prodded me. 'Where is Potapych then?!
Sortez, sortez!'* she herself began shouting to the young man.
I bent closer to her and told her in a firm whisper that one was
not allowed to shout like that here, and that it was even
forbidden to talk the tiniest bit loudly because it interfered
with the scoring, and that we would be thrown out straight
away.

'What a shame! The man's done for, it means he wants . . .
I can't look at him, I'm all upside-down. What a blockhead!'
and Grandmother hastily turned the other way.

There, on the left, on the other half of the table, a young
lady with a dwarf beside her stood out amongst the players.
Who this dwarf was, I do not know: maybe he was a relative
of hers, or she had just brought him along to make an
impression. I had noticed this woman before; she showed up
at the gaming table every day at one o'clock and left at exactly
two o'clock; she played for an hour each day. They already
knew her and quickly fetched her a chair. She took several
gold coins and several thousand-franc notes out of her pocket
and started staking them quietly and with composure, calculat-
ingly, noting down the numbers in pencil on a piece of paper,
and attempting to discover a system according to which the
chances were grouped at a given moment. She staked substantial sums of money. Every day she won one, two, at most three
thousand francs—no more, and having won, she immediately
left. Grandmother watched her for a long time.

'Well, that one won't lose! That one surely won't lose!
What's her background? Don't you know? Who is she?'

'She's a Frenchwoman, probably of you-know-what sort of
background', I whispered.

'You can tell a bird by the way it flies. You can see she's got
sharp claws. Now tell me what each spin means and how you
are supposed to stake.'

I explained to Grandmother, as best I could, the many
different combinations, red and black, even and odd, manque
and passe, and finally the various subtleties in the system of
numbers. Grandmother listened attentively, committed to
memory, repeated her questions, and learnt by heart. One
could immediately point to an example of any system of
staking, and so it was possible to learn and memorize a great

deal very easily and quickly. Grandmother was thoroughly satisfied.

'And what's this zero? That croupier there, the curly-headed one, the chief one, shouted zero just now, didn't he? And why has he raked in everything there was on the table? What a pile! Is it all his? What does that mean?'

'Zero means the bank wins, Grandmother. If the little ball lands on zero, then whatever has been betted goes to the bank, and nothing is paid out. It's true, there is another turn for anyone who has bet on evens to get their money back, but still the bank doesn't pay anything.'

'I see, I see! And I don't get anything?'

'No, Grandmother, if on that turn you'd staked on zero then you'd be paid thirty-five to one.'

'What's that, thirty-five to one, and it often comes up? How come everyone doesn't bet on it then?'

'The chances are thirty-six to one against it, Grandmother.'

'What nonsense! Potapych! Potapych! Wait a minute, I've got some money too, there!' She took a tightly packed purse out of her pocket and took out one gold friedrich. 'Put it on zero right now.'

'Grandmother, it has only just landed on zero,' I said, 'it won't do so again for a long time. It's a large stake to lose; wait a bit anyway.'

'Why, you're talking rubbish! Stake!'

'Excuse me, but it may not come up again until this evening, you may lose as much as a thousand, it's happened.'

'Oh, nonsense, nonsense! If you're afraid of the wolf don't go into the forest. What? I've lost? Stake again!'

And we lost the second gold friedrich; we bet the third. Grandmother could barely sit still. Her blazing eyes were simply devouring the little ball as it bounced along the notches of the spinning wheel. We lost the third as well. Grandmother was losing control, she couldn't keep still in her seat, and even thumped on the table with her fist when the croupier declared 'trente-six' instead of the anticipated 'zéro'.

'Oh, just look at it!' Grandmother said angrily. 'When is that blasted little zero going to come up? Upon my life, I'll sit here until it lands on zero! It's all the fault of that damned curly-headed croupier, it'll never land on it with him! Aleksey

Ivanovich, stake two gold pieces at once! Otherwise you'll have lost so much that even if zero does come up you won't break even.'

'Grandmother!'

'Stake, stake! It's not yours.'

I staked two gold friedrichs. The little ball flew round the wheel for a long time, and then it finally started to bounce over the notches. Grandmother froze and she squeezed my hand, and then all of a sudden: clonk!

'Zéro', announced the croupier.

'Look, look!' Grandmother quickly turned to me, all radiant and happy. 'You know I told you, I told you. And it was the Lord himself who gave me the idea of betting two gold pieces. Now, how much is it I'll get? Why aren't they paying up? Potapych, Marfa, where are they? Where have all our lot gone? Potapych! Potapych!'

'Grandmother, later on,' I whispered; 'Potapych is by the door, they won't let him in here. Look, Grandmother, they're giving you your money, you're getting it!' They tossed Grandmother an unwieldy roll of fifty gold friedrichs in notes, sealed in blue paper, and then counted out twenty loose gold friedrichs. I scooped it all up for her.

'Faites le jeu, messieurs! Faites le jeu, messieurs! Rien ne va plus?'* the croupier cried, inviting people to place their bets and preparing to spin the wheel.

'Oh, good Lord! I've missed it! He's going to spin it now! Stake, stake!' Grandmother said, getting fussed; 'come on, don't dither, quickly!' she said, quite beside herself, prodding me as hard as she could.

'Yes, but where shall I place the stake, Grandmother?'

'On zero, on zero! zero again! Put on as much as you can! How much have you got in all? Seventy gold friedrichs. No need to spare them, put on twenty gold friedrichs at a time.'

'Think what you're doing, Grandmother! Sometimes it doesn't land there for two hundred goes! I assure you, you're risking all your money.'

'Lies, lies! Stake! What tongue-wagging! I know what I'm doing', said Grandmother, beginning to shake in frenzy.

'According to the rules you're not allowed to stake more

than twelve gold friedrichs on zero, Grandmother; anyway, I've put them on.'

'What do you mean, it's not allowed? You aren't telling lies are you? Monsieur! Monsieur!' she prodded the croupier who was seated right beside her on the left, getting ready to spin the wheel, 'combien zéro? douze? douze?'*

I quickly explained the question in French.

'Oui, madame,' the croupier confirmed politely; 'in the same way no single bet must exceed four thousand florins, according to the rules', he added in explanation.

'Well that's it then, stake twelve.'

'Le jeu est fait!'* shouted the croupier. The wheel began to spin and landed on thirteen. We'd lost!

'Again! Again! Again! Stake again!' Grandmother cried. I no longer put up any opposition and, shrugging my shoulders, I staked another twelve gold friedrichs. The wheel spun for a long time. Grandmother was literally shaking as she followed the wheel. 'Surely she can't really think zero's going to win again', I thought, watching her in amazement. Her face shone with a positive conviction of winning, a clear expectation that at any moment they would cry 'zéro!' The little ball bounced into a compartment.

'Zéro!' the croupier shouted.

'What!!!' Grandmother turned to me in a frenzy of triumph.

I myself was a gambler; I felt it that very moment. I was trembling from head to foot, my head was throbbing. Of course, it was a rare occurrence that out of some ten goes it had landed on zero three times; but there was nothing particularly astonishing about it. Two days before, I myself had witnessed zero coming up three times *in a row*, and one of the players, who had been zealously noting down the winning numbers, commented loudly that only the day before this same zero had only come up once in the entire twenty-four hours.

Since she was the winner of a very considerable sum, Grandmother had her money counted out for her with particular care and attention. She was due to receive exactly four hundred and twenty gold friedrichs, that is to say four thousand florins and twenty gold friedrichs. She was given the twenty gold friedrichs in coin, and the four thousand in banknotes.

But this time Grandmother no longer called for Potapych; this was not her main concern. She did not even nudge anyone, or outwardly tremble. If one may express it in this way, she was trembling within. She was totally intent on one thing, and as such she took aim: 'Aleksey Ivanovich! Did he say that you can only stake four thousand florins at a time? Here, take this and put the whole four on the red', Grandmother decided.

It was useless to try and dissuade her. The wheel started to spin.

'Rouge!' the croupier announced.

Again a win of four thousand florins, so that made eight altogether. 'Pass four of them all over to me here, and put four on the red again', Grandmother commanded.

I staked four thousand again.

'Rouge!' the croupier announced once again.

'That's twelve in all. Pass them all over here. Pour the gold into my purse here, and hide the notes.'

'That's enough! Home! Wheel the chair away!'

CHAPTER 11

THE armchair was wheeled towards the doors at the other side of the hall. Grandmother was radiant. We all instantly crowded around her with our congratulations. However eccentric Grandmother's behaviour was, her triumph made up for a great deal, and the General was no longer afraid of being compromised in public because of his blood relationship to such a peculiar woman. He congratulated Grandmother with a smile that was both condescending and cheerfully familiar, as if he were soothing a child. However, he was clearly as taken aback as the rest of the onlookers. All around people were talking about Grandmother and pointing to her. Many of them walked past in order to take a closer look at her. Mr Astley was standing to one side talking about her with two of his English acquaintances. Several stately onlookers, women, were gazing at her in stately bewilderment, as if she were some sort of marvel. De Grieux simply showered her with congratulations and smiles.

'Quelle victoire!'* he said.

'Mais, madame, c'était du feu!'* added Mademoiselle Blanche with a flirtatious smile.

'Yes, I've just gone and won twelve thousand florins! What do I mean, twelve, what about the gold? With the gold it comes to almost thirteen. What's that in our money? It would be about six thousand, wouldn't it?'

I informed her that it was more than seven thousand, and at the present rate of exchange it might possibly be as much as eight.

'That's no joke, eight thousand! And you're just sitting there, like fools, doing nothing! Potapych, Marfa, did you see?'

'Madam, how did you do it? Eight thousand roubles', exclaimed Marfa, wriggling.

'Here you are, here are five gold pieces each from me, there!' Potapych and Marfa rushed to kiss her hands.

'And give the porters a gold friedrich each. Give them each a gold piece, Aleksey Ivanovich. Why is that footman bowing, and the other one too? Are they congratulating me? Give them each a gold friedrich as well.'

'Madame la princesse . . . un pauvre expatrié . . . malheur continuel . . . les princes russes sont si généreux',* said some whiskered personage, who was hanging around the armchair with a servile smile, dressed in a threadbare frock-coat and multicoloured waistcoat, holding his cap in the air . . .

'Give him a gold friedrich as well. No, give him two; well that's it now, or they'll never stop. Lift me up, carry me! Praskovia,' she addressed Polina Aleksandrovna, 'I'll buy you the material for a dress tomorrow, and I'll buy Mademoiselle . . . what is she, Mademoiselle Blanche, is it? I'll buy her the material for a dress too. Translate for her, Praskovia!'

'Merci, madame', Mademoiselle Blanche made an ingratiating curtsey, her face distorted in an ironic smile which she exchanged with de Grieux and the General. The General was somewhat embarrassed and was frightfully pleased when we reached the avenue.

'Fedosia, now just think how surprised Fedosia will be now', said Grandmother, remembering the General's nurse, whom she knew. 'She must have whatever she needs for a dress as well. Hey, Aleksey Ivanovich, Aleksey Ivanovich, give something to that beggar!'

Some ragamuffin with a hump back was walking past, looking at us.

'But, Grandmother, he might not be a beggar but some kind of rogue.'

'Go on! Go on! Give him a gulden!'

I walked over and gave it to him. He looked at me with wild disbelief; however, he took the gulden without saying a word. He stank of wine.

'And you, Aleksey Ivanovich, have you tried your luck yet?'

'No, Grandmother.'

'But your eyes were blazing, I could see.'

'I'll have a try, Grandmother, I certainly will.'

'And put it on zero straight away! Then you'll see! How much money have you got?'

'In all I've only got twenty gold friedrichs, Grandmother.'

'Not much. I'll lend you fifty gold friedrichs, if you like. Take this very packet here. Still, don't you expect anything, old chap, I won't give it to you', she said, suddenly turning to the General.

He was completely thrown by this, but he said nothing. De Grieux scowled.

'Que diable, c'est une terrible vieille!'* he muttered to the General through clenched teeth.

'A beggar, a beggar, another beggar!' Grandmother shouted. 'Aleksey Ivanovich, give this one a gulden as well.'

This time we had run into a grey-haired old man with a wooden leg, wearing a sort of blue frock-coat that reached the ground, and holding a long cane in his hand. He looked like an old soldier. But when I held the gulden out to him he stepped backwards and gave me a threatening look.

'Was ist's der Teufel!'* he cried, adding a dozen insults.

'Well, what a fool!' cried Grandmother, waving her hand. 'Let's go on! I'm starving! We'll have dinner straight away, then have a short rest and then back again.'

'Do you want to play again, Grandmother?' I cried.

'What do you think? That I want to sit here watching all of you moping?'

'Mais, madame,' said de Grieux, moving nearer, 'les chances peuvent tourner, une seule mauvaise chance et vous perdrez tout . . . surtout avec votre jeu . . . c'était terrible!'*

'Vous perdrez absolument',* twittered Mademoiselle Blanche.

'And what's that got to do with all of you? It's not your money I'll lose—it's mine! And where is this Mr Astley?' she asked me.

'He remained at the casino, Grandmother.'

'Pity; he's such a fine fellow.'

When we reached home Grandmother met the head waiter while she was still on the stairs, called to him, and boasted about her winnings. After that she called for Fedosia, gave her a gift of three gold friedrichs, and ordered her to serve dinner. During dinner Fedosia and Marfa simply sang her praises.

'I'm watching you, madam,' chirruped Marfa, 'and I says to Potapych, what is it our madam wants to do? And there's the money on the table, all that money, my oh my! In all my life I've never seen so much money, and all those ladies and gentlemen around, nothing but gentlefolk sitting there. And I says to Potapych, "wherever did all those ladies and gentlemen come from, Potapych?" And I'm thinking, may the Mother of God help her. I was praying for you, ma'am, and my heart kept missing a beat, missing a beat, and I'm shaking, all shaking. May the Lord help her, I'm thinking, and then the good Lord did send you luck. And ever since then I've been trembling so, I'm all trembling.'

'Aleksey Ivanovich, be ready to leave after dinner at about four o'clock. And now, for the time being, goodbye, and don't forget to fetch some wretched doctor for me, I must drink the waters as well. Otherwise I dare say it'll get forgotten.'

I was stupefied when I left Grandmother. I tried to imagine what was going to happen to all our party, and what course events would take now. I saw clearly that they (principally the General) had not yet had time to recover from even the first shock. The fact that Grandmother had appeared, instead of the telegram they waited for by the hour with the news of her death (and consequently of the legacy), had so upset their entire scheme and the decisions they had reached that they regarded Grandmother's further exploits at the roulette table with positive bewilderment, and a sort of stupor had descended on them all. Meanwhile, this second fact was almost more important than the first, since although Grandmother had repeated twice that she would not give the General any money, after all, who knows?—there was still no need to lose hope completely. De Grieux, who was involved in all the General's affairs, had not done so. I felt sure that Mademoiselle Blanche, also thoroughly involved (small wonder: the General's wife and a substantial inheritance!), would not lose hope and would use every bit of her seductive coquetry on Grandmother—in contrast to Polina, who was proud and intractable and incapable of being ingratiating. But now, now that Grandmother had accomplished such feats at roulette, now that Grandmother's personality had much such a clear and individualistic impression on all of them (an obstinate, power-loving old lady, *et tombée en enfance*)—now, perhaps, all was lost: after all, like a child, she was delighted to have thrown herself so greedily upon something and, as tends to happen, she would lose every last penny of it. 'My God!' I thought (with, may the Lord forgive me, the most malicious laugh), my God, after all every gold friedrich that Grandmother staked just now lay like a sore on the General's heart, infuriated de Grieux, and drove Mademoiselle de Cominges into a frenzy as she watched the cup being dashed from her lips. And there was yet another fact: even when, elated from her win, Grandmother was handing out money in delight to everyone and took every passer-by for a beggar, even at that moment she had come out with these words to the General: 'And as for you, I still won't give you any!' This meant that her mind had come to rest on that thought, she had dug her heels in, she had made a vow to herself—dangerous! dangerous!

All these considerations were going round in my head as I went up the main staircase from Grandmother's rooms to my own tiny room, on the very top floor. The whole thing intrigued me greatly; although, even before this, I had been able to guess at the more important and thicker of the threads linking the actors before me, I nevertheless did not know for certain what all the connections and secrets of this play were.

Polina had never entirely trusted me. Although it happened, it is true, that at times she opened her heart to me, almost involuntarily, I have nevertheless noticed that after these disclosures she very often, in fact almost always, either turns all she has said into a joke, or gets herself in a muddle with the intention of making it all look untrue. Oh! She has been concealing a great deal! In any case I suspected that the finale to this mysterious and tense situation was approaching. Just one more stroke and it would all be over and brought into the open. I was almost unconcerned about my own fate, which was also bound up with it all. I was in a strange mood: I have only twenty gold friedrichs in my pocket; I am far away in a foreign country without a job and without any way of supporting myself, without hope, without any prospects, and I am not worried about it! If it were not for the thought of Polina, I would quite simply give myself up entirely to the sheer comic interest of the impending denouement, and I would laugh as hard as I could. But Polina disturbs me; her fate is in the air, that I have sensed before, but I am sorry to say I am not in the least bit worried about her fate. I want to penetrate her secrets; I would like her to come up to me and say: 'You know, I love you', and if not, if this is inconceivable madness, then . . . well, what can I hope for? Do I even know what I want? I feel lost; I would like to be with her, within her aura, in her radiance, for eternity, always, all my life. Beyond that I know nothing. But can I really leave her?

On the second floor, in their corridor, something seemed to bump into me. I turned round and caught sight of Polina coming out of her door, twenty paces or so from me. She seemed to have been waiting for me and watching out for me, and she immediately beckoned to me.

'Polina Aleksandrovna . . .'

'Shh!' she warned me.

'Imagine,' I whispered, 'I thought that something had just bumped into my side; then I look around—it's you! It's as if you're giving off some kind of electricity!'

'Take this letter', said Polina, frowning anxiously, probably without hearing what I had said, 'and deliver it at once to Mr Astley in person. Quickly, I beg you. There's no need of an answer. He himself . . .'

She did not finish what she was saying.

'Mr Astley?' I repeated in astonishment.

But Polina had already disappeared through the door.

'Aha, so they're corresponding!' Of course, I ran off immediately to look for Mr Astley, first of all in his hotel, where I did not find him, and then in the casino, where I ran round all the halls; and then finally, when I was returning home, feeling annoyed and almost in despair, I met him by chance in a procession of English men and women, on horseback. I waved to him, stopped him, and gave him the letter. We did not even have time to look at each other. But I suspect that Mr Astley deliberately kicked the horse on.

Was I tormented by jealousy? But I was in the most utterly despondent frame of mind. I did not even want to find out what they were writing to each other. And so, he was her confidant! 'A friend is a friend,' I thought, 'and that is clear (and when he managed to become one)—but is there love here? Of course not', my reason whispered. But after all, reason on its own is not much help in these circumstances. In any case, this matter had to be cleared up as well. The thing was becoming unpleasantly complicated.

Before I managed to get into the hotel the doorman and the head waiter, who was coming out of his room, informed me that people were asking for me and looking for me, that three times they had sent someone to call me, and that I was wanted in the General's rooms as soon as possible. I was in the most vile mood. In the General's study, apart from the General himself, I found de Grieux, and Mademoiselle Blanche on her own without her mother. The mother was definitely a figurehead, only required for ostentation, and when it came to real business Mademoiselle Blanche took charge of things for herself. Anyway, it is doubtful whether her mother knew anything about the affairs of her so-called daughter.

The three of them were conferring heatedly about something and had even locked the door of the study behind them, which never happened. As I approached the door I could hear their loud voices, the insolent, biting tongue of de Grieux, the brazen abuse and shrieks of fury coming from Blanche, and the pitiful voice of the General, obviously trying to vindicate himself of something. When I appeared they all seemed to restrain themselves a bit and regain their composure. De Grieux straightened his hair and switched the anger on his face to a smile, that nasty, officially civil, French smile, which I so hate. The General's crushed, broken figure assumed a dignified air, but somewhat mechanically. Only Mademoiselle Blanche hardly modified the blazing anger that was written on her face and merely turned silent, fixing her gaze on me with impatient expectation. I must point out that up till now she had treated me with an almost unbelievable lack of courtesy; she had not even acknowledged my bow, and had quite simply taken no notice of me.

'Aleksey Ivanovich,' the General began in an affectionately reproachful tone, 'allow me to tell you that this strange, utterly strange . . . in a word, your behaviour regarding myself and my family . . . in short it is utterly strange . . .'

'Eh! Ce n'est pas ça', de Grieux interrupted in a tone of annoyance and contempt. (He was definitely in charge of everything!) 'Mon cher monsieur, notre cher général se trompe,* falling into that tone' (I continue his speech in Russian), 'but he wanted to say to you . . . that is to say, to warn you, or better still, to beg you as persuasively as possible not to ruin him—that's right, not to ruin him! I am choosing my words carefully . . .'

'But how, how on earth?' I interrupted.

'For pity's sake, you have undertaken to be a guide (or what should I call it?) for that old lady, cette pauvre terrible vieille,' de Grieux himself was getting in a muddle, 'but you know she'll lose; she'll lose every last penny! You saw yourself, you witnessed the way she played! If she starts to lose she won't leave the table, out of stubbornness and anger, and she'll keep on playing, and under those circumstances people never win back what they've lost, and then . . . then . . .'

'And then,' the General joined in, 'and then you'll ruin the whole family! Myself, and my family, we are her heirs, she has no closer relatives. I will tell you frankly: my affairs are in a bad way, a dreadfully bad way. You know some of the story yourself. If she loses a substantial sum, or even, perhaps, her entire fortune (oh, good Lord!), then what will happen to them, to my children' (the General glanced back at de Grieux), 'to me?!' (He took a look at Mademoiselle Blanche, who had turned away from him in contempt.) 'Aleksey Ivanovich, save us, save us! . . .'

'But how, General, tell me what I can do . . . Where do I come into all this?'

'Refuse, refuse, give her up! . . .'

'She'd only find someone else!' I cried.

'Ce n'est pas ça, ce n'est pas ça,' de Grieux interrupted again, 'que diable!* No, don't forsake her, but appeal to her conscience at least, persuade her, distract her . . . Well, at any rate don't let her lose too much, distract her in some way.'

'But how can I do that? If you yourself were to undertake to do that, Monsieur de Grieux', I added as naïvely as possible.

At that point I noticed Mademoiselle Blanche giving de Grieux a swift, fiery, questioning look. Something peculiar, something revealing that he could not hold back flashed across de Grieux's face.

'The fact is, she won't have me now!' cried de Grieux, with a wave of his hand. 'If only . . . then . . .'

De Grieux gave Mademoiselle Blanche a quick and significant glance.

'O mon cher monsieur Alexis, soyez si bon.'* Mademoiselle Blanche herself took a step towards me and with a seductive smile she took both my hands and pressed them firmly. The devil take it! That diabolical face of hers could change in a single second. At this moment her face looked so imploring, so sweet, smiling in a childlike, even mischievous way; as she finished the sentence she gave me a roguish wink, unnoticed by the others; did she want to fell me at a stroke? And she had pulled it off quite well, only it was crude though, very crude.

The General leapt up behind her, literally leapt up: 'Aleksey Ivanovich, forgive me for starting to talk to you as I did just now, I had no wish to say that at all . . . I ask you, I beg you, I bow down before you as a Russian, you alone, you alone can save us! Mademoiselle de Cominges and I beg you—you understand, after all you understand, don't you?' he implored, with a meaningful glance in Mademoiselle Blanche's direction. He was very pitiable.

At that moment there were three quiet, polite knocks at the door. It was opened; the boot boy had knocked, and Potapych was standing a few paces behind him. They had been sent by

Grandmother. They had been requested to seek me out and fetch me straight away. 'She's angry', Potapych informed me.

'But it's still only half past three, you know!'

'She couldn't sleep, she kept tossing about, then she suddenly got up, asked for her armchair and for you. She's already at the front entrance, sir . . .'

'Quelle mégère!'* de Grieux cried.

I did indeed find Grandmother already by the front door, losing her patience because I was not there. She could not wait until four o'clock.

'Well, lift me up!' she cried, and we set off again for the roulette.

CHAPTER 12

GRANDMOTHER was in an impatient, irritable mood; one could see that the roulette had gone to her head. She was inattentive to everything else and was generally distracted. For example, she did not keep asking about things as we went along, as she had before. Catching sight of a luxurious carriage that went whirling past us, she raised her hand and asked: 'What is that? Whose is it?' but she did not seem to hear my answer; her pensiveness was constantly interrupted by abrupt, impatient bodily movements and outbursts. When, as we were approaching the casino, I pointed out the Baron and Baroness Wurmerhelm from the distance, she looked at them in an absent-minded way, and said to me with complete indifference: 'Ah!' and turning swiftly to Potapych and Marfa, who were walking behind, she snapped at them: 'Why are you dogging my footsteps? I can't take you every time! Get back home! You're all I need', she added to me, as the others hastily bowed and returned home.

They were already waiting for Grandmother at the casino. They immediately cleared her the same place, next to the croupier. It seems to me that these croupiers, who are always so orderly and give the appearance of being the most ordinary kind of official, to whom it is almost completely irrelevant whether or not the bank wins, are really not in the least indifferent to the bank's losses and are, of course, provided with all sorts of instructions how to attract players and how best to protect the interests of the establishment—for which they certainly receive prizes and bonuses. At any rate, they already regarded Grandmother as fair game. And then, what the others had presupposed actually happened.

This is how it was.

Grandmother went straight for zero and immediately ordered me to stake twelve gold friedrichs at a time. We staked once, twice, three times—zero failed to come up. 'Stake, stake!' Grandmother prodded me impatiently. I obeyed.

'How many times have we lost?' she finally asked, grinding her teeth with impatience.

'That was already your twelfth stake, Grandmother. We've lost one hundred and forty-four gold friedrichs. I'm telling you, Grandmother, perhaps it will not be until this evening that . . .'

'Be quiet!' Grandmother interrupted. 'Stake on zero and put a thousand gulden on red straight away. Here's the note.'

Red came up, but zero failed again; we got back a thousand gulden.

'You see, you see!' Grandmother whispered, 'we've got back practically everything we bet. Stake on zero again; we'll bet ten more times and then give up.'

But by the fifth time Grandmother was quite tired of it. 'To hell with that filthy little zero. Here, stake all four thousand gulden on red', she commanded.

'Grandmother! That's too much; supposing it doesn't land on red?' I pleaded, but Grandmother almost struck me. (Anyway, she was prodding me so hard that one could almost say she did hit me.) There was nothing for it, I staked all four thousand gulden, so recently won, on red. The wheel began to spin. Grandmother was sitting calmly and proudly erect, never doubting that she was bound to win.

'Zéro', the croupier announced.

To begin with Grandmother failed to understand, but when she saw that the croupier had raked in her four thousand gulden, together with everything else that was on the table, and she realized that zero, which had not come up for so long and on which we had staked almost two hundred gold fried-richs, had sprung up as if on purpose the moment after she had been cursing it and given it up, she sighed and flung her hands in the air in view of everyone in the hall. People around even began to laugh.

'Goodness gracious! And that's when the cursed thing pops up!' Grandmother wailed. 'Look how damnable, damnable! It's you! It's all you!' she went for me ferociously, prodding me. 'It was you that talked me out of it.'

'Grandmother, I told you a fact; how can I be responsible for all the chances?'

'I'll give you a chance!' she whispered threateningly. 'Get away from me.'

'Goodbye, Grandmother', I turned round to leave.

'Aleksey Ivanovich, Aleksey Ivanovich, stop! Where are you going? But why, why? Look, you're angry! You fool! Well wait, wait a bit longer, no, don't get angry, I'm the fool! Come on, tell me, what do I do now?'

'Grandmother, I'm not going to take it upon myself to tell you anything, because you'll blame me. Play yourself; you give me the orders and I'll stake for you.'

'Well, well! All right, put another four thousand gulden on red! Here's my wallet, take it.' She took the wallet out of her pocket and handed it to me. 'Come on, take it quickly, here's twenty thousand roubles all in notes.'

'Grandmother,' I whispered, 'such large sums . . .'

'Upon my life, I'll get it back. Stake!' We staked and lost.

'Stake, stake, stake all eight!'

'It's not allowed Grandmother, the largest sum is four! . . .'

'Well, bet four!'

This time we won. Grandmother took heart.

'You see, you see!' she nudged me. 'Stake another four!'

We staked and lost; then we lost again and again.

'Grandmother, all twelve thousand have gone', I informed her.

'I can see they've all gone,' she said in a sort of calm fury, if one may so express it, 'I can see, my dear fellow, I can see', she muttered, staring intently before her, and apparently contemplating something. 'Eh! Upon my life, let's stake another four thousand gulden!'

'Yes, but we haven't got any money, Grandmother; here in your wallet you've got some of those five per cent government bonds of ours, and various money orders, but there's no money.'

'What about my purse?'

'Only small change, Grandmother.'

'Are there money-changing bureaux here? They told me they can change all our notes', Grandmother asked resolutely.

'Oh, as much as you want! But what you lose on the exchange like that . . . it would terrify a Jew!'

'Rubbish! I'll win it back! Take me. Call those blockheads!'

I wheeled the chair away, the porters appeared, and we wheeled out of the casino.

'Quickly, quickly, quickly!' Grandmother commanded. 'Show them the way, Aleksey Ivanovich, take the shortest . . . is it far?'

'A few steps, Grandmother.'

But at the turning from the square into the avenue we bumped into our entire group: the General, de Grieux, and Mademoiselle Blanche with her mama. Polina Aleksandrovna was not with them, neither was Mr Astley.

'Well, well, well! Don't stop!' Grandmother shouted. 'Well, what do you want? I haven't got any time for you now!'

I was walking behind. De Grieux dashed up to me.

'She's lost everything that she'd won and she's squandered another twelve thousand gulden. We're on our way to change the five per cent bonds', I hurriedly whispered to him.

De Grieux stamped his foot and rushed off to tell the General. We continued wheeling Grandmother along.

'Stop, stop!' the General whispered to me in a frenzy.

'You just try and stop her', I whispered to him.

'Auntie!' the General went up to her, 'auntie . . . we're just . . . we're just . . .', his voice trembled and faltered, 'hiring some horses and going into the country . . . The most ravishing view . . . the peak . . . we were just coming to invite you.'

'Oh, you and your peak!' said Grandmother, waving him aside irritably.

'There's a little village there . . . we'll have some tea . . .', the General went on, by now in total despair.

'Nous boirons du lait, sur l'herbe fraîche',* added de Grieux with savage spite.

Du lait, de l'herbe fraîche, is the absolutely perfect idyll of the Parisian bourgeois; as we know, that is his conception of 'la nature et la vérité'!*

'You and your milk! Swill it yourself, but it gives me a bellyache. And what are you pestering me for?!' Grandmother shouted, 'I'm telling you I'm in a hurry!'

'Here we are, Grandmother!' I shouted. 'Here!'

We rolled up to the house where the bank was. I went in to do the transaction; Grandmother waited at the doorway; de Grieux, the General, and Blanche were standing to one side, not knowing what to do. Grandmother looked at them angrily and they walked away in the direction of the casino.

I was offered such a terrible rate that I did not accept and went back to Grandmother to ask for her instructions.

'Ah, robbery!' she shouted, folding her arms. 'Well! Never mind! Change it!' she cried resolutely. 'Stop, call the banker out here to me!'

'Surely one of the clerks would do, Grandmother?'

'Well, a clerk then, it doesn't matter. Oof! the robbers.'

A clerk agreed to come out when he learnt that the request came from a frail old countess who could not walk. Grandmother spent a long time reproaching him in a loud angry voice for swindling her, and bartered with him in a mixture of Russian, French, and German, while I helped with the translation. The solemn clerk looked at us both in silence and shook his head. He stared at Grandmother with such intent curiosity that it was even impolite: in the end he started smiling.

'Well, off with you!' Grandmother cried. 'Choke yourself on my money! Change it with him, Aleksey Ivanovich, there's no time, otherwise we'd go to someone else . . .'

'The clerk says that others give even less.'

I do not remember exactly what the rate was but it was terrible. I received close to twelve thousand florins in gold and banknotes, got the receipt, and took it to Grandmother.

'Well! well! well!' There's no use counting it,' she said, waving her arms in the air, 'hurry! hurry! hurry!'

'I'll never again stake on that damned zero, nor on red', she said as we approached the casino.

This time I tried as hard as I could to impress on her that she should stake as little as possible, assuring her that when her luck changed there would always be time to stake larger amounts. But she was so impatient that, although to start with she agreed, there was no possibility of restraining her as the game went on. No sooner had she started to win stakes of ten or twenty gold friedrichs than she started nudging me: 'Well, look at that! Well, look at that! There, we've won. If we'd staked four thousand instead of ten, we'd have won four thousand, instead of, what is it we've got now? It's all because of you, you!'

And however filled with annoyance I was, as I watched the game, I finally resolved to be silent and not to give her any more advice.

Suddenly de Grieux came bounding up. All three of them were nearby; I noticed that Mademoiselle Blanche was standing to one side with her mother, paying court to the Prince. The General was clearly out of favour, virtually in the doghouse. Blanche did not even wish to look at him, although he was fidgeting beside her as hard as he could. The poor General! He went pale, blushed, then trembled, and was no longer even following Grandmother's game. Blanche and the little Prince finally left; the General ran after them.

'Madame, madame', de Grieux whispered to Grandmother in a honeyed voice, pressing right up against her ear. 'Madame, you can't stake like that . . . no, no, you can't . . .', he said in mispronounced Russian, 'no!'

'Well, how then? Teach me', Grandmother addressed him.

De Grieux suddenly started babbling away in very fast French, he started giving advice, making a great fuss, he said that she ought to wait for her moment, and he started doing calculations with various figures . . . Grandmother understood nothing. He kept turning to me for a translation; he was rapping his finger on the table, giving instructions; in the end he grabbed a pencil and was about to start working something out on paper. Grandmother finally lost her patience.

'Well, be off, be off! You keep talking rubbish! This

"madame, madame", and he doesn't understand a thing; be off!'

'Mais, madame', de Grieux twittered, and began prodding and pointing once more. He was already very carried away.

'Well, stake once as he says,' Grandmother ordered me; 'let's see: perhaps it will actually work.'

All de Grieux wanted was to distract her from placing high stakes; he proposed that she should stake on numbers either singly, or in combinations. Following his instructions I staked a gold friedrich on each number in the row of uneven numbers in the first twelve, and five gold friedrichs each on the groups of numbers from twelve to eighteen and eighteen to twenty-four: in all we staked sixteen gold friedrichs.

The wheel spun. 'Zéro', cried the croupier. We lost everything.

'What a blockhead!' cried Grandmother, turning to de Grieux. 'Vile little Frenchman! Look at his advice, the monster! Be off, go! He doesn't understand a thing, and comes fussing around here!'

Terribly offended, de Grieux shrugged his shoulders, looked at Grandmother contemptuously, and then walked away. He too was feeling ashamed at having got involved; he had not restrained himself sufficiently.

An hour later, for all our efforts we had lost everything.

'Home!' cried Grandmother.

Until we reached the avenue she did not utter a single word. In the avenue, when we were already approaching the hotel, she started spouting exclamations: 'What a fool! What a damn fool! You're old, you're an old fool!'

As soon as we reached her suite: 'I want some tea!' Grandmother shouted, 'and start getting ready right away! We're going!'

'Where are we going to madam, if you please?' Marfa began.

'What's that got to do with you? Mind your own business! Potapych, gather everything, all the baggage. We're going back to Moscow! I'm fifteen thousand roubles out of pocket!'

'Fifteen thousand, good gracious! My goodness me!' Potapych cried, folding his hands in a tender way, probably intending to help.

'Oh, oh, you idiot! You're already starting to whimper! Be quiet! Get ready! The bill, quickly, quickly!'

'The first train leaves at half past nine, Grandmother', I informed her to stop the panic.

'And what is it now?'

'Half past seven.'

'How annoying! But it doesn't matter! Aleksey Ivanovich, I haven't got a single copeck left. Here are these two notes, run to that place and change them as well. Otherwise I've got nothing for the journey.'

I set off. When I returned to the hotel half an hour later I found the rest of our party with Grandmother. Having discovered that Grandmother was leaving altogether for Moscow, they were apparently more astonished about that than her losses. Granted her departure would save her fortune, but on the other hand what would become of the General now? Who would repay de Grieux? And of course Mademoiselle Blanche would not wait for Grandmother to die and would now most probably slip off with the little prince, or with somebody else. They were standing in front of her, calming her and trying to talk her round. Once again Polina was absent. Grandmother was screaming atrocities at them.

'Leave me alone, devils! What business is it of yours? Why do you come poking that goatee at me,' she shouted to de Grieux, 'and you, you little peewit, what do you want?' she addressed Mademoiselle Blanche. 'Why are you playing up to me?'

'Diantre!'* whispered Mademoiselle Blanche, her eyes flashing with fury, but then she suddenly burst into laughter and left.

'Elle vivra cent ans!'* she cried to the General as she walked out of the door.

'Ah, so you're counting on my death?' Grandmother yelled to the General. 'Away with you! Chase them all away, Aleksey Ivanovich! What's it got to do with you lot? I've squandered my own money, not yours!'

The General shrugged his shoulders, bowed, and went out. De Grieux followed him.

'Call Praskovia', Grandmother instructed Marfa. Five minutes later Marfa returned with Polina. All this time Polina had been sitting in her room with the children and it seemed she had deliberately decided not to go out all day. Her face looked solemn, gloomy, and troubled.

'Praskovia,' Grandmother began, 'is it true, as I learnt by hearsay just now, that your fool of a stepfather wants to get married to that silly French flirt—an actress, is she, or something even worse? Tell me, is it true?'

'I don't know anything for certain, Grandmother,' Polina replied, 'but from what Mademoiselle Blanche herself has said, and she does not deem it necessary to be discreet, I gather . . .'

'Enough!' Grandmother broke in energetically, 'I understand everything! I've always thought he would do something like that, and I've always thought him a most shallow, frivolous person. He puts on all these airs because he's a General (he was promoted from Colonel on retirement) and he thinks he's important. My dear girl, I know everything, how you sent telegram after telegram to Moscow: "Is the old woman going to turn her toes up soon?" You were waiting for the inheritance; without the money that despicable wench—what's her name, de Cominges, isn't it?—wouldn't even have him for her lackey, and with those false teeth. They say she's got a heap of money of her own, and lends it out at interest, and lives quite well off it. I'm not blaming you, Praskovia; it wasn't you who sent the telegrams; and I don't want to talk about the past. I know that you've got a nasty little temper—like a wasp! And when you sting it swells up, but I'm sorry for you because I loved your deceased mother, Katerina. Well, what about it?— give up everything here and come away with me. After all, you haven't got anywhere to go now; and besides, it isn't fitting for you to be with them now. Wait a minute!' Grandmother stopped Polina, who had started to answer, 'I haven't finished yet. I shan't demand anything of you. As you yourself know my house in Moscow is a mansion, you can take over an entire floor and you needn't come down and see me for weeks if you don't like my temper. Well, do you want to or not?'

'First of all allow me to ask you: do you really mean to leave immediately?'

'What, do you think I'm joking, dear girl? I've said it and I'm off. I squandered fifteen thousand roubles today at that damned roulette of yours. Five years ago I promised that I would rebuild in stone this wooden church on my estate near Moscow, and instead of that I've been throwing my money away here. Now, dear girl, I'm going to go and build my church.'

'What about the waters, Grandmother? After all, you came to drink the waters.'

'Oh, bother you and your waters! Don't annoy me, Praskovia; are you doing it deliberately? Tell me, are you coming or not?'

'Thank you very, very much, Grandmother,' Polina began with feeling, 'for the sanctuary you're offering me. You've partly guessed my position. I'm so grateful to you for that, take my word, I'll come to you, it may even be very soon; but right now there are reasons . . . very important . . . and I am not able to make up my mind right now. If you were to stay even two weeks . . .'

'That means you don't want to?'

'It means I can't. Besides, I cannot leave my brother and sister, and since . . . since . . . since it might really be the case that they will be left abandoned . . . if you would take me together with the little ones, Grandmother, then of course I would come, and believe me I'd pay you back for it!' she added fervently, 'but without the children, I cannot, Grandmother.'

'All right, don't snivel! (Polina had no intention of snivelling; indeed, she never cried.) 'We'll find room for the chicks; it's a large hen-house. Anyway, it's about time they went to school. So won't you come now? Look out, Praskovia! I wish you well, but you see I know why you won't come. I know everything, Praskovia! That miserable little Frenchman will bring you no good.'

Polina blushed. I positively started. (They all know! I must be the only one who knows nothing!)

'Come on, don't scowl. I won't rub it in. The only thing is to take care that it doesn't end badly, do you understand? You're an intelligent young girl; I'd be sorry for you. Now that's enough, I wish I'd never set eyes on any of you! Off with you! Goodbye!'

'I can still see you off, Grandmother', said Polina.

'No need; don't interfere, I'm tired of you all.'

Polina kissed Grandmother's hand, but the latter withdrew her hand and kissed Polina on the cheek.

As she walked past me Polina threw me a swift glance and then looked away.

'And goodbye to you too, Aleksey Ivanovich! Only an hour until the train goes. I think you've had enough of me anyway. Take these fifty gold pieces.'

'I humbly thank you, Grandmother, my conscience . . .'

'Come on, come on!' cried Grandmother, but so vehemently and threateningly that I dared not oppose, and I accepted.

'If you are ever in Moscow looking for a job, come to me, I'll recommend you to someone. Well, be off!'

I went up to my room and lay down on the bed. I think I lay there for about half an hour, on my back with my hands behind my head. Catastrophe had struck, and there was much to think about. I decided that I must talk to Polina tomorrow. Um. The wretched Frenchman? So it must be true! But nevertheless, what could it be? Polina and de Grieux! Lord, what a match!

The whole thing was quite unbelievable. Suddenly, quite beside myself, I leapt up in order to go and find Mr Astley straight away and make him talk, come what may. He, of course, knew more about all this than I did. Mr Astley? There was another mystery to me.

But suddenly there was a knock at my door. I took a look— Potapych.

'Aleksey Ivanovich, sir, madam is asking for you!'

'What's that? She's leaving, isn't she? There's twenty minutes until the train goes.'

'She's worried, sir, she can hardly sit still. "Quickly, quickly!"—that's you, sir; for heaven's sake don't waste a second.'

I ran downstairs straight away. Grandmother had already been taken into the corridor. She was holding her wallet.

'Aleksey Ivanovich, lead the way, we're off! . . .'

'Where to, Grandmother?'

'Upon my life I'll win it back! Forward march, no questions! The play goes on until midnight there, doesn't it?'

I stopped dead in my tracks, thought for a moment, but I made up my mind immediately.

'Do as you like, Antonida Vasilevna, but I'm not coming.'

'Why's that? What's this now? Have you all gone crazy?'

'Do as you like: I would reproach myself afterwards; I don't want to! I don't want to be either a spectator or a participant; leave me out of it, Antonida Vasilevna. Here are your fifty gold friedrichs; goodbye!' And putting the roll of gold-friedrich notes right there on the little table next to where her chair was, I bowed and walked out.

'What nonsense!' Grandmother shouted after me. 'Don't come then, I'll find the way by myself! Potapych, come with me! Well, lift me up, carry me!'

I failed to find Mr Astley and returned home. Late that night, after midnight, I learnt from Potapych how Grandmother's day had ended. She lost everything that I had just changed for her, that is to say a further ten thousand roubles in our currency. The little Pole to whom she had given two gold friedrichs earlier on in the day latched onto her, and guided her play all the time. In the beginning, before the Pole appeared, she had tried to make Potapych place her bets, but she very soon got rid of him; and it was at that point that the wretched Pole leapt forward. As luck would have it, he understood Russian and even chattered away, somehow or other, in a mixture of three languages, so that they understood each other, after a fashion. Grandmother was mercilessly rude to him all the time, and although he kept 'laying himself at the good lady's feet', there was 'no comparison with you, Aleksey Ivanovich', Potapych told me. 'She treated you *just like a gentleman*, whereas he, well I saw with my own eyes, may the Lord strike me down if I didn't, he stole her money right in front of her on the table. She caught him doing it a couple of times, and did she shout abuse at him! She shouted every kind of abuse at him, sir, she even pulled his hair once, it's true, I swear, and there was laughter all round. She lost it all, sir, all; everything there was, everything you changed for her. We brought mother back here—she just asked for a drop of water to drink, crossed herself, and went to bed. Worn out, I should say, she fell asleep immediately. May the Lord send her sweet dreams! Oh, I loathe these foreign places!' Potapych concluded, 'I said it wouldn't lead to any good. If only we could get back to Moscow quickly! There's nothing at all we haven't got at home in Moscow. The garden, the flowers—types they don't have here—the scent, the ripening apples, space—but no: we had to go abroad! Oh, oh, oh! . . .'

CHAPTER 13

ALMOST a whole month has passed since I touched these notes of mine, begun under the influence of impressions which, even if disorganized, were powerful. The catastrophe which at that time I felt was imminent did actually occur, only a hundred times more dramatically and unexpectedly than I had thought. It was all strange, shocking even tragic, at any rate from my point of view. Several things happened to me that were almost miraculous; at least, that is how I still think of them, although looked at in another way, especially when one takes into account the whirl of events in which I was involved at the time, they were really nothing particularly out of the ordinary. But the most miraculous thing of all to me is my own reaction to all the events. I still cannot understand myself! And it all flashed by like a dream—even my own passion, and after all that was strong and sincere, but . . . what has become of it now? In truth: every now and then, still now, the thought flashes through my mind: 'Had I taken leave of my senses at the time, and was I not sitting somewhere in a madhouse, and perhaps that is where I am now, so that it all *seemed* to happen, and it still only *seems* . . . ?'

I have gathered together my pages and read them through . . . (Who knows, maybe it was to convince myself that I did not write them in a madhouse?) Now I am absolutely on my own. Autumn has arrived, the leaves are turning yellow. I am sitting in this depressing little town (oh, how depressing German towns are!) and instead of thinking about the next step, I am living under the influence of sensations that have only just passed, under the influence of such fresh memories, under the influence of that very recent whirlwind which caught me in its vortex and then threw me out somewhere. At times I still feel as if I am spinning around in that vortex and that at any moment the storm will come tearing by again, carrying me off on its wings as it passes, and once again I will lose all sense of order and proportion and I will start spinning, spinning, spinning . . .

However, I may perhaps settle down somehow and stop spinning, if I give myself the most accurate account that I can of all that has taken place during this month. I feel drawn to my pen again; and also at times there is absolutely nothing to do in the evenings. It is strange, but in order to find something to occupy myself with, I take out of the miserable library here Paul de Kock's* novels (in a German translation), which I can hardly endure, but I read them wondering at myself: it is as if I am afraid that a serious book, or some kind of serious occupation, will break the spell of what has just happened. As if that hideous dream, and all the impressions it has left behind, are so dear to me that I am afraid of going anywhere near it with something new in case it vanishes into thin air! Is it all so dear to me, then? Yes, of course it is dear; maybe even forty years from now I will still remember it . . .

And so, I will get down to writing. I can now recount it all only partially and briefly: the impressions were quite different . . .

*   *   *

First of all let us finish with Grandmother. The following day she really and truly lost everything. It was bound to happen: for anybody like her, once set on that path, it becomes just like sliding down a snowy hill on a sledge, going faster and faster. She played all day until eight o'clock in the evening; I was not present while she played and only know about it from what I was told.

Potapych stood in attendance beside her all day at the casino. The little Poles, acting as Grandmother's instructors, changed several times in the course of the day. She started by getting rid of the one of the day before, whose hair she had pulled, and she took hold of another one, who proved to be, if anything, even worse. Having dismissed him and once again taken on the first one, who had not left but spent his entire period of banishment right there behind her armchair, prodding away and continually popping his head forward at her, she finally fell into despair. Nor did the second banished Pole have the least intention of leaving; one of them settled on her right, the other on her left. They spent the whole time arguing and swearing at each other over the stakes and the manœuvres, calling each other 'scoundrel' and other Polish compliments, then making it up again and throwing money around at random, and giving useless orders. When they argued they would make opposite bets: for instance, one of them would bet on the red and the other would go straight on the black. They ended by making Grandmother so completely giddy and confused that she eventually turned to the elderly croupier, almost in tears, and begged him to protect her and make them go away. And indeed they were chased away there and then despite their shrieks of protest: they both shouted at once, claiming that Grandmother owed them money, that she had cheated them of something, had treated them dishonestly, meanly. The wretched Potapych told me all of this with tears in his eyes that very evening, after she had lost it all, and he complained that they had stuffed their pockets with money, that he himself had seen them stealing shamelessly and continually shoving it into their pockets. For example, one of them would request five gold friedrichs from Grandmother for his efforts and then immediately start staking at roulette, alongside Grandmother's bets. Grandmother would win, but he would shout that his stake had won and that Grandmother's one had lost. When they were thrown out Potapych stepped forward and informed her that their pockets were full of gold. Grandmother had immediately asked the croupier to deal with the matter, despite the Poles' outcries (they were like a couple of chickens caught in the hand); the police appeared and their pockets were instantly emptied for Grandmother's benefit. Until she lost everything Grandmother enjoyed a visible authority with the croupiers and the casino officials throughout the day. Bit by bit her fame spread all over the town. Visitors to the spa, of every nationality, both ordinary and distinguished people flocked to take a look at 'une vieille comtesse russe, tombée en enfance', who had already gambled away 'several millions'.

But Grandmother gained extremely little by getting rid of

the two Poles. Their place was immediately taken by a third Pole who put himself at her disposal, a man who already knew perfect Russian, dressed like a gentleman although he still resembled a servant with his large whiskers and his arrogance. He also 'kissed the lady's feet', and 'prostrated himself at the lady's feet', but he behaved haughtily to those around him, handling things in a despotic fashion. In short, he immediately established himself, not as Grandmother's servant, but as her master. Continually, at every manœuvre he addressed her, swearing with dreadful oaths that he was an 'honourable Polish gentleman' and that he would not take a single copeck of Grandmother's money. He repeated these oaths so often that she finally lost her nerve. But since in the beginning this gentleman really did seem to correct her game and she was starting to win, Grandmother could not leave him. An hour later, both of the previous Poles, who had been driven out of the casino, reappeared behind Grandmother's chair, once again offering their services, even if only to run errands. Potapych swore that the 'honourable Polish gentleman' winked at them and even handed them something. Since Grandmother had not eaten dinner and had scarcely got out of her armchair all day, one of the two Poles did indeed prove useful: he ran straight off to the casino dining-room and fetched her a cup of bouillon, and then a tea. Both of them were running around for her, however. But towards the end of the day, when it had already become obvious to everyone that she was going to lose her very last banknote, there must have been about six of these wretched Poles, none of whom had been seen or heard of before, standing behind her chair. As Grandmother lost her last coins, they all not only ceased listening to her but even stopped taking any notice of her. They stretched right across her to the table, snatched the money, took matters into their own hands, and staked, argued, shouted, and talked things over with the honourable Polish gentleman in a familiar tone, and the honourable gentleman almost forgot about Grandmother's existence. Even when, having lost absolutely everything, Grandmother was returning to the hotel at eight o'clock in the evening, there were still three or four Poles who would not leave her and who were running around the chair, on both sides, shouting at the top of their voices, babbling away, claiming that Grandmother had swindled them in some way, and must give them something back. And so it went on right until they reached the hotel, from which they were chased away with a kick.

In Potapych's reckoning that day Grandmother lost as much as ninety thousand roubles, apart from the money she had lost the day before. All her government securities—five per cent ones, her internal loans, all the stocks she had with her, had been changed one after the next. I expressed surprise that she had kept it up for those seven or eight hours, sitting in her chair, and hardly leaving the table at all, but Potapych told me that there were three occasions when she really had begun winning substantially; and carried away by renewed hope she could not bring herself to leave. Anyway, gamblers know that a person can sit for practically twenty-four hours in one place playing cards, without moving his eyes to either right or left.

Besides, throughout that day the most decisive things had also been happening in our hotel. Already in the morning, before eleven o'clock, when Grandmother was still at home, our group, that is to say the General and de Grieux, had decided on the final step. Having learnt that Grandmother was no longer thinking of leaving, but was on the contrary setting off for the casino again, all of them (except Polina) came to see her in conclave, in order to talk things over with her finally and *openly*. The General, his heart wavering and sinking at the prospect of the terrible consequences to himself, actually went too far: after half an hour of prayers and entreaties, having openly admitted everything, that is, all his debts to everyone, as well as his passion for Mademoiselle Blanche (he lost his head completely), the General suddenly adopted a threatening tone and even began to shout and stamp his feet at Grandmother; he shouted that she was disgracing the family name, had become the scandal of the whole town, and lastly . . . lastly: 'You are bringing shame upon the name of Russia, madam!' the General yelled, 'and there are police for that sort of thing!' Grandmother finally chased him away with a stick (a real stick). The General and de Grieux conferred once or twice in the course of the morning; what preoccupied them was precisely the question whether they could not in fact use the police somehow. Here, they would say, was an unfortunate but respectable old woman who had lost possession of her faculties and was gambling away the last of her money, etc.; in a word, would it not be possible to contrive to place her under some sort of surveillance or arrest? . . . But de Grieux simply shrugged his shoulders and laughed in the face of the General, who was by now talking absolute gibberish as he darted up and down the study. In the end de Grieux gave it up as hopeless and vanished somewhere. In the evening they discovered that he had left the hotel for good, having first had a very crucial and mysterious conversation with Mademoiselle Blanche. As for Mademoiselle Blanche, she had taken final measures early that morning: she had completely given up the General and would not even allow him within her sight. When the General ran after her to the casino and found her arm in arm with the little Prince, neither she nor Madame veuve Cominges recognized him. The Prince did not bow to him either. All that day Mademoiselle Blanche sounded the Prince out and worked on him until he finally said something definite. But alas! She was cruelly deceived in her plans for the Prince! This little tragedy took place in the evening; it was suddenly revealed that the Prince was as poor as a church mouse, and that he was counting on borrowing money from her in exchange for a promissory note in order to play roulette. Blanche indignantly told him to go away and locked herself in her room.

On the morning of that same day I went to see Mr Astley, or rather I should say I spent the whole morning looking for Mr Astley, but could not find him. He was neither at home, nor in the casino, nor in the park. He did not dine in his hotel on this occasion. Towards five o'clock I suddenly caught sight of him walking off the platform at the railway station and heading straight for the Hôtel d'Angleterre. He was hurrying and seemed extremely preoccupied, although it is difficult to distinguish anxiety or any other kind of confusion in his face. He cordially held out his hand to me, with his usual exclamation: 'Ah!' but he did not stop and walked on at a rather rapid pace. I latched onto him; but he contrived to answer me in such a way that I did not manage to find anything out. Besides, I found it terribly embarrassing to talk about Polina; and he did not ask about her at all. I told him about Grandmother; he listened attentively and seriously and shrugged his shoulders.

'She will lose everything', I remarked.

'Oh yes,' he replied, 'you know, she had already begun playing before I left, and I knew for certain that she would lose. If there is time I will drop in at the casino and have a look, because it's a curious . . .'

'Where have you been?' I cried, astonished that I had not yet asked him.

'I've been in Frankfurt.'

'On business?'

'Yes, on business.'

Well, what else could I ask him? However, I kept walking alongside him, until he suddenly turned off into the hotel 'De Quatre Saisons', which stood by the roadside, gave me a nod, and disappeared. As I returned home it gradually dawned on me that even if I had spoken to him for two hours I would have discovered absolutely nothing, because . . . I had nothing to ask him! Of course, that was it! I could find no way of formulating my question.

Polina spent the whole of that day either walking with the children and the nanny in the park, or sitting indoors. She had been avoiding the General for some time and barely spoke to him, at least about anything serious. I had noticed that a long time ago. But knowing the position the General was in today I thought that he would be unable to avoid her, that is to say that there would have to be some sort of serious family discussion. However, when on my way back to the hotel after my conversation with Mr Astley I met Polina with the children, her face reflected the most serene calm, as if only she were escaping this storm involving the entire family. She responded to my bow with a nod. I went to my room feeling very angry.

Naturally, I had been avoiding speaking to her, and had not had a single meeting with her since the occurrence with the Wurmerhelms. To some extent this was bravado and affectation on my part; but the more time went on, the more I seethed inside with genuine indignation. I thought that even if she did not love me at all, she should nevertheless not tread on my feelings in that way, or accept my avowals with such indifference. After all, she knows that I truly love her; after all, she was the one who allowed, who permitted me to speak to her like that! It is true that things began in a strange way between us. A long time ago, perhaps a couple of months before, I had started to notice that she wanted me to be her friend, her confidant, and that she was indeed partially testing me out. But for some reason things did not get going between us at the time; instead we were left with our present peculiar relationship; that was the reason why I began speaking to her as I did. But if she finds my love objectionable, why not simply forbid me to talk about it?

I was not forbidden; at times she had even invited conversation and . . . of course, she did it for a joke. I know for certain, I quite definitely noticed that—she enjoyed listening to me, exasperating me to the point where it hurt, and then suddenly disconcerting me with some outburst of extreme contempt and disregard. And, you see, she knows that I cannot live without her. It is now three days since the episode with the Baron, and I am already unable to bear our *separation*. When I bumped into her just now near the casino, my heart pounded so strongly I turned white. After all, she cannot go on living without me either! She needs me, and—well, surely not just as a buffoon like Balakirev.*

She has a secret—that is clear! Her conversation with Grandmother stung me to the bottom of my heart. I have challenged her to be sincere with me thousands of times, and you see she knew that I really was prepared to lay down my life for her. But she always shunned me, almost contemptuously, and instead of the sacrifice I have offered her, she has demanded pranks like that one with the Baron! Surely that is disgraceful. Could this Frenchman really mean the world to her? What about Mr Astley? But that was where the whole thing became absolutely incomprehensible, and in the meanwhile—God, how tormented I was!

When I reached home, in a fit of fury, I grabbed my pen and scribbled the following to her:

Polina Aleksandrovna, I can see clearly that things have come to a head, and will of course affect you too. I repeat for the last time: do you or do you not need my life? If you need me for *anything* at all— I am at your disposal, but in the meanwhile I will sit in my room, at any rate most of the time, and I will not go anywhere. If it is necessary then write, or call for me.'

I sealed the note up and sent it with the bellboy, instructing him to deliver it straight into her hands. I did not expect an answer, but three minutes later the bellboy returned with the message that 'she sends her regards'.

Towards seven o'clock the General sent for me.

He was in his study, dressed as if he were preparing to go out somewhere. His hat and stick were lying on the sofa. It seemed to me, as I walked in, that he was standing in the middle of the room, with his legs apart, and his head drooping, saying something aloud to himself. But the moment he caught sight of me he rushed towards me almost shrieking, so that I involuntarily stepped backwards and was about to run off; but he grabbed both my hands and dragged me over to the sofa; he sat himself down on the sofa and put me in an armchair straight opposite him without letting go of my hands, and with trembling lips, and tears suddenly shimmering on his eye-lashes, he said to me in an imploring voice: 'Aleksey Ivanovich, save me, save me, have mercy on me!'

For a long time I failed to understand a thing; he kept on talking and talking and kept repeating: 'Have mercy, have mercy!' Finally I guessed that he was expecting something like advice from me, or should I say, abandoned by everyone, in anguish and trepidation he had remembered me and called for me, in order to talk, talk, talk.

He had gone mad, or at any rate was absolutely beside himself. He was clasping his hands and was on the verge of throwing himself on his knees before me, asking me (what do you think?) to go straight to Mademoiselle Blanche and request her, prevail upon her conscience, to come back to him and marry him.

'For heaven's sake, General,' I cried, 'I shouldn't think Mademoiselle Blanche has noticed my existence yet. What can I do?'

But it was useless to object: he did not understand what was being said to him. He fell to talking about Grandmother, but utterly incoherently; he stuck to the idea of sending for the police.

'We, we,' he began, suddenly boiling with indignation, 'in a word, in Russia, in a well-organized state, where there are authorities, they would have immediately arranged to put an old woman like that under surveillance! Oh yes, my dear sir, yes sir!' he continued, suddenly lapsing into a reproving tone, jumping up from the sofa and pacing up and down the room; 'you still do not know, my dear sir,' he said, addressing some imaginary dear sir over in the corner; 'now you'd better learn about it . . . yes sir, in our country old women like that are brought under control, under control, yes sir, oh, damn it!'

And he threw himself onto the sofa once again, but a minute later, breathless and practically sobbing, he hurriedly told me that Mademoiselle Blanche was not going to marry him because instead of the telegram Grandmother had arrived, and it was now obvious that he was not going to receive the inheritance. He seemed to think that I did not yet know anything about all this. When I started talking about de Grieux, he made a dismissive gesture: 'He's gone! Everything I had is pawned to him; I'm as poor as a church mouse! The money you went to fetch . . . that money, well I don't know how much there is there, I think there's about seven hundred francs left and—oh! that's enough now, that's all there is to it, and beyond that—I don't know, I don't know, sir!'

'How are you going to pay your hotel bill?' I cried in alarm. 'And then, what after that?'

He was looking thoughtful, but he did not appear to have understood, and may even not have heard me. I tried to raise the subject of Polina Aleksandrovna and the children; he hurriedly answered: 'Yes! Yes!' but then he started off again about the Prince and about how Blanche was now going to go off with him and then . . . and then . . . 'What am I to do, Aleksey Ivanovich?' he suddenly turned to me, 'I swear to God! What am I to do? Tell me, after all, that's ingratitude! Isn't that ingratitude?'

In the end he dissolved in floods of tears.

There was nothing one could do with a man like this; it was also dangerous to leave him alone; something might well happen to him. I did, however, somehow manage to get away from him, but I informed the nurse that she must call in on him at frequent intervals, and I also spoke to the bellboy, a very sensible young chap; he also promised me that he would keep an eye open.

I had barely left the General when Potapych appeared with a summons from Grandmother. It was eight o'clock and she had only just returned from the casino after her final loss. I set off for her rooms: the old lady was seated in the armchair, completely exhausted and evidently ill. Marfa was serving her a cup of tea, which she almost forced her to drink. Both Grandmother's voice and her intonation were quite changed.

'Greetings old chap, Aleksey Ivanovich,' she said, inclining her head slowly and with dignity, 'excuse me for disturbing you once again, forgive an old woman. I left it all there, my dear friend, practically a hundred thousand roubles. You were right in not coming with me yesterday. Now I have no money, not a single farthing. I don't want to delay a single moment, I'm leaving at half past nine. I've sent for that Englishman of yours, Mr Astley or whatever he's called, and I mean to ask him to lend me three thousand francs for a week. So, if you would persuade him not to think the wrong thing and refuse. My dear friend, I'm still fairly rich. I have three villages and two homes. And there's still some money too, I didn't bring all of it with me. I'm telling you all this so that he won't have any doubts . . . Ah, here he is! You can tell he's a fine person.'

Mr Astley had hurried over at Grandmother's first call. Without giving it much thought or saying very much he immediately counted out three thousand francs against a promissory note, which Grandmother duly signed. The business over, he bowed and hurried away.

'And now you too must go, Aleksey Ivanovich. I have little more than an hour left and I would like to lie down, my bones ache. Please forgive an old fool. Now I won't accuse the young of being reckless any more, and at this point it would be sinful for me to blame that unfortunate General of yours. I'm still not going to give him any of the money he wants because, in my opinion, he really is just a silly idiot, only I'm no more intelligent myself, old fool that I am. Truly, God brings even the old to account and punishes their pride. Well, goodbye. Marfa, help me up.'

But I wanted to see Grandmother off. Apart from which I was in such a state of suspense, I kept expecting that something would happen any minute. I couldn't sit in my room. I went into the corridor and even ventured out into the avenue for a quick stroll. The letter I had written to her was clear and decisive, and the present catastrophe was, of course, conclusive. In the hotel I heard about de Grieux's departure. If in the end she rejects me as a friend, maybe she won't reject me as a servant. You see, she does need me, if only to run errands; I might prove useful, how can it be otherwise?!

When it was approaching the time for the train to leave I ran down to the platform and helped Grandmother into her seat. They were all sitting in a special family compartment. 'Thank you, old chap, for your unselfish concern,' she said as we parted, 'and remind Praskovia of what I was saying to her yesterday—I'll be expecting her.'

I went home. As I walked past the General's rooms I met the nanny and enquired after the General. 'Oh, he's all right, sir', she replied in a dejected tone. I went in, but at the door to the study I stopped in total amazement. Mademoiselle Blanche and the General were roaring their heads off with laughter about something. Veuve Cominges was sitting there on the sofa. The General was evidently out of his mind with joy: he was babbling all kinds of nonsense and breaking into long fits of nervous laughter, which covered his face with an innumerable quantity of wrinkles into which his eyes seemed to disappear. I learnt afterwards from Mademoiselle Blanche herself that, after she had driven the Prince away and heard about the General's tears, she thought she ought to go and comfort him and went up to pay him a brief visit. But the poor General did not know that at that very same moment his fate had been decided and that Blanche had already begun packing in order to rush off in the morning, on the first train to Paris.

After standing for a short time in the doorway to the General's study, I changed my mind about going in and left unnoticed. I climbed up to my own room, opened the door, and in the semi-darkness I suddenly noticed a figure sitting on a chair in the corner over by the window. The figure did not get up when I appeared. I swiftly walked over, took a look, and—my breath was taken away: it was Polina!

CHAPTER 14

I JUST yelled.

'What is it? What is it?' she asked strangely. She was pale and looked sombre.

'What do you mean, what is it? You? Here in my room!'

'If I come, *all* of me comes. That is my custom. You'll see now; light the candle.'

I lit the candle. She got up, walked over to the table, and placed an open letter before me.

'Read it', she instructed me.

'It's, it's de Grieux's hand!' I cried, seizing the letter. My hands were shaking, and the lines were dancing before my eyes. I have forgotten the precise wording of the letter but here it is, if not word for word, then at least thought for thought.

'Mademoiselle,' wrote de Grieux, 'unfortunate circumstances force me to leave without delay. Of course, you yourself will have noticed that I have deliberately avoided giving you any final explanation until all the circumstances were clarified. The arrival of your elderly relative (de la vieille dame) and her absurd behaviour have settled all my doubts. The sorry state of my own affairs utterly forbids me from nurturing any longer those sweet hopes in which I have allowed myself to revel for some time. I regret the past, but I hope that you will find nothing in my behaviour that is unworthy of a nobleman and honourable person (gentilhomme et honnête homme). Having lost almost all my money in loans to your stepfather, I now find myself absolutely compelled to make use of what I have left: I have already told my friends in Petersburg to arrange rapidly the sale of the property mortgaged to me. Knowing, however, that your frivolous stepfather has squandered your own money, I have decided to let him off fifty thousand francs and I am returning to him part of the mortgages on his properties, so that you are now in a position to recover everything that you have lost by claiming your estate through the legal system. I hope, Mademoiselle, that in the present state of affairs, my action will be wholly to your advantage. I also hope that through this action I have completely fufilled my obligations as a man of honour and nobility. Rest assured, I will hold your memory in my heart for ever.'

'Well then, that's all clear enough,' I said, turning to Polina, 'surely you couldn't have expected anything else?' I added with indignation.

'I didn't expect anything', she replied, seemingly calm, but still with a sort of tremor in her voice. 'I made up my mind a long time ago; I read his thoughts and discovered what he was thinking. He thought that I was searching . . . that I would insist . . .' (She stopped and, without finishing what she was saying, bit her lip and said nothing for a moment.) 'I deliberately redoubled my contempt for him,' she started up again; 'I waited to see what he would do. If a telegram had arrived about the inheritance I would have thrown him the debt that idiot (my stepfather) owed him and then shooed him away! For a long, long time I have found him loathsome. Oh, he was not like that before, a thousand times different, but now, now! . . . Oh, now with what delight I would fling those fifteen thousand in that mean little face of his, and I would spit . . . and then rub the spit in!'

'But the paper, the mortgage document for fifty thousand that he returned, it's with the General, isn't it? Get it and return it to de Grieux.'

'Oh, that's not the same! It's not the same! . . .'

'Yes, you're right, it's not the same thing. And besides, what could the General do now? And Grandmother?' I suddenly cried.

Polina looked at me in a somewhat distracted and impatient way.

'Why Grandmother?' Polina said in annoyance. 'I can't go and see her . . . Neither do I wish to ask forgiveness of anybody', she added irritably.

'What's to be done?!' I cried. 'And how, just tell me how you could have loved de Grieux?! Oh, the scoundrel, the scoundrel! Well, if you want I'll kill him in a duel! Where is he now?'

'He's in Frankfurt and will spend three days there.'

'Just one word from you and I'll go there, tomorrow even, on the first train', I said, with rather silly enthusiasm.

She started laughing.

'But he might perhaps say: first give me back the fifty thousand francs. And anyway, why should he want to fight? . . . What a lot of nonsense!'

'But, where, wherever can we get these fifty thousand francs?' I repeated, grinding my teeth, as if one could suddenly just go and pick them up off the floor. 'Listen: what about Mr Astley?' I asked, turning to her as a very strange idea began to dawn on me.

Her eyes were sparkling.

'What's this, surely *you yourself* don't want me to leave you for that Englishman?' she said, looking me straight in the face with a piercing glance, and a bitter smile. For the first time in her life she had addressed me with familiarity as 'thou'.

I think her head was spinning with emotion at that moment and she suddenly sat down on the sofa, apparently exhausted.

I felt as if I'd been struck by lightning; I stood and I could not believe my eyes, I could not believe my ears! Why, then, that must mean she loves me! She has come to see *me* rather than Mr Astley! She, a young girl on her own, has come up to my room, in a hotel—which means she has compromised herself publicly—and I am standing before her and I still cannot understand it!

A wild idea flashed through my head.

'Polina! Give me just one hour! Wait here for one hour and . . . I'll be back! It's . . . it's essential! You'll see! Stay here, stay here!'

And I ran out of the room without answering her astonished, questioning look; she shouted something to me but I did not turn round.

Yes, at times the wildest of ideas, the most impossible-looking idea, becomes so entrenched in one's mind that in the end one assumes that it is feasible . . . Moreover, if the idea coincides with a strong, fervent desire, then perhaps one may eventually accept it as something fated, inevitable, pre-destined, as something that simply must be, and must happen! Perhaps there is something else to it, some kind of combination of presentiments, some kind of exceptional strength of will, a self-intoxication by one's own fantasy, or something else—I do not know; but that evening (which I will never in my life forget) something miraculous happened to me. Although it is in no way a mathematical improbability, I nevertheless still find it miraculous. And why, why had that conviction taken such a deep and powerful hold on me, and so long before? Indeed, I had been thinking about it, I repeat, not as a chance which could be numbered amongst others (and which, consequently, might also not happen), but as something that was absolutely certain to happen!

It was a quarter past ten; I went into the casino with such firm hope and at the same time in a state of excitement such as I had never before experienced. There were still quite a number of people in the gaming halls, although half as many as in the morning.

After ten o'clock only the genuine, desperate players are left around the gaming tables, those for whom the only thing that exists at the spa is the roulette, and who have come for that alone, those who barely notice what is going on around them and who take no interest in anything throughout the whole season, who do nothing but gamble from dawn to dusk, and who would happily gamble through the night until daybreak if it were possible. And they always disperse with annoyance when the roulette is closed down at midnight. When at about twelve o'clock, before closing down the roulette, the head croupier announces: 'Les trois derniers coups, messieurs!'* they are sometimes ready to stake everything they have in their pockets on these last three turns—and that is just when they lose the most. I went over to the very same table where Grandmother had been sitting not long before. It was not very crowded, so I very soon found a place to stand at the table. Straight ahead of me, on the green cloth, the word 'passe' was inscribed. 'Passe' refers to the series of numbers from nineteen to thirty-six inclusive. The first series, from one to eighteen inclusive, is called 'manque'; but what had that got to do with me? I had not been calculating, I had not even heard what the ball had landed on the last turn, neither did I ask when I started playing—as any even marginally prudent gambler would have done. I pulled out my entire twenty gold friedrichs and threw them on 'passe', which happened to be in front of me.

'Vingt-deux',* shouted the croupier.

I had won, and once again I staked everything: both the previous stake and what I had just won.

'Trente et un',* shouted the croupier. Another win! That meant I now had eighty gold friedrichs in all! I moved all eighty of them over to the twelve middle numbers (pays three times, but the chances are two to one against), the wheel spun, and twenty-four came up. They laid out three rolls of fifty gold friedrichs for me, and ten gold coins; in all, together with what I had before, I now had two hundred gold friedrichs.

Feeling delirious I moved the whole pile of money onto the red—and then I suddenly came to my senses! And for the only time during the whole of that evening, during the entire game, an icy fear came over me, making my hands and legs tremble. With horror I felt, and momentarily realized, what it would be like to lose now! My whole life was at stake!

'Rouge!' cried the croupier, and I drew breath, fiery goose-pimples breaking out all over my body. I was paid in bank-notes; there must have been four thousand florins and eighty gold friedrichs in total! (I could still keep count at that point.)

Next I remember once again staking two thousand florins on the twelve middle numbers and losing; I staked my gold and the eighty gold friedrichs, and lost. I was overcome with rage: I grabbed the two thousand florins that I still had left and staked them on the first twelve—just like that, at random, without giving it a thought, without any calculation! There was, however, one moment of waiting, in which my impressions were perhaps similar to those experienced by Madame Blanchard* when she plunged to the ground from a balloon in Paris.

'Quatre!' cried the croupier. Together with the former stake I now found myself once more with six thousand florins. I already looked like a conqueror, I was now afraid of absolutely nothing, and I flung the four thousand florins on the black. About nine other people followed suit, also staking on black. The croupiers were talking amongst themselves and exchanging glances. All around people were talking and waiting.

It landed on black. At this point I lost track of the amount and order of my stakes. I only remember, as if in a dream, that I had already won something like sixteen thousand florins; then suddenly in three unlucky rounds I lost twelve of them;

then I moved the remaining four thousand to 'passe' (but by
now I hardly felt anything at all as I did it; I just waited,
somewhat mechanically, without thinking)—and I won again.
Then I won a further four times in a row. All I can remember
is that I gathered in money by the thousands; I also remember
that the middle numbers came up most often, so I stuck to
them. They somehow came up regularly, three or four times
in a row without fail, then they disappeared for a couple of
turns, then came back again three or four times in succession.
This astonishing regularity sometimes comes in bursts—and it
is this that throws the inveterate gamblers, who make their
calculations with a pencil in their hands. And what terrible
ironies of fate occur at times!

I do not think that more than half an hour had passed since
my arrival. The croupier suddenly informed me that I had won
thirty thousand florins, and that since the bank would not
accept responsibility for more than that on one occasion, the
roulette would therefore be closed until the next morning. I
grabbed all my gold, shoving it into my pockets, then grabbed
all the banknotes and went over to another table in a different
hall, where there was another game of roulette; the entire
crowd surged after me; a place was cleared for me at once and
I set about staking once again, haphazardly and without
counting. I do not understand what saved me!

At times, however, calculations began flashing through my
mind. I stuck to various numbers and chances, but soon
abandoned them and staked again, hardly realizing what I was
doing. I must have been very distracted; I remember that on
several occasions the croupiers corrected my play. I made some
flagrant mistakes. My brow was drenched with sweat and my
hands were shaking. The wretched Poles were jumping up to
offer their services, but I did not listen to anybody. My luck
held! All at once there was loud talk and laughter all around.
'Bravo, bravo!' they were all shouting, some of them even
clapping their hands. I had broken the bank here as well by
winning thirty thousand florins, and once again the bank
closed until the next day!

'Leave, leave', a voice on my right whispered to me. It was
some Jew or other from Frankfurt; he had been standing

beside me the whole time, and I believe that at times he had been helping me play.

'For God's sake, go!' another voice whispered over my left ear. I gave a fleeting glance. It was a woman of about thirty, dressed very modestly and properly, and with a rather unhealthily pale, weary face which still bore traces of her former splendid beauty. At that moment I was stuffing my pockets with banknotes, all crumpled up, and gathering up the gold that was still on the table. Seizing the last roll of fifty gold friedrichs in notes I hastily slipped it to the pale lady, completely unnoticed; I had a terrible desire to do it and I remember how her delicate, thin little fingers squeezed my hand as a sign of her keen gratitude. It all happened in a flash.

Having collected everything, I quickly walked over to the trente-et-quarante.

The aristocratic members of the public sit at the trente-et-quarante table. It is not roulette, it is a card-game. Here the bank will pay up to a hundred thousand thalers at a time. Here too the most one can bet is four thousand florins. I did not know the game at all and hardly knew any of the ways of betting, apart from red and black, which it also has. I stuck to these. The whole casino was crowding around. I do not remember whether I even once thought about Polina during all this. At the time I experienced some sort of irresistible pleasure in snatching and raking in the banknotes, which were piling up in front of me.

It really was as if fate was prompting me. On that occasion, as if deliberately, something occurred that actually happens fairly often in this game. Luck stays with red, for instance, for about ten or even fifteen turns. Two days before, I had heard that during the previous week red had won twenty-two times in succession; nobody could remember that ever having happened at roulette, and people spoke about it with amazement. Of course, everybody immediately leaves red and by about the tenth go practically nobody bets on it. But at that point none of the experienced players will bet on black, the opposite to red, either. The experienced player knows what this 'capricious luck' means. For instance, one would think that after red had come up sixteen times it is bound to be black on the seventeenth. Newcomers to the game fall for this in crowds, doubling and trebling their stakes and losing dreadfully.

But owing to some strange sort of waywardness, after I had noticed that red had come up seven times in a row, I deliberately stuck to it. I am convinced that half of it was vanity; I wanted to astonish the spectators by taking crazy risks, and—oh, what an odd sensation!—I distinctly remember that without even the slightest prompting from vanity, a frightful craving for risk suddenly took hold of me. It may be that by going through so many sensations the soul does not feel satisfaction but is only exasperated by them, and demands yet more sensations, and stronger and stronger ones, until it is finally exhausted. And I promise I am not lying when I say that if the rules of the game had allowed me to stake fifty thousand florins at a time, I would certainly have done so. All around people were shouting that it was a folly, that red had already come up fourteen times.

'Monsieur a gagné déjà cent mille florins',* someone's voice beside me rang out.

I suddenly came to my senses. What? I had won a hundred thousand florins that evening! What more did I want? I fell upon the banknotes, crammed them into my pockets without counting them, raked in all my gold, together with all the bundles of money, and dashed out of the casino. Everyone around was laughing as I walked through the halls, looking at my bulging pockets and at my uneven gait which resulted from the weight of the gold. I think there must have been well over a stone of it. Several hands stretched out towards me; I gave it away in handfuls, as much as I could get into my fist. Two Jews stopped me by the door.

'You are brave! You're very brave!' they said to me, 'but you must leave tomorrow morning without fail, otherwise you'll lose absolutely all of it . . .'

I did not listen to them. The avenue was so dark that I could not even see my own hands. It was less than half a mile to the hotel. I have never been frightened of thieves or robbers, not even when I was a small boy; neither did I think about them now. However, I do not remember what I thought about on the way; my mind was blank. I only felt some sort of frightful delight—success, victory, power—I do not know how to express it. The image of Polina flashed through my mind; I remembered and grasped the fact that I was going to her, that any moment now I would be with her and would tell her and show her . . . but I had already almost forgotten what she had just said to me and why I had gone, and all those recent sensations that had occurred only half an hour before now seemed to me to belong to the distant past, emended, obsolete—something we would no longer remember, because now everything would be starting afresh. When I was almost at the end of the avenue I was suddenly struck with fear: 'What if I am murdered and robbed now?' My fear doubled with every step. I was almost running. Suddenly at the end of the avenue there was our hotel glittering, illuminated by its numerous lights—thank God: home!

I ran up to my floor and quickly flung open the door. Polina was there, sitting on my sofa in front of the burning candle, her arms folded. She looked at me in amazement and, of course, I looked strange enough at that moment. I stopped in front of her and began flinging my entire pile of money onto the table.

CHAPTER 15

I REMEMBER that she looked at my face terribly intently, but without moving from her seat, or even changing her position.

'I won two hundred thousand francs', I cried as I threw down my last roll. The table was covered with an enormous heap of banknotes and rolls of gold coins, which I could not take my eyes off; for minutes on end I completely forgot about Polina. One moment I was sorting out the piles of banknotes, stacking them up together, the next putting all the gold to one side in a general pile; then I would leave it all and start pacing up and down the room with rapid strides, deep in thought, and then I would suddenly go back to the table again and start counting the money once more. Suddenly, as if I had just come to, I rushed to the doors and hastily locked them, turning the key twice. Then I stopped in hesitation in front of my little suitcase.

'Should I put it in the suitcase until tomorrow?' I asked, suddenly turning to Polina, and suddenly remembering about her. She was still sitting there motionless, in exactly the same place, but her eyes were following me intently. The expression on her face was rather odd; I did not like that expression! I am not mistaken if I say that there was hatred in it.

I walked swiftly to her.

'Polina, here are twenty-five thousand florins, which is fifty thousand francs, or even more. Take them and throw them in his face tomorrow.'

She did not answer.

'If you want I'll take them myself, early in the morning. All right?'

She suddenly burst into laughter. She laughed for a long time.

I watched her with surprise and a feeling of sorrow. This laughter was very much like the laughter with which she had mocked me so often recently, and which always coincided with my most passionate declarations. Eventually she stopped, and frowned; she looked at me sternly, glowering.

'I will not take your money', she said contemptuously.

'What? What is the matter?' I cried out. 'Why ever not, Polina?'

'I do not take money for nothing.'

'I offer it to you as a friend; I offer you my life.'

She gave me a long, searching look, as if she wanted to pierce me with it.

'You are giving too much,' she said, grinning; 'de Grieux's mistress is not worth fifty thousand francs.'

'Polina, how can you speak to me like that?!' I cried reproachfully. 'I'm not de Grieux, am I?'

'I hate you! Yes . . . Yes! . . . I do not love you any more than de Grieux', she shouted, her eyes suddenly beginning to sparkle.

And then suddenly covering her face with her hands, she became hysterical. I rushed over to her.

I realized that something had happened to her in my absence. She did not seem to be altogether in her right mind.

'Buy me! Is that what you want? Do you? For fifty thousand francs, like de Grieux?' she broke out, sobbing convulsively. I embraced her, kissed her hands and feet, and went down on my knees before her.

Her hysteria was passing. She placed both her hands on my shoulders and scrutinized me intently; it seemed as if she was wanting to read something written on my face. She was listening to me but evidently did not hear what I said to her. A rather troubled and thoughtful expression appeared on her face. I was afraid for her; I definitely thought that her mind was disturbed. At one moment she would suddenly begin to draw me quietly towards her, a trusting smile already wandering across her face; and then suddenly she would push me away and start staring, giving me dark looks.

All at once she threw herself at me in an embrace.

'But you do love me, don't you?' she said. 'After all you, after all you . . . wanted to fight the Baron for my sake!' And she suddenly burst out laughing—as if something amusing and sweet were suddenly flashing through her memory. She was crying and laughing at the same time. But what could I do? I myself felt as if I was delirious. I remember she started saying something to me, but I could hardly understand anything. It was a sort of delirium, babbling—as if she wanted to tell me something as quickly as possible—a delirium occasionally interrupted by the most cheerful laughter, which was beginning to frighten me. 'No, no, you dear person, you dear!' she repeated. 'You are my faithful one!' and she once again placed her hands on my shoulders, scrutinizing me, and she kept repeating: 'You love me . . . you do . . . will you love me?' I did not take my eyes off her; I had never before seen her in such a fit of tenderness and love; true, it was of course a delirium, but . . . having noticed my passionate glance, she suddenly began to smile slyly; and then for no reason at all she began talking about Mr Astley.

However, she had repeatedly started to say something about Mr Astley (especially when she had been trying so hard to tell me something just before), but I could not grasp what exactly it was. It seemed that she was even laughing at him; she kept on repeating that he was waiting . . . and did I know that he was probably standing beneath the window right now? 'Yes,

yes, under the window, well go on, open it and have look, have a look, he's here, here!' She pushed me over to the window, but the moment I made a movement towards it she burst into peals of laughter and I stayed beside her whilst she rushed to embrace me.

'Shall we go? We're going tomorrow, aren't we?' the thought suddenly entered her troubled mind. 'Well' (and she stopped to think), 'we'll catch up with Grandmother, don't you think? I should think we'll catch up with her in Berlin. What do you think she'll say when we catch up with her and she sees us? And Mr Astley? . . . Well, I don't think *he* would jump off the Schlangenberg, do you?' (She broke into laughter.) 'But listen: do you know where he's going next summer? He wants to go to the North Pole to make some scientific studies and he has asked me to join him, ha, ha, ha! He says that we Russians would know nothing were it not for the Europeans and we wouldn't be able to do anything . . . But he's also a kind man! Do you know he makes excuses for the General?—he says that Blanche . . . that passion— well, I don't know, I don't know', she suddenly repeated, as if she were carried away and had lost her thread. 'The poor things, I do feel sorry for them, and Grandmother . . . Come, listen, listen, how could you kill de Grieux? Did you really, really think you would kill him? Oh, fool! How could you possibly have thought that I would let you fight de Grieux? You won't kill the Baron either', she added, suddenly beginning to laugh. 'Oh, how ridiculous you were with the Baron; I was watching you both from the bench. And how reluctant you were to go when I sent you. Oh, how I laughed, how I did laugh!' she added, roaring with laughter.

And then all of a sudden she kissed me and embraced me again, pressing her face tenderly and passionately against mine. I no longer thought about anything, or heard anything. My head was spinning . . .

I think it was about seven o'clock in the morning when I woke up; it was broad daylight in the room. Polina was sitting beside me, looking around in a rather strange way, as though she had just emerged from some kind of gloom and was collecting her thoughts. She too had only just woken up and was looking intently at the table, and the money. My head felt heavy and was aching. I tried to take Polina's hand; she suddenly pushed me away and jumped up from the bed. The start of the day was overcast; it had been raining before dawn. She walked up to the window, opened it, and thrust out her head and shoulders, supporting herself with her hands, leaning her elbows against the window-frame, and she remained like that for about three minutes, without turning round to me or listening to what I was saying to her. A fearful thought came to me: what is going to happen now, and how will it all end? She suddenly climbed down from the window, walked up to the table, and looking at me with an expression of infinite hatred, her lips trembling with malice, she said to me: 'Well then, give me my fifty thousand francs.'

'Polina, again, again!' I began.

'Or have you changed your mind? Ha, ha, ha! Maybe you're already regretting it?'

There were twenty-five thousand florins that had already been counted out the day before lying on the table; I took them and gave them to her.

'Anyway, they are already mine, aren't they? Well?' she asked me spitefully, holding the money in her hands.

'Why, they've always been yours!' I said.

'Well, here are your fifty thousand francs.' She brandished the money and threw it at me. The packet of money gave me a painful blow in the face and scattered over the floor. Having done it, Polina ran out of the room.

I know at that moment she was not in her right mind, although I cannot understand this temporary madness. It is true that even now, one month later, she is still ill. However, what was the reason for this condition, and more importantly for this episode? Was it wounded pride? Was it despair at having resorted to turning to me? Had I perhaps given her the impression that I was glorying in my good fortune and that, like de Grieux, I wanted to get rid of her by giving her fifty thousand francs? But after all, that was not the case, I know that from my own conscience. I think that her vanity was partially to blame: it had prompted her not to trust me and to insult me, although all this had probably been very unclear to her. In that case, I, of course, was answering for de Grieux and became guilty without any great guilt. It is true this was all just a delirium; it is true too that I knew she was raving and

. . . that I paid no attention to that fact. Perhaps that is what she cannot forgive me for now? Yes, but that is now; but then, then? After all, her delirium and illness were not bad enough to make her completely forget what she was doing when she came to me with de Grieux's letter. She must have known what she was doing.

I hastily and haphazardly shoved all my notes together with the pile of gold onto the bed, covered it, and left my room about ten minutes after Polina. I was certain that she had run home and I wanted to steal my way quietly into the entrance hall and ask the nursemaid about the young lady's health. And how amazed I was when I met Nurse on the staircase and learnt that Polina had not yet returned home and that she herself was on her way to my room to find her.

'Just now,' I told her, 'she left me just now, about ten minutes ago; where could she have got to?'

Nurse looked at me reproachfully.

Meanwhile a regular scandal had erupted, and was already making its way round the hotel. In the porter's lodge and the head waiter's room it was being whispered that at six o'clock that morning the Fräulein had run out of the hotel in the rain, and rushed off in the direction of the Hôtel d'Angleterre. From what they said and from the hints they dropped, I noticed that they already knew she had spent the night in my room. However, the whole of the General's family had already been under discussion: it had become known to all that the General had taken leave of his senses the day before and had been crying all over the hotel. They were also saying that Grandmother was his mother, who had deliberately come all the way from Russia to forbid her son to marry Mademoiselle de Cominges, and to disinherit him if he disobeyed; and as he had in fact disobeyed her, the Countess had in his eyes deliberately gambled away all her money at roulette so that he really would get nothing. 'Diese Russen!'* the head waiter repeated indignantly, shaking his head. The others laughed. The head waiter was preparing the bill. The news had already got round of my winnings; Karl, my bellboy, was the first to congratulate me. But I had no time for them. I rushed over to the Hôtel d'Angleterre.

It was still early. Mr Astley was not receiving anyone; but

learning that it was me, he came out into the corridor and stopped in front of me, fixed his pewter-coloured eyes on me, and waited in silence for what I was going to say. I asked about Polina straight away.

'She's ill', replied Mr Astley, staring at me as before, and refusing to take his eyes off me.

'So, she's actually here with you?'

'Oh yes, with me.'

'And so you . . . you intend to keep her with you here?'

'Oh yes, I intend to do that.'

'Mr Astley, this will lead to a scandal; it's impossible. Besides, she's not at all well; perhaps you haven't noticed?'

'Oh no, I've noticed and I've already told you that she's ill. If she wasn't ill she wouldn't have spent the night in your room.'

'So you know about that too?'

'Yes, I do. She was to come over here yesterday and I would have taken her to a relative of mine, but because she was ill she made a mistake and went to you.'

'Can you imagine?! May I congratulate you, Mr Astley? By the way, you've made me think of something: were you standing beneath our window all night? Throughout the night Miss Polina kept making me open it and look to see whether you were standing there beneath the window, and she laughed dreadfully.'

'Really? No, I wasn't standing beneath the window; but I was waiting in the corridor and walking about.'

'But you see she needs treatment, Mr Astley.'

'Oh yes, I've already called the doctor, and if she dies, then you'll answer to me for her death.'

I was astounded. 'Excuse me, Mr Astley, what is it you want?'

'Is it true that you won two hundred thousand thalers yesterday?'

'It was only a hundred thousand florins.'

'Well, there you are, you see! And so, you will leave for Paris this morning?'

'Why?'

'Every Russian with money goes to Paris', Mr Astley

explained, in a voice and tone that made it sound as if he was reading from a book.

'What would I do in Paris now, in the summer? I love her, Mr Astley! You know that.'

'Really? I'm sure you don't. Besides, if you stay here, you'll be certain to lose it all, and you won't have anything left to go to Paris with. Anyway, goodbye, because I'm absolutely certain that you'll go to Paris today.'

'Very well, goodbye, only I'm not going to Paris. Just stop and think, Mr Astley, what will happen to us now. In a word, the General . . . and now this escapade with Miss Polina—you see, it will be all over the town.'

'Yes, all over the town; but I don't really think the General is thinking about that—he's got other things on his mind. And anyway, Miss Polina is absolutely entitled to live wherever she wants. As far as the family is concerned you might well say that the family no longer exists.'

I walked along, chuckling to myself at the Englishman's strange certainty that I would go to Paris. 'But he will want to kill me in a duel if Mademoiselle Polina dies,' I thought; 'and what a commission *that* would be!' I swear I felt sorry for Polina, but it was odd—from the very first moment I touched the roulette table the day before, and began raking in piles of money, my love had retreated into the background, so to speak. I say this now; but at the time I was still unable to see it clearly. Am I really in fact a gambler, did I in actual fact . . . love Polina so strangely? No, to this day I still love her, God's my witness! But at the time, when I had left Mr Astley and was walking home, I genuinely suffered and blamed myself. But . . . at this point a very strange and silly thing happened to me.

I was hurrying to see the General when suddenly, not far from their apartments, a door opened and somebody called out to me. It was Madame veuve Cominges and she was calling me at Mademoiselle Blanche's instruction. I entered Mademoiselle Blanche's rooms.

Their suite was a modest one, just two rooms. I could hear Mademoiselle Blanche laughing and shouting in her bedroom. She was getting up.

'A, c'est lui!! Viens donc, bêta! Is it true, que tu as gagné une montagne d'or et d'argent? J'aimerais mieux l'or.'*

'Yes, I did', I replied, laughing.

'How much?'

'A hundred thousand florins.'

'Bibi, comme tu es bête! Come on, come in here, I can't hear anything. Nous ferons bombance, n'est ce pas?'*

I went into her room. She was lolling about beneath a pink satin bedspread, from beneath which protruded her swarthy, robust, stunning shoulders—the sort of shoulders one only dreams about—carelessly covered with a lawn blouse, trimmed with shining white lace, which suited her dark skin wonderfully.

'Mon fils, as-tu du cœur?' she cried, catching sight of me, and she burst into laughter. She always laughed very cheerfully, and sometimes even sincerely.

'Tout autre . . .',* I was about to begin, playing on Corneille's words.

'You see . . . vois-tu,' she suddenly started to gabble, 'first of all find my stockings, help me to put my shoes on, and secondly si tu n'es pas trop bête, je te prends à Paris.* You know, I'm leaving at once.'

'At once?'

'In half an hour.'

Everything had indeed been packed. All her suitcases and things were standing there ready. The coffee had already been served long before.

'Eh bien! If you want, tu verras Paris. Dis donc, qu'est ce que c'est qu'un outchitel. Tu étais bien bête, quand tu étais outchitel.* Where are my stockings? Get them on me, come on!'

She exhibited a truly delightful little foot, dark-skinned, dainty, and not misshapen like practically all those feet that look so charming in shoes. I started laughing and began pulling on her silk stocking for her. Meanwhile, Mademoiselle Blanche was sitting on the bed prattling away.

'Eh bien, que feras-tu, si je te prends avec? Firstly, je veux cinquante mille francs. You can give them to me in Frankfurt. Nous allons à Paris; we will live together there et je te ferai

voir des étoiles en plein jour.* You'll see women such as you've
never seen before. Listen . . .'

'Stop a moment! So I'll give you fifty thousand francs, and
what will be left for me?'

'Et cent cinquante mille francs, you have forgotten, and on
top of that, I'm prepared to live in your flat for a month or
two, que sais-je!* Of course, we'll get through these hundred
and fifty thousand francs in two months. You see, je suis
bonne enfant and I'm telling you beforehand, mais tu verras
des étoiles.'*

'What! Spend all of it in two months?'

'What! Does that scare you? Ah, vil esclave!* And do you
know that one month of that life is better than your entire
existence? One month—et après, le déluge.* Mais tu ne peux
comprendre, va! Go, go, you're not worth it. Ai, que fais-tu?'*

At that moment I was putting a stocking on the other foot,
but could not refrain from kissing it. She snatched it away and
started hitting me in the face with the tip of her toes. In the
end, she chased me away altogether. 'Eh bien, mon outchitel,
je t'attends, si tu veux;* in quarter of an hour I'm leaving!' she
shouted after me.

Returning home, I was already in a whirl. Surely it was not
my fault that Mademoiselle Polina had thrown the whole
bundle of money in my face and had already preferred Mr
Astley to me yesterday? Several of the fallen banknotes were
still lying scattered over the floor; I picked them up. Just at
that moment the door opened and the head waiter himself
appeared (hitherto he had never bothered to look at me) with
an invitation: would I care to move downstairs to a superb
suite, where Count V. had just been staying?

I stopped and thought.

'My bill!' I shouted, 'I'm leaving right away, in ten minutes'
time.' 'To Paris, then, to Paris!' I thought to myself, 'it means
it was destined to happen!'

A quarter of an hour later we were indeed sitting together as
a threesome in a group compartment: there was myself,
Mademoiselle Blanche, and Madame veuve Cominges.
Mademoiselle Blanche was looking at me and roaring with
laughter, almost hysterically. Veuve Cominges was seconding
her; I cannot say that I felt cheerful. My life had been broken

in two, but since yesterday I had already grown accustomed to
staking everything on cards. Perhaps it really was true that all
that money had been too much for me and had gone to my
head. Peut-être, je ne demandais pas mieux.* It seemed to me
that for a time, but only for a time, I needed a change of scene.
'But in a month's time, I'll be back, and then . . . and then
you and I can sort things out, Mr Astley!' No, as I recall it
now, at the time I was terribly sad, even though I laughed
back at that little idiot Blanche.

'But what's wrong with you? How silly you are! Oh, how
silly you are!' Blanche kept crying, interrupting her laughter
and starting to reproach me in earnest. 'Well yes, well yes,
yes, we'll spend your two hundred thousand francs, but on the
other hand, mais tu seras heureux, comme un petit roi;* I'll
tie your tie for you, and introduce you to Hortense. And when
we've spent all our money, you'll come here and break the
bank again. What did the Jews say to you? The most important
thing is courage, and you've got that, and you will bring back
money to Paris for me, more than once. Quant à moi, je veux
cinquante mille francs de rente et alors . . .'*

'What about the General?' I asked her.

'The General, as you yourself know, goes out every day at
this time to get a bouquet of flowers for me. This time I
deliberately told him to find me some very rare flowers. The
poor old thing will return to find the bird has flown. He will
fly after us, you'll see. Ha, ha, ha! I'll be very pleased. He'll
be useful to me in Paris; Mr Astley will settle up for him
here . . .'

And so that was how I came to leave for Paris.

CHAPTER 16

WHAT can I say about Paris? Of course, the whole thing was
madness and folly. I spent a little over three weeks in Paris,
and my hundred thousand francs were completely finished
during that period. I am speaking only of a hundred thousand;

the other hundred thousand I gave to Mademoiselle Blanche in cash—fifty thousand in Frankfurt, and after three days in Paris I gave her a further fifty thousand in the form of a promissory note, for which, however, she got money from me a week later, 'et les cent mille francs qui nous restent, tu les mangeras avec moi, mon outchitel'.* She kept calling me 'tutor'. It is difficult to imagine anything in the world more calculating, stingy, and miserly than the class of beings like Mademoiselle Blanche. But that is regarding her own money. As for my hundred thousand francs, later on she told me quite frankly that she needed them to get herself set up in Paris. 'So I have now started on a very respectable basis once and for all, and now nobody should topple me for a long time—at least, not the way I've arranged things', she added. However, I hardly set eyes on that hundred thousand; it was she who kept the money all the time, and in my wallet, which she went through every day, no more than a hundred francs ever accumulated, and there was nearly always less.

'Well, what do you need money for?' she would say at times, in the most simple way, and I did not argue with her. On the other hand, she decorated her apartment pretty nicely with the money, and when she took me across to her new abode she said, as she showed me the rooms: 'See what careful reckoning and good taste can do with the most scanty means.' This 'scantiness', however, amounted to exactly fifty thousand francs. With the remaining fifty thousand she acquired a carriage and horses; we also gave two balls, that is to say two evening parties, attended by Hortense, Lisette, and Cléopâtre—remarkable women in a great many ways, and far from stupid. I was obliged to play the utterly ridiculous role of host at these two evening parties, to receive and entertain the dullest little *nouveaux riches* merchants' wives, various unbelievably ignorant and shameless lieutenants, pitiful writers and journalistic insects who appeared wearing the most fashionable tails and pale yellow gloves, and who had a degree of egocentricity and conceit that would be unthinkable even among us in Petersburg—and that is saying quite a lot. They even presumed to laugh at me, but I got myself drunk on champagne and collapsed in the back room. I found the whole thing loathsome in the extreme. 'C'est un outchitel,' Mademoiselle

Blanche said about me, 'il a gagné deux cent mille francs,* and without me he wouldn't know how to spend them. And afterwards he'll go back to teaching again; does anyone know of a post for him? I must do something for him.' I began turning to champagne not infrequently, because I kept feeling melancholy, and unutterably bored. I was living in the most bourgeois and mercantile surroundings where every sou was calculated and weighed up. Blanche did not like me in the least for the first two weeks, I noticed that; true, she dressed me like a dandy and tied my tie for me each day, but in her soul she sincerely despised me. I did not pay the slightest bit of attention to that. Bored and depressed, I got into the habit of going to the Château des Fleurs, where I regularly, every evening, got drunk and learnt the cancan (which they dance quite disgustingly there), and in the end I even acquired a certain reputation in that respect. Blanche finally saw through me: earlier on she had somehow had the idea that during our period of living together I would follow her around with pencil and paper in hand, adding up how much she spent, how much she had stolen, how much she was going to spend and going to steal, and of course she had already convinced herself that there would be a battle between us over every ten-franc piece. And she had already, well in advance, prepared a retort to each of the attacks she anticipated from me; but when she saw there was no sign of any attack coming from me, to start with she defended herself anyway. Sometimes she began with tremendous fervour, but then seeing that I did not say anything—more often than not I was lolling on the couch, staring at the ceiling, motionless—she would end up being even quite astonished. To begin with she thought that I was just stupid, 'un outchitel', and merely cut short her explanations, probably thinking to herself: 'After all, he's stupid; no point putting ideas in his head, if he doesn't understand anyway.' She would go away, but ten minutes later she would return once more (this took place during the period of her frenzied expenditure, expenditure that was way beyond our means: for example, she exchanged the horses and bought another pair for sixteen thousand francs).

'Well, my pet, so you aren't angry?' she said, walking over to me.

'Not at all; you just weary me', I said, pushing her away with my hand, but she found this so intriguing, she immediately sat down beside me: 'You see, if I decided to spend so much, then it's because they were a bargain. They can be resold for twenty thousand francs.'

'I'm sure they can, I'm sure; they are beautiful horses; and now you've got a superb turn-out; it will be useful; well, that's enough.'

'So you aren't angry?'

'Why should I be? It's wise of you to stock up with a few things that are essential to you. It will all be useful to you later on. I can see that you do really need to set yourself up in this sort of fashion; otherwise you'll never make a million. This hundred thousand francs of ours is just the beginning—a drop in the ocean.'

To Blanche, who was not in the least expecting this sort of argument from me (but rather outcries and reproaches!), this was like a bolt from the blue.

'So you . . . so that's the sort of person you are! Mais tu as de l'esprit pour comprendre! Sais-tu, mon garçon,* you may only be a tutor, but you ought to have been born a prince! So you don't regret that our money is going quickly?'

'Oh, get rid of it as quickly as possible!'

'Mais . . . sais-tu . . . mais dis donc, but you aren't rich, are you? Mais sais-tu, after all you despise money too much. Qu'est-ce que tu feras après, dis donc?'*

'Après I'm going to Homburg and I'll win another hundred thousand francs.'

'Oui, oui, c'est ça, c'est magnifique!* And I know that you will certainly win and come back here with it. Dis donc, why you'll succeed in making me actually love you! Eh bien, because that's the way you are, I will love you all the time and I won't be unfaithful to you once. You see, I may not have loved you all this time, parce que je croyais, que tu n'est qu'un outchitel (quelque chose comme un laquais, n'est-ce pas?), but I have nevertheless been true to you, parce que je suis bonne fille.'*

'Oh, but you're lying! What about that Albert, that swarthy little officer, didn't I see you with him last time?'

'Oh, oh, mais tu es . . .'*

'Well, you're lying! You're lying! Come on, you don't think I'm angry, do you? I don't care a damn; il faut que jeunesse se passe.* You're not to chase him away if he was here before I was, and you love him. Only see that you don't give him any money, do you hear?'

'So you aren't angry about that either? Mais tu es un vrai philosophe, sais-tu? Un vrai philosophe!' she cried in ecstasy. 'Eh bien, je t'aimerai, je t'aimerai—tu verras, tu sera content!'*

And indeed, from then on she did actually seem to become attached to me, even friendly, and that is how we spent our last ten days. I did not see the promised 'stars'; but in certain respects she did in fact keep her word. Moreover, she introduced me to Hortense, who was a truly remarkable woman in her own way, and whom we used to call Thérèse-philosophe in our little circle . . .

However, there is no need to enlarge on that; the whole thing could constitute a separate story, with its own separate flavour, which I do not wish to include in this story. The fact was that I longed with my whole being for it to come to an end quickly. But, as I have already said, our one hundred thousand francs lasted almost a month—which truly surprised me: Blanche spent at least eighty thousand of it on things for herself, and we certainly had no more than twenty thousand left to live on—and yet we managed. Blanche, who towards the end became almost open with me (at any rate there were some things she did not lie to me about), declared that at any rate those debts she had been forced to incur would not fall on me. 'I didn't make you sign any bills or promissory notes,' she told me, 'because I was sorry for you; someone else certainly would have done and would have sent you packing to prison. You see, you see, how much I've loved you and how kind I am! That damned wedding alone is going to cost me goodness knows what!'

We really did have a wedding. It took place at the very end of our month, and one must assume that the very last dregs of my hundred thousand francs went on that; and that was where it ended, at least that was when our month came to an end, and after that I formally retired.

It happened like this: a week after we had established

ourselves in Paris the General arrived. He came straight to
Blanche and from the very first visit he practically lived with
us. He did, however, have his own small flat somewhere.
Blanche greeted him cheerfully, with shrieks of delight and
laughter, and even threw herself at him in an embrace; as it
turned out, it was she who would not let him go, and he had
to follow her everywhere: on the boulevards, in her carriage,
to the theatre, and to visit friends. But the General was still
very good at that sort of thing; he was fairly imposing and
decorous—he was almost tall, with dyed side-whiskers and a
large moustache (he had formerly served in the Cuirassiers),
and a distinguished face, even if it was rather flabby. His
manners were superb and he wore evening dress very comfort-
ably. He began wearing his decorations in Paris. To walk along
a boulevard with someone like this was not just a possibility,
but if I may say so, it was *recommendable*. The kind-hearted,
muddled General was extremely pleased by all this; he had
certainly not been counting on it when he appeared at our
place on his arrival in Paris. He arrived almost shaking with
fear; he thought that Blanche would start screaming and order
him to be sent away; and so this turn of events sent him into
ecstasy and he spent the whole month in a state of mindless
rapture; and that is how I left him. When I was already back
here I learnt in detail of how, after our very sudden departure
from Roulettenburg, he had some sort of a fit the very same
morning. He fell, unconscious, and then for a week he was
almost like a madman, and rambled in his speech. The doctors
were treating him, but then he suddenly threw it all up, caught
a train, and rolled up in Paris. Of course, Blanche's reception
proved to be the best possible treatment for him; but signs of
his illness remained for a long time afterwards, despite his
joyous and rapturous frame of mind. He was by now quite
unable to reason, or even to conduct a slightly serious conversation; in this event he just kept saying 'hm!' to everything, and
nodding his head—and he avoided the issue in that way. He
frequently laughed, but it was a sort of nervous, sickly
laughter, like a fit of hysterics; on another occasion he would
sit for hours on end, sullen as the night, knitting his thick
eyebrows. There were many things that he completely forgot;
he had become unbelievably absent-minded and had adopted

the habit of talking to himself. Only Blanche could bring him to life; and so his attacks of gloom and depression, when he took refuge in a corner, simply meant that he had not seen Blanche for a long time, or that Blanche had gone off somewhere, without taking him with her, or that she had not caressed him when she left. On these occasions he could not say what he wanted, and he did not even realize that he was being gloomy and sullen. After sitting for an hour or two (I noticed this a couple of times, when Blanche had gone out for the entire day, probably to see Albert), he would suddenly begin to look around, fidget, glance back, remember something, and then appear to try and find someone; but seeing no one and not remembering what it was he wanted to ask, he once again fell into oblivion until the moment when Blanche suddenly appeared again, gay, playful, dressed up, with her resounding laugh; she used to run up to him and start teasing him, or she might even kiss him—something she seldom bestowed on him, however. Once the General was so pleased to see her that he even burst into tears; I was quite astonished.

From the moment of his arrival Blanche immediately started pleading his cause with me. She had even lapsed into eloquence; she would remind me that she had betrayed the General because of me, that she was practically his bride, she had given him her word; that he had abandoned his family for her sake, and finally that I had been employed by him and that I ought to remember it, and that—wasn't I ashamed of myself? . . . I remained completely silent and she spoke an awful lot of nonsense. In the end I burst into laughter, and that was how the thing ended, that is to say, first of all she had thought I was a fool, and by the end she reached the opinion that I was a very fine, accommodating person. In short, I had the good fortune, finally, of definitely winning that worthy young lady's good favour. (As it happens, Blanche was in actual fact an extremely sweet-natured person—in her own little way, of course; I had not appreciated that at first.) 'You're an intelligent, kind person,' she used to say to me at the end, 'and . . . and . . . it's only a pity that you're such a fool! You'll never, never become rich!'

'Un vrai Russe, un Calmouk!'* Several times she sent me out to walk around the streets with the General, exactly as if we were her lackey and her Italian greyhound. Nevertheless I escorted him to the theatre, to Bal-Mabile, and to restaurants. Blanche even gave me the money for this, although the General had his own, and he absolutely loved taking out his wallet in the presence of others. Once I nearly had to use force to stop him buying a brooch for seven hundred francs which had caught his eye in the Palais-Royal and which he had set his heart on giving to Blanche. Well, what was a seven-hundred-franc brooch to her? The General had no more than a thousand francs in all. I never managed to find out where he got them from. I presume from Mr Astley, especially since it was he who settled their hotel bill. As for the General's attitude towards me all this time, it seems to me that he did not even have a suspicion about my relations with Blanche. Although he had heard in a vague way that I had won a large sum of money, he probably assumed that I was something like a private secretary, or maybe a servant, to Blanche. At any rate he always spoke to me in the same haughty manner as before, imperiously, and sometimes he would even set about giving me a thorough talking-to. One morning in our apartment while we were having our coffee he made us laugh no end. He was not exactly a touchy person; but, all of a sudden, he took umbrage at me. Why? I still do not know. But of course he himself did not know. In short, he delivered a speech without either a beginning or an end, *à bâtons rompus*,* shouting that I was an urchin, that he would teach me a lesson . . . that he would make me understand . . . and so on and so forth. But nobody understood any of it. Blanche broke into peals of laughter; finally he was somehow calmed and taken out for a walk. I noticed on a number of occasions, however, that he looked sad, that he felt sorry for someone or something, was missing someone, despite the presence of Blanche. Once or twice in these moments he began speaking to me, but was never able to make his meaning clear, as he recalled his years in service, his late wife, his family affairs, his estate. He would stumble on a particular word which pleased him and he would repeat it a hundred times in a day, although it had no bearing on either his thoughts or his feelings. I tried to get him onto the subject of his children; he would evade the question by lapsing into rambling speech as before, and rapidly move on to a different subject: 'Yes, yes! the children, the children, you're right, the children!' On one occasion only, when we were going to the theatre, did he express any concern for them: 'Those are unfortunate children!' he said all of a sudden, 'yes, sir, yes, they are unf-fortunate children!' And later on that evening he repeated several times the words 'unfortunate children'. Once when I started to talk about Polina he went into a fury: 'She's an ungrateful woman,' he exclaimed, 'she is wicked and ungrateful! She has put the family to shame. If there were laws here I would make her knuckle under! Yes, sir, oh yes!' As for de Grieux, he could not even bear to hear his name. 'He has brought me to ruin,' he said, 'he has robbed me, he's been the undoing of me! He's been a nightmare to me for two whole years. For months on end he has haunted my dreams. That—that, that . . . Oh, don't ever talk to me about him!'

I could see that things looked to be going well for them, but as usual I said nothing. Blanche was the first to let me know: it was exactly a week before we parted. 'Il a de la chance,'* she prattled away to me, 'Grandmother really is ill now, and will certainly die. Mr Astley has sent a telegram; you must admit that he is her heir, all the same. And even if he isn't, he won't interfere at all. First, he has his own pension, and secondly he will live in a side room and be quite happy. I will be "madame la générale". I will enter into a good social circle' (Blanche was always dreaming about this), 'and then I will be a Russian landowner, j'aurai un château, des moujiks, et puis j'aurai toujours mon million.'*

'And if he starts getting jealous, he'll demand . . . God knows what—do you realize that?'

'Oh no, non, non, non! How would he dare? I have taken precautions, don't worry. I have already made him sign several promissory notes in Albert's name. The slightest thing—and he will be punished immediately; oh no, he won't dare!'

'Well, marry him . . .'

The wedding took place without any great ceremony, a quiet, family affair. The only people invited were Albert and one or two friends. Hortense, Cléopâtre, and the others were resolutely excluded. The bridegroom was exceedingly concerned about his position in society. Blanche tied his tie and pomaded his hair herself, and in his tails and white waistcoat he looked 'très comme il faut'.*

'Il est pourtant très comme il faut',* Blanche herself declared to me as she came out of the General's room, as if the idea of the General being 'très comme il faut' startled even her. I paid such little heed to the details, participating as a mere idle spectator, that I have forgotten a great deal about what happened. I remember only that Blanche turned out not to be a Cominges at all, just as her mother was in no way a veuve Cominges, but a Du Placet. Why they had been de Cominges up until then, I do not know. But the General was very pleased about this as well, and he even liked Du Placet more than de Cominges. On the morning of the wedding, already completely dressed, he kept pacing up and down the hall, repeating to himself, with an unusually serious and pompous air: 'Mademoiselle Blanche Du Placet! Blanche Du Placet! Du Placet! Miss Blanca Diu Plaset! . . .' And a certain satisfaction shone on his face. In the church, at the mayor's, and at the reception at home, he was not only happy and satisfied, but even proud. Something had happened to both of them. Blanche had begun to assume a look of particular dignity.

'Now I need to behave in a completely different way,' she told me extremely seriously, 'mais vois-tu, I never thought about one awful thing: imagine, I still can't get the hang of my new surname: Zagoriansky, Zagoziansky, madame la générale de Sago-Sago, ces diables des noms russes, enfin madame la générale à quatorze consonnes. Comme c'est agréable, n'est-ce pas?'*

We finally parted, and Blanche, that silly Blanche, even shed a few tears when she said goodbye to me. 'Tu étais bon enfant', she said, snivelling. 'Je te croyais bête et tu en avais l'air,* but it suits you.' And having pressed my hand for the last time, she suddenly exclaimed: 'Attends!' She rushed to her boudoir and a moment later brought back two thousand-franc notes for me. I would never have believed that! 'This will be useful to you; you might be a very learned outchitel, but you are a terribly stupid person. Not for anything will I give you more than two thousand francs because you'll gamble it away in any case. Well, goodbye! Nous serons toujours bons amis, but if you win again be sure to come back to me, et tu seras heureux!'*

I still had five hundred francs of my own left; besides which, I have a magnificent watch worth a thousand francs, some diamond cuff-links, and so forth, so that I can still hold out for quite a long time without worrying about anything. I have deliberately settled down in this little town, in order to sort myself out, and more importantly to wait for Mr Astley. I found out for certain that he will be passing through here and will stay for twenty-four hours on business. I shall find out about everything . . . and then—then I'll go straight to Homburg. I shall not go to Roulettenburg, unless perhaps next year. Indeed, they say it brings bad luck to try one's fortune at the same table twice in a row, and in Homburg there is real play.

CHAPTER 17

A YEAR and eight months have passed since I glanced at these notes, and it is only now, out of anguish and grief, that I chanced to read them, with the idea of distracting myself. So, I left off at the point where I was going to Homburg. God! With what a light heart, comparatively speaking, I wrote those last lines! That is to say, not really with a light heart, but with what self-assurance, what unshakeable hopes! Did I doubt myself at all? And so, more than a year and a half has gone by, and in my opinion I am far worse off than a beggar! So much for beggars! To hell with beggars! I have simply destroyed myself! But there is almost nothing to draw a comparison with and it is useless to moralize to oneself! Nothing could be more absurd than moralizing at a time like this. Oh, self-satisfied people: with what proud self-assurance these chatterboxes are prepared to deliver their maxims! If only they knew to what extent I myself understand how completely loathsome my present situation is, then of course they would not lash out at me, in the hope of teaching me. But what, what can they tell me that is new, that I do not know? And is that really the point? Here the point is that, one turn of the wheel and—everything changes, and these same moralists would be the first (I am sure of this) to come and congratulate me with friendly jest. And they would not all turn away from me as they do now. Yes, to hell with them, with all of them! What am I now? Zéro. What can I be tomorrow? Tomorrow I may rise from the dead and start to live again! I may find the man in me, before he is lost for ever!

I did indeed go to Homburg that time, but . . . afterwards I was in Roulettenburg again, and in Spa; I was even in Baden, where I went as a valet to councillor Hintze, a scoundrel and my former master here. Yes, I was even a footman for five whole months! That happened immediately after prison. (I went to prison, you see, in Roulettenburg for a debt I incurred here. An anonymous person bought me out—who was it? Mr Astley? Polina? I do not know; but the debt was repaid, all two hundred thalers, and I was set free.) What was I to do? And so I went to this Hintze. He is a young, empty-headed person, fond of doing nothing, and I can speak and write in three languages. At first I went to him as a sort of secretary, for thirty gulden a month; but I ended up being his footman: he found he did not have the means to keep a secretary, and he decreased my salary; I had nowhere to go and I stayed—and thus I turned myself into a footman. I did not have enough to eat or drink in his service, but on the other hand I saved seventy gulden in the five months. One evening, in Baden, I informed him that I wished to leave; that same evening I set off to play roulette. Oh, how my heart pounded!! No, it was not the money that was precious to me! At that time the only thing I wanted was for all those Hintzes, all those head waiters, all those splendid women in Baden, to be talking about me the next day, telling my story, marvelling at me, praising me, and admiring my new winnings. These were all childish dreams and concerns, but . . . who knows? perhaps I might even meet Polina, and I would tell her, and she would see that I was above all these absurd twists of fate . . . Oh, it was not the money that was precious to me! I am sure that once again I would have thrown it all at some Blanche, and once again would have driven around in Paris for three weeks with my own sixteen-thousand-franc pair of horses. You see, I know perfectly well that I am not mean; I think I am even extravagant—and yet, with what trepidation, with what a sinking heart I listen to the croupier's cry: 'trente et un, rouge, impair et passe', or 'quatre, noir, pair et manque'! With what avarice I look at the gaming table, along which are strewn louis d'or, gold friedrichs, and thalers, at the little columns of gold as the croupier's shovel scatters them into piles that glow like fire, or at the columns of silver, two feet long, that are lying around the wheel. As I am still approaching the gaming hall, two rooms away, as soon as I begin to hear the clinking of money being poured out—I almost go into convulsions.

Oh! that evening when I took my seventy gulden to the gaming table was also quite remarkable. I started with ten gulden and once again with passe. I am prejudiced in favour of passe. I lost. I had sixty gulden in silver coins left; I stopped and thought and preferred zero. I began staking five gulden at a time on zero; on the third stake zero suddenly came up, and I almost died of joy when I received a hundred and seventy-five gulden. I was even happier than when I had won a hundred thousand gulden. I instantly staked a hundred gulden on red—and won; all two hundred on red—and won; all four hundred on black—and won; all eight hundred on manque—and won; counting what I had before there was now one thousand and seven hundred gulden—and this in less than five minutes! Yes, in such moments one forgets all one's previous failures! You see, I had achieved this at the risk of more than my life, I had dared to take the risk and—now I was once again among the ranks of men!

I took a room at the hotel, locked my door, and sat till about three o'clock counting my money. When I woke up in the morning I was no longer a footman. I decided to go to Homburg that very same day: I had not worked as a lackey or been in prison there. Half an hour before the train departed I set off to place two bets, no more, and lost fifteen hundred florins. All the same I did go to Homburg, and I have now been here a whole month . . .

I live, of course, in a constant state of anxiety, play for the smallest stakes, and wait for something to happen, make calculations, stand for days on end at the gaming table *observing* the play; I even dream about the game, but for all that it seems to me as if I have grown stiff, as if I were stuck in some sort of mud. I reach that conclusion from my experience on meeting Mr Astley. We had not seen one another since that time and the meeting took place by accident. This is what happened. I was walking in the garden and working out that I had almost no money, but had fifty gulden—and besides I had settled my bill with the hotel, where I occupied a little attic room, two days before. Thus, I was now left with the possibility of only one more go at the roulette table—if I won something I could carry on playing; if I lost I would have to go back to being a footman, if I did not immediately find a Russian family needing a tutor. Preoccupied with this thought I set off on my usual daily walk across the park and through the woods into the neighbouring principality. Sometimes I would spend as much as four hours doing this and arrive back in Homburg tired and hungry. I had just entered the park from the gardens when I suddenly saw Mr Astley sitting on a bench. He had noticed me first and hailed me. I sat down beside him. Noticing a rather pompous air about him, I immediately moderated my delight—for at first I had been terribly pleased to see him.

'And so, you are here! I just thought I would meet you', he said to me. 'Don't bother to tell me: I know, I know everything; your entire life during this last year and eight months is known to me.'

'Ha! So that's how you keep up with old friends!' I replied. 'It does you honour that you don't forget . . . Wait a moment though, you've made me think of something—was it you who bought me out of prison in Roulettenburg, where I was being held on account of a debt of two hundred gulden? An anonymous person paid the money for me.'

'No, oh no; I didn't pay for you to get out of the Roulettenburg prison, where they put you because of a debt of two hundred gulden, but I knew that you went to prison for a debt of two hundred gulden.'

'That means that you know who it was who got me out, all the same.'

'Oh no, I can't say I know who got you out.'

'Strange; I'm not known to any of the Russians, and anyway I dare say none of the Russians here would buy me out; it's at home, in Russia, that the Orthodox buy out the Orthodox. But I just thought that it was some odd Englishman who did it out of eccentricity.'

Mr Astley listened to me with a certain degree of surprise. I think he thought he would find me dejected and broken.

'I'm very pleased, though, to see that you have completely retained your independence of spirit and even cheerfulness', he uttered with a fairly unpleasant air.

'That is to say, you're seething with annoyance inside, because I'm not crushed and broken', I said, laughing.

He did not understand straight away, but when he did, he smiled.

'I like your remarks. I recognize in these words my former, clever, enthusiastic, yet at the same time cynical, old friend; only Russians can combine in themselves so many contradictions at the same time. People really do like seeing their best friends humiliated; a large part of a friendship is based on humiliation; and that is an old truth, well known to all intelligent people. But in the present case, I assure you that I am genuinely pleased that you have not lost heart. Tell me, you aren't intending to give up gambling?'

'Oh, to hell with that! I'd give it up at once, if only . . .'

'If only you could win back what you've lost? That is what I thought; no need to finish what you're saying—I know. You said that accidentally, and consequently you spoke the truth. Tell me, do you do anything else apart from gambling?'

'No, nothing . . .'

He began to quiz me. I knew nothing; I hardly ever looked at the newspapers and had definitely not opened a single book since I had been there.

'You've become dull,' he commented; 'you have not only renounced life, your own interests and those of society, your duty as a citizen and a man, your own friends (and you did have friends)—you've not only renounced every aim whatsoever in your life except for winning at gambling, you've even renounced your memories. I remember you at a passionate and intense period of your life; but I am sure that you have forgotten all your best impressions of that time; your dreams, the most urgent of your present desires, do not go beyond even and odd, rouge, noir, the twelve middle numbers, and so on and so forth, I'm sure of it!'

'Enough, Mr Astley, please, please, do not remind me!' I shouted with annoyance, practically with spite; 'let me tell you, I have forgotten almost nothing! I've simply put it out of my head for a while, even the memories—until I have radically improved my circumstances; then . . . then you'll see, I'll rise from the dead!'

'You'll still be here ten years from now', he said. 'I'll lay a bet that I'll remind you of it on this very same bench if I'm alive to do so.'

'Well, that's enough,' I interrupted impatiently, 'and to show you that I'm not so forgetful of the past, allow me to ask: where is Miss Polina now? If it was not you who bought me out of prison, then it must have been her. I've had no news of her since that time.'

'No, oh no! I don't think that it was she who bought you out. She is in Switzerland at the moment, and you would do me a great favour if you would stop questioning me about Miss Polina', he said emphatically, even angrily.

'That means that she has hurt you as well!' I laughed involuntarily.

'Miss Polina is the finest of all creatures worthy of respect, but, I repeat, you would be doing me an enormous favour if you would stop asking me questions about Miss Polina. You have never known her, and I consider it an offence to my moral sensibilities to hear her name on your lips.'

'Is that so? However, you are wrong; and besides, what is there for me to talk to you about except her? Tell me! After all, that is what all our memories consist of. However, do not worry, I do not need to know any of your inner, secret affairs . . . I am only interested in, so to speak, Miss Polina's external situation, just her present outward circumstance. You can tell me of that in two words.'

'Agreed, so long as these two words will be the end of it. Miss Polina was ill for a long time; she is still ill now; for some time she lived with my mother and sister in the north of England. Six months ago her Granny—you remember, that crazy woman—died and left her, personally, a fortune of seven thousand pounds. Now Miss Polina is travelling with the family of my sister, who has married. Her younger brother and sister were also provided for in Granny's will and are studying in London. The General, her stepfather, died from a stroke a month ago in Paris. Mademoiselle Blanche treated him well, but she managed to transfer everything he got from Granny into her own name . . . that, I think, is all.'

'And de Grieux? Is he also travelling in Switzerland?'

'No, de Grieux is not travelling in Switzerland, and I do not know where de Grieux is; besides, I am warning you once and for all to avoid hints and ignoble comparisons of that kind, otherwise you'll certainly have me to answer to for it.'

'What! Despite our former friendly relations?'

'Yes, despite our former friendly relations.'

'I beg your forgiveness a thousand times over, Mr Astley. But allow me, nevertheless; there is nothing offensive or ignoble about it; after all, I don't blame Miss Polina for anything. Besides—a Frenchman and a Russian lady, generally speaking, is a combination that neither you nor I could explain or fully understand, Mr Astley.'

'If you will not mention de Grieux's name in conjunction with the other name, then I will ask you to clarify what you imply by the expression "a Frenchman and a Russian lady". What sort of a combination is that? Why should it be specifically a Frenchman and why does it have to be a Russian lady?'

'You see, it does interest you then. But that is a long story, Mr Astley. One would need to know a lot of things beforehand. However, it is an important question—however amusing it may all seem at first glance. A Frenchman, Mr Astley, is the epitome of beautiful form. You, being British, may not agree with that; I, being Russian, am also in disagreement, although it is perhaps through envy; but our young ladies might think differently. You may find Racine* affected, corrupt, and perfumed; you probably cannot even bear to read him. I also find him affected, corrupt, and perfumed, from one point of view even funny; but he is charming, Mr Astley, and more importantly he is a great poet, whether or not you and I like it. The French national form, that is to say, the Parisian, had begun to structure itself into an elegant form while we were still bears. The Revolution took over from the nobility. Nowadays even the most vulgar little Frenchman can have manners, poise, expressions, and even ideas that are thoroughly elegant in form, without either his initiative, his soul, or his heart participating in the form; he has acquired it all by inheritance. In their own right they can be the shallowest of the shallow, and the most despicable of the despicable. But, Mr Astley, I'll tell you now that there isn't a creature in the world more trusting and open than a kind, intelligent, not too affected young Russian lady. A de Grieux, appearing in some role, appearing in disguise, may capture her heart with exceptional ease; he has elegant form, Mr Astley, and the young lady takes this form for his very spirit, for the natural form of his spirit and heart, rather than a garment he has inherited. To your extreme displeasure I must admit that for the most part Englishmen are angular and inelegant, and Russians are fairly sensitive to beauty and have a penchant for it. But in order to distinguish beauty of the soul and originality of character one needs incomparably more independence and freedom than our women have, still less our young ladies—and in any case more experience. Miss Polina then—excuse me, but once said it's said—will need a very, very long time to resolve that she prefers you to that villain de Grieux. She will appreciate you, she will become your friend, she will open her heart to you; but that loathsome scoundrel, that nasty, petty money-lender de Grieux will still reign in that heart. It will even go on, so to speak, out of sheer obstinacy and vanity, because at some time this de Grieux appeared to her wearing the halo of an elegant marquis, a disillusioned liberal ruined (supposedly?) by helping her family and the empty-headed General. All those tricks of his were revealed later. But it does not matter that they came to light: go and give her the old de Grieux now—that's what she wants. And the more she hates de Grieux as he is now, the more she pines for the former one, although this former one only existed in her imagination. You are a sugar-refiner, aren't you, Mr Astley?'

'Yes, I am a partner in the well-known sugar-refining company Lovell & Co.'

'Well, there you are, Mr Astley. On one hand sugar-refining, and on the other an Apollo Belvedere;* somehow none of it fits together. And I'm not even a sugar-refiner; I'm just a petty gambler at roulette, and I've even been a footman, which is probably already known to Miss Polina, because she seems to have good spies.'

'You're embittered and that's why you're saying all this rubbish', said Mr Astley coolly, having thought for a moment. 'Besides, there's nothing original in what you say.'

'I agree. But the dreadful thing is, my noble friend, that all these accusations I'm making, however obsolete, however trite, however much they seem to belong to vaudeville, are nevertheless true. You and I have nevertheless achieved nothing!'

'That's vile nonsense . . . because, because . . . I'll tell you then!' Mr Astley said in a trembling voice, his eyes flashing. 'Let me tell you, you ungrateful, unworthy, petty, miserable man, that I came to Homburg on her instruction, deliberately to see you, to have a long and sincere talk with you, and then tell her everything—your feelings, thoughts, hopes and . . . memories!'

'Really! Really?' I cried, and tears poured from my eyes. I could not keep them back and I think that was the first time it had happened to me in my life.

'Yes, you wretched man, she loved you, and I can reveal this to you, because you are ruined! What's more, even if I tell you that she still loves you—you'll stay here all the same! Yes, you've destroyed yourself. You had certain talents, a lively personality, and you weren't bad-looking; you could even have been useful to your country, which is so lacking in men, but— you will remain here and your life is finished. I am not blaming you. In my view all Russians are like that, or inclined to be like that. If it isn't roulette then it's something else similar. The exceptions are only too rare. You are not the first to fail to realize what work entails (I am not speaking now about your peasantry). Roulette is principally a Russian game. Up until now you have been honest and you preferred to become a footman than thieve . . . but I dread to think what might happen in the future. That's enough, farewell! You need money, of course? Here are ten louis d'or for you, and more than that I won't give you because you'll lose it all the same . . . Take it and goodbye! Take it!'

'No, Mr Astley, after all that's just been said . . .'

'Ta-a-ake it!' he shouted. 'I am sure you are still a man of honour, and I'm giving it to you as one true friend to another.

If I could only be certain that you would give up gambling and
Homburg straight away and go to your own country, I would
be prepared to give you a thousand pounds right away in order
to start a new career. But the very reason I'm not giving you a
thousand pounds, but only ten louis d'or, is that at the moment
a thousand pounds and ten louis d'or amount to the same thing
to you; it's all the same—you'll lose it. Take it and goodbye.'

'I'll take it if you will allow me to embrace you on parting.'

'Oh, with pleasure!'

We embraced each other sincerely, and Mr Astley walked
away.

No. He's not right. If I was harsh and stupid about Polina
and de Grieux, then he was sharp and quick-tempered about
the Russians. Of myself I shall say nothing. However . . .
however, for the moment all that is beside the point. It's all
words, words, and words, whereas one needs deeds! Switzerland is the most important thing now! Tomorrow even—oh, if
only it were possible to set off straight away tomorrow! To be
reborn, to rise from the dead. I need to prove to them . . . To
let Polina know that I can still be a man. All I need to do is
. . . it is late now, however—but tomorrow . . . Oh, I have a
presentiment and it cannot be otherwise! I've now got fifteen
louis d'or, and it was fifteen gulden that I started off with! If I
start carefully . . . but surely, surely I can't be such a child!
Surely I'm not forgetting that I'm a ruined man. But why can't
I rise up again? Yes! All I need to do is to be careful and
prudent, just once in my life, and—that's all! All I have to do
is to keep control of myself for once, and I can change my
whole destiny in just one hour! The most important thing is
strength of character. I need only recall what happened to me
in this respect seven months ago in Roulettenburg, just before
I finally lost everything. Oh, that was a remarkable instance of
determination! I had lost it all, then, everything . . . As I am
walking out of the casino, I look—there is still one gulden
tinkling about in my waistcoat pocket: 'Ah, so I will be able to
have something for dinner!' I thought, but, after walking a
hundred paces I changed my mind and turned back. I staked
the gulden on manque (that time it was manque) and, it is
true, there is something peculiar in the sensation, when you
are alone in a foreign country, far from home and friends, and

not knowing what you will eat that day, you bet your last gulden, your very, very last! I won and twenty minutes later I walked out of the casino, with a hundred and seventy gulden in my pocket. That is a fact, sir! That is what your last gulden can mean at times! But what if I had lost heart, if I had not dared to make that decision? . . .

Tomorrow, tomorrow it will all be over!

EXPLANATORY NOTES

Notes from the Underground

9 *collegiate assessor*: eighth grade in the Civil Service of tsarist Russia, equivalent to the rank of major in the army.

10 *all that is beautiful and sublime*: a reference to Hegel's aesthetic theory of 'the sublime and beautiful', and to V. Chernyshevsky's thesis 'Aesthetic Relations of Art and Reality' (1855), in which he refuted Hegel's theory and made an apologia for reality at the expense of art. Dostoevsky abhorred this denigration of aesthetics begun by Chernyshevsky with his utilitarian attitude to literature and taken still further by Pisarev and Dobroliubov.

13 *the wall*: stands here as a symbol of the Hegelian beliefs of contemporary utilitarians and rationalists like V. Chernyshevsky and N. Dobroliubov, against whom much of the polemic in this section is directed.

l'homme de la nature et de la vérité: a somewhat derisive reference to J.-J. Rousseau's 'universal man', the forefather of the 'noble, happy savage' which became a cult amongst the romantics of the nineteenth century. On Rousseau, see note to p. 39 below.

17 *Waggenheims*: a common name for dentists in St Petersburg in the nineteenth century.

21 *the artist Gey*: Nikolay Nikolaevich Gey (1831–94) belonged to the 'School of Wanderers' founded by I. Kramskoy. Their aim was to advocate social reform to the country at large through exhibitions of realistic paintings. The reference here is to one of his religious paintings, *The Last Supper*, a work of art that made a particularly strong impression on Dostoevsky and which shocked the Orthodox Church. Like many of Gey's paintings with a religious subject it is executed in a mawkishly sentimental style that blends detailed realism with tortured melodrama.

To one's Satisfaction: refers to an article written in 1863 by Mikhail Evgrafovich Saltykov-Shchedrin (1826–89), a notable Russian novelist, satirist, and editor of the *Fatherland Notes*, who wrote a complimentary article in response to N. Gey's paintings.

24 *Buckle*: Henry Thomas Buckle (1821–62), an English historian, known for his *A History of Civilisation in England*. One of the

principles Buckle supports in his writings is that with civilization man becomes continually better and less aggressive, something the underground man rejects.

Napoleon . . . the contemporary one: Charles Louis Napoléon Bonaparte (1808–73), who became Napoleon III. He was elected president of the French Republic in 1848 and declared himself Emperor in 1852. He was deposed in 1870 following France's débâcle in the Franco-Prussian war.

Schleswig-Holstein: during the nineteenth century a whole complex of diplomatic and other issues arose out of the relations of the two contiguous duchies of Schleswig and Holstein, to the Danish crown on the one hand and the German Confederation on the other. The issues became the object and pretext of European power struggles.

25 *Stenka Razins*: Stepan (Stenka) Razin (*c.*1630–71) was leader of the rebelling peasants in the Russian Peasants' War (1670–71) and was renowned for his butchery. He was ultimately captured and put to death.

26 *the Crystal Palace*: an unusual steel and glass edifice designed by the English architect Sir Joseph Paxton (1803–65) which served as the main pavilion at the London World Fairs of 1851 and 1862. It became a symbol of the dreams of the Russian Utopian socialists and nihilists and was used by V. Chernyshevsky in his novel *What is to be Done?* as an image of Utopia. The dream of Chernyshevsky and others was one of earthly paradise and universal well-being, founded on the basis of the rational agreement of wills, acting out of utilitarianism. The underground man's objection to the Crystal Palace, and all that it stands for, is part of Dostoevsky's polemic against Chernyshevsky and the socialist utilitarians of the day.

the bird of Kagan: a bird that Siberian exiles refer to. In this instance it is another way of saying a bird of paradise.

30 *the Colossus of Rhodes*: a gigantic statue of Helios, the Greek sun god, on the island of Rhodes, completed *c.*280 BC to commemorate the successful defence of the island. It is regarded as one of the Seven Wonders of the World.

Mr Anaevsky: A. E. Anaevsky (1788–1866) was the author of various miscellaneous pieces. He was often derided by journalists because of the poor calibre of his work.

33 *aux animaux domestiques*: to domestic animals.

39 *Heine*: Heinrich Heine (1797–1856), a German romantic poet, journalist, and satirist.

Rousseau: Jean-Jacques Rousseau (1712–78), French author, philosopher, and political theorist often regarded as the father of nineteenth-century Romanticism. His *Discours sur les sciences et les arts* and his *Discours sur l'origine et les fondements de l'inégalité* protest against existing society, showing how the growth of civilization corrupts natural goodness, and how the growth of society reflects the growth of inequality. These works identified him with the cult of the noble, happy savage. In his later years Rousseau wrote *Les Confessions*, a romantic autobiography, certainly misleading in fact, but highly revealing of his psychology.

43 *Nekrasov*: Nikolay Alekseevich Nekrasov (1821–77) was a poet whose works were primarily concerned with the plight of the peasant masses and with social justice. He was also a prominent editor of radical literature, working from 1846 onwards on the *Petersburg Gazette* (with Dostoevsky), *The Contemporary*, and (from 1868) *Fatherland Notes*.

47 *Kostanzhoglos*: Kostanzhoglo is the ideal landlord in the second and uncompleted volume of Nikolay Gogol's *Dead Souls*.

Uncle Petr Ivanoviches: Petr Ivanovich is the very practical and pragmatic uncle who aids in the socialization of his romantic, idealistic nephew in *A Common Story*, a novel written by Ivan Goncharov (1812–91).

51 *Gogol's Lieutenant Pirogov*: a character in Gogol's story *Nevsky Prospect*, written in 1835. He is an officer and self-styled cavalier who pursues a German woman for her favours, only to be thoroughly beaten by her enraged husband. Pirogov will not challenge the man to a duel but complains to the police and to his commanding officer.

52 *Fatherland Notes*: a literary and political monthly journal published in St Petersburg between 1839 and 1884. It contained some of the best literature of the day and advocated progressive social ideas. It was forcibly closed because its editorial policy was deemed too liberal.

58 *Manfredian*: Manfred is the central figure of the dramatic poem 'Manfred', written by Lord Byron (1788–1824) in 1817. He sells himself to the devil and lives in a splendid and proud solitude without any human sympathies.

Austerlitz: the scene of a battle in 1805 at which Napoleon inflicted a heavy defeat on the combined Russian and Austrian forces.

Villa Borghese: one of the residences of the enormously wealthy and politically powerful Borghese family. The family held considerable influence over the Pope and in 1803 Camillo Filippo Ludovico Borghese married Pauline, sister of the Emperor Napoleon.

61 *Zverkov*: Dostoevsky gives two of the 'school-fellows' names that are meaningful to the Russian reader. 'Zverkov' suggests something like 'Mr Brute', and 'Trudoliubov' is transparently 'Mr Industrious'.

63 *Trudoliubov*: see previous note.

82 *Silvio*: the central character in 'The Shot', a short story by A. S. Pushkin (1799–1837) written in 1830. After having his pride damaged by a wealthy young count who refused to take a duel seriously, Silvio sacrifices everything for revenge. When the Count marries, Silvio decides to reconvene the duel. He is satisfied when he sees the Count's fear and embarrassment in front of his young bride, and magnanimously wastes his shot in a gesture to show the Count that he could have taken his life.

Masquerade: a romantic play written in 1835–6 by Mikhail Lermontov (1814–41). The play tells the story of a romantic egoist called Arbenin who poisons his wife when he suspects that she has betrayed him, and who goes insane when he learns of her innocence.

106 *George-Sandish*: George Sand was the pen-name of Amantine Lucie Aurore Dupin Dudevant (1804–76), a French author who wrote romantic works examining free love, humanitarian reforms, Christian socialism, nature, and rustic manners. She was one of the strongest literary influences on Dostoevsky. This is revealed in his notebooks of 1876–7: 'How many of my admirations and enthusiasms go back to this poet, how much joy and happiness she afforded me! I do not hesitate in my choice of words, for this is literally true.'

107 *Alexander of Macedon*: the Emperor Alexander the Great (356–323 BC) conquered the civilized world, extending Greek civilization to the East and ushering in the Hellenistic Age.

The Gambler

129 *outchitel*: the Russian word for 'tutor', given in the Russian text in this French transliterated spelling for ironic effect; pronounce as 'uchitel'.

130 *Opinion Nationale*: Parisian political daily paper published 1859–79.

131 *Cela n'était pas si bête*: 'That was not such a stupid thing.'

132 *General Perovsky*: General Vasily Alekseevich Perovsky (1795–1857), a Russian military figure who detailed in his *Memoirs* the horrors inflicted on the Russians by the retreating French army during the war of 1812.

133 *la baboulinka*: this represents Russian *babulenka*, a diminutive of the word for 'grandmother'.

150 *Vater*: German for 'father'.

151 *Rothschild . . . Hoppe & Co.*: famous family banking concerns; the latter was based in Amsterdam.

156 *le coq gaulois*: 'the cock of Gaul', symbol of France.

162 *j'ai l'honneur d'être votre esclave*: 'I have the honour of being your slave'.

Hein!: 'Eh?'

Jawohl: 'Yes.'

Sind Sie rasend?: 'Have you gone mad?'

171 *mon cher monsieur, pardon, j'ai oublié votre nom, monsieur Alexis? . . . n'est ce pas?*: 'my dear sir, do forgive me, I have forgotten your name, Alexis? . . . Isn't that it?'

172 *le baron est si irascible, un caractère prussien, vous savez, enfin il fera une querelle d'Allemand*: 'the Baron is so irascible, a Prussian type, he will pick a quarrel over nothing'.

que diable! un blanc-bec comme vous: 'the devil take it! A milksop like you.'

174 *peut-être*: 'perhaps'.

179 *Barberini*: a famous noble patrician family, especially powerful during the sixteenth and seventeenth centuries.

un beau matin: one fine morning.

186 *à la barbe du pauvre général*: under the poor General's nose.

187 *Oui madame . . . et croyez, je suis si enchanté . . . votre santé . . . c'est un miracle . . . vous voir ici, une surprise charmante . . .* : 'Yes, madame . . . and believe me, I'm so delighted . . . your good health . . . it's a miracle . . . to see you here, a charming surprise . . .'.

191 *Cette vieille est tombée en enfance*: 'This old lady has reverted to childhood.'

Mais, madame, cela sera un plaisir: 'Why madam, it will be a pleasure!'

196 *seule elle fera des bêtises*: 'if left alone she will do something stupid'.

200 *Sortez, sortez!*: 'Leave! go on, leave!'

202 *Faites le jeu, messieurs! Rien ne va plus?*: 'Place your bets, gentlemen! No more?'

203 *combien zéro? douze? douze?*: 'how many zero? Twelve, is it? Twelve?'

Le jeu est fait!: 'No more bets!'

205 *Quelle victoire!*: 'What a victory!'

Mais, madame, c'était du feu!: 'Why madam, that was very impulsive!'

Madame la princesse . . . un pauvre expatrié . . . malheur continuel . . . les princes russes sont si généreux: 'Madam Princess . . . a poor émigré . . . constant misfortune . . . Russian princes are so generous'.

206 *Que diable, c'est une terrible vieille!*: 'The devil take it, she's a frightful old lady!'

Was ist's der Teufel!: 'What the devil is it?!'

207 *Mais, madame . . . les chances peuvent tourner, une seule mauvaise chance et vous perdrez tout . . . surtout avec votre jeu . . . c'était terrible!*: 'But, madam, one's luck can change; one unlucky move—and you lose everything . . . especially with your kind of stake . . . it was dreadful!'

Vous perdrez absolument: 'You will lose utterly and completely.'

211 *Ce n'est pas ça . . . Mon cher monsieur, notre cher général se trompe*: 'That is wrong . . . My good sir, our General is mistaken.'

212 *Ce n'est pas ça, ce n'est pas ça . . . que diable!*: 'That's not it, that's not it . . . oh, to hell!'

O mon cher monsieur Alexis, soyez si bon: 'Oh, my dear Alexis, would you be so good?'

213 *Quelle mégère!*: 'What a shrew!'

217 *Nous boirons du lait, sur l'herbe fraîche*: 'We are going to drink milk on the cool grass.' Dostoevsky uses this expression to express the impoverished ideals of the bourgeoisie who have been torn from the soil.

la nature et la vérité: 'nature and truth'. Dostoevsky frequently uses this expression, taken from J.-J. Rousseau's *Confessions*, in an ironic way. Whereas Rousseau's eighteenth-century 'homme de la nature et de la vérité' had existed only as a noble ideal, the reference here is to his nineteenth-century counterpart, who had now become a reality as a result of the growth of a genuine bourgeoisie, but who had by contrast rather trivial aspirations.

220 *Diantre!*: 'Devil take it!'

Elle vivra cent ans!: 'She'll live to be a hundred!'

226 *Paul de Kock*: French novelist (1793–1871) remarkable for his vivid and detailed portrayals of Parisian life.

232 *Balakirev*: Ivan Aleksandrovich Balakirev (1699–1763), a servant to Peter I and jester to the Empress Anna Ivanovna. He wrote a notorious book of anecdotes based on his exploits.

240 *Les trois derniers coups, messieurs!*: 'Last three goes, gentlemen!'

Vingt-deux: twenty-two.

241 *Trente et un*: thirty-one.

Madame Blanchard: Sophie Blanchard (1778–1819), wife of Jean-Pierre Blanchard, a pioneering balloonist, who ascended many times herself.

244 *Monsieur a gagné déjà cent mille florins*: 'Monsieur has already won a hundred thousand florins.'

250 *Diese Russen!*: 'These Russians!'

253 *A, c'est lui!! Viens donc, bêta. Is it true, que tu as gagné une montagne d'or et d'argent? J'aimerais mieux l'or*: 'Ah, it's him!! Come in then, you silly old thing. Is it true that you won a mountain of gold and silver? I would rather have gold.'

Bibi, comme tu es bête! . . . Nous ferons bombance, n'est ce pas?: 'My pet, how stupid you are! . . . We can have a bonanza, can't we?'

Mon fils, as-tu du cœur? . . . Tout autre . . . : 'My son, have you courage?' . . . 'Anyone other . . .'. Lines taken from Corneille's tragedy *Le Cid*.

si tu n'es pas trop bête, je te prends à Paris: 'if you aren't too silly I will take you to Paris'.

tu verras Paris. Dis donc, qu'est ce que c'est qu'un outchitel? Tu étais bien bête, quand tu étais outchitel: 'you'll see Paris. Hey, what is a tutor? You were very stupid when you were a tutor.'

Eh bien, que feras-tu, si je te prends avec? . . . je veux cinquante mille francs . . . Nous allons à Paris . . . et je te ferai voir des étoiles en plein jour: 'But what will you do if I take you with me? . . . I want fifty thousand francs . . . We'll go to Paris . . . and I will make you see stars in broad daylight.'

254 *que sais-je?!*: 'goodness knows for how long!'

je suis bonne enfant . . . mais tu verras des étoiles: 'I'm a nice young lady . . . but you will see stars'.

Ah, vil esclave!: 'You abject stooge!'

et après, le déluge: 'and after, the deluge'. This is a rephrasing of a reply to King Louis XV of France after the defeat of the French armies by Frederick the Great of Prussia in 1757 during the Seven Years War. Madame de Pompadour is alleged to have said 'Après nous le déluge'.

Mais tu ne peux comprendre, va! . . . Ai, que fais-tu?: 'But you would not understand that! . . . Hey, what are you doing?'

Eh bien, mon outchitel, je t'attends, si tu veux: 'Well, my tutor, I will be waiting for you, if you wish.'

255 *Peut-être, je ne demandais pas mieux*: 'Maybe I could not have asked for more.'

mais tu seras heureux, comme un petit roi: 'but you will be as happy as a little prince'.

Quant à moi, je veux cinquante mille francs de rente et alors . . .: 'As for me, I want an income of fifty thousand francs and then . . .'.

256 *et les cent mille francs qui nous restent, tu les mangeras avec moi, mon outchitel*: 'and as for the hundred thousand francs that we have left, you and I will go on a spending spree with them, my tutor'.

C'est un outchitel . . . il a gagné deux cent mille francs: 'He's a tutor . . . he's won two hundred thousand francs.'

258 *Mais tu as de l'esprit pour comprendre! Sais-tu, mon garçon . . .*: 'But it seems that you are intelligent enough to understand. You know, young man . . .'.

Mais . . . sais-tu . . . mais dis donc . . . Mais sais-tu . . . Qu'est-ce que tu feras après, dis donc?: 'But . . . you know . . . tell me . . . But you know . . . What are you going to do afterwards?'

Oui, oui, c'est ça, c'est magnifique!: 'Yes, that's right, it's wonderful!'

parce que je croyais, que tu n'est qu'un outchitel (quelque chose comme un laquais, n'est-ce pas?) . . . parce que je suis bonne fille: 'Because

I thought you were just a tutor (some kind of servant, isn't it?) . . . because I'm a good girl'.

258 *Oh, oh, mais tu es . . .* : 'Oh, oh, but you are . . .'

259 *il faut que jeunesse se passe*: 'one must live one's youth'.

Mais tu es un vrai philosophe, sais-tu? Un vrai philosophe! . . . Eh bien, je t'aimerai, je t'aimerai—tu verras, tu sera content!: 'But you're a real philosopher, you know. A real philosopher! . . . Well, I'll love you, I really will—you'll see, you'll be pleased.'

261 *Un vrai Russe, un Calmouk!*: 'A true Russian, a Kalmyk!'

262 *à bâtons rompus*: completely incoherently.

263 *Il a de la chance*: 'He is lucky'.

j'aurai un château, des moujiks, et puis j'aurai toujours mon million: 'I'll have a château, peasants, and then I'll still have my million'.

264 *très comme il faut*: quite the part.

Il est pourtant très comme il faut: 'And yet he really does look quite the part.

mais vois-tu . . . madame la générale de Sago-Sago, ces diables des noms russes, enfin madame la générale à quatorze consonnes. Comme c'est agréable, n'est-ce pas?: 'but you see . . . madam the wife of the General of Sago-Sago, these Russian names are devilish; in short, the general's wife with fourteen consonants! How lovely it is, isn't it?'

Tu étais bon enfant . . . Je te croyais bête et tu en avais l'air: 'You were a good young fellow . . . I thought you were stupid, and you looked it.'

Nous serons toujours bons amis . . . et tu sera heureux: 'We will always be good friends . . . and you will be happy.'

271 *Racine*: Jean Racine (1639–99), a French classical dramatist.

272 *Apollo Belvedere*: a fourth-century BC statue of Apollo, the Greek god of light, beauty, and the arts. The statue was made by Leochares, an Athenian sculptor. A copy now stands in the Vatican Museum.

The Oxford World's Classics Website

www.worldsclassics.co.uk

- Information about new titles
- Explore the full range of Oxford World's Classics
- Links to other literary sites and the main OUP webpage
- Imaginative competitions, with bookish prizes
- Peruse the Oxford World's Classics Magazine
- Articles by editors
- Extracts from Introductions
- A forum for discussion and feedback on the series
- Special information for teachers and lecturers

www.worldsclassics.co.uk

American Literature

British and Irish Literature

Children's Literature

Classics and Ancient Literature

Colonial Literature

Eastern Literature

European Literature

History

Medieval Literature

Oxford English Drama

Poetry

Philosophy

Politics

Religion

The Oxford Shakespeare

A complete list of Oxford Paperbacks, including Oxford World's Classics, Oxford Shakespeare, Oxford Drama, and Oxford Paperback Reference, is available in the UK from the Academic Division Publicity Department, Oxford University Press, Great Clarendon Street, Oxford OX2 6DP.

In the USA, complete lists are available from the Paperbacks Marketing Manager, Oxford University Press, 198 Madison Avenue, New York, NY 10016.

Oxford Paperbacks are available from all good bookshops. In case of difficulty, customers in the UK can order direct from Oxford University Press Bookshop, Freepost, 116 High Street, Oxford OX1 4BR, enclosing full payment. Please add 10 per cent of published price for postage and packing.